BEGINNINGS

WORLDS
OF
HONOR
#6

Baen Books by David Weber

Honorverse Novels:
On Basilisk Station
The Honor of the Queen
The Short Victorious War
Field of Dishonor
Flag in Exile
Honor Among Enemies
In Enemy Hands
Echoes of Honor
Ashes of Victory
War of Honor
At All Costs
Mission of Honor
Crown of Slaves
(with Eric Flint)
Torch of Freedom
(with Eric Flint)
The Shadow of Saganami
Storm from the Shadows
A Rising Thunder

Honorverse Anthologies:
More than Honor
Worlds of Honor
Changer of Worlds
The Service of the Sword
In Fire Forged
Beginnings

**Honorverse Young
Adult Novel:**
A Beautiful Friendship
Fire Season (forthcoming)

Empire from the Ashes
Mutineers' Moon
The Armageddon Inheritance

Heirs of Empire
Empire from the Ashes (omnibus)

Path of the Fury
In Fury Born

The Apocalypse Troll

The Excalibur Alternative
Oath of Swords
The War God's Own
Wind Rider's Oath
War Maid's Own

With Steve White
Insurrection
Crusade
In Death Ground
The Shiva Option
The Stars at War I
The Stars at War II

With John Ringo
March Upcountry
March to the Sea
March to the Stars
We Few

With Eric Flint
1633
1634: The Baltic War

With Linda Evans
Hell's Gate
Hell Hath No Fury

To purchase these and all other Baen Book titles in e-book format,
please go to www.baen.com.

BEGINNINGS

WORLDS OF HONOR #6

DAVID WEBER

WITH
CHARLES E. GANNON
TIMOTHY ZANN
JOELLE PRESBY

BEGINNINGS

Copyright © 2013 by Words of Weber, Inc.
"By the Book" Copyright © 2013 by Charles E. Gannon, "A Call to Arms" Copyright © 2013 by Timothy Zahn, "Beauty and the Beast" Copyright © 2013 by Words of Weber, Inc., "Best Laid Plans" Copyright © 2013 by Words of Weber, Inc., "Obligated Service" Copyright © 2013 by Joelle Presby.

A Baen Books Original

Baen Publishing Enterprises
P.O. Box 1403
Riverdale, NY 10471
www.baen.com

ISBN 13: 978-1-4516-3903-2

ISBN 13: 978-1-4516-3924-7 (Signed Edition)

Cover art by David Mattingly

First printing, July 2013

Distributed by Simon & Schuster
1230 Avenue of the Americas
New York, NY 10020

Library of Congress Cataloging-in-Publication Data

Beginnings : worlds of honor #6 / By David Weber.
    pages cm. -- (Worlds of honor ; #6)
"A Baen Books Original."
ISBN 978-1-4516-3903-2 (hc)
1. Science fiction, American. 2. Harrington, Honor (Fictitious character)--Fiction. I. Weber, David, 1952-
PS648.S3W383 2013
813'.0876208--dc23
                          2013005693

Printed in the United States of America

10 9 8 7 6 5 4 3 2 1

CONTENTS

BY THE BOOK

Charles E. Gannon

BY THE BOOK

Four days out from Hygeia, August 12, 2352 AD (250 PD)

The ship's youngest rating, Brian Lewis, sighed so heavily that the inside of his faceplate fogged for a moment. "So, that's it, Skipper. We're locked out."

Lieutenant Lee Strong stared at the uncooperative external airlock door in front of them.

The other rating, three-year veteran Roderigo Burns, asked, "Well, why don't we just set some charges and blow our way into the ship?"

Lee's senior NCO and EVA specialist, Jan Finder, made a reply that was more growl than human speech. "Because, idiot, if we blow a hole in the side of this tin can, we can't be sure who'd be left alive inside."

"But the internal door—"

"Listen, recruit, and listen good. Since we can't see into the airlock, we can't *know* that the inner hatch is dogged. And we can't assume what we can't see. Even our green looey here figured that out—and a whole lot more, besides."

Which was exactly the kind of backhanded—and therefore, safe—compliment Lee had come to expect from Finder. He'd watched how most NCOs worked with new lieutenants. If they hated them, it was all respectful formality to their face and subtle undermining behind their back. On the other hand, if they liked the new officer, they ribbed him gently at first—like this—but always in a way that reminded the ratings that even though their CO was a newbie, he was a *smart* newbie, and they'd better respect both his intelligence and his rank.

Burns sounded obstinate. "Well, even if the airlock's inner hatch *is* open when we blow the hatch, then when we blow the outer hatch, the environmental sensors will detect the exposure to vacuum and seal the emergency bulkheads automatically."

"Only if the internal sensors are still functioning, Roderigo," Lee said quietly. "And since we know this ship was seized violently, we've got to assume that any of its systems could be compromised."

"Uh . . . well, yeah, Sir. I guess there's that."

Lee heard the smile behind Finder's affirming grunt. He glanced at his overage top kick, whose squat, powerful form was a black silhouette against the starfield, with Jupiter an intensely bright star staring over his left shoulder. "Your thoughts, Sergeant?"

There was no sign of motion in the floating black outline. "We could try cutting." The silhouette shrugged. "It's safer. But it takes longer, so they'll know we're coming. Not good."

"Sounds like you're speaking with the voice of experience, Sergeant Finder."

"Yep. When I was a green recruit, an officer tried doing that in a situation like this."

"And the hijackers heard you coming and killed the hostages?"

"Worse than that, Lieutenant. They let us get on board, then executed a young girl right in front of us. Threatened to shoot more if we came any closer. That suckered our officer into talking, negotiating. Meanwhile, they worked most of their men around behind us, using the environmental conduits. They killed half our team."

"And no hostages rescued, I'll wager."

"You'd win that bet, L.T.—if you could find someone stupid enough to take it. Now, Burns here is none too smart, but he's said to be a betting man—"

"Hey—" complained Roderigo.

"That's enough," Lee ordered. "We can't use demolition charges, and we can't use cutting torches."

"So, we're stuck outside," Lewis repeated in a voice full of quiet vindication. "We're done."

"No, Lewis, we're not," corrected Lee. "There's another way." He studied the length of the outsystem passenger liner. Extending aft from the forward collection of habitation and command modules where they were floating, there was a midsection girdle of sausage-like fuel tanks and then a long, thin boom, bracketed by four support trusses. They all terminated at the rearmost engine decks. Pointing aft, Lee uttered the timeless, two-word order that junior officers had been uttering for millennia: "Follow me."

He pushed off the hull of the liner—the *Fragrant Blossom*, two weeks out from Mars—and used his suit jets to angle astern, toward the engine decks.

❈ ❈ ❈

They stared "up" into the large black hole in the belly of the liner's primary thrust module.

"You're not serious," breathed Roderigo Burns.

"You might say he's deadly serious," Finder quipped.

"I don't think you're helping matters, Sergeant," Lee said.

"Sorry, sir. But this *is* nonstandard."

"'Nonstandard'?" Brian Lewis croaked. "Sirs, this is directly against regs. This is a class-one radiation hazard, and if—"

"Lewis," Finder said from far back in his throat where he apparently cached a ready supply of gravel, "shut up. Those regs are superseded by emergency rescue ops. And don't you ever call me 'sir' again. I'm not an officer; I work for a living. Now, you will give your undivided attention to the L.T. or I will give your ass the undivided attention of my boot."

Lee was inspecting the edges of the large black hole. "No signs of recent wear. Probably hasn't been used since they did the post-production trial run."

"Great," muttered Lewis with a shiver.

"Calm down, Brian," said Lee. "That test is performed with an inert core. It's just to prove the ejection system functional. Sergeant, get me a REM reading."

Finder rumbled assent.

Roderigo Burns looked dubious, his eyes wide through the tinting of his photosensitive faceplate. "But sir, I thought they used this hole to vent radioactive wastes."

Lee suppressed the urge to declaim the official fear-mongering that the Earth Union called "truth." "No, Burns. A nuclear drive's core-ejection tube has one use, and one use only: to dump the business part of a malfunctioning reactor." Which, as an automatic protocol, was pretty stupid in and of itself. But that was the Earth Union for you. Ever since the Greens and Neo Luddites had come to power almost two centuries ago, the words "nuclear power" had become functionally synonymous with "demonic arts." The notion of exposing a human body to radiation of any kind had become such an object of fetishistic fear that many of the extreme Neo Luddite groups refused any medical diagnostics that involved X-rays (or even magnetic resonance imaging, despite repeated assurances that such tests did not involve any radioisotopes). Consequently, their life expectancy statistics were usually about ten years less than other groups living in the same communities.

Finder put away his palm-sized combination Geiger counter/radiance sensor. "Readings indicate eighteen REM per hour, holding steady."

Lee turned to the ratings. "We'll be in and through in ten minutes. That a total exposure of three REM, tops. No physical effects."

Burns and Lewis tried to look reassured but failed miserably; a lifetime of indoctrination was not overcome in a single minute.

Finder edged closer. "Okay L.T.; we go in the hot pipe. Then what? Sure as hell there can't be an airlock at the other end."

"No, Sergeant, but there are access panels. Now, follow me."

The carrier signal changed subtly; another subaudial hiss had popped into existence alongside the general tactical channel. "Sir," said Finder, using the private link reserved for NCO-officer communications. "I'm the EVA expert. And I'm the meat-headed Sarge. So let me go in first, okay?"

Lee fought two contending reactions: a wise readiness to accept respectful advice from a career sergeant versus the powerful desire to show his men—by example—that he'd do anything he asked them to do, and that in this case, there was no danger in what he was ordering. Well, not from radiation, at least.

But Lee managed to resist that second, stronger impulse. He cleared his throat, and used his chin to shut off the private channel, sending his next statement to the entire team. "Sergeant Finder, on second thought, you lead with your radsensor. If it gets any hotter as we go, we'll want to know right away."

"So we can bug out?" asked Burns anxiously.

"No: so we can double-time it to our objective." Lee unholstered his large-framed ten-millimeter handgun. "Let's go."

※ ※ ※

The core ejection tube showed no sign of wear—or maintenance. Evidently, the fearsome legends of the nuclear dragon residing at the other end of this man-made cave had kept visitors away—even the ones whose duty it was to periodically check that the tube was unobstructed and functional. It was yet another example of the dangers of the excessive fear often inculcated by the Greens and Neo Luddites. As the terror of a technology became primal, the maintenance of it devolved into a collection of dread rituals, not clear-eyed technical practices.

Had the Greens found any other technology to provide inexpensive and swift space travel beyond the moon, Lee had no doubt they would have seized upon it. But, unwilling to focus either public attention or funds upon advances in new technology, the Green leadership in almost every country had reluctantly agreed to approve nuclear thermal rockets for limited use beyond cis-lunar space. Unfortunately, that approval came with so much dire rhetoric of the technology's implicit dangers that all too few people born on Earth had the interest—indeed, the courage—to master it. So it was left—as so many dirty jobs were—to the Upsiders, that very small population that lived either on the moon, on Mars, or in the rotational habitats. It was they who maintained the satellites, mined the belt, or helped to build the slower-than-light starships that sent feckless, and usually obstreperous, bits of the human race off to colonize other star systems.

Of course, that still didn't mean there were a *lot* of vessels with nuclear plants. Even now, there were probably not more than four dozen operating in the system, all marks and missions included. But whereas cargos could be shuttled from one far-flung point of the system to another with VASIMIR drives, and shorter trips could be made by slightly higher power magnetoplasmadynamic thrusters, deep space personnel movers had to be equipped with nuclear thermal rockets. Otherwise, journeys that currently took a few weeks would take months, even years, to complete.

But since the leadership of Earth always viewed nuclear rockets as a deal with the devil, they never became comfortable with them. If anything, their necessity was an infuriating goad to the Greens and the Neo Luddite camps alike, prompting a steady derogation of anything—or anyone—having anything to do with them.

And so, trailing at the rear of the four-man boarding team, Lee Strong watched his otherwise technically competent ratings—Burns and Lewis—superstitiously flinch away from contact with the sides of the tube. Lee half expected to see one of them make a warding sign in the direction of the fission plant itself.

At the end of the tube, Finder counter-puffed his suit jets until he hung motionless before an oversized hatch fitted with immense bolts. On the private channel, he reported, "REM now up to twenty-three an hour. Rising slowly. What now, L.T.? I didn't bring a big enough wrench to unbolt this monster."

"We don't need one. We're not going in there."

"No?"

"Nope. Look to your left. See the panel, flush with the wall?"

"Yeah. Okay. Recessed bolts. But it looks like we'll need a special key wrench to unlock them for manual removal, and I don't—"

"You don't have the right-shaped wrench-head," Lee completed for Finder as he drifted forward between Burns and Lewis. "But I do." He undid a small velcro-sealed pocket on the inside of his left wrist, and carefully withdrew the lanyarded key-wrench.

"Huh." The sergeant had gone back to the private channel. "Guess that's why you're the officer." Finder's quick smile sent a glint of teeth even through his semi-tinted visor.

"In this case, yeah. The big wigs in Geneva don't like advertising anything about nuclear access. Particularly a backdoor like this one."

"So they entrust it to a lieutenant who'd never seen a nuke pile before leaving Luna. No offense, sir, but a lot of you guys from Earth—well, you're not exactly brimming with good sense. Current company excepted, of course."

"Of course. And I can't say I disagree with you, Sarge." Which was not just polite banter with the NCO whose help or hindrance would either save or undo him during his first year in deep space. In this case, the sergeant's Upsider prejudices were sadly accurate. After ensuring that every child grew up hearing an unceasing flood of invective against the dangers of technology, of space, and of nuclear power, the Earth Union's Space Activities subdivision had a hard time finding enough capable young men to serve as officers. Women were not permitted to work in the Customs Service or any of the other official spacefaring divisions of the Earth Union. Their ovaries had to be protected from the electromagnetic rapine of spaceside radiation exposure. And among the men, Lee had to admit that few of his training class had showed half as much technical aptitude as political shrewdness. Consequently, although they often failed to grasp the practical realities of life in space, they understood full well why, in services populated almost exclusively by native-born Upsiders, only natural-born sons of Earth were allowed to wear the gold braid of the officer ranks: they were the watchdogs of Dirtside interests. They were to ensure that those lesser humans born in space, and who performed all the dirty work there, never found themselves unsupervised long enough to consider turning the tables on their terrestrial masters.

Lee had finished unlocking the bolt covers with the key wrench. "They'll give to hand tools easily enough, Sarge."

Burns' voice was hushed as he asked on the other circuit, "L.T., if the mutineers, or hijackers, or pirates, or whoever took over the *Blossom* hear us back here, could they—well, could they wash us out of this tube with radioactive gases?"

Resisting the impulse to shake his head at the depth of ignorance implicit in the question, Lee toggled his mic back to the general circuit. "No, Roderigo. That's not how these engines work. A particle bed nuclear rocket is designed so that all its radioactives are sealed within a shielded subassembly. At need, that 'core' can be jettisoned through this tube, but it's a fairly specialized process, and the activation codes are only known to a few crewmembers. And I doubt any of the criminals currently in control of the hull are hanging back here in the Engineering section."

"Okay, but if they were—I figure there's got to be some manual release, right, Skipper?"

It was reassuring that, only two months into his first year on his deep space tour, senior crewmembers were calling him "skipper." "Well, in the event that the subassembly is, for some reason, frozen in place, there are ways for technicians to jettison it manually. But that would be a suicide mission, given the exposure levels."

Finder had removed the bolts, and drifted a curved section of tube outward, revealing a narrower, rectangular passageway beyond. Half a dozen meters on, it turned to the right.

Roderigo Burns peered over Lee's shoulder. "Is the airlock around that bend?"

Lee shook his head. "Still no airlock. Just beyond that corner, there's another access panel that will put us in a safety-venting and access conduit that runs all around the unit. Then two double access panels before we reach the interior. Now, let's go—unless you want to increase your exposure time."

Burns' eyes widened and, kicking off from the opposite side of the tube, he jetted into the exposed passageway.

"A good officer always knows how to motivate his men," drawled Finder, "After you, Lieutenant."

※ ※ ※

When they turned the bend in the narrow passageway, they found a plainly marked access panel in front of them. Hazard hatchings of yellow and black surrounded the six orange-colored bolts securing it in place.

Lewis was staring at the panel. "So, in order to get inside, we have to trigger these six explosive bolts and let this hunk of metal shoot straight into our faces?"

Lee shook his head. "Those six orange spots aren't explosive bolts, Lewis. They're frangible nuts. We can trigger them ourselves, one at a time, from the outside. That will not only control the release of the panel, but allow the inert gases on the other side to bleed off without blowing us halfway back down the ejection tube."

Burns turned to stare at Lee. "Hey, Skipper, how do you know all that stuff?" He sounded genuinely respectful, even a little relieved.

"I know it because I read the specs less than an hour ago."

"And," added Jan histrionically, "it is also because he is a hand-picked officer, and a member of our beloved Customs Patrol: humanity's most elite formation of misfits, political undesirables, and problem children. All hail the Customs Patrol."

"All hail," echoed Burns and Lewis with a level of enthusiasm that they usually reserved for latrine duty.

"That's the spirit," Lee drawled with a grin at Finder. "Now, let's get going."

※ ※ ※

The terminal access panel—the one into the engine room itself—was still responsive to commands. Lewis hot-wired the keypad and bled out most of the atmosphere while Lee deployed the rest of the team for an assault entry. "I'll take point," he said, glancing back at Finder. Who apparently understood from that look not to debate the point. "The Sergeant will provide covering fire while you follow me in, Burns. We skim low and to the center of the room. There's plenty of cover around the power plant itself." Burns nodded nervously, probably more at the notion of proximity to a nuclear reactor than armed adversaries. "Lewis, we go on three. One, two . . ."

On "three," Lewis triggered the panel release; it swung out toward them. Lee angled around its opening arc, got low, kicked hard. He skimmed across three meters of deck, reached the reactor housing, and curled himself behind a control panel. A moment later, Burns jammed himself into the same space. "Okay, Roderigo," Lee muttered, "you check our twelve; I'll scan our six."

They peeked around the manifolds, control surfaces, and shielding of the nuclear rocket. No movement. Lee chinned open the circuit to Finder. "Sarge, talk to me."

"I would if I saw anything, L.T. All quiet."

"Okay. You and Lewis enter, seal the panel behind you. Then sweep the room from opposite directions. Burns and I will provide bases of fire."

"Aye, aye, Skip."

Twenty tense seconds later, the engine room was secure, and Finder was able to report a whopping three millirem per hour exposure level.

"So no leaks," breathed Lewis gratefully.

"And no bodies," Finder pointed out. "What next, L.T.?"

Lee glanced at the entry to the passageway that ran the length of the ship's keel-boom, up to the habitation modules. "We go forward. Right down the middle of that damned fifty-meter shooting range."

"Right," said Finder quickly. "Okay, now listen up, ratings. L.T. says we're going forward. Burns, swap weapons with Lewis; I want you on point with me for this one. Lewis, you use the bullpup to provide a base of fire. You follow the lead element at ten meters. Stay close to the outer wall of the passageway; no reason to line ourselves up like duckpins. Right, L.T.?"

Lee nodded while he wondered, *what was Finder doing*? Granted, Lee had indicated the next objective, and tactical deployment was the top kick's duty, but Finder had jumped in too quickly, as if he wanted to make sure that his deployment outline was the one used. And besides, Lee thought, toggling the private channel with his chin, Burns, not Lewis, was the best shot with the bullpup carbine they had brought. "Sarge," he began—

Finder's response on the private channel was curt. "Trust me, L.T. I know Lewis isn't the better shot, but that's not what's important here."

"Then what *is* importa—?"

"L.T., trust me. Please."

"All right, Sergeant—with the proviso that we're going to have an after-action chat."

Finder nodded. "You're the boss, Boss." Finder switched back to general address. "Okay, Lewis, since you're our base of fire the rest of the way, you're our point-man into the passage. Get to the side as soon as you're in, and once the entry is secured, tuck down to the right; L.T. you'd go in last, and tuck down to the left. Sir, we go on your count."

Lee nodded. "Lewis, you go on 'three.' One, two—"

On "three," Burns tripped the door release and Lewis drift-stepped into the passageway, Lee felt a fumbling at his left hand. Looking down, he saw Finder sneaking an odd-looking pistol into it. Well, pistol was a charitable term. It looked like a long, anorexic tube with a magazine at the rear and the manufacturing characteristics of a zip gun.

"What the—?"

Finder's voice on the private channel was a fast hiss, "Eight rounds. Gyrojet ammo. Recoilless for zero-gee. Don't use your ten-millimeter. Stay alive." And then Finder was popping through the entry after Burns, barking orders. Lee was still so surprised he almost forgot to follow.

When he did, he discovered the rest of the team towing themselves down into crouched positions; Lee did so too, tugging his body into a ball to the left of the door.

"All clear, L.T.," reported Finder. "Pretty quiet, for a hijacking."

Lee kept his eyes up the corridor that dwindled away from them. "Yes and no. I wasn't expecting to find any bad guys back here, only crew bodies. One of which may be there." Lee pointed.

Burns, squinting, nodded. "Yeah. Looks like a floater. Almost at the other end of the tube."

"Twenty-three meters away," reported Lewis, who was just taking his right eye away from the carbine's laser rangefinder.

"Active sensors off, Lewis," Lee snapped. "They may not be patrolling this part of the ship, but they could have seeded with automated detection systems. So from here on, we go in old school: no sensors, no comm, hand signals only."

"But L.T.," Burns began.

Lee made a throat-cutting gesture with the edge of his left hand. Burns got the idea and shut up.

Finder nodded, pointed to Lee and Lewis, made a push-back gesture with his palm, raised all his fingers, held out a stationary thumbs up and waited.

Simple enough. Finder was simply reconfirming the order that Lee and Lewis were to follow at a range of ten meters. Lee replied with a thumbs up.

Finder nodded, tapped Burns on the shoulder and pushed firmly off the deck at a shallow angle, drifting to the right. Burns copied him, but drifted to the left. Lee waited until they were about eight meters away, then nodded to Lewis and copied Finder's jump.

However, being the only native Dirtsider in the team, Lee's free-jump was not as precise. He had to push back from the wall just before reaching the spot where the dead crewman was floating, Finder had already sent Burns ahead to secure the entry into the inhabited areas and now pointed at the corpse's wounds. Lee squinted through a diffuse cloud of small red globules. A small crossbow bolt had hit the crewman just above the hip. But that had not been the fatal injury. The two stab wounds to either side of the sternum and the slashed neck were the obvious causes of death.

Lee tugged himself lower so he could see the shoulder tabs on the corpse's coveralls. As he suspected, an engineer, who'd probably been baby-sitting the reactor when the hijacking began. Either he had heard calls for help and was hustling forward, or the hijackers had baited him out. Either way, he had been surprised and probably disabled by the crossbow hit. Then his attackers had finished their job up close and personal. And since they had used a knife in zero-gee, it made it quite likely they were not Earth-born. Zero-gee melee was a very exacting skill, possessed only by those who already had a great deal of experience living and working in low or no gravity environments.

Finder leaned over until his helmet's faceplate touched Lee's. Through the glass, he heard the sergeant's voice, hollow and muted. "This was the work of Upsiders, no doubt about it."

"Yes—this one killing was. But that doesn't mean that *all* the hijackers are Upsiders."

Finder raised an eyebrow, then nodded. "True enough, L.T. Now, we're going to leave Lewis a little farther behind, okay?"

"More for us to chat about later on, then."

Finder shrugged, smiled, turned to Lewis, and made a push-back gesture holding up ten and then five more fingers. Then he tapped Lee on the shoulder and readied to jump. As soon as Lee had postured himself identically, Finder nodded and they pushed off, gliding down the remaining corridor at waist height.

Lee's jump was a little better this time, partly because he felt there was less reason to stick close to the wall. Reading the unfolding evidence, he doubted that the mutineers felt any need to patrol this part of the ship. Indeed, their absence here suggested that they were confident they had accounted for all the passengers and crew. And that prompted a number of surmises that began to coalesce into a coherent tactical picture.

Firstly, the attackers were clearly willing to kill the crew given little or no cause to do so. There was no sign that the dead engineer had been carrying a weapon. Or that he had been moving to help the other crew or passengers. Or that he had intended to hole up in Engineering, where he could have plagued the attackers with environmental shutdowns, bulkhead lockouts, and a dozen other things that would have made their takeover both dangerous and uncertain. On the contrary, it seemed far more likely that the attack had been so quick and fierce that none of the crew had had the chance to warn him. The unrumpled condition of his clothes and still-combed hair supported the conclusion that the floater had been accosted and bushwhacked by someone he trusted enough to come close to.

Which further suggested that some of the crew were in on the mutiny, either as the ringleaders, or as accomplices to the attackers who had masqueraded as passengers. And since there was no sign that anything had gone awry with the hijacking, that prompted Lee's last grim conclusion: that the mutineers had not been interested in hostages. They had not made any demands for ransom or concessions in exchange for the hostages. Indeed, the mutineers had not contacted the authorities at all. The only reason Lee had known to investigate was because the *Fragrant Blossom*'s captain had missed a privately arranged check-in call with his friend, Callisto's Chief Administrator for Outbound Operations. By deduction then, it seemed unlikely that there were any passengers or crew left to rescue.

Arriving at the entry to the hab modules, Lee stopped his forward glide with an outthrust left hand. Finder signaled for a huddle; they leaned their helmets together. "Okay," he said, "what do you want me to do next, L.T.?"

"Not a lot of choice, Sergeant; we go room-to-room. And we go fast. I don't think they've bothered with guards, except in the forward section where they'll be manning the bridge and watching our ship. And waiting for their ride."

"Huh?" said Burns.

"Their ride," repeated Lee. "If they meant to take this hull somewhere, they wouldn't just be drifting here. Since coming on site, we've ascertained that they've got control over enough systems to keep the airlock sealed against us, and that their engines are in fine working order. So if it was part of their plan to take this ship somewhere else, they'd already be doing so. Which means that there's company coming."

Lewis and Burns exchanged wide-eyed looks. Finder merely smiled. "I see we got lucky and drew a good CO. For a change. What else, sir?"

"Their lack of contact with us, and particularly their failure to warn us off by threatening the lives of hostages, means they probably don't have any left to threaten. So I suspect that we are in a free-fire situation. However, we can't be sure of that, and we definitely want to take these bastards alive, both because that's in accordance with regulations, and because we really—*really*—need to interrogate them."

"What? Why?" Lewis asked.

"Because even among the few cases of deep-space hijacking or mutiny on record, this one is the oddball outlier. They're not after hostages, or the ship itself, so they're playing some other game—and we need to talk to a few of them if we're ever going to learn what that game is. Set up our entry, Sergeant."

"Yes, sir. Burns, you will lead the room breaches using the spray-gun."

Roderigo was already pulling what looked like a wide-muzzled, sawed-off grenade launcher off his shoulder.

"Open the choke for maximum dispersion, and use the heavy tranq rounds."

"Uh, Sarge, the chemical warfare experts told us that if a target is small, wounded, or has a coronary condit—"

Finder fixed Burns with a sharklike stare. "If the bastards die, the bastards die. We'll take every precaution, but with that tube of yours set on wide dispersal, you can't count on multiple hits. One gel bead is going to have to take any target down. So today you're serving up double-strength sleepy-time cocktails."

"Roger that, Sarge."

"The L.T. and I will be carrying the lethal firepower to clear the passageways, moving forward by leapfrog advance."

Lewis frowned. "What about me?"

"You keep a tight hold on that carbine, Lewis. You're our ace in the hole. If the spray gun jams, or we bypass some hostiles and they come out on our rear, you're going to be our fire brigade. As needed, we'll call you forward to outflank them, or add your heavier firepower to ours."

"So I stay all the way back here?"

"Yes—which also guarantees that if everything goes south and we have to beat ass out of here, you're holding the exit open for us."

Lewis shrugged. "Yes, Sarge."

"Good. Lieutenant, whenever you're ready, just give the word."

Lee nodded. "The word is given."

※ ※ ※

It was pretty much what Lee had expected. They entered the forward decks unopposed—except for the silent scrutiny of reangled video pickups, and the accusing stares of floating bodies.

The hijackers had killed crew and passengers alike. One of the latter—a Loonie, judging from her unnaturally lean build—couldn't have been more than fourteen years old. Maybe not even that much. Lee clamped his molars down hard and pushed on through the mid-air sargasso sea of corpses and blood globules.

Tagging closed stateroom hatches with small opening alarms to alert them to anyone emerging into their rear, they propelled themselves toward the bridge at best speed—

And were met halfway by two ill-shaven men who had obviously seen them coming on the realigned security cameras. The good news was that the enemy's armament was fairly light. One had a regulation ten-millimeter pistol, the other had what looked like a repeating compressed-air spear gun made out of spare parts. The bad news was that they were in their space suits: Roderigo's spray gun would be useless unless it hit them in the face.

Damn it, Lee thought, even as he shouted, "Burns, switch to lethals. Fire at will."

As in most meeting engagements, most of the shots went wild. As in most zero-gee combat, the shots were wilder than usual. Burns was late swapping weapons, got a small spear *cum* crossbow bolt in the left shoulder of his hard-suit. It was impossible to tell from his grunt whether it had penetrated or merely thumped him mightily. Either way, he was now trying to correct a modest backward tumble.

Finder pitched forward, so that he was aimed face-and-shoulders-first at his attackers. Lee did the same, appreciating how this nonregulation "prone posture" both minimized his body's silhouette and put it in line with the recoil of his weapon. There would be push-back, yes, but little if any tumble.

And that seemed to be helping Finder's marksmanship. As the enemy's own ten-millimeter rounds spanged and sparked overhead, the sergeant fired twice, paused and then fired a third time. The pistol-wielding thug went backward, struggling, trying to bring his pistol around to bear again. Finder ended that attempt with a fourth shot.

But Lee was too busy to see the outcome. Sighting down through his own weapon's basic peep sight, he lined up the man with the spear gun and fired. The gun didn't kick at all, but there was a brief wash of pressure on both the inner and outer surface of his gloved wrist. It was the angled backblast from the charge that kicked the round out of the barrel, equalizing the propulsive force both forward and back. An instant later, the tail of the round lit up like a tracer as its gyrojets kicked into life and sent it jumping forward.

And straight into the bulkhead behind the crossbowman. But now Lee understood why Finder had paused after taking two shots. He had been comparing the trajectory of his fire to the three-dimensional drift of his target. But now Lee's target was raising the reloaded spear gun. Lee fired two rounds.

The spear gunner spun sharply to the right as Lee's first bullet hit him in that arm. The second shot, a blind miss, extinguished whatever fleeting flare of triumph the young lieutenant had felt. Sighting carefully, Lee prepared to spend a fourth bullet on this target—

From behind him, a ten millimeter automatic barked three times. At least one of the rounds hit the wounded spearman in the center of mass. Blood erupted like a thin stream from a child's bubble-making toy, and the man's movements diminished into fitful writhing.

Lee turned to thank the now-pistol armed Roderigo Burns—but the rating was desperately reaching out for the wall, trying to stop the tumble imparted by his own quick sequence of shots. Lee stretched to help him—

Finder's voice was a respectful, if curt, reminder. "You wanted a fast advance, right, Lieutenant?"

Lee paused, nodded, turned back toward the bridge and snapped his hips down so that his feet contacted the deck; as they did, he kicked.

Arrowing forward ahead of his sergeant, he couldn't help smiling at Finder's appreciative mutter over the private circuit, "Not half bad—for a newb."

⚜ ⚜ ⚜

Taking the bridge was pure anticlimax. Although the last two mutineers were armed with ten-millimeters, they blasted away at a stray suit glove that Finder spun lazily through the doorway. Only three shots from each, but that was all the advantage the top-kick needed. Swimming around the rim of the hatchway with the fell purpose of a stubby piranha, he watched as the hijackers tried to correct their tumbles and took careful aim.

Lee chinned the private circuit. "If they're helpless enough, we could take them pris—"

"Negative, L.T. Look at them; they're reorienting already. They're either Upsiders or have enough training to recover from the tumble. We'll have lost our advantage in another three seconds."

Lee sighed, "Fire at will."

They both did: two rounds from each of them finished the job.

That was when one of the door-opening alarms went off to their rear. Tugging themselves around into sharp 180-degree turns, Lee and Finder kicked and soared back the way they had come.

Before reaching the site of the first gun battle, they saw Burns taking cover in a hatchway, the distinctive bark of a ten-millimeter causing him to flinch back even farther. Just then, a series of sharp, higher-velocity cracks echoed at them from even farther up the corridor.

"All clear," signaled Lewis on the open circuit. "There was just one of them. Probably asleep when we came in. I got 'im. Sarge, I hit him all three times, even though the recoil had me—"

"Great, Lewis, that's great." Finder turned to Lee. "Well, there goes your chance to interrogate a prisoner, L.T."

Lee shook his head. "Rotten luck, Sarge, rotten luck."

Finder switched to private circuit. "That presumes the death of that last hijacker was a matter of luck—that there was no intent involved. Sir." Finder's glance in Lewis' direction was dour.

Yes, Lee reflected, he and the sergeant would have an awful lot to chat about later on . . .

❊ ❊ ❊

Arriving back on the bridge of his customs cutter, Lee relieved the acting XO, Bernardo de los Reyes, with an exchange of lazy salutes.

"Started worrying about you out there, Skipper," said de los Reyes.

Lee finished pulling off his suit gloves. "Had to go to radio silence before we took out the hostiles about two hours ago. There were five of them."

"And why so shy during the last two hours?" de los Reyes asked in an almost bored drawl, which was an act for the benefit of the bridge ratings. Bernie knew damned well that the extended radio silence meant something unusual was up. Probably something dangerous.

"No time to chat about that just yet, Bernie. We still have some work to do."

Finder clumped onto the bridge as well, still in his vacc suit. "Lieutenant Strong's working on a pretty interesting hunch, Bernie."

"You don't say?" muttered the much-younger de los Reyes. The two were pals from way back, and by all rights and measurements of seniority, it should have been Finder, not Bernie, serving as the brevetted noncom XO aboard their cutter, the *Venerated Gaia*. However, Finder's wit was not only barbed, but occasionally injudicious. Previous Dirtsider officers had put enough demerits and reprimands into his record to ensure that he never became anything more than he was right now: First Sergeant and EVA team leader.

Lee drifted across the bridge to hover behind the shoulder of the nav rating. "Navigator?"

"Yes, Lieutenant?"

"Run a plot for me: trajectory of the *Fragrant Blossom* for the next three weeks."

"But sir, the *Fragrant Blossom* is adrift. She's not under power or on course for any—"

"I know, Rating. Indulge me."

"Yes, Sir."

As the first navigator worked, both Bernie and Finder drifted over to watch the process.

The computer flicked between subroutines, cleared, then showed a course plot that intersected one red circle: a possible rendezvous with a charted object.

"Throw that up on the main plot, Navigator," Lee said with a nod at the computer screen.

Which showed that the trajectory of the *Fragrant Blossom* would carry it out of the Jovian side of the asteroid belt, and very close to one nearby planetoid, the red-circled 216 Kleopatra.

Lee turned to his two senior subordinates. "The hijackers weren't just drifting. If they had been, they'd still have been more or less on course for Callisto. But they're not. Which means that, after they took the *Fragrant Blossom*, they used some corrective thrust to put them on a coasting trajectory to that collection of rocks," he pointed at 216 Kleopatra.

"Why there?" wondered the First Navigator.

"Because," supplied Lee, "that's where their friends are waiting."

※ ※ ※

Bernie and Finder were the only ones who accompanied Lee into the claustrophobic CO's ready room. As they entered, Bernie reached under the light table—already displaying the projected course to 216 Kleopatra—and flicked a switch. The room was suddenly filled with what sounded—or more accurately, felt—like a pitchless hum: a white-noise generator.

Lee glanced at Bernie. "Well, today seems to be the day for nonregulation surprises."

Bernie met the glance sheepishly and shrugged. "Guess so, Sir. Now, how long do we have before we're on top of 216 Kleopatra?"

"Two hours and eight minutes," Lee answered. "Meaning I've got no time to catch you up on what we found aboard the *Blossom*. Hell, we don't even have time to get instructions from, or clear a farther ops plan with, the brass back on Mars."

Bernie nodded. It was a little over twenty light minutes to Mars, which would guarantee at least a full hour's lag time.

"They're not going to be able to offer any worthwhile input before we have to commit to *some* plan of action," he agreed. "So we either do this on our own—which means we carry the can for not waiting for confirmation if things go wrong. Or else they send us loose, provisional orders based on the first batch of incomplete data. So that, if things go wrong, they can blame the failure on our sketchy reporting and poor execution. That about what you were thinking, Skipper?"

"Something like that," Lee acknowledged.

"Which leaves the steaming turd in our laps, either way," Finder grumbled.

"In my lap, gentlemen, in my lap." Lee sighed. "I'd be happy to share the inevitable blame with you both, but this is my command, my call, my court-martial."

Bernie looked at Finder and expelled a histrionic sigh. "Jan, I meant to ask you, are we *still* having trouble with the lascom array?"

Finder was blank-eyed for a moment, then nodded sadly. "Oh. Yeah. That. Can't seem to figure out what's wrong with it."

"And did you log it as being off-line yesterday, when we first discovered the malfunction?"

"I don't think so. I'll have to go back in the records and check. I might need to make a retroactive correction." Finder was now beaming with positively malicious glee.

"I should report you both," Lee said, managing not to smile.

"You should, Skipper," Bernie agreed with a somber nod, "you really should."

Lee grinned. "Okay, so the lascom will 'finally' come back on-line after we get to 216 Kleopatra: too late for us to give a sitrep to, or get orders from, the brass on Mars. But just in time to send them word of what we found both there and here. And of course, we can't send by radio because we can't put out an active EM signature while there might be a hostile hull in our area of operations."

"Aye, aye, Sir," agreed Bernie. "As per regs. Which we always follow around here."

"So I have observed."

Finder looked up. "You suspected there was something hinky bout the *Blossom*'s hijacking from the start, L.T.—but why?"

Lee shrugged. "Logically, with an intact drive, the bad guys should have made best speed toward a hidey-hole as soon as they could. Just as logically, we'd have spotted their engine signature—or their residual temperature, if we only came across them after they stopped boosting. Either way, they'd have been lit up like a neon sign on our sensors, once we arrived in the area. But they made sure they weren't."

Bernie frowned. "So are you saying they *knew* we'd be here? But how?"

"That's the hinky part. The only way they could know we'd be here, running dark, was if they had access to classified information. Specifically, our projected patrol plot."

"Damn," breathed Finder, "that's nontrivial access."

"Yes, but everything points to it. They not only knew we were in the area, they were also prepared for any conventional boarding attempt."

Bernie frowned. "What do you mean?"

Finder shrugged. "After we took down the mutineers and secured the ship, we found out that they'd booby-trapped all the logical ingress points—except the one they either didn't know, or forgot, about."

"You mean the core-ejection tube?" Bernie shook his head. "Hell, they just probably figured no one was crazy enough to try it."

Lee smiled. "You mean, they figured no one would be able to look past their superstitious fears and focus on the physics."

"Yeah." Bernie scratched an ear. "While we're on that topic, L.T., me and Sarge here couldn't help notice that you're not exactly—well, you're not like the other officers Earth has sent to us."

"To put it scientifically, you are trying to ascertain why I'm not an arrogant prick?"

Finder guffawed. Bernie smiled broadly. "Uh, yeah . . . something like that."

"Long story, but let's just say my family isn't exactly beloved by the 'globally-appointed' politicos back home."

"And home is where, for you?"

"Tacoma, then Vancouver, then Amherst."

Finder and Bernie exchanged knowing looks. "Another New World troublemaker, eh?" Bernie asked.

Lee shook his head. "Not me. But my folks were. They're part of a dying breed, I'm afraid."

Bernie shrugged. "Seems to me the independent spirit doesn't die too easily in 'the colonies.'"

"Perhaps not"—Lee tried to smile genuinely but felt rue pulling down the corners of his mouth—"but die it does, nonetheless. There are a lot of disincentives for free-thinkers. You don't get prompt access to social services if you're known to be a card-carrying 'recidivist.'"

Bernie and Finder exchanged long glances. "Yeah. We know."

Lee leaned back. More and more it seemed that the "long chat" he was going to have with Finder had probably better include Bernie as well. "You guys have been watching me, haven't you?"

Finder smiled as he filled a liquid-bulb with coffee. "You're just figuring that out now? A smart guy like you—Sir?"

"No, I just didn't realize how methodical you've been. And how much more there must be for me to learn."

Bernie shook his head. "Lieutenant, you don't know the half of it."

"I'm sure you're right—but it's going to have to wait." Lee glanced at the clock. "We'll be drifting past 216 Kleopatra in only two hours, and we've got a lot of work to do."

"Like what?" asked Bernie. "Seems to me we should just back well away from the *Blossom* without altering its heading, match course, and lie doggo until an extraction ship comes out to pick up the mutineers. Then we hit them while they're in the middle of their personnel transfers and—"

Lee shook his head. "You're presuming that upon reaching Kleopatra 216, they'll have to stop for a long rendezvous, and that the mutineers will stay inside the *Blossom*, waiting for pick up. But they may go EVA beforehand, and get fetched by a small ROV tug. That way, the enemy ship could stay in the shadows of Kleopatra the whole time."

Stares went back and forth between Bernie and Finder again. Finder was the first to shake his head and admit, "He's right."

"Damned if he's not," muttered Bernie. "Imagine, being schooled in space ops by a Dirtsider. My Ma on Mars will never let me live it down."

"Then don't tell her," suggested Lee. "But that EVA pick-up is not the scenario I'm most worried about."

"Oh?" Finder leaned forward, coffee suddenly forgotten.

"Nope. Since the hijackers weren't interested in hostages, or the ship itself, that means they have other motivations. Motivations we haven't seen yet."

Bernie shrugged. "Okay, but how does that change anything?"

"It changes things because, if they do have access to our patrol plot, then this is just the messy part of some bigger covert operation. An operation that someone is trying to hide, or to keep plausibly deniable. Which means it has to be perfectly sanitary." He paused. "Which means that the tools they used to carry it out might need to be sterilized. With extreme prejudice."

"Damn," breathed Finder, "the kid—I mean, the lieutenant is right. For all we know, the rendezvous at 216 Kleopatra may only be to get information or proof of mission success. Once the extraction team gets what they need, their next move might have been to grease the hijackers themselves."

"Yeah," Bernie agreed with a nod, "it fits." He folded his arms. "Okay, skipper, so what's the game plan?"

"Are all of our own ROV tugs available?"

"One hundred percent readiness, sir."

"Excellent. And how many remote passive sensor packages do we have in stores?"

"Six, Sir. Of different marks."

Lee nodded, then leaned over the light-table plot. "Okay, then. Here's what we're going to do . . ."

❀ ❀ ❀

Almost two hours later, the crew of the *Venerated Gaia* was at general quarters, and wondering why the hell Lieutenant Strong was not maneuvering more aggressively. But the cutter—which they had long ago rechristened the *Venereal Gato*—continued to match the slow progress of the *Fragrant Blossom*, drifting side by side with the larger hull, fully in its shadow.

Couch-sized debris tumbled along with them. Having originated from the *Blossom*'s cargo decks, it angled away from the twinned craft, the gap between junk and ships widening steadily.

The *Gato* was almost as silent as the space through which she glided. The hum of computers and the dampened vibration that resulted from running on batteries were unusually noticeable in the absence of human banter. The possibility of an engagement not only had the crew tense, but evoked a sense of the surreal, so rare was space combat. That the potentials of the adversary were wholly unknown only kept their eyes more firmly riveted to their screens, their fingers tense with waiting for orders to act.

The bridge crew had another object to stare at, however. There, in the main viewscreen, 216 Kleopatra—shaped like a 217-kilometer long dog-bone with a maximum width of 94 kilometers—loomed steadily larger. Tumbling end-over-end every five hours, it was a fairly kinetic rock, accompanied at some distance by two planetisimals—three and five kilometers in diameter, respectively. Intermittent sampling and mining ejecta accompanied it as well, the individual objects ranging in size from a handball to a house. And so, depending on the size of the enemy ship—assuming there was only one, of course—it could be hidden behind any of several dozen rocky slabs or lumps in the area, including, of course, the immense Kleopatra herself.

"Kleopatra is now within the outer engagement envelope of our missiles, Skipper," the first gunner rasped, his throat evidently too dry to get out the words easily.

"Sensors, report," Lee ordered, not turning to look at the rating in question.

"No change, sir. Of course, we'd get better data if we lit up the active arrays—"

Lee's interruption was quiet but sharp. "Don't even think that thought, Rating. We run dark until I give the word."

"Yes, Sir, but—"

"I'm well aware that passive sensors don't give us full detection capabilities, much less targeting. For now, just maintain the lascom links to our passive assets and keep me apprised."

"Yes, Sir."

Bernie drifted closer. "Lieutenant, you know it's possible that the hijackers don't have anyone waiting for them here, that they just planned to switch to a smaller craft that they stashed here in some little crevice where we'll never see it."

"It's possible," Lee admitted.

"But you don't buy it," Bernie completed the implicit reservation.

"No, I don't. Given all the trouble they went to in setting this up, I just don't—"

"Lieutenant—!" The tense exclamation was in reaction to a sudden orange glow limning the far rim of 216 Kleopatra: a false-colored superimposition of a new heat signature's halo.

"I see it, Sensors. Get me a triangulation on the probable point-source."

"Can't do it, sir—not with the remote sensors we're depending upon currently."

Bernie chewed his lip, staring at the orange glow. "That's a lot of juice, if we can see it as this range with portable passive sensors. What do you think—?"

"Nuke drive," Lee answered flatly.

"Sounds like you were expecting it," Finder said from the back of the bridge.

Lee turned, barked. "Sergeant, your post is in auxiliary for the duration of all combat. If this bridge is destroyed—"

The faces around Lee suddenly became pale. Finder snapped a salute. "I'm on it, Sir."

Bernie smiled—until Lee swiveled around to face him. "Mr. de los Reyes, you are the only man on this bridge who is not secured in an acceleration couch. Do so at once."

Bernie gulped, nodded, sat, and pulled at the straps.

The Mars-lean crewman manning the Sensors sounded as if he was being strangled. "That halo is heating up, Sir. Readings suggest high-energy particles—"

"I'll bet they do," muttered Lee. "Prepare to re-angle the passive sensors—but be careful not to impart any vector change to the debris we mounted them on."

"Aye, sir. The ROV tugs are ready to rotate the debris and converge the scanning cones of the individual sensors."

And not a moment too soon. From over the rim of 216 Kleopatra, the orange halo coalesced as it rose, shrinking and concentrating into an angry red blob.

"Vampire, vampire!" shouted the Sensor Rating. "Moving at—holy shit!"

Lee ignored the profanity. "Gunnery, sensors are now under your direct control. Triangulate upon the emissions with the passive sensors."

"That won't get us a serviceable target lock, sir."

"I am aware of that, Rating. I'm not trying to get a hard lock with them—yet. And with our on-board active arrays still dark, he doesn't even know we've got him located. Unless he has ESP and knows that the junk paralleling us is concealing passive sensor packages."

Bernie breathed appreciatively. "And working almost like a phased array of thermal detectors."

"That's the idea. Let's hope it works. Helm, stand ready. Navigator, plot a direct retreat from that vampire."

"We—we're *running*, sir?"

"No, we are opening the range. And if you wait another second to plot that course, I will cite you as derelict in your duty, mister."

"Sir, plotting new course, *Sir!*"

The engineering rating licked his lips. "Do I bring our own power plant on-line?"

"Not yet. Right now, we're putting out less radiant energy than the plant on the *Blossom*. I want to keep it that way."

Bernie smiled. "So we're hiding in the liner's thermal shadow."

"Hopefully. Gunnery, ready a wide missile spread."

"How many birds, Sir?"

"Salvo all."

"Sir?"

"Given how fast that ship is approaching, do you think we're going to get a chance to shoot twice?"

Gunnery gulped. "Salvo all, aye, Sir."

The red blob seemed to have angles now, but was more intensely red—and it was growing visibly.

"That damn thing has twice our thrust," muttered the helmsman.

"More like five times, and unless I'm very wrong, it's leaving a rad trail so hot that it almost glows in the dark."

"Damn—yes Sir, I think it is," said the sensor rating.

"Gunnery, do we have a preliminary target lock?"

"Still working, Sir. Interpolation is pretty messy with these portable sensors—"

"Sensors, has the vampire lit up its active targeting arrays yet?"

"No—but he should have done it, Sir. He's in range. Is he damaged—?"

"He probably has home-brewed missiles with shorter range than ours. So he's hoping we'll panic when we see how rapidly he's closing on us, and that we'll go for a Hail Mary shot from extreme range."

Bernie nodded. "Yeah, he wants us to launch while he's still just a thermal smudge. And once we do, he'll go active, get a fast reciprocal lock on us by tracking back along our own active sensor emissions, and run a missile up our ass."

Lee nodded; he felt his armpits growing unpleasantly wet. "I say again, Gunnery, do we have a preliminary lock?"

"Not ye—Lock! It's fuzzy and unsteady, but I've got a piece of him. Not enough to guarantee a hit, though, Sir."

"Salvo all, Gunnery. Set missiles to follow our guidance datafeed."

"But Sir, if they're to have any chance of hitting him, we've got to light up our own arrays, get an active lock with our on-board sensors."

"Negative. Not until fifty percent of our missiles' flight time has elapsed."

"Which is happening . . . right . . . *now!*"

"Active arrays on," ordered Lee. "Send that new datafeed straight to our missiles: give them a solid lock. Engineering, power to full. Helm, best speed away from the vampire."

Gunnery whooped. "Missiles are transferring over to active array target lock. Eighty percent of them are still inside a possible intercept footprint pattern and are closing."

Out in space, the missiles were no longer following the imprecise and irregular targeting data being relayed from the tactical thermal sensors riding the ROVs slaved to the *Blossom*'s detritus. Now that they were using the active arrays' clean, infinitely superior guidance datastream, they rode it straight toward their target. The crude guidance from the passive arrays had put eight of the ten missiles close enough to adjust to a true intercept course—even though they had already closed sixty percent of the range to target.

Obviously, the enemy craft had expected the *Gato* to launch and engage her active arrays at the same time—the latter being the target they had been waiting for. Now, with eight missiles already bearing down upon it, the vampire attempted to evade, tumbling ninety degrees and using its extraordinary thrust to alter its vector as abruptly as possible. But the tremendous delta vee it had already invested in closing the range to its target now worked against it. Although the enemy hull could side-vector dramatically, it was still closing with the oncoming missiles, which tracked along with its vector changes unwaveringly.

The adversary discharged a desperate flurry of its own missiles—and then was gone in a short, vicious flash.

The elated whoops on the bridge died at the sound of Lee's harsh question. "Inbound missiles?"

"Three, sir. Jamming, but they're still on us."

"Probably flying by simple on-board sensors now, looking for our emissions. Deploy decoys; put in a heavy mix of thermals."

Bernie nodded. "Another reason you kept our own rockets cold for so long. If we had been building up engine heat over the past hour, their birds might have been able to distinguish us from our decoys."

That was the very moment that the countermeasures rating reported that one of the enemy missiles had spent itself homing in on an RF emitter decoy; the other two expended themselves on the thermal flares.

Lee undid his seat-straps and stood. "Secure from general quarters." He leaned over to the voice-activated comm system. "Sergeant Finder to the bridge on the double. Helmsman?"

"Yes, Sir?"

"As senior rating present, you have the con. I will be in the ready room with Mr. de los Reyes, preparing an after-action report and waiting for the sergeant to join us."

※ ※ ※

As soon as the ready room's door closed behind Finder, Lee turned to face his two NCOs. "Okay, gentlemen, now that we have a few minutes to talk, you have some explaining to do. Specifically, I need to know the origins of the gyrojet zip gun that you passed to me on the sly, Sergeant Finder, and why you made sure Rating Lewis was left out of the team that went into the forward section of the *Blossom*. Who, you later intimated, may have shot the last hijacker three times not out of nerves but in order to ensure that we had no prisoners left to interrogate. And then there's the white-noise generator that you obviously had installed in this room, Mr. de los Reyes. A pretty unusual modification for a man who 'always follows regulations.'"

Lee sat down. "So I need both of you to remedy my Dirtsider ignorance about these matters. Right now. Before Mars can respond to the after-action report I just sent." He folded his arms and waited.

"Wow," breathed Bernie after blinking. "We had you pegged for the mild-mannered type, L.T."

"Sorry to surprise you. Now, it's time to share your surprises with me. What the hell is going on out here?"

Finder massaged a calloused palm. "L.T., just to make sure that we don't waste time reinventing any wheels that are already spinning between your ears, what do you *think* is going on out here?"

"Well, what I already *know* is that what we Dirtsiders are told about Upside is incomplete and slanted to flatter the dominant political party on Earth, the Greens. Who have a penchant for information control, whereas the Neo Luddites don't have the clout, organization, or—most of all—the patience to oversee the necessary subtleties and nuances. What I *suspect* is that despite all the rhetoric, the Customs Patrol Officer corps isn't the Earth Union's only 'loyal eyes and ears' in space. The Union has to have other, less obvious methods of surveillance."

Bernie shrugged. "We know where our officers' loyalties lie, given where all of you come from. No offense intended, L.T."

"None taken. But that means you're more worried about informers from inside your own, Upside ranks." Lee turned toward Finder. "So that's what was going on with Lewis. You suspect him of being an informer for the Earth brass."

Finder nodded soberly. "Yeah. He's new and no one knows his family—not even the other Loonies."

"He's a Loonie? He doesn't look it."

"That's because he's not lunar-born. But his zero-gee skills are too good for him to have been born Dirtside."

Lee thought about Finder's assertion. "Could he have grown up on one of the rotational habitats—like you, Sergeant?"

Finder smiled. "So you pegged me already? Good for you."

Lee shrugged. "I've heard your accent in the mess. Sounds like one of the L-4 hab rings. And you didn't get that build living anyplace that had less than a one-gee equivalent. Means one of the big toruses.

Which could be where Lewis' family came from. That would explain his Upsider skills, but why he'd be a first-generation Loonie, even so."

Bernie nodded. "Which would also make him a perfect candidate for the Greens to recruit as a snitch."

"Why?"

"The Earth Union maintains strict immigration limits between the different Upside communities. But there are ways to increase your chances of getting permission to move."

"Such as a demonstrated willingness to 'cooperate'?"

Bernie nodded. "They extort a lot of favors that way—particularly when people have a real need to change where they live. Medical needs, for instance."

"Such as?"

Bernie leaned forward, legs wider, hands rubbing roughly between his knees. "You sure you want to hear all this, L.T.? Might change your world view more than you think. Might make it hard to go back."

Lee breathed out. "Not sure I want to go back Dirtside. Not sure I want to live Upside, either."

"Hell," grunted Finder, "ain't like there's much in between."

Lee smiled. "And there you have the crux of my dilemma, Sergeant. But go ahead, Bernie: tell me how the Earth Union uses medical blackmail."

Bernie shrugged. "Okay—and remember: you asked. So, when I was growing up on Mars, we had some neighbors, two domes farther down the main tube. Nice folks, two kids, one a daughter. Guess I had a bit of crush on her. Anyway, when she was twelve, they diagnosed her with environmentally-induced leukemia."

Lee frowned. "I thought the habitats on Mars all had to meet rigorous radiation protection standards."

"Yes, and all our nonexistent pigs have wings, too. Look, L.T., maybe the protections passed spec when they were built. But in some cases, that's more than two centuries ago. Materials get compromised, shielding wears away, berms get eroded. Bottom line is we have to maintain them as best we can, but Earth always finds excuses to delay or cancel crucial cargos."

"They delay shipments of basic shielding?"

"They delay shipments of everything. Including—and here we return to my story—specialty medications. My cute neighbor with the leukemia should have been getting her meds weekly, but the supply on Mars ran out after five weeks. She had to wait ten weeks before another batch arrived. If that had gone on, she'd have been dead in two years, three at the outside."

Lee unclenched his teeth. "So her parents made a deal."

"Of course they did. Wouldn't you? They got permission to go to one of the low-gee rotational habitats out near Earth's Trojan asteroids. And I'm guessing they're still there, working as snitches for the Earth Union. Lewis is a more typical candidate, though."

"Why?"

"Well, frankly, because he's a Loonie. See, Loonies are generally the wealthiest Upsiders. They get lots of shipments from Earth, they get lots of loyalty perks, they have a lot of regular contact with Dirtsiders. And because it's only a light-second away, and it's part of the same public data net, and because you Dirtsiders see a lot of it on your screens, the Earth Union has got to make life on the moon look nice. So Loonies tend to enjoy the same social services and access to needed supplies. And where that kind of money and privilege is flowing, it's always easier to find sympathetics for the Earth regime."

"If there's an Earth Union snitch on board a ship," grumbled Finder, "it's even odds that he's a Loonie. Which is why we're careful sharing secrets with them. Like our home-made zero-gee pistols."

Lee leaned back. "This isn't exactly what they teach us in school about Upside life."

"Yeah," Finder said gruffly, "we know. Remember; we've dealt with a long line of your predecessors, a new one every year. And that's touches on the mystery *we've* been trying to solve, L.T. How did you become so—um, 'open-minded'?"

Lee shrugged. "Well, some of my relatives are Fifthers."

Now it was Bernie's turn to stare blankly. " 'Fifthers?' "

"Yes. As in 'I invoke my rights as guaranteed under the Fifth Amendment'?"

"What's the Fifth Amendment?" asked Bernie.

Finder frowned. "If I remember correctly, that's the part of the American Constitution that gives people the right to refuse to respond to a question, even in a court of law, if it would incriminate them."

"Wow," wondered Bernie. "Whatever happened to *that* right?"

Lee shrugged. "It still exists in the U.S.—technically. But back about a hundred years ago, when the Greens were consolidating their hold on power before revamping the UN into the Earth Union, they managed to get the equivalent of loyalty oaths passed in most countries. In some places, like northern China, you *had* to respond. In others, if you didn't respond, it was the old 'silence grants consent' construance. In a small number of countries, you could still refuse to take the oath. You had to explain why, however—except in the U.S. There, you could still just fold your arms and shut your mouth, as per your Fifth Amendment rights. Ever since then, anyone in the U.S. who doesn't roll over for the powers that be is dubbed a Fifther."

"Huh. So you come from a long line of troublemakers," observed Bernie. "I knew there was something I liked about you, L.T. But that doesn't explain why you're—well, competent."

Lee shrugged. No reason not to tell them. "Probably because I grew up reading all the radical books in my great-grandfather's library—half of which you can't even find anymore."

Bernie mused. "What sort of books have the Greens and Neo Luddites weeded out of Dirtside circulation?"

"Lots. Decent history of any kind. Fiction—or plays or poems—that had heroes whose behavior didn't 'exemplify the spirit of communal cooperation.'"

"What?" Finder exclaimed, "No Shakespeare?"

"Oh, that's different. Anything from before the nineteenth century is now considered 'primitive' literature."

"Damn," said Bernie with a stare, "I though they were called the 'classics' of literature."

"Yeah, well that was before the Behavioral Standards committees made sure that all our society's heroes unfailingly demonstrated 'model-worthy behavior.' So the earlier heroes are relegated to semi-barbarian status. No fault of theirs, of course. They lived in the benighted epochs before the Green Awakening."

Finder was frowning. "Didn't the Russians try to control book availability during their Communism phase?"

Lee shook his head. "Can't say. It's hard to find much accurate history from 1800 onward. We had a little in great-granddad's library, but mostly books about America's past and its military campaigns. But novels—" Lee pictured the dark wood shelves that went on and on, that had been silent gateways into worlds other than his drab, narrow reality, in which bold ideas or actions were viewed as destabilizing and dangerous. In the books, characters had saved cities, built or broken empires, discovered continents, explored planets . . .

"L.T., you still with us?"

Bernie's quiet prompt jarred Lee out of his fond recollections. "So I decided I was going to live as much of that life as I could."

Finder's bushy eyebrows climbed toward his receding hairline. "And how did you do that?"

Lee shrugged. "After college, I enlisted in the only service that still went in harm's way: the Coast Guard. Search and rescue. And the Earth Union is always glad to find people willing to sign up for that kind of duty, particularly officer material. Not a lot of folks with good grades are willing to take those kinds of risks anymore—not even to save someone else's life."

Bernie nodded. "Well, that explains why you didn't get rattled on the bridge when we started trading shots with those bastards. Damn, even us Upsiders don't head straight into danger. If it's coming toward us, we sensibly run like hell. If we can."

Finder smiled. "So you prequalified for the Customs Patrol by sailing into hurricanes."

Lee smiled back. "Pretty much. That was the only way they were ever going to let me go Upside."

"Which you wanted to do . . . why?"

Lee glanced at Bernie. "To do this. To go to a place where I figured the global bureaucracy couldn't have everything under its constant scrutiny and control."

"Well," exhaled Bernie, "welcome to the shit, Lieutenant Strong. Because that's what you asked to swim in, and that's where you are."

"Skipper," the communications rating broke in, "incoming signal from the brass."

"Speaking of shit—" drawled Finder.

Lee cut a sharp look at him as he responded to the rating, "Pipe it in here."

"Sir, there isn't really anything to pipe. It's a request for a retransmission of your after-action report, sir—to new lascom coordinates."

"New coordinates? For where?"

"Best guess, sir? Hygeia."

Bernie and Finder looked as surprised and puzzled as Lee felt. "Very well, Rating. Comply with the request." He toggled the channel off, turned to the other two. "Hygeia?"

Bernie shrugged. "The outermost of the Belt's big rocks. Observation post, watering hole, fuel station, gathering place for off-contract prospectors and small-claim miners."

"That I know. I've read the charts. But what do you mean, 'off-contract'?"

"I mean what everyone out here knows, L.T., your superiors included. Not every person born off-Earth is duly reported to the authorities, nor is every business, or every ship, or every community."

"So, by off-contract, do you mean they're not part of a legitimate commercial contract, or not part of the greater social contract?"

"Both. They only continue to exist because they stay under the radar."

"Ah. And some of these—independents—come to Hygeia to trade?"

"That, and more. A lot of matchmaking goes on there. Talk to a Belter sometime about the about the difficulty of *really* long-distance relationships."

Lee smiled. "I see your point. But then why would the brass order us to retransmit our report to Hygeia?"

Finder looked at his big feet. "Well, there are rumors, Skipper."

Bernie looked over at him, surprised. "Okay, Jan, what've you been holding out on me?"

Finder looked up at him. "Listen, Bernie, if I told you everything I knew, then you'd be as smart as I am. Almost. So allow an old man his secrets." He turned to Lee. "Skipper, word is that there are a few Earth Union ships—larger than cutters—which lurk around out here, and that they have hidden support caches on or near some of the major planetoids. Like Hygeia."

Lee frowned. "You mean, other Customs Patrol craft?"

"Yes and no. Reportedly, these ships are under the control of a secret branch of the Customs Patrol, one that reports directly to the senior Green politico on the Earth Union Steering Committee. And these ships are crewed by guys like you, former cutter skippers and other Dirtsiders who got a little actual experience out here."

Lee felt his frown deepen. "And what's their mission?"

Finder looked glum. "Whatever the politicos tell them it is."

Lee felt his hands and feet suddenly go cold. "A spaceside Praetorian Guard?"

"Or Cossacks. So the rumor runs."

Bernie stared at Finder. "I thought that was just an old wives' tale, bogeymen for scaring the kids."

Finder's eyes rolled round toward the younger man. "If the tales I hear are true, they don't show up to scare people. Only to kill them."

Lee started doing the forensic math. "If such ships really exist, it makes sense that one might be lurking nearby—particularly if our guess is right that the hijacking of the *Blossom* is just part of some larger covert conflict."

"Okay," said Bernie, "but if this Cossack Patrol is in on that action, then were the hijackers working for Upside or Dirtside interests?"

Lee nodded. "Or are there other players in the game?"

Bernie frowned. "Like who?"

The comm system squawked. "Incoming message, Sir. And be advised, there's a total exchange delay of forty seconds."

"Acknowledged. Pipe it in, Rating."

Bernie rubbed an index finger across his full upper lip as he did the math. "Twenty light-seconds range. A little closer than Hygeia, but not by much."

The screen on the aft bulkhead flickered into life, revealing a plain-featured man, wearing an extremely conventional suit, seated stolidly in front of a nondescript background.

"Greetings, Lieutenant Strong. I am the Regional Customs Patrol Coordinator, Stephan Mann."

With no outgoing signal to be sent until they were done watching this transmission, Bernie wasn't shy about filling in what he knew about their caller. "I've heard of this guy. Swiss-Belgian, been out here about five years. Every time he shows up, something funky has, or will, hit the fan. No friend of us Upsiders, and as Green as they come."

Lee nodded and added silently, *And not on any table of organization I've ever seen for the Customs Patrol. This guy handles special jobs only. Careful, now.*

"We are in receipt of your after-action report, Lieutenant. You are to be commended on your competent performance."

"I think he means, 'enthusiastically congratulated for kicking bad-guy ass,'" muttered Bernie.

Mann's time-delayed image had not paused. "However, your failure to maintain necessary system readiness on your vessel compels us to append a negative comment to your performance. We trust you will ensure that such a failure does not recur."

"System failure?" echoed Finder. "What system failure?"

Lee grinned sideways at him. "The lascom that you recorded as malfunctioning 'yesterday.' Remember?"

Finder's puzzled frown was replaced by the same sheepish look that was already on Bernie's face. "Oh, yeah, that. Sorry we didn't see this glitch coming, L.T."

"So I don't get a cookie from Mr. Bad Suit. Big deal."

The spare administrator in the admittedly bad (or at least, utterly dull) suit, was continuing. "What was of greater concern to us, however, was that you were unable to secure any prisoners. It would have been helpful to interrogate any of the perpetrators of the senseless and depraved criminal act that was carried out against the *Fragrant Blossom*."

Lee raised an eyebrow. *Senseless and depraved?* That seemed to obliquely suggest that Mann was satisfied that the unexceptioned slaughter of both passengers and crew was an act of wanton savagery, not ruthless premeditation. It was a puzzling—or maybe telling—conclusion.

Mann droned on. "Concerning your speculation that the ship you destroyed was equipped with a reconfigurable nuclear thermal rocket—specifically, a gas model that could shift between closed and coaxial operating modes—our engineers point out that such a technology is hypothetical only. Your speculation also presupposes that there are rogue Upside engineers and shipbuilders who have achieved this high-performance technology independently, and have amassed sufficient radioactives to operate it. Our threat projection analysts deem both conjectures insupportable and not worthy of further examination. However, if you have further evidence to support your speculations, please transmit it now." The message ended.

Lee looked at his senior ratings. "Am I going nuts, or did he just tell me that what I hypothesized is absolutely impossible, but then ended by asking me to send more evidence to support my hypothesis?"

"Uh, yeah, pretty much," nodded Bernie.

Lee shook his head, and signaled to the communications rating. "Prepare to send reply."

"Sir, your comm pickup is live and sending."

Lee stood slightly straighter. "Coordinator Mann, I am happy you have received my reports and data so promptly. In the matter of the capabilities and origin of the enemy craft, I base my conjecture on theoretical work that dates back almost three centuries, and the Customs Patrol's known inability to maintain complete overwatch on Upside activities this far from Earth."

He felt Bernie's and Finder's eyes upon him, watching, measuring, wondering how much he was going to tell or reveal about what he was learning about the real circumstances of Upside existence.

"However, while I can offer no concrete evidence of production facilities or personnel operating away from the supervision of the Customs Patrol or other duly appointed Earth Union authorities—"

—he heard two faint, relieved sighs behind him—

"—it is nonetheless noteworthy that the intensely radioactive nature of the threat vehicle's expended propellant and its ability to generate such a profound energy spike so quickly points to a fundamentally different nuclear thrust technology, one that would be consistent with the projected performance ratings of a reconfigurable nuclear thermal rocket. I close by pointing out that it would be the perfect vehicle for their operation, able to change power levels quickly, and seize the offensive initiative with a five-hundred-percent thrust advantage over us, at least during our brief engagement.

"Finally, while our understanding of the *Fragrant Blossom*'s hijacking is limited to what we can reconstruct from the forensic evidence, I must point out that although the felons showed depraved indifference to life, their actions are hardly seem 'senseless.' Each step of their plan was deliberately and methodically executed, right down to the long drift they undertook to reach 216 Kleopatra a few days after the event, rather than making a fast getaway. The discipline evident in their actions leads me to conclude that this may not be the work of mere pirates, but of political radicals among the Upsider communities." He switched off the comm hub, sat down . . . and suddenly noticed that both Finder and Bernie were carefully avoiding his eyes. "Okay," Lee said in a low voice, "what now? *Is* there an organization of renegade, radical Upsiders?"

"Well," answered Finder, "it's not so much an organization, as it is a loose collective. They call themselves the Spacers."

"Why that?"

Bernie rubbed his hands anxiously. "Because, L.T., it's their way of saying you're wrong to think that the dirt is humanity's real home. The most extreme of them insist that humanity's prevalent obsession with living on a green planet is not only outdated, but dangerous. They believe that's why Dirtsiders treat Upsiders like crap: because they feel superior, because they live on Earth, the holy womb of the race."

Finder nodded. "And their answer is to turn their backs on Earth and let it drown in its own sewage and self-importance."

Damn, I really do *have a lot to learn about what's going on out here,* Lee thought.

"But I'm not sure the Spacers are militant enough to resort to hijacking, Skipper," finished Bernie. "On the other hand, you're dead right that whoever took down the *Blossom* wasn't doing it to get money, to get the ship, or even to get the short-term concessions that hostages can buy. So we've gotta wonder, what *were* they after?"

Finder nodded with the whole upper half of his body. "Yeah, and why was there an illegal, nuke-engined, missile-laden hot rod waiting in the weeds to spirit them away?"

Lee nodded. "We have too many questions and not enough answers—but I don't think we're going to find any new ones just by combing the ship again. I think we have to expand the search."

"To where?" Finder asked.

"To the one place that might have answers, and which we can get to: Callisto. That's where the *Fragrant Blossom* was heading."

Bernie nodded. "And you think that the 'mutiny' was planned to make sure she didn't get there?"

"More specifically, to make sure that something or someone on board didn't get there."

Finder frowned. "So you think someone on Callisto was waiting to receive the goods? Maybe the guy who sent the warning about the *Blossom* being overdue?"

Bernie shook his head. "No, that would be too obvious. And

besides, Callisto doesn't get a lot of ships in—maybe four a year, tops. So a lot of people are going to be eagerly waiting on each one of those hulls for supplies, building materials, new personnel, forwarded cargo."

Lee nodded. "Yes, but somewhere in the haystack of the *Blossom*'s cargo hold, there just might be that one incriminating needle of evidence that will point to someone who was waiting for something *not* on the manifest, something secret."

The communications rating called through the ready-room door. "Skipper, incoming reply to your last transmission."

"Thank you, Rating. Pipe it in."

The screen brightened. Mann was seated as before but appeared to be on the verge of fidgeting. "Lieutenant Strong, it is my professional opinion that your comparative youth and the uncommon stress of the last few hours has you imagining perfidies, plots, and political renegades where none exist. It is an understandable after-effect of combat, but you must put these phantasms behind you. You have work to do and a patrol route to complete. You are to take the *Fragrant Blossom* in tow and make for the nearest secure Earth Union facility at best speed. You are not to conduct any further forensic surveys of the ship's contents; that will be carried out by the on-site authorities. Farther communications on this matter are prohibited, except insofar as you must coordinate with the Earth Union facility at which you will turn over the derelict ship. If, since your initial report, you have detected anything anomalous or unusual on board the *Fragrant Blossom*, you are to report it now. I await your final transmission."

After a few seconds, the communications rating prompted over the intercom, "Sir, do you wish to record your reply?"

Lee exhaled slowly, leaned back from the communications hub. "I will not be sending a personal reply. Simply transmit that I have nothing further to report, that I have received and understood my orders, and will be underway to the nearest secure Earth Union Facility within the hour. Conclude with my regards to Coordinator Mann, and my thanks."

Finder jerked his head toward the now-blank screen. "That bastard Mann should have let you follow up on the evidence, finish this investigation."

Lee smiled. "Oh, but he did." He punched the intercom stud, feigning obliviousness to the matched stares on the faces of his senior staff. "Helm?"

"Yes, Skipper?"

"Make fast the *Fragrant Blossom* for towing. Navigator?"

"Here, Sir!"

"Plot a course for Callisto. As soon as the helmsman signals that the *Blossom* is securely in tow, execute at best speed."

"Yes, sir!"

Lee turned back to his goggling senior staff and smiled.

"You're trying to get yourself court-martialed," hypothesized Bernie.

"I am obeying orders," corrected Lee. "You said it yourself, we always follow regulations on the *Gato*. To the letter, in this case."

Finder's face brightened with comprehension. "Because Mann told you to head to the *nearest* secure Earth Union facility. Which, given our current position, is Callisto."

"Yes, it's the closest—by about a thousand kilometers."

Bernie stared balefully. "Skipper, you know Mann wasn't including Callisto in the list of options."

"Do I, Bernie? He said 'the closest.' If he had any exceptions in mind, it was—by regulations—his responsibility to make them explicit."

"Lieutenant, Callisto is off-limits. We're not even allowed to go there."

"That's where you're wrong, Bernie. *You're* not allowed to go there. No Upsider is, unless they are on a government contract to help build the Outbounders' interstellar colony ships. But as a Customs Patrol *officer*, I have clearance to go to the facility and inspect it, if I deem it necessary to ensure its security."

"And do you currently have any concerns for its security?"

"I don't have to, Bernie. On the one hand, I have the clearance. On the other hand, I was just given an explicit order by Coordinator Mann to go to the closest facility—Callisto."

Bernie glanced at Finder, who shrugged. "Hey, he's following regs, as far as I can tell."

"Sure, Skipper's following the letter of the law—but is completely twisting the intent of it." Bernie turned back toward Lee. "Listen,

Lieutenant Strong, we don't get a lot of officers like you. So you'll forgive me if—for purely selfish reasons, and for the good of the crew—I ask you to reconsider this course of action. You know they're going to slow-roast you for going to Callisto—for bringing us Upsiders that close."

Finder leaned forward. "Skipper, I hate to say it, but Bernie's right. Much as I'd like to see you get to the bottom of whatever happened on the *Blossom*, the Earth Union has made it painfully clear to us Upsiders that we're not allowed close enough to see the technology that's being used to build the Outbounder ships. And you can understand why. If your hunch is right, then our own off-contract communities found a way to improve on nuclear thermal rocket technology and build the raider that almost blew us to dust a few hours ago. What do you think they'd do with the fusion drive and power-plant technologies used for the Outbounders' STL colony ships? Or the waste-heat radiation systems? Or the robotics and automated systems?" He spread his hands wide. "L.T., your bosses know that if we Upsiders got our hands on those systems in their entirety, not just the little bits and pieces we fabricate separately, we'd have monkey copies operating in a few years. And we'd have improvements within a decade. And then how long would it be before the Spacers would decide to turn away cutters like this one—or vaporize them, if they refused to listen? With fusion-based energy and engines, we'd own space almost overnight. And you know what that means."

Lee nodded. "Ultimately, you'd own Earth, too. Or can at least threaten it with annihilation."

Bernie leaned close. "So don't push the letter of the regs on this one, L.T. The Earth Union will burn you for it, even if they have to trump up charges and falsify evidence. They can't afford to let you thumb your nose at them."

Lee nodded. "True—but on the other hand, they can't afford to reprimand me if I find, and can prove, that there was a deeper conspiracy behind the hijacking of the *Blossom*. Hell, you know how they'll spin it then: Coordinator Mann 'displayed extraordinary foresight in ordering Lieutenant Strong to take the unusual step of towing the *Fragrant Blossom* to Callisto, thereby enabling him to surreptitiously conduct the investigation that ultimately revealed the identity and purpose of the saboteurs.'"

Bernie shook his head. "But L.T., you don't *have* to do that. You're taking a hell of a risk. And for what? Because you'll be able to prove your fellow Dirtsiders wrong?"

"No," Lee said, looking steadily at Bernie, "because it's the right thing to do. Because it's our duty to find out who was ultimately behind the deaths of all those innocent people on the *Blossom*. No matter what our gutless superiors say, that is Job One. So that's the job we're going to do."

"Damn," breathed Finder, "you really do sail straight into hurricanes, don't you?"

※ ※ ※

"Administrator Perlenmann is on open channel, sir. Exchange delay is minimal."

Lee leaned toward the audio pickup. "Hello, Mr. Perlenmann. I'm sorry to come to your facility under these sad circumstances."

"Lieutenant, as I understand the regulations, you are not supposed to come to my facility under *any* circumstances. We are off limits to all Upsiders."

"That is true, Mr. Perlenmann. But firstly, I am not an Upsider. Secondly, I was given clear orders to tow the *Blossom* to 'the nearest secure Earth Union facility.'"

"And why was I not informed of your arrival earlier?"

"Again, orders. I was instructed not to send any transmissions relevant to the disposition of the *Blossom* until such time as I was ready to transfer her to the closest facility."

"I mean no inhospitality, Lieutenant, but your presence here, and those orders, are most irregular. However, we are grateful you have brought the *Blossom* to us, both for operational and personal reasons."

"I understand that several of her passengers were late-arriving members of Outbounder families already working here on-site."

"That is correct. They will want to take possession of those bodies as soon as it is practicable. What is your ETA to Callisto, Lieutenant?"

"Just under three hours, sir."

"Very well. After our navigational controllers have settled you into orbit, I will send a shuttle to dock with the *Blossom* and—"

"Mr. Perlenmann, I'm sorry, but that isn't going to be possible."

A long pause. "And why not?"

"Unfortunately, in handling some suspicious containers that the hijackers evidently smuggled aboard the *Blossom*, a hermetic seal was broken and it is possible that a bioagent was released."

Lee glanced at Finder, who, at that signal, opened a spoiled ration pack. He wrinkled his nose at the faint stench, and whispered, "Uh-oh. Could be a biohazard, Skipper."

Lee rolled his eyes, tried not to smile, and heard a note of concern creep into Administrator Perlenmann's voice. "It is not a particularly virulent pathogen, I hope?"

"It's too early to say, Mr. Perlenmann. We're still trying to type it. But until we do, and assess how effective our efforts at containment have been, I'm afraid I have to impose a quarantine."

"Which puts us at a most difficult impasse, Lieutenant. We cannot safely come to you, and you are not permitted to come to us."

"That's not quite accurate, Mr. Perlenmann. I have had no personal contact with the possible pathogen, and, as a Dirtsider and officer of the Customs Patrol, I am authorized to travel to Callisto."

Another long silence. "Very well, but that does not answer the issue of reclaiming the deceased family members of our Outbounders, nor our timely access to necessary supplies. We get only four shipments from cis-lunar manufacturers per year. They fabricate all the proprietary systems that go into the Outbound colony ships. Without those components, we're unable to work."

"I think I have a way to solve those problems, Mr. Perlenmann," Lee said. "Upon arriving, I will shuttle down to Callisto to present the paperwork necessary for releasing the bodies to their next of kin. The bodies themselves will need to remain under observation for seventy-two hours to ensure that they are not harboring elements of the unknown biohazard." *During which time we'll ensure that the incriminating needle we're looking for isn't being carried inside one of those bodies.*

Perlenmann sounded thoughtful. "And so at that point, either my personnel or yours could transfer the contents of the *Blossom* to my shuttles?"

"Well, sir, we'll need to be a little more methodical than that with the cargo."

"I don't understand, Lieutenant."

"Mr. Perlenmann, the hijackers compromised the *Blossom's* computers. Among the most heavily damaged files were those containing the ledgers of the ship's manifest, stores, and personal effects. Unfortunately, we have not been able to locate any hard-copy backups. Consequently, because some of the contents of the *Blossom's* hold were bound for locations other than Callisto, we can't simply release everything to you. Instead, I must ask you to forward an itemized list of what you expected to be receiving from the hold—or from the personal belongings of the deceased. While we wait out the seventy-two hours of quarantine, we will locate the items you indicate and ready them for conveyance to you." *And sift through all that junk for the evidentiary needle we're seeking.*

Perlenmann did not respond immediately. Bernie and Finder waited hopefully; Finder even had his fingers crossed. The silence dragged on—

"Very well, Lieutenant, although this is most inconvenient. Now, when did you say you would be arriving with the paperwork for releasing the bodies?"

❧ ❦ ❧

Perlenmann met Lee at the entry to Callisto's cavernous ice separation and processing facility. Over the sustained, throbbing moan of the catalytic water crackers, he shouted an inaudible greeting and waved for Lee to follow. As he did, spacesuited workers turned to watch him pass, the exposed faces no more readable than the ones concealed behind sealed visors. Although the volatiles refinery was a shirtsleeve environment, it was separated from the murderous surface of Callisto by only one bulkhead wall. Suits were required, no exceptions.

Lee was turning to ask his bearded host about their daily production capacity when the immense hydrogen-purification tank on the far side of the processing facility exploded. The shock wave slammed into Lee like a whole-body battering ram and sent him tumbling forward. His left shoulder hit the rocky floor first, his torso cinching at the waist. His feet continued arcing away from the source of the blast, dragging him head-over-heels into a punishing low-gee somersault.

Instincts took over—instincts that had been drilled into him during his training on Luna, and that had been acquired at a high price in bruised bones and suppressed vomit. As Lee's momentum spun him back into a heads-up position, he stretched his legs wide, thereby making his longest axis perpendicular to the direction of his tumble. His rotation became faster but less powerful. At the same time, his left hand (the expendable one) went out in front of him, elbow bent, wrist relaxed: a shock absorber for what was sure to be a nasty impact. His right hand caught the lower lip of his helmet's raised faceplate, pulled down sharply—

Burning hydrogen roared over and around him just after the faceplate clanked into place. The force of the fiery wash accelerated his forward tumble; he landed hard on his left hand, felt several bones bow, one crack. Lighting streaks of pain sprinted up his arm.

He managed to keep his legs wide and his hips cantilevered forward as his chin and chest slammed into the floor. His heels tried to rise again, struggling to unclench his abdominal muscles and pull him into another somersault.

But Lee fought back, kept his waist bent and legs down. His rotational momentum bled away and he started sliding forward, his left arm out for drag and stability while his right hand protected the faceplate. A few more skittering bumps and then he felt himself drifting to a halt. He rolled over, kicked his legs out and up, and came to a buttock-bruising stop.

The wash of burning hydrogen had been brief but every worker in the high-roofed chamber had been knocked flat by the force of the explosion. Most were swaying to their feet, some weren't. Uncertain hands fumbled to secure faceplates as snow began to materialize in the cold, thinning air; a clear sign that the explosion had caused a pressure breach, probably somewhere behind the shattered purification tank. Considering the leisurely pace at which the white specks were migrating in that direction, the breach was probably no worse than a small crack in the berm-covered bulkhead.

Lee rose into the almost nonexistent gravity, looked for Perlenmann, and spotted him rising to his hands and feet a few meters away. Lee dusted off his spacesuit, skim-walked over to the administrator, and helped him up.

From behind a cracked faceplate, Perlenmann nodded his thanks, silver-gray forelock bobbing limply. He smiled crookedly at Lee; "Welcome to Callisto, Lieutenant."

❈ ❈ ❈

Steam oozed out of the drinking tube which protruded from the top of Lee's coffee bulb. The ostensibly disposable bulb looked even older than the ones on the *Gato*. It had been washed and reused so many times that the plastic rim's innumerable hairline cracks resembled a thick forest of denuded saplings.

Directly across the table, Administrator Perlenmann stared down at nothing in particular as his chief engineer concluded his report. The news was not good.

"—so I figure we're down to forty-eight percent production capacity, Mr. Perlenmann, since that was our largest purification unit."

Perlenmann nodded slowly. "Can we reconfigure any of the standard tanks to function as purifiers?"

The engineer nodded and rubbed his blistered cheek; he had been at the processing plant when the explosion occurred and hadn't gotten his faceplate down in time. "Can't do it, Mr. Perlenmann."

"Why?"

The engineer scratched his reddening cheek, winced, snapped his hand away from his face. "Because storage tanks can't be retooled for refining. They're too thin-skinned to take the pressures generated during purification."

"Very well, Mr. Carroll." Perlenmann turned toward a man and a woman who were sitting at the far end of the table. He inclined his head slightly toward the woman. "Doctor Iseult?"

The woman, about thirty and pixieish, straightened in her seat, an action that was more suggestive of a porcupine bristling than a mere effort to improve posture. "Casualties were much lighter than they might have—or rather, *should* have—been. One fuel operations worker, Grigori Panachuk, is still in the infirmary."

"Frankly, it is a miracle that Panachuk didn't wind up in the morgue. He was standing within thirty meters of the tank when it exploded, with his faceplate open and his gloves off. Luckily, he was facing the other way, adjusting his collar communicator with both hands. Otherwise—"

"—Otherwise, Panachuk wouldn't have a face or hands left to worry about," finished the man who was sitting near Iseult.

The doctor shot him an annoyed look, but nodded assent. "Mr. Parsons' assessment is correct. As it is, Panachuk has serious burns and a number of internal injuries. A piece of debris punctured his suit and lodged in his back. Seventeen personnel have been treated for second degree burns, another eighteen for fractures—nineteen, counting Lieutenant Strong." Her eyes, sharp and unfriendly, flicked in Lee's direction. "The pain has subsided, yes?"

Before Lee could nod and lift his splinted hand in thanks, Iseult was finishing her report. "First degree burns and other, minor traumas—I don't even have a final count on those yet."

Perlenmann nodded toward the man next to her. "Mr. Parsons?"

Parsons shifted his blocky frame, stared down at his coffee bulb, and wiped a greasy hand on the front of his faded gray coveralls. He didn't seem in a hurry to answer, or to be particularly impressed with Perlenmann's authority.

A faint German accent intruded upon Perlenmann's otherwise perfect diction; "Your report, Mr. Parsons." *Parsons* now sounded like *Parsuntz.*

Parsons shrugged. "My report? Okay, here's my report. The casualties were predominantly fuel ops techs. All Upsiders. All *my* people." There was a distinct tone of accusation in Parsons' voice.

"As I understand it, Mr. Parsons, there were also half a dozen flight technicians and two environmental maintenance workers in the processing area when the explosion occurred, all of whom sustained some level of injury. All Dirtsiders. I therefore doubt that this explosion was targeted specifically against your personnel."

Lee stopped in mid-drink; a *targeted* explosion? Terrorism? Sabotage? Here too?

Parsons' face was split by a humorless grin. "Perlenmann, if you weren't such a book-loving Green, sometimes I'd swear you were in cahoots with the Sols yourself. How can you even doubt they were behind this? It was Sol sabotage, pure and simple."

Lee put down his coffee bulb with a sharp *clack.* Eyes turned towards him. "Excuse me, but would somebody mind telling me what the hell is going on at this 'secure' facility? Specifically, who or what are the 'Sols'?"

Iseult, Parsons, and Carroll all exchanged brief, awkward glances. Perlenmann seemed to be waiting. In the end it was Parsons who leaned forward, incredulity in his voice. "Don't they tell you guys anything before they send you out here? Oh wait a minute, I forgot. It's beneath a Dirtsider's dignity to learn about Upside."

Parsons was clearly looking for trouble. Lee held his tongue until he was sure of his resolve not to give it to him. "Mr. Parsons, prior to my assignment to the *Gato*, I read everything I could about Upsider communities and issues. And you're right, the info we're given on Earth is incomplete and slanted. However, I've been fortunate enough to be included in some Upsider conversations, so I know about some of the less-obvious issues, and about political movements like the Spacers." Parsons blinked. *Hah, gotcha.* "But I have never heard mention of the Sols, so maybe you'd be kind enough to clue me in."

Parsons guffawed. "I don't know any way to 'clue in' an inherently clueless Dirtsider, but I'll give it a try. Ignoring the Greenie administration in charge of this facility," he glared briefly at Perlenmann, "you've got at least three distinct groups on Callisto. The smallest is made up of Dirtside contract workers. The largest is comprised of Upsiders like me, some of whom are probably undisclosed Spacers. Then you've got Outbounders, who just can't wait to get on their colony ship and abandon us Upsiders to the tender mercy of Earth's Greens and Neo Luddites. It's also possible that you've got a small number of Sols here, who think that Upsiders like me are soft, and that Outbounders are craven traitors."

Iseult scoffed, looked away. Lee seized the opportunity. "You have a different perspective, Dr. Iseult?"

She turned to look at Lee, apparently trying to decide whether he was worth talking to. Eventually, she shrugged and offered her version. "Many of the personnel here do express one of two primary political sympathies: pro-Upside or pro-Dirtside. However, their differences have never been violent. The great majority of the Upsiders want to stay on Callisto and keep the Outbound operations running. They rightly believe that if it wasn't for the opportunity to send Earth's most wealthy Dirtsider dissidents off to the stars, the Green and Neo Luddite political alliance would probably discontinue all space-based activities altogether.

"The Dirtsiders are the technicians sent here from Earth to carry out the confidential engineering on the colony ships, or the Outbounders themselves. The Outbounders fear the same outcome that the Upsiders do, but rightly believe the way to prevent the closure of Callisto's shipyard is to offer strong support to the mostly moderate

Greens of the Earth Union Steering Committee. As long as they stay in power, Callisto stays open and the starships keep leaving."

"And the Sols?"

"They are the wild cards in this strange game. The Sols—the self appointed 'star-chamber' of the entire off-Earth population—think that Outbound activities should be ended so that the moderate Upsiders are no longer seduced by the contracts they get from Earth. Then, they believe, the Upsiders would become desperate and help them overthrow the Earth Union." Iseult shrugged. "I do not approve of their methods, but you can hardly blame them. They know what's coming."

They know what's coming. Strange that such a simple sentence could have so ominous a sound. "They know *what* is coming, Dr. Iseult?"

Her fine-boned face was very grave. "War."

"With whom?"

"*Mon Dieu*, can you be so blind? Why, with Earth, of course. Upsiders may resent Earth, but they work with it—and have done so for almost three centuries, now. And over that time, the Upsiders have been accumulating power, gathering the knowledge and means to independently produce technologies which will soon reduce, maybe eliminate, their dependence upon Earth. However, when that day comes—" Iseult shivered although the room was warm.

"And the Sols believe that things are getting so bad that it's better to trigger a war now, to openly engage in sabotage?"

Perlenmann volunteered the answer. "Lieutenant, even out on Callisto, we hear the protectionist rhetoric in the speeches coming out of the Steering Committee in Geneva. The Behavioral Standards Committees have even gone so far as to retroactively restrict the books that may be distributed or owned Upside, including those that will comprise the now-stunted libraries of the Outbounder colony ships we launch.

"The last century's trend toward gradual improvements in freedom of trade and information is now reversing rapidly. And the Sols are not willing to stand by and let that happen. If they are behind today's bombing, it would be to call attention to the creeping return of tighter controls and the danger of Upsider complacency in the face of a potential conflict with Earth."

"There isn't going to be any such conflict, and the Sols know it." Parsons' growl swelled in both volume and disdain. "Let's be realistic. You Dirtsiders know that with us already sitting on the moon, ready to pull another Heinlein 'drop-the-rock' maneuver, you can only push us so far. The Sols are making a mountain out of a molehill. When push comes to shove, the Earth Union will back down."

Iseult shook her head. "Before Lieutenant Kotsukov was 'transferred' he said the same thing about Upsiders: that they would ultimately kowtow to the Earth Union's increased restrictions because the Upsiders are simply not self-sufficient in most regards." The doctor smiled bitterly. "Parsons, if the leaders on both sides are as hardheaded as you and Kotsukov, then there *will* be war."

Parsons snorted disdain but offered no rebuttal.

Lee kept his attention focused on Iseult. "Doctor, who is Lieutenant Kotsukov, and why was he 'transferred'?"

Another uncomfortable silence. Perlenmann ended it, his voice not much more than a murmur; "Lieutenant Kotsukov was our on-site chief of security. He was ex-Customs Patrol and was given a small detachment to help him in his duties here."

"A detachment of Upsiders?"

"No: Dirtsiders, like him. They were drawn from the domestic security administrations of several of the nations of the Earth Union."

Lee kept his reaction from showing on his face. "Domestic security administration" was just a nice word for the paramilitary rent-a-thugs who hunted down unlicensed inventors and roughed up dissidents. "So Lieutenant Kotsukov was a strong supporter of the Green and Neo Luddite coalition?"

"He was a god-damned Dirtsider fascist," snarled Parsons, "He didn't give a damn about politics except in one way: that Earth was to remain the object of all human veneration and the source of all authority." Parsons snorted. "Hell, he didn't make it any secret that in his opinion, the Greens were too soft, and the Neo Luddites too boneheaded to be trusted. That didn't go over too well with the home office, I guess."

Lee frowned. "I'm curious, Mr. Parsons. How did the Earth Union find out about Kotsukov's political sympathies? As Mr. Perlenmann observed, this *is* a rather out-of-the-way facility."

Parsons' smile was feral. "I guess some concerned citizen must have sent a complaint to his regional advocate."

So it was Parsons himself who had been responsible for Kotsukov's "reassignment." Interesting—and valuable cautionary information, reflected Lee as he picked up his coffee bulb.

"Okay, so you've got potentially violent extremists in both the Upsider and Dirtsider communities, resentment toward Earth, resentment toward the Outbounders, and someone sabotaged one of your quarterly cargo runs when they took over the *Fragrant Blossom*—which I'm guessing would have shut you down for quite a while out here."

Perlenmann nodded. "All true."

"So why do you think it happened now? Which individuals might be behind it?"

Perlenmann smiled. "That is precisely what we hope to learn from your investigation, Lieutenant."

Lee paused in mid-drink; hot coffee slid to a stop in the vicinity of his larynx and burned there. "I beg your pardon?" he croaked.

Perlenmann simply continued to smile—and Parsons jumped into the silence with all the docility of a scalded wolverine.

"Jesus H. Christ on a pogo stick, Perlenmann. You're going to turn the investigation over to *him*?" Parsons' finger fired an acrimonious beam at Lee. "To another undereducated and inexperienced Dirtside shavetail who's been here for less than three hours?"

Before Lee's shock at the frankness of the insults could transform into indignant rage, Perlenmann was halfway through a counter. "Lieutenant Strong's dossier indicates that he is not, as you would suggest, a 'reject,' Mr. Parsons."

"Then what the hell is he doing all the way out here? They only send losers to staff the deep-space cutters of the Customs Patrol. Everybody knows that."

Lee didn't bother to keep the edge out of his voice. "Mr. Parsons, my parents are American—Fifthers who are active in the Constitutional Return movement. My assignment here was, I am sure, partly motivated by the Earth Union's willingness to distance me from such a 'recidivistic environment.'"

Parsons rolled his eyes. "Great; now we've got an American version of Kotsukov: a Yankee Doodle Dirtsider ready to give it up for the red, white and blue. What did you do, Perlenmann—put in a special order for this guy?"

Lee kept his own voice level. "Mr. Perlenmann had nothing to do with my arrival here, Mr. Parsons. That was strictly coincidental. Farthermore, I myself am not involved in the Constitutional Return movement. However," he said, turning toward the Administrator, "insofar as any investigations are concerned, Mr. Perlenmann, I would be going well beyond my jurisdiction if I were to take charge of a civilian inquiry."

Perlenmann smiled wanly—and Lee had the distinct premonition that he was about to learn that his jurisdictional knowledge was imperfect. Perlenmann did not disappoint him.

"Lieutenant, I must point out that while our charter here is through a non-security-related agency, the Outbound Operations Administration, we are also officially classified as an Earth Union 'secure facility.' The safety and secure operation of such facilities are the direct responsibility of the Customs Patrol. Under those terms, I believe your authority in this matter is quite clear."

Damned if it isn't at that, thought Lee. If Callisto had only been a commercial refueling depot in the Belt, then it would be a local matter. But since the Callisto facility was where the Outbounder ships were built, and that necessitated the application of proprietary technologies that were subject to security monitoring and protection, it was— officially—a security asset, as well. That meant the investigation was Lee's responsibility.

He cleared his throat. "You realize, of course, that if you turn this matter over to me, the crime in question can no longer be investigated or tried as industrial sabotage. It becomes an act of treason."

Only Perlenmann nodded. The others seemed surprised and suddenly uncomfortable. Lee pressed on, "Mr. Perlenmann, everyone here assumes that the explosion was the result of sabotage, rather than a mechanical failure. Why is that?"

Perlenmann shrugged. "Because, I am afraid, we have already experienced one smaller incident of sabotage here on Callisto. Our secure document scanner was sabotaged about four months ago. The replacement I asked for should be on board the *Blossom*. Did you happen to notice it when you reviewed the cargo?"

Lee nodded. "Actually, I did, because it was a rather surprising item. From what fragmentary records we have"—Lee suppressed a sudden impulse to cross his fingers as he said that—"it was actually included in the priority cargo manifest. But, Mr. Perlenmann, I have to wonder if the two incidents are really connected. After all, why would a Solist, or a Spacer, or a militant Dirtsider bother to sabotage your secure scanner?"

Perlenmann folded his hands. "The Earth Union authorities require that we use our document scanner as a primitive data firewall to protect our mainframe. All incoming data is run though a standalone computer and converted into image files or hard copy. Those images or hard copies are then run through the secure scanner, which is able to analyze any suspicious code elements without those elements becoming resident on any drive as executable data packages. That way, if viruses or trojans are found, they never make it to the mainframe."

Lee nodded. " But how would it be in anyone's particular interest to sabotage that?"

Parsons snorted. "Because all the extremists on this rock have their own worries about the administrator receiving a message they don't get to hear first. If there's no secure scanner, then coded orders can't be sent here, because there's no other means of decryption. So if the Earth Union Steering Committee gets taken over by Neo Luddite extremists and orders that Callisto is to be shut down, the Earth Union would have to send it in the clear, which gives the Outbounders a fair amount of warning."

"And the Sols?"

Iseult shrugged. "They fear the opposite: that the most moderate Greens in the Earth Union Steering Committee might begin reversing the current crackdowns and even order the reacceleration of the Outbounder hull-construction programs. The Sols would see that as undermining the urgency of their own radical anti-Earth agenda, so, given advance warning, they might successfully undermine that trend with key acts of terrorism."

"Okay, so there's reason to suspect both sides of sabotaging the scanner. I'm assuming you already investigated and came up empty-handed?"

Perlenmann nodded.

"Okay, so do you at least know how today's explosion was rigged, what kind of bomb was used?"

Jack Carroll, the blister-faced engineer, pulled a small plastic sleeve out of his breast pocket, pointed at the blackened mass inside the bag. "There was no bomb involved. The saboteur used that electric igniter, slaved to a common wristwatch."

Iseult leaned forward. "*Que?* How can one have an explosion without an explosive?"

"When there's still some hydrogen in a fuel tank, you don't need an explosive, Doctor. Just a spark." Carroll frowned, thinking. "My guess is that the saboteur's first move was to rig the fuel tank's level indicator so that it would read 'empty' a little prematurely. That would keep the pumps from completely purging the tank after a processing run, which means that some of the liquid hydrogen would remain at the bottom of the tank.

"But, when the level indicator registers the tank as empty, the cryogenics shut off. So the tank begins to heat up a little—enough to cause the liquid hydrogen to evaporate into its very flammable gaseous form. At that point, all you need is one little spark and *wham*—you get one hell of an explosion."

Lee frowned. "Who on Callisto would have the knowledge and technical expertise to set this up?"

Carroll's face did not betray what his voice suggested; that only a rank newbie would ask such a question. "Everyone, Lieutenant—with the possible exception of Dr. Iseult and some of her staff. And all the various models of igniters are easy to acquire, since we use them for so many tasks: for burning off waste gases, as starters for auxiliary power plants. They're ubiquitous."

Lee sighed. *No easy answers there.*

Parsons rose noisily. "If we're just about done, I've got some people in the infirmary that I'd like to visit."

Perlenmann hadn't even completed his nod of acquiescence before the fuel-ops chief was out the door. Iseult and Carroll were close behind. Lee rose to follow.

"Lieutenant, a moment—if you please." Lee regained his seat slowly. Perlenmann smiled. "I trust you've had warmer welcomes, Lieutenant. Although I confess surprise that you are out here at all."

"Just luck, Mr. Perlenmann. It was my turn in the patrol rota—"

"You misunderstand me, Lieutenant. I mean I find it unusual that you are in the Customs Patrol."

"Oh. That. Well, unless you were bluffing earlier, you've already seen my dossier."

Perlenmann smiled faintly. "I have. Which is precisely why I'm asking what you're doing out here. A history major, with a minor in literature? And with dissident parents? I'm surprised you were even allowed to go to college."

Lee smiled, knew it was crooked. "Administrator, that's not the kind of—er, 'politically incorrect candor' I am accustomed to hearing from a Green official."

Perlenmann shrugged. "I don't recall saying that I am a Green. Or anything else, for that matter. However, you will find in the course of your investigation, Lieutenant, that there is a great penchant for affixing labels around here. I suspect you aren't particularly susceptible to that kind of blind partisanship, but allow me to emphasize what you probably already know. It will not help an investigator to assume that labels are either useful or accurate."

"Probably no better than it does a facility administrator—even one so unusually articulate as you, Mr. Perlenmann. So tell me, what are *you* doing in this plush job?"

The administrator stroked his beard. "Watching myself grow old, Lieutenant. In some ways, my story resembles your own. I started out as a young professor at Cambridge—Political Science—and was a bit of a radical in the eyes of my employers. I insisted on using unabridged original works, which was not a welcome pedagogical method when the books in question were treatises such as *The Federalist Papers* and Rousseau's *Social Contract*."

"You're English?"

"Half. My mother was from Munich, which is where I grew up before going to school in Italy. I'm something of an EU mutt, I'm afraid. At any rate, I was accused of proffering the forbidden fruit of free thought—so they sent me here."

"It would seem Milton takes a back seat to the Earth Union when it comes to devising suitable punishments for liberty-spouting Lucifers."

Perlenmann laughed. "Lieutenant, despite the sabotage and political skullduggery, I am glad to have you here. Please feel free to come by if you need any assistance—or if you wish to borrow a book." He swept a hand behind him, indicating the innumerable volumes of every height, width, and color, which covered all four walls in serried, sawtoothed ranks.

Lee had a sudden reminiscent flash of standing in the doorway that led into his great grandfather's library. "I just might take you up on that offer, Mr. Perlenmann."

"Good. And, Lieutenant, you might wish to introduce yourself to the on-site security personnel. They are, after all, under your direct command while you are on Callisto. Here are their dossiers. You might also be interested in learning that I haven't notified them of your arrival." Perlenmann smiled. "Nothing like a surprise inspection to boost morale, eh?"

❊ ❊ ❊

The duty officer's room was in complete disarray: overflowing ashtrays, dishes clotted with ossified leftovers, and a clutter of papers held together by the seamy brownish lacquer of old coffee spills. Through the far door, the tittering of girlish laughter was plainly audible. Moving softly on the balls of his feet, Lee approached the doorway.

Two double bunks faced away from the door, offering a direct view of the videoflat which had been set up (in defiance of regulations) on the wall opposite. The current cinematic fare: a buxom starlet in a Little Bo Peep costume halfheartedly fending off the advances of three leering, leather-clad adolescents.

The lower levels of both bunks were occupied. On the left, a broad torso (with a decidedly large central bulge) spanned the width of the mattress. To the right, a small and almost cadaverously lean man was cheering on the video studs in some mishmash of English and Portuguese.

"Tennnnnn-*HUT!*"

The little stick figure on the right jumped so hard and high that he hit the ceiling, rebounded at an angle, caromed off the upper left bunk—and crashed straight into his larger companion, who was just rising. The stick figure went down in a heap. The larger man tottered and unsuccessfully aimed a meaty leg at the stick figure's head. Steadying himself, the big one spat a Slavic growl—"*Izvierk!*"—and then turned toward Lee, the growl metamorphosing into English. "And who the hell do you think you—?" The big man's mouth froze in a fishlike gape as his eyes hit the gold bar on Lee's left shoulder.

"You were about to ask me a question, Sergeant Bulganin?"

The broad Russian snapped his mouth shut—so hard that Lee could hear his teeth clack. Then: "*Nyet*—I mean, no, Sir. No question." Bulganin had pushed himself to attention, but his chin stayed down and his dark brown eyes had hardened into stubborn, lusterless black beads.

Lee turned his attention to the smaller trooper, whose stare was rapidly shuttling back and forth between the Russian and the American. Eager, observant, waiting to see how things would work out. This one would follow whoever established himself as the top dog, rank notwithstanding. Lee turned his attention back to the Russian. "I take it, Sergeant, that you were not informed of my arrival."

"That is correct . . . Sir."

A long pause on the "sir"; the challenge was starting already. Good. Best to get this over with right away. "And is this the condition in which you maintain your quarters?"

Bulganin shrugged, did not answer. Lee could feel the little guy's growing excitement; stick-figure smelled a fight brewing.

"I asked you a question, Sergeant."

Bulganin, who hadn't uttered a sound, sneered. "I said 'No, Sir.' My apologies; my speech must be too soft for you to hear." Stick man giggled.

Lee took a step closer to the Russian. "That's odd, Sergeant. My hearing is quite good and you don't seem like the quiet type. But, perhaps your speech has become soft"—Lee lowered his eyes to Bulganin's sagging midriff—"along with the rest of you."

The black eyes flared then smoldered. "The Lieutenant will please pardon my inquiry: I have seen a uniform and insignia of rank, but I have not seen papers."

Lee admired the way the Russian refused to surrender the initiative. Bulganin was tenacious, if sloppy. There was probably a good soldier lurking underneath the blubber. Lee tossed his ID packet on Bulganin's bunk. "Lieutenant Lee Strong, Customs Patrol, USA, New World Collective. Now in charge here."

Bulganin smiled faintly, smugly. "I see," he said.

"No, you don't—but you will." Still looking straight at Bulganin, Lee barked, "Cabral!"

The stick man jumped, rammed back to attention, his eyes wide. "Sir!"

Lee recited the dossier from recent memory. "Cabral, Eduardo. Senior Rating, Third Interurban Security Force, Brazil. Currently on detached duty to the Customs Patrol." A rent-a-thug from the *favelahs*, probably; might as well check. "From Rio, Cabral?"

"Yes, Sir!"

"Enjoying this assignment, Rating?"

"Yes, Sir!"

"Then you don't have the brains you were born with. *Bulganin!*"—the Russian didn't even flinch as Lee turned back toward him, roaring his name—"First name: Arkady. Sergeant, 18th Security and Protection Group. Twenty-four-year service record. Demerits for brawling, drunken-and-disorderly conduct, and 'political agitation'—*nyet, tovarisch?*"

Bulganin's eyes narrowed at Lee's drift into his nation's contemporary hardline Neo Luddite vernacular. "If we are foregoing standard military address, Sir, I prefer *gospodin.*"

Stubborn and insubordinate, but Bulganin had balls. "Perhaps I should include your mention of that preference when I make my first report, Sergeant. The Neo Luddite regime in Moscow might find it somewhat disturbing."

"I am already in exile, sir." Bulganin's eyes swept the dismal environment. "Where can they send me that's worse than here?"

Lee smiled. "They can send you out an airlock, Arkady. Things are tightening up back in Mother Russia. Neo Luddites—and their preindustrial Communalism—are busy looking for counter-revolutionaries. Some things never seem to change." He stepped back. "And at this moment, I don't give a damn whether they ever do. The only thing I'm concerned with is what's going on right here, right now."

"Sir, with all due respect,"—Bulganin's tone suggested that this was a minuscule amount—"I must ask. What *do* you know about what is going on right here, right now?"

"I know that discipline has gone down the drain and that this unit is currently incapable of carrying out its assigned mission."

"Lieutenant, this 'unit,' as you call it"—Bulganin glanced sidelong at Cabral, and then back—"has carried out its duties, even though we have been forced to struggle along without an officer for over a year now." Bulganin allowed himself a slow, sarcastic smile.

Lee smiled back. "So you're in full readiness? Even for emergency duty in a full grav environment? Tell me, Sergeant,"—Lee looked down at Bulganin's overly-thick midriff—"have you been putting in the mandatory one hour per day in the spin gym?"

Bulganin's smile diminished, faded away.

"Have you, Sergeant?"

The Russian glanced sideways. "There have been—mechanical failures."

"Have there? Well, then you'll be glad to learn that I stopped by the spin gym on my way here and found it to be in full working order. So I'll expect you to report for double-shift PT, Sergeant."

Bulganin's eyes betrayed a hint of dread. "When?"

Lee's smiled widened. "Right now."

※ ※ ※

Iseult cast a curious glance at Lee as she picked up Bulganin's feet and helped her orderlies carry the unconscious Russian out of the spin gym. Cabral stood to one side, watching, panting, and dripping perspiration. One calf was shaking spasmodically—a sign of over-exertion and electrolyte depletion—but the little Brazilian had stayed the distance.

"Cabral."

The wiry private spun away from the door and came to attention. "Sir!" His chin was up, his eyes straight ahead and fixed, his body tensed with readiness. Lee restrained a smile. The top dog barks and Cabral listens.

"At ease, Rating."

Cabral fell into the "at ease" position, which looked even more uncomfortable than his previous stance.

"No, no—stand down, Rating. Take ten."

Cabral's eyes flicked sideways, evidently double-checking Lee's expression against Lee's words: was the American trying to trick him or was this a genuine invitation to relax?

Lee wandered over to a bench, and flopped down. Cabral breathed a sign of relief and joined him.

"So what do they call you, Cabral?"

"Me, sir? Eduardo."

"No, I mean your nickname."

Eduardo smiled, a flash of white teeth. "They call me Fast Eddie, Sir."

"Well, Fast Eddie, you didn't do too badly today. How long has it been since you put in"—Lee checked his watch—"fifty minutes in the gym?"

Cabral paused, then admitted, "A long time, sir."

"Well, we'll be doing at least an hour every day, now. From here on in, we're going by the book."

Cabral laughed suddenly, unexpectedly.

"Did I say something funny, Private?"

"Oh no, Sir. I mean, yeah, you did say something funny, but I guess you didn't know it. You said 'by-the-book,' Sir. That's what the workers call Mr. Perlenmann."

Lee leaned back on his elbows. "Why do they call Perlenmann 'by-the-book'?"

"Well, it's sort of a double meaning, sir. I mean, he has all those books, right? Thousands of them. But it's also a joke about how he does things. Everything with Perlenmann is 'by-the-book,' you know?"

Lee licked salty perspiration off his upper lip; odd, Cabral's description didn't quite jibe with his own perception of Perlenmann. "Tell me, Eddie, what do you think of all this sabotage business? Who do you think is behind it, the hardline Dirtsiders or the Sols?"

The Brazilian shrugged. "I don't know, Lieutenant. Could be either one, I guess."

"What about the rank and file Upsiders? Are there any of them that might have a reason to shut down Callisto?"

Fast Eddie frowned. "I dunno, Sir. I don't see why they would."

"Me neither. What about the Outbounders?"

"The Outbounders? But why, sir? If there isn't enough fuel, they can't leave."

That's true, Eddie—which is also why no one would ever suspect them of destroying fuel to frame the group that was most likely to prevent them from leaving the system and *resorting to violence: the Sols.*

"Besides," Eddie was continuing, "The Outbounder leaders—Briggs, Kerkonnen, even Xi—they're real nice, real *pacifico.* They've never done nothing that was, like, harmful or sneaky."

Well, if this line of inquiry was to bear fruit, it certainly wouldn't be as a consequence of Fast Eddie's political perspicacity. Might as well get back to basics. "Rating, how long since you've done any shooting?"

"Long time, Sir; months." Fast Eddie's eager smile was a testimony to the fact that he liked guns—a lot.

"Then it's about time we got you back in practice, Rating. What do you use for a range around here?"

※ ※ ※

Early the next day, Callisto's comm specialist paged Lee in his planetside quarters. "Incoming message from the *Gato*, Lieutenant Strong. Shall I match encryption?"

"Yes, please do. Put them through."

A moment later, Bernie and Finder were crowding their faces into his screen. "Hi, Skipper. How's the chow down there?"

"Indistinguishable from what you're having up there."

"Ouch. That bad? Well, so much for officer perks, I guess."

"I guess. Do you have an update for me, Bernie?"

"Sure do. Skipper, this whole hijacking incident is getting weirder and weirder."

Lee wondered how that was possible. "In what way?"

"Well, when we sent the hijackers' digitized DNA samples back to Earth, they assigned it the lowest priority status in their search queue."

"That's odd. That search isn't hard and we should be at the top of the priority list."

"That's what I thought. So we took the liberty of sending the samples to a pair of our Upside friends. One works database management on L-5, and the other is in charge of immigration record-keeping on Mars. They got us concrete results—and very fast."

"Fast means that the hijackers were already part of the population that is pre-flagged for scrutiny."

"Bingo. Seems the hijackers were all either convicted or accused felons."

"Pawns for someone else, then. Not surprising."

"No, but this is: every single one of them were Upsiders. They were either from cis-lunar or Belt communities. And all genuinely anti-social types, some with diagnoses of possible sociopathia. What do make of it all, Skipper?"

"Nothing conclusive. They're all Upside-born, so perhaps they were tapped by other Upsiders—Spacers, maybe—who needed cold-blooded killers. But on the other hand, it sounds like someone on Earth was involved, someone who had enough clout to get these brutes out of jail or off parole in exchange for doing this job."

"But why?"

"Until we find what they were after on the *Blossom*—until we find that needle in the haystack—I don't think we're going to get any closer to having an answer to that question, Finder. About which: has there been anything interesting on the cargo claim lists send up from Callisto?"

"Nothing particularly riveting, Skipper. We've been examining every piece they've asked for, including sensor scans for hidden compartments. If they have electronic components, we've run full data analyses. So far, nothing."

"What about tantrums by the brass? Has anyone had a coronary about my decision to divert to Callisto?"

"So quiet it's scary, Lieutenant. We've received dispatches and routine orders, but that's all."

"What orders?"

"Just the ones we were expecting. First a message to resume our patrol route ASAP, then a correction to that order, in response to Perlenmann's indication of our quarantine situation. He bought us an extra one hundred hours on-station. And I got us two extra days beyond that."

"How'd you do that, Bernie?"

"Well, with Callisto's deuterium refinery down, I explained that we didn't have sufficient authorization to draw on Callisto's reserve fuel cache, since every frozen drop is now reserved for the next Outbound colony ship. At least until their main purifier is running again, and they've built up a sufficient surplus."

Lee frowned. "I'm surprised the brass didn't kick that upstairs to get you the necessary permission."

"We didn't give them the chance, sir. In the same communiqué, we indicated that we had made preparations to transfer the fuel from the *Blossom* to our own tanks. Pending their approval, of course, since that could be construed as tampering with sealed evidence."

Lee was impressed at Bernie's inspired chicanery. "So what did they do with that pile of tangled prerogatives and priorities?"

"What bureaucrats do best: they passed the buck to Perlenmann. Who sat on the request for a while, and then sent notice to command—and us—that he was authorizing us to tap the *Blossom*'s tanks and take on her fuel. Which, as you know, is a very long process unless you have specialized fuel-tending apparatus."

"True, but Perlenmann has a tender module. Several, I think."

"So I gathered. But he didn't offer and we didn't ask."

Lee smiled. "How long can you reasonably extend the refueling operations?"

"Brass tells us that due to the 'situational impediments,' we have an additional two days to take on fuel. So we can stay on station for another six days, all told. Then you'll have to interrupt your Callistan vacation and—"

"Negative, Bernie. I'm staying."

"Sir, I'm not sure I heard you correctly. Did you say you're staying?"

"Perlenmann has tapped me to investigate the sabotage that took out their fuel production. It's a matter of regulations: I can't say no. But that could be to our advantage. Did the brass say *I* had to take the *Gato* back out in six days?"

"Well, no, but you are the CO and I think they assumed—"

"That's their problem, then. If I haven't wrapped up here in six days, you resume our patrol roster as the acting CO. That gives me more time on Callisto to see if there's some connection between what happened to the *Fragrant Blossom* and the sabotage here. If they're two pieces of the same puzzle, then in the process of my investigation, I might find whoever was supposed to take possession of that lost needle you're still looking for aboard the *Blossom*."

"Maybe, Skipper. I suppose I don't have to tell you that this is another decision that won't earn you brownie points with the brass."

"This time, they'll have to complain to Perlenmann." Lee told himself that would shield him from the worst of his superiors' probable wrath. Knowing himself to be a poor liar, he was not convinced. "If I'm not back on board in six days, head toward Hygeia first, quarter speed."

"Why there, Sir?"

"So that you'll still be close when I call you back for a pickup."

"Got it, Skipper. Anything else we can do for you?"

"Not unless you believe in the power of prayer or have a lucky rabbit's foot."

"A what?"

"A barbaric Earth tradition."

"Sounds Neo Luddite."

"It probably is. Keep on looking for that missing needle of evidence, Bernie."

"Will do, Skipper. You just keep your head down."

"Sound advice. Out."

❈ ❈ ❈

It took the better part of a week to get Cabral and Bulganin reaccustomed to one-gee centrifuge exercise and military discipline. Bulganin remained silent and somewhat surly, but was obedient and seemed to acquire a grudging respect for Lee.

Which was more than could be said for the Upsiders among the facility personnel. Their written responses to Lee's inquiries about the explosion were terse to the point of uselessness. In the corridors, they avoided meeting his eyes, kept responses to his social greetings as brief and closed-ended as possible. The Dirtsiders weren't much better, and the Outbounders already seemed to be living in another world, simply eager to leave the incessant Upsider/Dirtsider bickering behind them.

The only individual who seemed willing to help was Perlenmann, who opened up his personal log for Lee's perusal. According to the administrator's accounts, the Upsider/Dirtsider factionalism on Callisto had never broken out into violence or sabotage before. However, since the explosion, Parsons' Upsider fuel-ops technicians had provoked at least two public confrontations with Dirtsiders, intimating that if they discovered the bombing had been specifically directed against them, they would retaliate. It was far less certain that they would exert much care in ensuring that their retribution was directed only against the guilty parties.

By the middle of the second week, Jack Carroll had finished his forensics report on the technical details of the saboteur's methods—a report which Lee and Perlenmann decided to keep under wraps until the case was nearing its resolution. A general disclosure now would only tell the perpetrator how much the investigators did (or, rather, did *not*) know.

As he leafed through Carroll's report, Lee sighed, letting his last hopes for an easy investigation escape along with his breath. Ten days of thorough research had turned up nothing. The time had come to press some personal buttons and to see what happened when he did.

❈ ❈ ❈

The cavernous gut of the damaged hydrogen purification tank was alive with the echo of distant work crews. Lee craned his neck to look up at the "ceiling" ten meters overhead, and moved deeper into the vast space, angling toward the intermittent white-blue glow of workers' torches.

A dozen steps later, he found himself approaching a stocky silhouette, its hands-on-hips stance backlit by the intermittent light of the welding. Parsons' voice was less pleasant than usual. "What do you want here, Dirtsider? My people have filled out your idiot reports, so leave 'em alone."

"I wish I could, Mr. Parsons, but I'm afraid 'your people' didn't complete the questionnaires I gave them. To be specific, not a single one of them provided the names of any individuals that they suspected of being radicals—either Dirtsiders or Upsiders. Now I wonder why that would be."

"Wonder all you like, Patrolman." Parsons spat; the impact of the saliva made a flat sound, like a pebble ricocheting off slate. "We're not snitches on this station. And if that's what you require of us, then you can go to hell."

"If you, or any of your people, have any relevant suspicions, I advise you not to withhold them. Anyone who does so knowingly is obstructing an official investigation, which in this case makes them accessories to sabotage—and guilty of endangering the lives of the workers at this facility."

As Lee had guessed, that was the right button to press; Parsons' voice grew taut, his words coming out in a rush. "You're going to accuse my men of endangering their fellow fuel workers? All of whom are Upsiders? Well, take your best shot, Patrolman. But I'll tell you this: we watch out for our own here on Callisto, and if we have any problems, we sort it out ourselves. You don't understand how things work out here—and it's real easy for newcomers to get hurt by things they don't understand. Don't you agree?"

"Threatening a Customs Patrol officer is a serious offense, Mr. Parsons, and it makes me wonder if I shouldn't expand my investigation to include you as a prime suspect."

Parsons' laugh was soft and deep. "Did I threaten you, Lieutenant? Gee, I can't remember saying anything threatening. I was just commenting on how outsiders can find this sort of political problem to be difficult—even dangerous—to handle. And as for investigating me," Parsons snorted derisively, "be my guest. Let me guess. You're convinced that I'm a deep-cover operative for the radical Dirtsiders, right?" His teeth shone as he sneered. "Yeah, while the Dirtside Greens and Neo Luddites are slowly strangling this facility out of existence, you'll waste time investigating the people who need to keep it running in order to survive."

Parsons' tone grew more strident. "You make life hard for us and who knows, maybe production will suffer. Maybe that will make life hard for the Greenie bigwigs on the Steering Committee by giving the Neo Luddite hardliners just that much more ammunition to criticize their handling of Callisto. Maybe that will mean an inquiry, and maybe that will make life hard for *you*—very hard." He paused and leaned closer. "You get my drift?"

Lee leaned into Parsons' face. "Yes, and I hope you're getting mine. I'm here to uphold the law and find the saboteur. And that's exactly what I'm going to do—with or without your help."

Their faces were less than three inches apart, the scratchy hiss-and-whine of torches intermittently piercing the silence. Then Parsons changed his stance, which gave him an excuse to lean back and laugh. "Suit yourself, Patrolman; it's your court-martial." He turned into the glow of the torches and drift-walked away across the belly of the fuel tank, shouting orders as he went.

❧ ❧ ❧

Doctor Iseult arched an eyebrow when Lee entered her office. "And to what do I owe the honor, Lieutenant?" The crisp tone added about a foot to her diminutive frame.

Lee smiled tentatively. "Might I take a seat, Doctor?"

Iseult impaled him with a glare that suggested she was seriously considering a negative response; then she sighed and waved him into the chair on the other side of her desk. "Well, you are sitting. What is it?"

"Doctor, I'm sure it's no secret that I'm not making a lot of progress with my investigation."

Iseult's smile was genuine, if wry. "You have a talent for understatement, Lieutenant. From what I hear, you are making no progress at all—although you are making a number of enemies."

Lee nodded. "I was hoping you might be a little more willing to help me."

Iseult's smile now included a measure of incredulity. "Oh? And why is that?"

"Because you're a doctor."

"Which would tend to make me resent paramilitary bullies such as yourself, *non*? After all, I get to clean up the messes made by you uniformed children."

Lee shrugged. "I suppose so. But I thought that, given the increasing potential for violence on Callisto, you'd want to help me prevent further bloodshed, rather than just patch it up when it occurs. But I guess I was wrong."

Iseult's smile had disappeared, although her teeth were still displayed—now in a rictus of rage. "*Merde!* The gall—that you would attempt to extort cooperation from me in such a manner!"

"Like I said, Doctor, I just wanted to give you the opportunity to save lives." Lee rose to leave.

"*Mon Dieu*, you are arrogant—no, sit. Sit down, damn you." One tiny fist clenched and went white as she regained her composure, a process which took almost half a minute. Then she looked up, her eyes cold and bright. "Unfortunately, you are also right. Parsons' people are getting edgy. I am afraid that they will convince themselves that they must preempt the Dirtsiders—and even the Outbounders—by attacking them first. Physically."

"And that concerns you."

She blinked. "Of course it concerns me. As you so astutely observed, I'm a doctor."

"No, I mean it concerns you because you sympathize with the Outbounders."

Her eyes widened, then narrowed. "Do you wish me to help you— or simply to sit still for an interrogation?"

"Possibly a bit of both, Doctor. I do recall that, when I first arrived, you seemed to stick up for the Outbounders when Parson was bad-mouthing them."

Iseult drummed her slender fingers against the tabletop, stared at them while she weighed her next statement. Finally: "I suppose I do support the Outbounder point of view, somewhat—as well as other moderates. It's the extremists and their pawns who are the real danger to us. Spacers and Customs Patrol, Sols and pro-Earth fascists—you'll all kill each other yet. And when your final war starts, Callisto and every other innocent spaceside community will be caught in the middle.

"And even if you do not have your idiotic war, it is still true that we live on a razor's edge here on Callisto. If the political mood on Earth worsens, then the Outbounder colonization program will be disbanded, and this facility will be closed. And the same will happen to many of the deep-space facilities which exist to supply us. In that scenario, many—most—of those displaced Upsiders will have to be relocated to Earth. No other place can absorb such a sudden increase in population."

"But what about the Upsiders who were born in low- or zero-gee, who can't survive on Earth, even in neutral buoyancy pools?"

"Lieutenant, I am a doctor, not a social planner. I do not have such answers—if any exist." Frustrated, she looked away, her mouth leaned against her fist.

Lee stole a fast, assessing look at her. *She cares, but she's genuinely torn about what to do. She doesn't have the dogmatic certainty of a political factionalist. Time to back off.* "I'm sorry, Doctor; I didn't mean to upset you."

"Lieutenant, it is bad manners to lie, particularly if you lie so badly. You most certainly *did* mean to upset me."

Lee felt his face grow uncomfortably warm. "Yes, Doctor. I'm sorry—but I had to."

"Well, at least you can be embarrassed enough to blush about it. Perhaps you are human after all, Lieutenant Strong."

"Lee."

She almost smiled. "Very well. Lee. You may call me Genevieve if you are done provoking me."

"I believe I'm quite finished, Genevieve."

"Good. Now, how can I help?"

A new voice intruded. "You can help by giving Mr. Panachuk a sedative, Doctor; he's a bit too eager to get out of bed and back to work." Perlenmann emerged from the infirmary, pushing open the door and leaning against the jamb. "How goes the investigation, Lieutenant?"

"It's going, Mr. Perlenmann, but not very fast or very far. I was hoping Dr. Iseult could give me some new insights, particularly into the Outbounders."

The administrator shook his head. "I find it hard to believe that the Outbounder leaders—Mr. Briggs and Mr. Kerkonnen—would advocate violence of any type."

"What about Ms. Xi?"

Perlenmann shrugged. "She is the most temperamental of the Outbounders, but that makes her almost too obvious a suspect, don't you think?"

"Maybe she didn't do it herself. Maybe she got somebody else fired up enough to do it for her." Out of the corner of his eye, Lee saw Iseult frown skeptically.

Perlenmann shrugged again. "Perhaps, but the only reasonable underlying motive—that the Outbounders are trying to frame and discredit the Sols or Spacers—seems a bit far-fetched. Now I must regrettably return to my office; I'm swamped with paperwork."

Perlenmann drift-walked out of Iseult's office. Lee stared after him, and when the door had closed, asked, "What about him?"

Iseult cocked her head. "What do you mean?"

"Could he be—well, a secret Dirtsider fascist, someone who's been waiting for a reasonable excuse to get this facility shut down?"

"Perlenmann? A fascist or Neo Luddite plant? Are you mad?" Iseult's full laugh was a pleasant, musical sound.

"What's so funny?"

"Lieutenant, even if Perlenmann had sympathies for any of the extremist factions, he would never act upon them. Everything with him is by the book, and his mandate is quite clear: to keep Outbounder operations running at 'the maximum sustainable level.' And despite the supply reductions and delays that the Neo Luddites have caused by their filibustering in Geneva, he has managed to stay close to the original ship-launching schedule. Which is no mean feat, believe me."

"I do."

"Well, then, there's your answer, too. Perlenmann's mandate is spelled out clearly and he does not deviate from its rules."

Lee nodded. "Yeah—but it's the exception that makes the rule. Maybe this is the exception."

Iseult shook her head once, sharply. "No. Listen, Lee: I know enough people who either speak to, or are undeclared, radicals. I'm not in on any of their plans, but they trust me—enough for me to know that they all consider Perlenmann to be a stooge for the moderate Greens who are in power back home. Upsiders, Dirtsiders, Spacers, Outbounders: the one thing they *can* agree on is that Perlenmann won't break the rules."

Lee shrugged. "Well, I had to ask."

"Yes, you did. Is there any other way I can help?"

"Not right now." Lee rose into the almost nonexistent gravity.

"Good; then it's your turn to help me." Iseult rummaged in her desk, produced a small bottle of pills and handed them to Lee. "For Sergeant Bulganin," she explained.

Lee smiled. "Weight-loss pills?"

Iseult's face became stern. "That is not funny, Lieutenant. Kindly make sure that the sergeant gets these. Promptly."

Lee frowned. "What are they?"

Iseult, who had directed her eyes to her computer, looked back up at Lee, surprised. "You don't know?"

Lee shook his head.

"He didn't tell you?"

Lee shook his head again.

"*Mon Dieu*, men are so childish! Lee, Sergeant Bulganin suffers from asthma, and all that exercise you've been pushing him through has been making it worse. Much worse."

Lee's thoughts were suddenly cluttered with images of Bulganin in the spin gym, his stony face alternately florid and pale, but always creased by rigid lines of suppressed pain. Lee had attributed the strain to the Russian's excess weight, but now he realized why Bulganin's gray sweatshirt was always black with perspiration, why neither his running time nor his endurance had improved: he wasn't getting enough air.

Lee closed his hand around the bottle. "Thank you, Doctor. I'll see that he gets these immediately."

❧ ❧ ❧

Bulganin stood to attention as Lee entered the now-pristine duty officer's room. The American waved him down.

"Be at your ease, Sergeant. Have a seat and take ten." Bulganin eyed Lee suspiciously and then slowly sank into his chair. He turned back toward the computer on his desk.

Lee extended his hand across the table, uncurled his fingers to reveal the medicine bottle. "Sergeant, I believe these are for you." Bulganin's face reddened and his jaw locked in place. His bearish paw reached out, removed the bottle with slow dignity, and stashed it in his breast pocket. He nodded faintly and shifted in his seat to readdress the computer.

"Sergeant, why didn't you inform me about your condition?"

Bulganin's jaw worked silently for a moment before he muttered, "It is not serious, Sir."

"Damn it, Bulganin, that's not true and you know it. More to the point, now I know it, too."

Bulganin's eyes did not meet Lee's. "You are removing me from duty, then?"

Lee shook his head. "Hell, no, Sergeant. Even if I wanted to, I couldn't. I can't afford to lose you." Bulganin's eyes grew slightly less hard. "But I do want to know how long you've had this condition and why—*why*—you didn't tell me."

Bulganin looked away from the computer, considering. Then: "May I speak frankly, Sir?"

"I insist upon it."

"I did not tell you about my condition because I will not be humiliated by being excused from your physical training requirements—Sir."

"*I* did not set those standards, Sergeant, and you know it. They are Customs Patrol regulations."

Bulganin nodded slightly. "Yes, that is true. But after your arrival, I—I did not wish to receive any special treatment from you, Sir."

Lee nodded. "I think I understand, Sergeant. But hopefully we've gotten beyond our initial friction—at least somewhat. I'm still going to expect an hour of 1-gee PT from you each day. However, you are now to fulfill that requirement by spending three separate twenty-minute periods in the gym, with at least an hour of nonphysical duties preceding each of those PT periods."

Bulganin had his mouth open to protest, but Lee held up his hand. "That is an order, Arkady."

Bulganin closed his mouth, stared, and then smiled slightly. "It will be nice to breathe again."

Lee smiled back. "I imagine it will. How long have you had this condition, and why isn't it on your records?"

Bulganin frowned. "It's not on my records because I've never reported it."

"Christ, Bulganin, that's taking a hell of a chance."

The Russian shrugged. "I would have been taking a bigger chance if I reported it. As you pointed out, my record has some rough patches, including anti-Neo Luddite protests. What do you think would happen if they found out I had severe asthma? Discharged from the service. And then what? I don't know how to do anything other than be a soldier. So I requested spaceside duty and tried to volunteer for the most isolated posts."

"—Hoping that on those assignments, you could either conceal your asthma, or that your CO wouldn't bother to report it."

"*Da*—I mean, yes. That is it exactly."

"Well, don't worry, Arkady; I'm not going to add any health reports to your record."

Bulganin blinked and then beamed. "*Spaseebo*, Lieutenant." Then he looked away, uncomfortable.

"What is it, Sergeant?"

"Sir, I am afraid I have—er, 'forgotten'—to tell you something that might be relevant to your investigation."

Ah hah; now maybe I can get somewhere. "I understand how something might have slipped your mind, Sergeant. It's been a very busy ten days."

Bulganin smiled gratefully. "It's about Kotsukov, Sir. He was involved with the Outbounders. Although they did not share his fervor for Earth's continuing dominion, they were certainly interested in ensuring the continuation of the Outbound operations."

"So I've heard. But why would Kotsukov associate with them? Logically, he'd consider them traitors, right?"

Bulganin nodded. "And so he did. But Kotsukov was practical. They had the same foes: the Sols. Besides, for the time being, Kotsukov was only too glad to see Earth ridding herself of dissidents so disaffected that they would rather take their chances traveling to the stars." Bulganin shrugged. "Towards the end, he even helped them to arrange their secret meetings."

"Secret meetings? Why secret?"

"Well, I think the Outbounders were starting to make contingency plans, trying to decide what they should do if Earth terminated work on the current colony ship."

"Were they considering militant options?"

"I'm not sure, Sir, but I think some of them were. And Kotsukov, he . . . well, he . . ."

"Yes?"

Bulganin swallowed. "He told me where they held the meetings."

※ ※ ※

As the ventilation fan cycled to a slow halt, Bulganin uncoupled the unit's hinge. A heavy push, a scratchy squeal of breaking rust, and then the fan and its mounting bracket swung inward, revealing an air shaft approximately one meter in diameter. Bulganin squeezed himself into the aperture and waved for Lee to follow.

It was a tight crawl. On three separate occasions, Lee regretted that Fast Eddie wasn't familiar with the ventilation system. He would have been a much faster duct-crawler than Bulganin.

After half an hour of crawling, Bulganin came to a dead end where the vent broadened and was blocked by a rapidly spinning fan. After cutting power to the fan and waiting for the blades to drift to a halt, the Russian freed the hinge and yanked the fan inward. It swung back, revealing a tight-meshed grate. The two men crawled forward until they were within inches of the mesh.

Beyond the black metal grille-work, about thirty-five individuals were sitting in an irregular semicircle. Bulganin pointed once, twice, three times; "Briggs, the leader and the smartest. Kerkonnen, his right hand. Xi, good spokesperson. She's only twenty-seven; holds more appeal for the younger ones." The other individuals represented a broad mix of age, ethnicity, and profession.

Lee drew his sidearm: he was once again carrying a standard issue ten-millimeter caseless automatic. Concerned that the homebrewed Upsider gyrojet pistol might raise some eyebrows and unwanted speculation about his own loyalties, he kept it well out of sight.

Lee's attempt to eavesdrop on the Outbounders' debate was unsuccessful. "Bulganin, can you hear what they're saying?"

"No, Sir. Too much noise out there and too much echo in here."

Lee checked his watch. "Well, we'll have the opportunity to inquire about the topic of tonight's meeting soon enough. Coming up on the two-minute mark. Check your weapon and make sure you've got tranq rounds loaded."

Bulganin frowned. "Are you sure you want the tranq, Sir?"

"Quite sure, Sergeant. Besides, we'll have another option on call if we need it."

Bulganin nodded, produced his own ten-millimeter automatic, and sat so that his legs were curled up between his body and the grille.

Lee watched the seconds tick away. "Follow me in as soon as you can. And don't try jumping for distance, Arkady, just a good landing."

"And 'safety-on' until I'm steady."

"Right. Okay, it's show time. Make it a good kick."

Lee, alongside Bulganin, rose into a scrunched parody of a sprinter's crouch. The sergeant pulled his legs back and kicked the grate—hard.

As the grate tumbled out and away—pinwheeling in the low-gee— Lee launched himself forward. His fast, level glide carried him about seven meters, at which point he swept his bent legs up and then stamped down; a *whump* and he was grounded. He snapped the handgun's safety off—and could barely keep from grinning at the semicircle of open mouths before him.

"In accordance with Earth Union Legal Code 1770B2, I am detaining all persons here assembled, effective immediately. Please do not—"

Xi and two others launched into a long, floating run toward the room's main entrance, a large door directly opposite the vent Lee had come through. Bulganin, landing with a thump just a few feet behind Lee, made a guttural inquiry. "Drop them?"

"Not necessary, Sergeant. Just flank out."

Xi and her companions reached the door just as it opened inward, revealing two panicked adolescents. They began screaming about a raid and were then forcibly propelled forward into the room, courtesy of Fast Eddie's booted feet. Xi turned and bolted back the way she had come.

But the other two exits were now blocked by Lee and Bulganin respectively. Xi completed her last leaping step just a few feet away from where she had started, her lips a taut line, her almond-shaped eyes wide and bright—and locked on the pistol Bulganin had pointed at her. Behind Xi, Briggs and Kerkonnen exchanged looks and raised their hands slowly into the air.

Lee holstered his weapon, but left the safety off. "Much better. And now, if you don't mind, I've got a few questions . . ."

※ ※ ※

Perlenmann stared at Lee over steepled fingers and across a table littered with open books. "So where does that leave us?"

"Just about back where we started."

Perlenmann closed a few books, revealing more open ones beneath, as well as the new scanner that had been offloaded from the *Gato*. "You're sure none of the Outbounders were involved in the sabotage?"

"Am I *sure*? I don't know if I'm sure of anything." Lee sighed, wondered what the scanner was doing mixed in with Perlenmann's precious books. "I can tell you this much, however. If any of the Outbounders *were* involved in some elaborate false-flag sabotage plot, they're keeping it a secret from their own leaders."

"What about Ms. Xi? She seems to be their political firebrand; could she be more militant than she appears?"

Lee shook his head. "Not likely. And she's got a pretty good alibi for the seventy-two hours prior to the explosion."

"Oh?"

"She was home with a nasty virus that's been going around; confined to bed per Iseult's orders. Lots of folks visited her, so she's got wall-to-wall witnesses who can testify that she was at home constantly during the three days preceding the explosion."

Perlenmann shrugged. "I suppose we must conclude, then, that the Outbounders were not the saboteurs."

"Leaving who? The Sols—if any of them are even on Callisto? Or a lone psychopath?"

Another shrug. "Maybe the former, but I doubt the latter. The Earth Union bureaucracy screens for mental aberrations before allowing access to Callisto."

"Well, then, I'm fresh out of possible suspects."

Perlenmann re-steepled his fingers. "Well, presuming the explosion is not an expression of madness, it must still advance the objectives of the saboteur, who is evidently *not* a Dirtsider, an Outbounder, and probably not a Sol."

"Apparently."

Perlenmann shrugged. "So maybe it is no longer effective to go looking for the culprit. Maybe we must trick him into standing forth where we can see him."

Lee frowned. "I don't understand—"

And then, with the suddenness of an eye snapping open, Lee understood—and not just about the sabotage, but about the *Fragrant Blossom's* hijacking, as well. "Mr. Perlenmann, I'm going to make a quick, private call to the *Gato*. Then I'm going to confer with Dr. Iseult before we call for a closed-door meeting . . ."

❧ ❧ ❧

Lee made sure that his face was set in grim lines when he reentered Perlenmann's briefing room later that day. His nod of greeting was returned by Iseult and the administrator. Parsons scowled at him from the far end of the table. Briggs and Xi simply looked worried.

Lee shoved aside a few books as he sat down. "Thanks for coming on such short notice."

Parsons' scowl deepened. "Yeah, well, I got a lot of work to do, so—"

"Then we might as well get straight to it. Dr. Iseult?"

Genevieve folded her hands in front of her but did not look up. Her voice was small and tight. "Mr. Panachuk died a few hours ago."

Perlenmann's eyes widened slightly. Briggs looked saddened, Xi looked concerned, and Parsons, open-mouthed, struggled to get out a single word: "What?"

Iseult explained. "When the tank exploded, Panachuk was evidently hit by a needlelike fragment traveling at very high speed. It must have entered on the same trajectory as the larger fragment we removed. Consequently there was no separate entry wound. The smaller fragment entered high in his left lung. When Panachuk later reported intermittent coughing with slightly bloody sputum, we presumed he had come down with the same bug that recently affected Ms. Xi and so many others—all the more likely since Panachuk's burns taxed his immune system and made him particularly susceptible to opportunistic infection.

"Possibly Panachuk didn't feel the fragment working its way inward with each cough because of the the pain medication he was receiving for his burns. Or possibly, he did feel it but didn't want to risk being invalided out of his job here. Either way, the first warning we had was when we found him unconscious with rapidly deteriorating coronary function." Iseult looked away. "The fragment ultimately worked its way into his heart. By the time we isolated the problem and prepped him for surgery, he was dead."

Parsons had grown very pale. "Jesus Christ. Poor Panachuk. His wife Marta is—"

"That will have to wait, Mr. Parsons," Lee interrupted. "We've got a bigger problem to deal with."

Parsons frowned. "What do you mean?"

"Panachuk's death means that this is no longer merely material sabotage; the crime now includes murder—the murder of one of *your* people. How long do you think your workers are going to wait for the wheels of justice to turn? That's why I've asked you all to assemble here. If we don't find the killer fast, your workers may take matters into their own hands and lynch some scapegoat. Fortunately, I think we have a strong suspect."

Briggs blinked; Xi looked wary. "Who?" she asked.

"Jack Carroll, chief engineer."

"Jack?" Parsons stared blankly at Lee. "You've got to be kidding."

"I'm not. He's got the know-how, he had the opportunity, and we have evidence that he tampered with the forensics results."

"In what way?"

Lee leaned back. "Well, in his report, Carroll claimed that he couldn't establish the make of the commercial watch that the saboteur used as the timer for the electric igniter. I went over the evidence myself and I'm pretty sure I have been able to type the watch—which is identical to one which Carroll owned, and which he reported as missing about a week before the explosion."

Parsons shuddered, then shook his head. "You're wrong. Even if Carroll did it, he wouldn't have killed anybody. He could—and would—have prevented that from happening."

Lee frowned. "I'm not sure I understand how you reach that conclusion, Mr. Parsons."

Parsons scowled "Because if he really wanted to kill people, he'd have used a spark-gap igniter to touch off the hydrogen, not one of those dinky magnetic-induction igniters—"

Parsons stopped. Lee was smiling and Perlenmann's left eyebrow had risen precipitously.

Lee leaned forward. "Tell me, Mr. Parsons, how did you happen to know—*know*—that the saboteur used a magnetic-induction igniter rather than a spark-gap igniter?"

Parsons' complexion—already pale—became corpselike.

Lee continued. "You couldn't know about it from Carroll's final forensic report; I had that sealed, pending the conclusion of this investigation. And you couldn't have identified the igniter at our first staff meeting; it took Carroll two hours with a microscope to determine that what kind of igniter it was. So I ask you again, Mr. Parsons: how did *you* happen to know that the igniter used was a magnetic-induction model?"

Parsons didn't say anything; his eyes went around the room, starting at Lee and ending at Perlenmann. Then, he started to rise—

The door opened and Fast Eddie leaned in from the corridor, ten-millimeter automatic held securely in both hands. It was centered on Parsons' chest. Parsons sank slowly, carefully, into his seat.

Lee leaned back with a sigh. "Mr. Parsons, I'm going to ask you this question just one more time . . ."

※ ※ ※

The flood of admissions came quickly once Parsons was informed that Panachuk was not only still alive, but scheduled to be released later that day. Parsons was also angry—but relieved—to learn that Carroll had never been a suspect; despite his other failings, Parsons clearly didn't want anybody else paying for his act of sabotage.

Parsons' tale unfolded along the lines Lee had expected. Although Parsons felt the Sols were dangerous extremists, he was an ardent undisclosed Spacer, and so was also concerned by the Upsiders' accommodation with their Dirtside masters. So he concocted a scheme designed to correct both problems.

By crafting the fuel-tank sabotage to look like a Solist political statement, Parsons was certain that the Earth Union would crack down broadly in response to the sabotage and thereby spawn an Upsider backlash against Dirtside oppression.

However, Parsons had planned to simultaneously rally the

Upsiders to mount "vigilance patrols" that would ultimately be credited with successfully suppressing farther "Sol violence" on Callisto. The moderate Greens would no doubt crow over the "elimination of treason on Callisto" and proudly point to the self-policing Upsiders as the means whereby it was eliminated, thereby making them poster children for the argument that, with proper incentives, spaceside communities could be made to aid Earth Union interests.

Of course, that would demonstrate to those same "exemplary" Upsiders that they could wrest concessions from the Dirtsiders if they were organized and proactive. In the long run, Parsons had hoped that the Earth Union would entrust more of the operation of Callisto to Upside hands, and in so doing, make the confidential technologies more accessible to the Spacers who would then carry that information to their independent enclaves in the Belt. There, those technologies would be developed and disseminated to increase the collective power position of the Upsiders in relation to their terrestrial masters.

"But I had nothing to do with the scanner sabotage," Parsons finished. "Not as though that will help me much now. So let's just get it over with."

Perlenmann cocked his head. "Get what over with?"

"Don't toy with me, Perlenmann. I know what happens next. I've confessed, you sentence. That's part of your job as administrator."

Lee released a slow sigh. He was glad his part in this mess was over. Maybe now things would start settling down . . .

Perlenmann's words ruined that nascent hope. "Mr. Parsons, I am willing to suspend your sentence and permanently seal the record of these proceedings—and of Lieutenant Strong's investigation—if you will agree to undertake a special community service project."

Iseult looked from Perlenmann to Lee. "Can he do that?"

Lee nodded, his mind racing ahead, trying to see where this was all leading. "Yes, he can, Doctor. Even though I was running the investigation, Mr. Perlenmann is this facility's *de facto* judicial authority."

Perlenmann nodded to acknowledge the correctness of Lee's comment. "Just so. Mr. Parsons, are you interested in this solution?"

Parsons was still staring at Perlenmann as though the administrator had grown another head. "Uh . . . sure. Yes."

"Then, Mr. Parsons, here is what you must do. You must convene an open forum comprised not only of Upsiders and Spacers, but Outbounders and Dirtsiders, as well. And your first collective act must be to renounce violence. After that, you are to use the forum to air your concerns to the entire community. This means that the entire community will also hear the often-contending concerns and viewpoints of your adversaries. If you achieve no more than that, I will be satisfied. We need to exchange views, not blows, here on Callisto."

Perlenmann glanced over at Lee, smiling. Lee smiled back and nodded. Yes, it was all becoming clear now. Very clear.

Perlenmann was concluding. "Do you agree to these terms, Mr. Parsons?"

Parsons nodded, dumbfounded. "Y-yes. Sure."

Lee nodded at Perlenmann. "And it's all by the book, isn't it?"

Perlenmann smiled again. "Yes; quite." Then he stared at Parsons and proclaimed. "Mr. Parsons, having agreed to fulfill the service required, you are free to go. But fair warning: if you perpetrate, incite, or encourage any farther violence to persons or property on Callisto, I shall reopen the file on this matter, have you incarcerated, and remand you to Earth for appropriate sentencing on the charges of sabotage and treason."

Parsons stood, looked anxious to be off. Lee smiled. *He probably wants to get the hell out of this room before Perlenmann comes to his senses and throws the book at him. Which is what should have happened.*

Perlenmann nodded. "You may go."

Parsons exited, followed closely by Briggs, Xi, and Cabral. The little Brazilian still kept his eyes on Parsons—and one hand on his holstered gun. Iseult, with another raised-eyebrow glance at Lee, followed them out.

As the door closed behind them, Lee shook his head. "Bravo, Mr. Perlenmann. A command performance."

Perlenmann's smile dimmed somewhat. "I'm afraid I don't understand you, Lieutenant."

"Mr. Perlenmann, you understand me so well that you have been able to control me like a marionette without my knowing it. Except that you *did* step over the line of legality one time—and that's what gave you away."

Perlenmann smiled. "And what is this purported oversight of mine?"

"Oh, it wasn't an oversight; you just didn't have a choice. The scanner, Perlenmann. *You* sabotaged the scanner."

The smile widened. "And why would I do such a thing?"

Lee indicated the cluttered table. "Well, partly because of the books—which the current Earth Union censorship prevents from being distributed anymore."

Perlenmann shrugged. "I fail to see your reasoning. Why scan books that I already have, as do a number of Upside libraries?"

"You're not worried about Upside readers, Mr. Perlenmann. Your concern is with Outbound readers, particularly those in coming generations who would otherwise be deprived of the true depth and breadth of human thought, innovation, and imagination. So, since the Dirtside censors control what goes into the colony ships' data banks, you realized that the only way to work around their restrictions was to create your own, uncensored graphical library.

"But the old secure scanner wasn't the right tool for that job. It was too slow. So you got something that can capture pages in the blink of an eye. And all those images are probably hidden with false file names, or mixed into other data records on the Outbounder colony ships."

Perlenmann smiled. "Better than that. The library files are hidden among compressed backups of earlier versions of navigational software. The Outbounders will not even be aware of them until several years into their journey. At a preset date, the archives will unfold themselves and alert the crew to their existence." He leaned back. "So, you have discovered my heinous crime. I am at your mercy."

"You might not want to make a joke of that just yet, Administrator Perlenmann, because I'm not done. You see, I started thinking about how your sabotaging the secure scanner might answer some of the other mysteries I've been grappling with. Like how it might be related to the hijacking of the *Fragrant Blossom*."

Perlenmann raised an eyebrow; his tone was wry. "So those pirates were after my scanner, too? I was not informed that it has such an inexplicably high market value."

"Actually, it's you who had the inside information on its value, and it was the hijackers who didn't. But let's stop calling them that; they were paid assassins, sent to retrieve something they never found. Because it was hidden in that scanner, right there." Lee pointed at the unit.

Perlenmann's smile vanished.

Lee tapped the scanner in a slow rhythm. "It's been said that the best place to hide a big crime is deep within a small one. And that's what you did. Sure; you wanted the new scanner. And if you had been caught, you could always have blushed and smiled a little and all would have been well. And no one would have thought to look any closer at the new secure scanner—which was in fact a data mule. Oh, I know you intend to use it to digitize your library, too, but its *real* purpose was as a means of transmitting illegal, even treasonous, data, stored as coded 'test images' on the scanner's chip. And unless I'm much mistaken, that's what the assassins on the *Blossom* were actually after. They were there to intercept that data. That's why they didn't give a damn about hostages, or stealing the ship. It's why they had to stay aboard her, letting her drift, attracting no attention, while they tried to locate the hidden data. It's why they had an armed, high-speed getaway ship waiting at 216 Kleopatra to retrieve the information, debrief the hijackers, and then probably liquidate them."

"And yes, we found a large store of test images in the scanner. We made a record of them, but they didn't make any sense to us until now. But I suspect that if we had the right cipher, we'd discover why someone was willing to send assassins to retrieve that information— and why, as its recipient, you're willing to live a double life that smacks of treasonous intent."

"I'm curious, Lieutenant. What led you to conjecture that I was the recipient for such secret data?"

Lee shrugged. "Part of my research involved going over your confidential logs, which include the base's comm records. I went back and checked the transmissions to and from the *Fragrant Blossom* during its prior arrivals. There was almost no communication between you. But this time, from the moment the *Fragrant Blossom* left her orbital berth at Mars, you were in constant contact with her." Lee smiled. "Obviously, you and her captain had a lot to talk about. And that was a lucky coincidence for you, because if you hadn't set up a regular call-in schedule with the *Blossom*'s CO, you'd have never learned about the hijacking in time to alert us."

"Oh, luck had nothing to do with our frequent communications, Lieutenant Strong. That was our attempt to discourage the assassins we already feared might be on board the *Blossom*."

Lee stared. "What do you mean?"

"Lieutenant Strong, although the *Blossom*'s captain did not have any definitive proof, he had considerable reservations regarding several late-booking passengers, as well as one or two replacement crewmembers. He communicated these reservations to me and so we made a very public point of establishing a relatively frequent check-in schedule, which included information that we hoped would deter any potential mutineers. For instance, I mentioned several times that your cutter was within the area, as well as your sister-ship, the *Revered Timberland*. Clearly, we underestimated the determination of our opponents."

Lee heard the self-recriminatory tone. "Don't blame yourself, Mr. Perlenmann. These assassins weren't going to let anything interfere with their plans."

Perlenmann nodded, stared at Lee. "I'm not sure you know the full truth of your own words, Lieutenant Strong. Only two days prior to their attack, the *Revered Timberland*—or *Ravenous Tiburon*, in your parlance—was called away to provide emergency medical aid to a small, temporary mining outpost deeper in the asteroid belt."

"So what? We get those calls all the time."

"I'm sure you do—but not about outposts that don't exist. But this hoax had a most impressive pedigree. The message had a valid Customs Patrol authorization code affixed to it. And when the *Tiburon* departed, it also ensured that yours was the only ship left in the area."

Lee felt cold streak down his spine. "What are you implying?"

Perlenmann held out his hands. "I should think it is obvious. The closest of the two ships that could have come to the aid of *Flagrant Blossom* was officially ordered to a distant location only two days before the hijackers acted. So who was left alone in the approximate vicinity of the attack site? Why, a junior commander. A commander with no prior combat experience. A commander from a family with questionable political affiliations. A commander who, by all reports, was getting along entirely too well with the crew of the *Venerated Gaia*, a.k.a. *Venereal Gato*." Perlenmann looked at Lee over steepled fingers. "You know, don't you, that positive reviews and reactions from your Upsider crew is actually a matter of grave concern to your superiors?"

Lee swallowed. He hadn't known that, but given everything he'd learned in the past weeks, it made sense. From the Earth Union perspective, if an Upsider crew adopted and confided in a Dirtsider officer, that could evolve into a Very Risky Situation indeed. "I find your conjectures . . . disturbing," Lee admitted, his mouth suddenly very dry.

Perlenmann nodded. "I thought you might."

Lee had recovered a bit. "Logically, then, whoever drew off the *Tiburon* has agents inside the Customs Patrol. And, being behind the hijacking, they almost certainly advised the assassins and their recovery ship on our position and isolation. Which is why the assassins didn't bother to change their game plan. They figured we'd be too far off to detect anything amiss, or stumble across them—as long as the crew of the *Blossom* didn't get off a cry for help, and they continued to drift along quietly. And that's also why the assassins were ready for every conventional boarding method we might have tried. Someone told them exactly what to prepare for."

Lee regarded Perlenmann closely. "But we'd have never been there at all—never learned about the *Fragrant Blossom's* troubles—if it hadn't been for you. None of the people plotting to seize the *Blossom* could anticipate that you would contact me directly, that you were keeping close tabs on the situation—and my position." Lee shook his head. "I should have known something wasn't kosher when your message about the *Blossom* came directly to our own lascom. You would only have had such precise coordinates on us if you'd already been tracking and taking regular fixes on our position. Just like the bad guys were."

Perlenmann nodded. "And you see the implications that logically follow from your conjectures, of course."

"You mean that you're part of some larger clandestine organization? Sure, but what organization? And which side is it working for?"

"The organization I work with does not support any one faction. Our concern is for the welfare of this whole solar system. And for the whole system to be healthy, all parts of it must enjoy equal freedoms.

And the most fundamental of all those freedoms is this: that persons must be free to read, write, say, and think what they will. Without that, all other freedoms are not merely meaningless, they are shams."

Lee smiled crookedly. "Now you're starting to sound like my parents."

Perlenmann returned the smile. "That was not my intention, but it does not surprise me."

Lee leaned back, realizing that, for the first time since puberty, he was completely uncertain as to the outcome of his present conversation, or where it might take him. "So, what's in the scanner: your secret plans, or your enemies'?"

Perlenmann sighed. "Unfortunately, both—but that was not our intent. Our own plans were the last covert package to be carried by the *Blossom*, and would have attracted no attention. But events dictated that another data package—plans for a top secret operation being prepared by the Greens—had to be shipped out here along with it."

"Okay, so let's go through this one step at a time. What is this about a secret Green operation?"

Perlenmann sighed. "The Greens have devised a clandestine plot to simultaneously wipe away the increases in Upside self-sufficiency while simultaneously eliminating the recent political gains of the Neo Luddites. It's quite an ingenious scheme actually, dubbed 'Case Red.'"

"And how did it come to be on the *Blossom*?"

Perlenmann shrugged. "Apparently, one of our agents got unexpected access to the plans—probably as a target of opportunity—and had to get them beyond the clutches of the Green security apparatus."

"Don't you mean the Earth Union security apparatus?"

Perlenmann shook his head. "No. The Greens couldn't afford to use Earth Union forces to reclaim the file. If they did, the contents would be examined—which would reveal their attempt to undermine their supposed political allies, the Neo Luddites."

"So the Greens have their own secret security apparatus. And that's probably who was behind the hijacking, the raider ship, and the radio call that pulled away the *Ravenous Tiburon*."

"Unquestionably. All done to keep their perfidy concealed from both the Upsiders and the Neo Luddites. So, when Case Red fell into the hands of our operatives, I suspect their only choice was to get it off-world as quickly, and as far, as possible."

"So they gave it to the captain of the *Blossom*."

"Yes, who the Greens apparently knew was part of our organization. What they didn't realize was that his only role in the organization was as a courier, bringing a series of secret documents out to me on Callisto. And so, without any intention of doing so, we suddenly had all our most crucially secret eggs in one fragile basket: the *Blossom*."

Lee nodded. "And although the Greens tracked Case Red to the *Blossom*, they couldn't take open action before she departed. Everything in port is under official scrutiny at all times."

"Exactly. So the Greens deposited a mix of operatives and amnesty-bribed thugs on board the *Blossom* instead. The operatives went as replacement crew, the thugs masqueraded as legitimate passengers. The captain suspected as much, of course, but could do nothing. The infiltrators had impeccable false identities and credentials, supplied by Greens who control the necessary personal record databases."

Lee saw how these circumstances had led to what he had discovered on the *Blossom*. "So the infiltrators waited until the liner was in deep space, took her, interrogated both the crew and passengers in an attempt to locate the Case Red file, and failing that, eliminated them and continued the search on their own. And it's entirely possible that Coordinator Mann deflected us from investigating more deeply because he is an agent for the Green conspirators. In fact, he might be the one who set the hijacking to begin with."

"There is no way to be certain, but he had the opportunity and authority to do so."

Lee stared around at the books. "Now, about your own secret file—the one the scanner was carrying as test images: what the hell is it?"

Perlenmann folded his hands. "The images are graphical copies of a computer code—a code too important and sensitive to be transmitted *as* code. So we have been shuttling it out here to Callisto, piece by piece."

"And what makes this code so important?"

"Do you know what a backdoor is, Lieutenant?"

"Sure. It's code put into a program—usually an operating

system—so that the code writer can access and control the system later on without having to log on or go through any other security protocols."

"Precisely. Well, we have been recompiling the code of a long-unused backdoor for almost five years."

"What is it a backdoor to?"

"The market and financial management software used by the Earth Union."

Lee stared. "How did your agents get access to that kind of code? That should be completely inaccessible."

"It is. Even to the Greens themselves."

"Mr. Perlenmann, you're going to have to stop talking in riddles, please."

"Actually, I'm stating the simple truth. The Greens are no longer aware that this backdoor exists. You see, several decades before the economic collapse of the twenty-first century, the programmers who wrote the financial tracking and exchange software used by the major markets of the world realized that there could come a day when world leaders might need to intervene to forestall an imminent fiscal crash. So they put a backdoor in all their programs."

"And the security subroutines of those programs never tweaked to it?"

Perlenmann smiled. "That would have been a most difficult task, since the backdoor was nested inside the security subroutines themselves."

"Oh," said Lee, who did not feel particularly intelligent at that moment.

"When the markets did collapse a generation later, the backdoor codes were mostly forgotten by the new market managers, and what remained was lost in the chaos.

"That would have been the end of the story if there had not been a collection of nations—mostly in Europe—which, by nationalizing their debts and shifting to an emergency command economy, remained stable enough to continue trading amongst themselves. In time, the global markets—now under Green control—reasserted.

"However, in the technophobic culturescape arising from the collapse, there was no interest in creating new programs to integrate and manage dataflow between the world's markets. So they simply retained the old software and rebuilt the old machines which ran it."

Lee goggled. "And they're still using that system today? Almost two hundred years later?"

Perlenmann shrugged. "Why not? It works, and to replace it would mean a significant investment, appropriated over the objections of the Neo Luddites, many of whom detest the entire notion of money, anyway. The software has evolved, of course, but its core program is still the same. And the backdoor is still there."

"And your organization found the code for it? How?"

Perlenmann's smile was sly; Lee pictured him suggesting to Eve that she might enjoy just one tiny bite of that shiny, ripe apple. "It was never entirely lost, although its full potential was not understood. The access code itself was split up shortly after the Greens began their initial rise to power. For generations there was no opportunity, and no pressing reason, to reassemble or use it. Until the recent retrenchments, it was conceivable that, over time, the Greens would relent and humanity would reattain a reasonable balance between eco-consciousness and technological advancement, despite the resistance of the Neo Luddites.

"But then we started getting fragmentary reports of a clandestine Green operation dubbed 'Case Red.' Named for how it will begin—the inciting and then crushing of a 'popular revolt' on Mars—the plan is designed to strip away every bit of autonomy the Upside communities have managed to accrue and set them back about a century. It is also structured so that it will appear to be a purely Neo Luddite plot."

"So you began reassembling the pieces of the backdoor code in order to cripple the fiscal structures of the Earth Union before they could make the Upsiders their serfs once again."

"Well, yes. But we are not doing this just to save the Upsiders. We are trying to save Earth, as well."

"How does destroying Earth's markets save it?"

Perlenmann feigned surprise. "I thought you were a student of history, Lieutenant Strong."

"I am. And what you're doing will have an effect as profound as the Great Depression of the twentieth century, or even the currency collapse of the late twenty-first century, which is what brought the Greens to power in the first place."

"Just so. But tell me, weren't there even worse social cataclysms in history?"

Lee shrugged. "Of course there were. The collapse of the Roman Empire led to the Dark Ages. Centuries of misery, decline, and belief that humanity was now debased, fated to live in the shadows of a greatness that could not be regained."

"Just so. Now, what made the Roman fall so much greater than the economic collapses of the twentieth and twenty-first centuries?"

Lee started. "Well, you can't really compare them at all. A market collapse is the failure of just one element in a larger, integrated system." And then Lee saw what Perlenmann was driving at. "They didn't cause a complete social implosion because, however bad they looked at the time, they weren't complete system failures. They were corrections of a flawed element within the system."

"Exactly. Of course, it doesn't feel like a mere 'correction' to the people living through those events. But we can be sure of this: they were far less terrible than being alive in the Europe of 500 AD, enduring a squalid, wretched existence among ruins, lost in a deep night of decline and despair."

Lee nodded. "Which, if the Greens and the Neo Luddites succeed with Case Red, is exactly where Earth is headed. By smashing the Upsiders, they're smashing the few injections of innovation and growth that stave off complete cultural and economic stagnation, and ultimately, implosion."

Perlenmann nodded and folded his hands. "Lieutenant Strong, let us even presume that the Greens fail to execute Case Red. If the Earth Union continues on its current course for another century, what is likely to become of it?"

Lee's throat became uncomfortably dry and tight. "The same thing: stagnation and implosion. The Great Depression, the Dark Ages, and the Fall of Rome, all rolled into one social cataclysm. Anarchy. Savagery. Barbarism."

"Horribly so. An unavoidable and unpreventable certainty. As in Rome, the system has accrued so much power and inertia that, if left to its own devices, it will not merely stumble to a halt: it would crash into a thousand, irreclaimable pieces."

Lee looked up sharply. "So are you trying to sell me the idea that your backdoor sabotage is actually some kind of perverse mission of mercy?"

"Admittedly, it does seem perverse. A market collapse now will kill thousands and generate much misery. However, left to fester for another fifty to a hundred years, it will become a great fall that will kill billions and generate unparalleled suffering and barbarism. Or are you beginning to doubt your own conclusions, Lieutenant Strong?"

Lee shook his head, considered. "And now I understand why you've been recompiling the code out here. Because Callisto is Ultima Thule, the far Marches of the Empire. It's a place where ships come only four times a year, where Earth Union oversight is almost nonexistent, and where the presence of the Customs Patrol is so rare that our visits are memorable events. So where better to put such a code back together, and who better than the local eye and arm of Earth Union authority, the facility administrator?"

Perlenmann nodded, watched Lee, said nothing, seemed to be waiting.

Lee nodded back, understanding. "And now that the backdoor code is fully compiled, you want me to carry it back in-system for you, where others of your organization can spread it for maximum effect before you activate it."

Perlenmann shrugged. "I cannot compel you to carry it in-system. But I would not use coercive means even if they were at my disposal. To do so would make me the very thing I strive to defeat."

"And if I refuse to work as your courier?

"Perhaps another means of conveying the code to where it is needed will present itself. Perhaps not. However, I must be frank: we are now in a desperate race against disaster."

"What do you mean?"

"I mean that the Greens must presume that Case Red has been compromised. They will almost certainly move up the timetable for its implementation. What they had thought to initiate in five or six years might well be accelerated to two or three years—maybe less."

"And you'll do nothing?"

"The only thing we can do is spread and activate the backdoor code as quickly as possible. Which means, Lieutenant, that you have a decision to make, and very soon."

Lee considered. If he became a courier for either the backdoor code or Case Red, he was committing treason. If he simply boarded the *Gato* and did nothing, he was still aiding and abetting treason. Either way, he was breaking his oath of service unless he arrested Perlenmann immediately.

Of course, the Earth Union had broken its vows in so many ways, so profoundly, and with such callous disregard for the people it was supposed to protect and serve, that his oath of service to it had begun to feel like a contract made with a con man. But still, if he was going to break with the Earth Union and his oath, shouldn't he take the moral high ground and do it openly—?

"Lieutenant, I have spent many years observing expressions on the faces of other people. If I were to guess, I would say you are in the throes of a conflict of conscience. Perhaps I can clarify things for you. If you openly repudiate your oath of service, you will undo all we have worked for. Such a statement will attract the very attention we must avoid. I am sorry to say that I require not only your services as a courier, but your silence—at least until you have delivered the data."

Lee considered. Well, yes; that certainly did make it simpler—in a way. If he was going to break an oath, he would have to go all the way and become a coconspirator. Not merely an open enemy of the state, but a covert traitor, a spy. He almost wished he had not decided to come out and see what real life was like, out among the Upsiders.

Perlenmann's smile was sad. "Lieutenant, I believe there is not much middle ground in the choices before you. You know what I am guilty of. You must either uphold your oath and arrest me, or not."

Lee leaned back, let his eyes wander across the books, across Perlenmann's face—creased with a slight suggestion of anxiety—and finally let his gaze rest upon the scanner. "All this scanning—even with a new machine—must still take forever."

Perlenmann shrugged; "It's not too bad, but it is rather tedious; scan, turn a page, scan, turn another page—"

Lee nodded, rose, picked up a book. Hesse's *Magister Ludi*. "Given all the work ahead of you, it sounds like you could use another pair of hands."

"Yes, I can use another pair of hands, Lieutenant. In more ways than one." Perlenmann handed Lee a thinner volume: Sun Tzu's *The Art of War*. "In more ways than one."

❄ ❄ ❄ ❄ ❄

The sudden, virtually overnight breakdown of the entire financial network of Old Earth on July 26, 252 PD (2354 Old

Style), inflicted catastrophic damage on Old Earth's markets and national economies. The "Economic Winter," as it came to be known, effectively wiped out over a third of all major corporations within the first thirty-six hours. Efforts to control or even slow the rolling collapse of the planetary economy proved fruitless, and by August 1, well over half of the world's transnational corporations had been driven into failure. Old Earth had never seen such a tidal wave of bank and corporate bankruptcies, and every effort to restart the economy or somehow impose financial order failed in the face of massive collapses within the world trading networks as the software which had provided the sinews of the financial system crumbled, apparently overwhelmed by the sheer cataract of disaster.

Claims by the ruling political parties that the onslaught of ruin was the result of some sort of bizarre plot, delberately inflicted by "terrorists," were greeted intitially with incredulity and then with rage as the political leadership's obvious effort to scapegoat someone else—*anyone* else—for its own failures sank home. Mobs took to the street, initially inchoate and fueled solely by rage and desperation, but leaders soon emerged. Within weeks, the first of the Committees of Renaissance was organized in North America; within months, the ruling Greens and Neo Luddites of the GRASP coalition found themselves fighting for their lives. The ruling elites' longstanding plans to retreat to Old Earth's orbital habitats in the face of disaster failed; officers of the Customs Service ordered to support Earth Union police forces against the Committees' armed supporters either refused or were forcibly prevented from obeying by their crews; the Upsider community, from Mars to Callisto, declared its support for the insurrection; and after three weeks of bitter fighting on Luna, the Lunar habitats also joined the united opposition.

By January 253 PD, the Earth Union had effectively disintegrated. The old national units which had never been officially superseded asserted their sovereignty and independence once again, and the surviving leadership of the discredited Green and Neo Luddite parties had been driven entirely from power. The rage directed at them, sparked by the economic collapse, had grown nothing but fiercer and more burning as the citizens of Earth recognized the systemic stagnation and paralysis which had been ideolgically imposed upon them, and many of those political leaders were forced deep into hiding or even—in one of history's most bitter ironies—into seeking safety in interstellar flight once those flights were resumed in 257 PD.

The Economic Winter imposed untold suffering. It has been estimated that well over a century of accumulated wealth was destroyed in a period of less than two weeks. The actual death toll has never been fully assessed, but must have measured in the hundreds of thousands on a planet-wide basis. The individual citizens whose life savings were wiped away are literally beyond counting. And yet, despite the staggering blow the Sol System had taken, the tide of human capability and creativity rebounded dramatically in the period of restored individual liberties and representative government which blossomed in the wake of the Earth Union's destruction. By 261 PD, the system had almost completely recovered from the Economic Winter and charged ahead into two T-centuries of unparalleled economic, technological, and intellectual growth and expansion. Nor did the renaissance of humanity's home star system stop there. The nightmare of Old Earth's Final War still waited in the mists of the unseen future, but for the next six T-centuries, until the slide into the political and ideological madness of that cataclysm began with the Veronezh declaration of 850 PD, the light of human hope, dreams, and aspirations burned as strongly as that of Sol itself.

> — *From Darkness Back to the Stars:*
> *The Collapse of the Neo Luddites*,
> Ephraim Bousquet, Ph.D.
> Pélissard et Fils, Nouveau Paris,
> Haven, 1597 PD

A CALL TO ARMS

Timothy Zahn

A CALL TO ARMS

Epilogue

Growing up, Jeremiah Llyn had hated being short.

Not that he was *that* short. Not really. No more than nine or ten centimeters shorter than the planetary average. But ten centimeters had been more than enough to set off the jokesters in primary school, the brawlers in middle grade, and the more elaborate hazing during his teen years. Young adulthood had been marginally better, with at least a veneer of politeness and civilization covering up the derision. But even there, he could see the mental evaluation going on behind employers' eyes as he was passed over for promotions and the truly lucrative jobs.

Now, with the perspective and maturity that fifty T-years of life afforded a man, he found his lack of towering stature not only comfortable but valuable. People, even supposedly intelligent people, tended to underestimate shorter men.

In Llyn's current position, it was often very useful to be underestimated.

Across the desk, Cutler Gensonne shifted position, the prominent and self-awarded admiral's bars glinting on his shoulders with the movement. "Interesting," he said, his eyes still on the tablet he'd been studying for the past fifteen minutes.

Llyn waited a moment, wondering if there would be more. But Gensonne just flicked to the next page, his black eyebrows pressed together in concentration. "Is that a good interesting, or a bad interesting?" Llyn asked at last.

"Well, it sure as hell isn't good," Gensonne growled. "You realize this is a system that can conceivably field somewhere in the vicinity of *thirty* warships? Including six to nine battlecruisers?" He cocked his head. "That's one hell of a fighting force, Mr. Llyn."

Llyn smiled. It was a standard gambit among mercenaries, one that had been tried on him at least twice before over the years. By inflating the potential risks, the bargainer hoped to similarly inflate the potential payment. "You apparently missed sections fifteen and sixteen," he said. "The bulk of that fleet is in mothballs awaiting the scrapyard. What's left is either half armed or half crewed or both. Our estimate is that you'll be facing no more than eight to ten ships, with maybe *one* of those ships a battlecruiser."

"I *did* read sections fifteen and sixteen, thank you," Gensonne countered. "I also noted that the most recent data here is over fifteen months old."

"I see." Standing up, Llyn reached across the table and plucked the tablet from Gensonne's hands. "Obviously, you're not the group we're looking for, Admiral. Best of luck in your future endeavors."

"Just a moment," Gensonne protested, grabbing for the tablet. Llyn was ready for the move and twitched it out of his reach. "I never said we wouldn't take the job."

"Really?" Llyn said. Time for a little gamesmanship of his own. "It certainly sounded like the job was too big for you."

"There *is* no such job," Gensonne said stiffly, standing up as if prepared to chase Llyn all the way through his office door if necessary to get the tablet back. The fact that Llyn was making no move to leave seemed to throw him off stride. "I was simply making the point that your intel was stone cold, and that *any* merc commander would want an update before taking action."

"Was *that* what you were saying?" Llyn said, feigning a puzzled frown. "But then why did you imply that the odds—?" He broke off, letting his frown warm to a knowing smile. "Oh, I see. You were trying to amp up your price."

Typically, Llyn knew, people hated to see their stratagems trotted out into the sunlight. But Gensonne didn't even flinch. A bull-by-the-horns type, with no apologies, no excuses, and no regrets, nicely consistent with Llyn's pre-meeting analysis of the man. "Of course I was," he said. "I was also seeking more information." He gestured to the tablet. "We can handle the job. The question is why we should bother."

"A good question," Llyn said. As if he was really going to let a grubby mercenary leader into the Axelrod Corporation's deepest thoughts and plans. "You'll forgive me if I respectfully decline to answer."

Gensonne's eyes narrowed, and for a moment Llyn thought the other was preparing to delve back into his bag of ploys and tricks. But then the admiral's face cleared and he shrugged. "Fair enough," he said. "You're hiring mercenaries, after all, not fishing for investors."

"Exactly," Llyn said, his estimation of the man rising another notch. Gensonne knew how to play the game, but he also knew when to stop. "So. Are the Volsung Mercenaries the ones for this job, or do I look elsewhere?"

Gensonne gave a little snort and an equally small smile. "The Volsung Mercenaries are very much the ones for the job, Mr. Llyn," he said. "Have a seat, and let's talk money."

I

"Mr. Long?" The gruff voice echoed down the passageway of HMS *Phoenix.* "Sir?"

Lieutenant (Senior Grade) Travis Uriah Long came to a reluctant halt, taking the calming breath he'd taught himself to do at times like this. Senior Chief Fire Control Tech Lorelei Osterman was a major pain in the butt, on a ship much of whose officer corps and enlisted personnel seemed to take a special pleasure in competing for honors in that position. "Yes, Senior Chief?" he replied, catching one of the corridor handholds and bringing himself to a floating stop.

Osterman was about twenty meters away, moving from handhold to handhold toward him, deftly avoiding collisions with the other crew members also moving through the narrow space. *Phoenix* had its share of first-tour crewmembers bumbling awkwardly in the zero-gee, but long-time veterans like Osterman made it look quick and efficient.

At the moment, though, Osterman didn't seem to be putting much effort into the *quick* part of that solution. In fact, now that Travis had stopped, she seemed to be taking her time about closing the rest of the gap between them. Travis waited, cultivating his patience and resisting the urge to order her to snap it up. He'd been on the other side of the line once, and remembered all too well what it was like to have officers barking at you.

Finally, after a few seconds and in her own sweet time, Osterman reached him. "I just wanted you to know, Sir," she said in a voice that skated the same not-quite-insubordinate line, "that Captain Castillo wants to see you."

Travis frowned, glancing at his uni-link to make sure it was active. It was. "I haven't heard any such orders."

"That's because he doesn't know it yet, Sir," she said calmly. "But I guarantee he's going to."

So even Osterman's department had heard. "Ensign Locatelli brought it on himself," Travis said firmly.

Or tried to say it firmly. Even in his own ears the edge of defensiveness was painfully obvious.

Apparently, it was obvious to Osterman, too. "It was one of *three* separate tracking sensors," she reminded him. "The next shift's diagnostic run would have spotted it in a minute."

"That diagnostic run was two hours away," Travis countered. "What would have happened if you'd had to fire one of your autocannon sometime during those two hours?"

Osterman raised her eyebrows. "At . . . ?"

"At whatever Captain Castillo decided needed shooting."

Osterman's expression was worse than any raised eyebrows could have been. And, to be honest, Travis couldn't blame her.

Because, really, there wasn't anything out there for *Phoenix* to shoot at. There were no invaders, no enemies—foreign *or* domestic—and the last boogieman who'd shown himself around these parts had vanished into the stardust nearly a century ago.

But that was beside the point. Men and women who wore the uniform of the Royal Manticoran Navy were supposed to *care* about their jobs, damn it.

Osterman might have been reading his mind. "And you think you're the only one who's getting it right, Sir?" she asked politely.

"No, of course not," Travis muttered. "But . . ."

He was saved by the twittering of his uni-link. He keyed it and raised it to his lips. "Long," he said briskly.

"Bajek," Travis's immediate superior's voice came. "Report to the captain's day cabin immediately."

Travis swallowed. "Aye, aye, Ma'am."

"Commander Bajek?" Osterman asked knowingly as he keyed off.

"Yes," Travis said sourly. Was the smug chief *always* right? "Carry on." Turning in the zero-gee, he gave his handhold a tug and once again launched himself down the corridor.

"Learn to play the game, Lieutenant," Osterman called quietly after him.

Travis glowered. Play the game. It was the same advice everyone else in the universe seemed ready and eager to give him. Learn to play the game. Never mind whether the game was good or bad or clean or rigged. Learn to play the game.

Like hell he would.

The lift ride through *Phoenix*'s spin section, as usual, was more than a little unpleasant, the rapid shift in effective gravity triggering Travis's abnormally sensitive inner ears. He kept his eyes straight ahead during the trip, thinking evil thoughts about whichever law of physics allowed stress bands that could create and mold huge gravitational fields, and compensators that could zero-out more than two hundred gees, but were only just now figuring out how to get a measly one gee pointed toward a warship's decks. Having a half-gee rotating section to live in was better than having to eat and sleep in weightlessness, but floating around the main duty stations like air-breathing fish was a royal pain in the butt.

Lieutenant Commander Bajek, the ship's weapons officer, was waiting in Captain Castillo's office when Travis arrived. "Come in, Lieutenant," Castillo said, his voice and expression stiffly formal. "I understand you want to write up Ensign Locatelli."

Travis was opening his mouth to answer when the phrasing of the comment suddenly struck him. No, he didn't *want* to write up Locatelli. He'd already done so.

Or so he'd thought. "Yes, Sir, I do," he said carefully. "Is there a problem?"

For a tense second he thought the question had put him over the line. Castillo's expression didn't change, but Bajek shifted her weight slightly in what was, for her, an unusually demonstrative show of discomfort.

"You're aware, I presume, that Ensign Locatelli's uncle is Admiral Carlton Locatelli," Castillo said. It wasn't a question.

"Yes, Sir, I am," Travis replied. For a brief moment he considered asking what Locatelli's genetic makeup had to do with following procedure, but decided he was in deep enough already. Besides, he was pretty sure he already knew the answer.

He was right. "Admiral Locatelli and his family have had a long and distinguished history of service with the Royal Manticoran Navy," Castillo said, in a way that reminded Travis of someone reading from a script file. "His nephew is this generation's representative to that line. The admiral is anxious that he achieve something of the same honor and distinction as his forebears." Castillo raised his eyebrows, in exactly the same expression Travis had gotten from Osterman a few minutes earlier. "Do you need me to spell it out for you?"

Travis took a deep breath. Unfortunately, neither he nor anyone else in the RMN needed it spelled out for them. "No, Sir," he said.

"There's a strong and growing movement in Parliament to gut the RMN even more than it already is," Castillo said. Apparently, despite Travis's assurances, the captain was in the mood for a spelling lesson. "Men like Admiral Locatelli and their families and allies are the ones standing up for our jobs. Standing up for *your* job, Lieutenant."

Which would mean a double handful of nothing, Travis thought blackly, if the cost of that protection was staffing the RMN with political animals who either couldn't or wouldn't do those jobs.

But that, too, was part of the spelling lesson. "Understood, Sir," he said.

"Good," Castillo said. "You have a promising career, Mr. Long. I'd hate to have it cut short for nothing." He pursed his lips briefly. "And bear in mind that there are other ways of dealing with incompetence and neglect, ways that don't involve the recipient's permanent record. You'd be well advised to learn them."

"Yes, Sir." In fact, Travis *did* know those other methods.

Sometimes they worked. Sometimes they didn't.

"Good." Castillo looked up at Bajek. "Is he still on duty?"

"Yes, Sir," Bajek said, never taking her eyes off Travis.

Castillo nodded and looked back at Travis. "Return to your station, Lieutenant. Dismissed."

The rest of the shift was tense, but not as bad as Travis had feared it would be. None of the men and women in his division said anything, though he did catch the edge of a couple of whispered conversations. Locatelli himself had the grace not to smirk. *Never ascribe to malice what can be explained by stupidity*, someone had once told Travis, and it was just barely possible that Locatelli wasn't so much arrogantly indifferent as he was a really slow learner.

Travis hoped it was the latter. Slow learning could be corrected with time and patience. Arrogance usually required something on the order of an exhibition bullwhip.

Still, by the time he started his final check of the systems under his watch, he was feeling more optimistic than he'd been earlier in the day.

Or at least he was until he discovered that the primary tracking sensor for the Number Two forward autocannon was once again miscalibrated.

Maybe, he thought as he headed wearily back to his quarters, it was time to go hunt up that bullwhip.

❄ ❄ ❄

"Freighter *Hosney*, you are cleared to leave orbit," the voice of Manticore Space Control came over the bridge com. It was an interesting voice, Tash McConnovitch thought, holding shades of both excitement and regret beneath the official tone. Excitement, because in a system where visitors typically dropped by less than twice per T-month, a Solly freighter was a welcome break from the drab routine of the controller's job. Regret, because with *Hosney*'s departure the boredom would be settling in again.

Patience, McConnovitch thought darkly in the controller's direction. *You'll be begging for boredom and routine before we're done with you.*

Or possibly not. The last data file Llyn had received from Axelrod's spies had put Manticore's fleet at somewhere around ten warships, with at most a single battlecruiser poised and ready to face combat.

But that data had been old. Dangerously old, as it turned out. For reasons McConnovitch had yet to pin down, King Edward had launched into an ambitious program of pulling RMN ships out of mothballs and pushing the boot camps and Academy to churn out enough warm bodies to put aboard them.

Still, Edward's revitalization was a work in progress. While the RMN might look fairly impressive on paper, none of the newly refurbished ships were even close to running at full strength. They should still be no problem for the Volsung Mercenaries.

Though of course the Volsungs themselves might not see it that way.

Fortunately, none of that was McConnovitch's concern. His job was simply to deliver the data to the rendezvous system where the mercenary task force was assembling. That snide little man Llyn was the one who would have to make the actual go/no-go decision.

"We're clear of the lane, Sir," the helmsman announced. "Course laid in."

"Good," McConnovitch said, and meant it. He was more than ready to show his kilt to this grubby, backwater little system. "Make some gees, Hermie. We wouldn't want to keep Mr. Llyn waiting."

❀ ❀ ❀

Travis had finished unsealing one of his boots and was starting on the other one when the young man lolling on the top bunk of their tiny cabin finally emerged far enough from the depths of his tablet to notice he was no longer alone. "*There* you are," Brad Fornier commented as he peered over the edge of the bunk. "Bajek have you on extra duty today? Or were you just starting the celebration early?"

"What are we celebrating?" Travis asked.

"Our upcoming R and R, of course," Fornier said. "Don't tell me you're not looking forward to a couple of weeks groundside."

Travis shrugged. "Depends on if the Number Two autocannon tracking sensor is slated for replacement. If so, yes. If not, not really."

"Mm," Fornier said. "At least you're not blaming Locatelli for that anymore."

Travis winced. No, he wasn't blaming the young ensign for the sensors' foul-up. At least not directly. "He still should have spotted the problem and either fixed it or reported it."

"Uh-huh," Fornier said, an annoyingly knowing tone to his voice. "How many people in your section, Travis?"

"Nine, including me."

"And how many of them are useless political appointees like Locatelli?"

Travis made a face. It wasn't hard to see where Fornier was going with this. "Maybe two."

"Maybe two," Fornier repeated. "So let's call it one and a half. One and a half out of eight—make it nine, since you're not political and I assume you consider yourself nonuseless. That comes to about seventeen percent. All things considered, that's really not all that bad."

"I suppose not," Travis conceded. Though Fornier was conveniently ignoring the fact that the political problem seemed to get worse the higher up the food chain you traveled. With one side of Parliament still pushing to defund and dismantle the Navy, all of those political animals—the ones who'd joined for the honor and glory—were scrambling to claw their way up the ladder to the coveted command ranks before the rug was pulled out from under them.

Maybe King Edward would turn that around. Certainly his "refit and recruit" program was showing progress.

But Travis had seen other such efforts fizzle out over the years. He wasn't really expecting this one to do any better.

And in the meantime, there were way more earls and barons in the command structure than anyone needed.

Maybe that was the end vector of all armed forces during protracted peacetime. Maybe the trend always drifted toward the political appointees, and the people who couldn't figure out what else to do, and the coasters who figured such service would be an easy and comfortable way to wander their way through life. Maybe the only way that ever turned around was if there was a war.

Still, much as it might be interesting to see how those three groups handled a sudden bout of real combat, Travis certainly didn't wish a war on the Star Kingdom. Or on anyone else, for that matter.

"Trust me, it's not bad," Fornier said dryly. "Certainly isn't a *travesty* or anything."

Travis glared up at him. "Not you, too," he growled.

"Sorry," Fornier said, not quite suppressing a grin. "It just suits you so well, that's all. How in the world did you pick up a signature phrase like that, anyway?"

"It's a long story," Travis said shortly, returning his attention to his boots.

"Okay, fine—don't tell me," Fornier said equably. "But seriously, take it from someone who did two years in retail before joining up. You keep track of every vendor, tradesman, bureaucrat, and official you meet during your two weeks groundside. I'll bet you a hundred that you'll find way more than seventeen percent who are jerks—"

Abruptly, the heart-stopping wail of the ship's klaxons erupted all around them. There were two seconds of full volume, and then the cacophony abruptly dropped to a relative whisper. "Battle stations!"

the voice of Commander Vance Sladek, *Phoenix's* executive officer, came sharply over the alarm. "Battle stations! Battle stations! All hands man battle stations!"

There was a thud as Fornier hopped off his bunk and landed on the deck. Travis was already at the emergency locker; pulling out the vac suits, he tossed Fornier's to him and started climbing into his own. "Hell of a time for a drill," Fornier said with a grunt.

"If it *is* a drill," Travis warned.

"Sladek didn't say it wasn't."

"He also didn't say it was," Travis countered. "Either way, he'll skin us alive if we're late, so move it."

Four of Travis's eight men and women were ready at their combat stations when he arrived. Ensign Locatelli, he noted darkly, wasn't one of them. "Diagnostics?" he asked, floating over to them in the zero-gee of the ship's bow.

"In progress," Ensign Tomasello confirmed. "Number Two's trackers are still coming up twitchy—"

"Long!" Bajek's voice boomed through the cramped space. "Lieutenant Long?"

"Here, Ma'am," Travis said, moving out from the partial concealment of a thick coolant pipe.

"Captain wants you on the bridge," Bajek said shortly. "I'm taking over here. Go."

"Yes, Ma'am." Maneuvering past her, Travis floated his way down the corridor toward the bridge, pulling himself hand over hand along the wall grips, a sinking feeling joining the resident tension already in his stomach. He had no idea what he'd done now, but for Castillo to be bothering with him at a time like this it must have been something big.

Like the other officers aboard *Phoenix*, Travis had been part of the bridge watch rotation ever since the early days of his assignment. But he'd never seen it during combat conditions, and the first thing that struck him as he maneuvered through the door was how calm everyone seemed to be. The voices giving orders and reports were terse, but they were clear and well controlled. Captain Castillo was strapped into his station, his eyes moving methodically between the various displays, while Commander Sladek held position at his side, the two of them occasionally murmuring comments back and forth.

All of the monitors were live, showing the ship's position, vector, and acceleration, as well as the status of the two forward missile launchers, the spinal laser, and the three autocannon defense systems.

In the center of the main tactical display was the approaching enemy.

It was a warship, all right. The signature of the wedge made that clear right from the outset. It was pulling a hundred twenty gees, which didn't tell Travis much—virtually any warship could handle that kind of acceleration, and most could do considerably better. The range marker put it just under four hundred thousand kilometers out, a little over twelve minutes away on their current closing vector.

His first reaction was one of relief. There was no way a warship could sneak up that close without *Phoenix's* sensors picking it up. Fornier had been right: this was indeed a drill.

But what kind of drill required Travis to be hauled away from his station onto the bridge? Was Castillo testing Bajek's ability to run the autocannon? That seemed ridiculous.

"Analysis, Mr. Long?"

Travis snapped his attention back. Castillo and Sladek had finished their quiet conversation, and both men were gazing straight across the bridge at him.

Travis swallowed hard. What were they asking *him* for? "It's definitely a warship, Sir," he said, trying frantically to unfreeze his brain as he looked around the multitude of displays. The sensor analysis should have spit out a data compilation and probably even an identification by now, but the screen was still showing nothing except the preliminary collection run-through. Probably another of *Phoenix's* chronic sensor glitches. "But it's not being overly aggressive," he continued, trying to buy himself some time. "The hundred twenty gees it's pulling is probably around seventy percent of its standard acceleration capability."

"So far, there's been no response to our hail," Sladek said. "How would you proceed?"

And then, to Travis's relief, the sensor ID screen finally came to life. The approaching ship was indeed one of theirs, a *Triumph*-class battlecruiser. Specifically, it was HMS *Invincible*, flagship of the Green One task force.

He had a fraction of a second of fresh relief at the confirmation that this was, indeed, just a drill. An instant later, a violent wave of fresh tension flooded in on him.

Green One was commanded by Admiral Carlton Locatelli. Uncle of Ensign Fenton Locatelli. The junior officer Travis was continually having to write up.

And here Travis was on *Phoenix's* bridge, being asked advice by his captain while Locatelli charged into simulated battle.

What the *hell* was going on?

"Mr. Long?" Castillo prompted.

With a supreme effort, Travis forced his brain back to the situation. "Do we know if she's alone?" he asked, again looking around the bridge. Everything he could see indicated *Invincible* was the only vessel out there, but he wasn't quite ready to trust his reading of the relevant displays.

"Confirmed," Sladek said. "There's nothing else within range—"

"Missile trace!" someone barked.

Travis snapped his gaze around to the tactical. A new wedge had appeared, the smaller, more compact wedge of a missile tracking straight toward *Phoenix*. "Acceleration thirty-five-hundred gees; estimated impact, two minutes forty seconds," the tactical officer added.

"Stand by autocannon," Castillo ordered calmly. "Fire will commence fifteen seconds before estimated impact."

Travis drew a hissing breath. That was, he knew, the prescribed response to a missile attack. With an effective range of a hundred fifty kilometers, the autocannon's self-guided shells were designed to detonate in the path of an incoming missile, throwing up a wall of shrapnel that could take out anything that drove through its midst, especially something traveling at the five thousand kilometers per second that a missile carried at the end of its run.

At least, that was the hoped-for outcome. Given that the missile would be entering the shrapnel zone barely two hundredths of a second before reaching its target, it was a tactic that either worked perfectly or failed catastrophically. Still, more often than not, it worked.

Only in this case, with *Phoenix's* Number Two autocannon not tracking properly . . .

"You have an objection, Mr. Long?" Castillo asked.

Travis started. He hadn't realized he'd said anything out loud.

"We've been having trouble with the autocannon, Sir," he said. "I'm thinking . . ." He stopped, suddenly aware of the utter presumption of this situation. He, a lowly senior lieutenant, was trying to tell a ship's *captain* how to do his job?

But if Castillo was offended, he didn't show it. "Continue," he merely said.

Travis squared his shoulders. He *had* been asked, after all. "I'm thinking it might be better to interpose wedge," he said, the words coming out in a rush lest he lose his nerve completely. "If the missile comes in ventral, there may not be enough autocannon coverage to stop it."

Castillo's lip might have twitched. It was hard to tell at that distance. But his nod was firm enough. "Helm, pitch twenty-six degrees positive," he ordered.

"Pitch twenty-six degrees positive, aye, aye, Sir," the helmsman acknowledged. "Pitching twenty-six degrees positive, aye."

On the tactical, *Phoenix's* angle began to shift, agonizingly slowly, as the ship's nose pivoted upward. Travis watched the display tensely as the incoming missile closed the distance at ever-increasing speed, wondering if his proposed countermove had been too late.

To his relief, it hadn't. The missile was still nearly twenty seconds out when the leading edge of *Phoenix's* floor rose high enough to cut across its vector.

"Continue countdown to missile impact," Castillo ordered. "Jink port one klick."

Travis frowned as the helmsman repeated the order. A ship had a certain range of motion within the wedge, particularly at the zero acceleration *Phoenix* was holding right now.

But moving the ship that way was tricky and cost maneuverability. What was Castillo up to?

"Missile has impacted the wedge," the tactical officer announced. "Orders?"

Castillo looked at Travis and raised his eyebrows. "Suggestions, Mr. Long?"

Travis stared at the tac display, where *Invincible* was now rimmed in flashing red to show that its position was based on the foggy gravitic data *Phoenix* was able to glean through the disruptive effects of its own wedge. For the moment, at least, the two ships were at a standoff.

Phoenix couldn't fire at something it couldn't see well enough to target, and with its wedge floor interposed between them the destroyer was likewise completely protected from any weapon *Invincible* cared to throw at them.

But *Phoenix* was a ship of the Royal Manticoran Navy. Its job wasn't to be safe. Its job was to protect the Star Kingdom's people. However Locatelli was grading them on this exercise, that grade wouldn't be very high if *Phoenix* continued to hide behind its wedge.

"Recommend we reverse pitch and reestablish full sensor contact, Sir," he said. "I'd also recommend we stand by to launch missiles." He hesitated, wondering if he needed to add that they would want the practice missiles, not the ones with full-bore warheads. Surely they already knew that.

"Agreed," the captain said. "Anything else?"

Travis frowned. From the tone of Castillo's question, he guessed there was indeed something else they should be doing. Wedge, sensor contact, missiles—

Of course. "I'd also suggest the autocannon begin laying down fire as we approach reacquisition."

"Good." Castillo gestured. "Pitch twenty-six degrees negative; prepare missiles and autocannon."

"Pitch twenty-six degrees negative, aye, aye, Sir."

"Prepare missiles and autocannon, aye, aye, Sir."

Once again, the tac display began to shift. Travis watched, his thumbs pressed hard against the sides of his forefingers. From somewhere forward came a muted rumble as the autocannon began firing. The flashing red rim around *Invincible* vanished as the sensors reacquired contact—

"Missile!" the tac officer snapped.

Travis blinked. The whole thing had happened way too fast for him to see, but the vector line on the tac display showed that the incoming missile had come in right along the edge of fire from the misaimed Number Two autocannon, shot past the wedge floor as it pitched back down, skimmed past *Phoenix* at a distance of eleven kilometers, then continued on to disintegrate against the wedge roof.

He was staring at the line in confusion, wondering how in the world a second missile had sneaked past the sensors, when the com display opened up and Admiral Locatelli himself appeared. "Well, Captain," Locatelli's voice boomed from the speaker, "I believe that gives me the kill."

"Very nearly, Admiral," Castillo said calmly. "But I think you'll find your missile didn't *quite* make it into full kill range."

The admiral frowned, his eyes shifting off camera. His smile soured a little, and he gave a small grunt. "Clever," he said reluctantly. "You're still blind, though—your whole tracking radar system would have been destroyed. Telemetry system, too."

"I can still launch missiles," Castillo pointed out.

"Only if there was another ship nearby you could hand them off to," Locatelli countered. "In this case, there isn't." He shook his head. "All in all, Captain, your response was a bit on the sloppy side. I suggest you consider upgrading your tactical officer's training and drill schedule."

"This wasn't my usual tac team, Sir," Castillo said. "One of my other officers was handling the action."

Locatelli sniffed audibly. "Your other officer has a lot to learn."

"Yes, Sir." Deliberately, it seemed to Travis, Castillo turned a studiously neutral look in his direction. "I believe he knows that."

Travis felt a swirl of disbelief corkscrew through his gut. He'd been prepared—almost—to believe that an admiral of the RMN might actually go out of his way to slap down a junior officer who had crossed him.

But for Travis's own captain to join in on the humiliation was beyond even Travis's usual level of reflexive paranoia. For Castillo to single him out this way, in front of the entire *Phoenix* bridge . . .

Travis swallowed, forcing back the stinging sense of betrayal. Castillo was still his commanding officer, and the captain was clearly expecting a response. "Yes, Sir," he managed.

"Perfection is a noble goal," Castillo continued, his eyes still on Travis. "We sometimes forget it's a journey, not a destination."

I never claimed to be perfect. Travis left the automatic protest unsaid. Clearly, this was his payback for insisting that Ensign Locatelli do his job, and neither Castillo or the admiral would be interested in hearing logical arguments.

Or pathetic excuses, which was what any comment would be taken as anyway. "I understand, Sir," he said instead. "I'll make it a point to remember today's lessons."

"I'm certain you will." Castillo turned back to the com display. "Any further orders, Admiral?"

"Not at this time," Locatelli said, a quiet but definite note of satisfaction in his voice. Whether this had been his idea or Castillo's, the admiral was obviously aware of the currents running quietly beneath the surface. "Resume your course for Manticore. I'll want a full analysis of your crew's response to this unscheduled exercise a.s.a.p."

"It'll be ready by the time you return from your training run, Sir," Castillo promised.

"Good," Locatelli said briskly. "Carry on." He reached somewhere off-camera, and his image vanished.

"Secure from Readiness One," Castillo ordered. "Resume course to Manticore, and get the spin section back up to speed."

He turned back to Travis. "First lesson of combat, Mr. Long: always be ready for the unexpected. In this case, because we weren't accelerating and were on a fairly predictable course, *Invincible* was able to slip a second missile into the wedge shadow of the first. If the attacker is very clever with his timing, he can arrange it so that the rear missile burns out its wedge at the same time the forward one impacts the target's wedge. With nothing showing, a pitched target will have just enough time to resume attitude as the second missile enters kill range."

"Sometimes the tell is a bit of the second wedge peeking through during the drive," Commander Sladek added. "Or it can show up as a sluggishness in the first missile's maneuvering as its telemetry control is eclipsed by the one behind it."

"Yes, Sir," Travis said. And if the missile was kicked out with a fusion booster there would also be a telltale flare when it was launched, as well as a slight decrease in the attacking ship's acceleration to give the missile time to get a safe distance before lighting up its wedge. All of that had been in his tactics classes back at Officer Candidate School, he belatedly remembered. In the heat of the moment, and with the role of command unexpectedly thrust upon him—

He cut off the train of thought. Rather, the train of excuses. He'd been given a job, and he'd failed. Pure and simple.

And if it hadn't been an exercise, with a practice missile instead of the real thing, he and everyone aboard *Phoenix* would probably be dead. "Yes, Sir," he said again. "I'm sorry, Sir."

Castillo grunted as he unstrapped from his station. "No need to be sorry, Lieutenant. There's just a need to learn." He waved at the tac display. "As I said, that kind of trick takes careful timing and a great deal of skill. But it also requires a fair amount of luck. Your job as an officer of the RMN is to cultivate both. And to always assume that your opponent has done likewise."

He floated out of his chair, steadied himself a moment, then gave himself a shove that sent him floating swiftly across the bridge. "Mr. Sladek, return ship to Readiness Five," he called over his shoulder. "Mr. Travis, you may return to your station for debriefing."

"Yes, Sir," Travis said. Lesson delivered, and lesson learned, and the captain was back to business as usual.

Travis *would* remember the day's lesson, he promised himself. Very, very well.

❈ ❈ ❈

For the next two days Travis walked around on figurative eggshells, waiting for the inevitable fallout from his part in the fiasco.

To his surprise, no such fallout materialized. Or at least nothing materialized in his direction. There were vague rumors that Captain Castillo was spending an unusual amount of time in his cabin on the com with System Command, but no details were forthcoming and Travis himself was never summoned into his presence. Given that *Phoenix* was about to settle in for some serious refitting, chances were good that that was the main topic of any such extended communications.

Phoenix was slipping into its designated slot in Manticore orbit, and Travis was finally starting to breathe easy again, when the shoe finally dropped.

❈ ❈ ❈

"You're joking," Fornier said, staring wide-eyed from across the cabin. "After all that, you're being *promoted*?"

"I'm being *transferred*," Travis corrected sourly. "I never said it was a promotion."

"Please," Fornier said dryly. "If *Casey* isn't a promotion, what the hell is it?"

"I don't know," Travis growled as he arranged his dress uniform tunic carefully at the top of his travel bag. "But if Locatelli's behind it, hell may very well be the relevant neighborhood."

Fornier shook his head. "You're way too young to be this cynical," he said. "Anyway, who says Locatelli's hand is anywhere near this? For all you know it was Castillo who recommended you for *Casey's* assistant tac officer slot."

"With my sterling performance on the bridge during that drill cementing it?" Travis snorted. "Not likely."

"Fine," Fornier said, clearly starting to lose his wedge-class patience level. "So maybe Castillo decided you needed a lesson in humility. Welcome to the human race. But maybe while he was delivering the message he also saw something he liked about you, some potential that hadn't come through before."

"I doubt it," Travis said. "About all I did was regurgitate what was in the manual. Or half of what was in the manual. No, given Heissman's reputation, I think they all just want me out from under Castillo's fatherly care and underneath a genuine hammer for awhile."

For a moment Fornier was silent. Travis looked around the cabin, mentally counting out the items he'd already packed and trying to figure out if he'd missed anything.

"There are two ways to approach life, Travis," Fornier said into his thoughts. "One: you can expect that everyone's out to get you, and be alert and ready for trouble at every turn. Or two: you can assume that most people are friendly or at least neutral, and that most of the time things will work out."

"Seems to me option two is an invitation to get walked on."

"Oh, I never said you don't need to be ready for trouble." Fornier grinned suddenly. "Hey, we're RMN officers. It's our *job* to be ready for trouble. I'm just saying that if you're always expecting that second shoe to drop, you're never going to be really able to trust anyone." He shrugged. "And speaking from my own experience, there are a fair number of people out there who are worth your trust. Not all of them. But enough."

"Maybe," Travis said, sealing his travel bag and picking it up. "I'll take it under advisement." He held out his hand. "It's been great serving and rooming with you, Brad. Keep in touch, okay?"

"Will do," Fornier promised, grasping Travis's hand in a firm grip and shaking it. "Best of luck."

II

"Hyper footprint," Captain Ngo announced. "From insertion vector, probably *Hosney*."

Llyn nodded, peering at the display. About time. The bulk of the Volsung task force had been sitting in this uninhabited red-dwarf star system for the past two weeks, with only one of the battlecruisers still absent, and Gensonne was starting to get twitchy. The fresh data McConnovitch was bringing in from Manticore should allay the admiral's lingering concerns about the particulars of the force he would be facing. "Any transmissions yet?"

"No, sir," Ngo said, an edge of strained patience in his tone. "It *is* still a light minute away."

"I wasn't asking about him," Llyn countered. "Gensonne's bi-hourly nagging call is almost due, and he'll have picked up *Hosney*'s footprint, too."

"No, sir, no transmissions from anywhere."

That silence wouldn't last long, Llyn knew. McConnovitch was a good man, and one of the best data scavengers in the business. But Gensonne didn't care about such things. He had his own ideas of how the universe was supposed to operate, and McConnovitch hadn't kept to that schedule, and the admiral hadn't been shy about sharing his view of such sloppiness with Llyn on a regular basis.

But all that was finally about to come to an end. Once McConnovitch confirmed the RMN's weakness, Llyn could turn the Volsungs loose and then head over to where his Axelrod superiors were waiting to hear that the operation was finally underway. By the time Gensonne had Landing and the Manticoran government under control, Axelrod's people would be on their way to take over.

"Transmission," Ngo called. "Incoming data packet from *Hosney*."

Llyn felt a prickling on the back of his neck. No greeting, no identification, just the data packet? That didn't sound like McConnovitch.

The report came up on his display. Frowning, Lynn began to read.

And as he did so, the prickling on his neck turned into a shiver.

Green Force One, scout unit: four ships.

Green Force Two, main Manticore/Sphinx defense unit: nine ships, including two battlecruisers. Not one, but two.

Red Force, Gryphon defense unit: four ships, including another battlecruiser.

The ten-ship, one-battlecruiser enemy that Gensonne was expecting to meet was in fact seventeen ships and no fewer than *three* battlecruisers. And that didn't even count the three battlecruisers and six other warships that were currently in refit.

Gensonne wasn't going to be happy about this. Not at all. In fact, he might be unhappy enough to take his ball and go home.

And given the unanticipated uptick in the RMN's numbers, the contract Llyn and Gensonne had signed not only allowed the Volsungs to bail, but also required Axelrod to pay them a hefty cancellation fee.

There was no way Llyn was going to let that happen. Not after coming this far. Taking a cleansing breath, he began combing methodically through the numbers.

It wasn't that bad. Not really. Green Forces One and Two were a formidable array, but the fact that they *were* split into two groups meant that Gensonne should be able to take them on one at a time. Even if he couldn't, it was still two RMN battlecruisers against the Volsungs' three. Even better, Red Force was way the hell over at Manticore-B and should be out of the picture until long after the battle was over. And of course, all the ships in dock for refit might as well not even be there.

No, Gensonne wasn't going up against anything he couldn't handle. Not with his three battlecruisers, his fourteen other ships, and his massive confidence.

There was certainly no reason to bother the admiral's little head with silly numbers and needless concerns.

He had finished editing McConnovitch's report when Gensonne finally called in. "Yes, Admiral, I've just decoded it," Llyn told him calmly. "I'm sending it to you now."

"Thank you," Gensonne said. "I trust nothing has changed since your last report?"

"Nothing of significance," Llyn assured him. "Nothing at all."

❈ ❈ ❈

Commodore Rudolph Heissman, commander of the light cruiser HMS *Casey* and the other three ships of Green Two, the task force callsigned Janus, was undoubtedly a very busy man. Nevertheless, from Travis's point of view at the far side of Heissman's desk, it looked like he was taking an extraordinarily long time to read through Travis's transfer orders. Seated beside him, Commander Celia Belokas, Heissman's exec, didn't look to be in any more of a hurry than her boss.

Finally, after a mid-size eternity, Heissman looked up. "Lieutenant Long," he said, his flat tone not giving anything away. "According to this, you have great potential."

He paused, as if expecting some kind of response. "Thank you, Sir," was all Travis could think to say. The words, which had sounded tolerably reasonable in his head, sounded excruciatingly stupid when he heard them out in the open air.

Heissman apparently thought so, too. "You know what I hear when someone uses the phrase *great potential*, Mr. Long?" he asked, his expression not changing in the slightest. "I hear someone making excuses. I hear someone who hasn't worked to reach the level of his or her ability. I hear someone who doesn't belong in the Royal Manticoran Navy. I hear someone who *absolutely* doesn't belong aboard HMS *Casey*."

"Yes, Sir," Travis said. That response didn't sound any better than the previous one had.

"I don't want to see potential," Heissman continued. "I want to see results." He cocked his head. "Do you know what a tac officer's job is, Mr. Long?"

"Yes, Sir." The words sounded marginally better this time. "To assist the captain in combat maneuvers and—"

"That's the job description," Heissman interrupted. "What a tac officer *does* is find patterns and weaknesses in the enemy, and avoid them in his own ship."

He gazed into Travis's eyes, his expression hardening. "Captain Castillo talks a lot about luck. I don't ever want to hear you use that word aboard my ship. Understood?"

"Yes, Sir," Travis said.

"Good," Heissman said. "As I said, part of your job is to know the weaknesses of your own ship and find ways to minimize them. Step one in that procedure is obviously to know your ship." He nodded to his side. "In light of that, Commander Belokas has graciously agreed to give you a tour. Pay attention and listen to everything she has to say. Afterward, you're going to need a lot of hours with the spec manual before you're anywhere near up to speed."

"Yes, Sir," Travis said. He shifted his eyes to Belokas. "Ma'am."

Heissman's eyebrows rose a fraction of a centimeter. "Unless, of course, you've already spent some time in the manual," the commodore continued, as if the thought had only just occurred to him. "Have you?"

"As a matter of fact, Sir, yes, I have," Travis confirmed, trying not to grimace. He'd only spent eighty percent of his waking hours during his two weeks of groundside time poring through everything he could find on *Casey* and her equipment. Which, considering all the bureaucratic hoops he'd had to jump through to even get the manuals, Heissman almost certainly already knew. "Just the surface information, of course—"

"In that case, *you* can give the tour," Heissman said. "You'll tell Commander Belokas everything you know, and she'll start on her list of everything you *don't* know. That sound fair to you?"

"Yes, Sir," Travis said.

"Good," Heissman said. "You have two hours before you're to report to Lieutenant Commander Woodburn, so you'd better get to it." He nodded briskly and lowered his eyes to the report. "Dismissed."

III

"Admiral Gensonne?"

His eyes and attention still on Llyn's report, Gensonne reached over and keyed the com. "What is it, Imbar?"

"Hyper footprint, Sir," Captain Sweeney Imbar, commander of *Odin*, reported. "Looks like *Tyr* has finally arrived."

Gensonne grunted. About fraggy time. They'd been waiting on Blakely to get his butt here for four solid weeks, and the rest of the captains were getting antsy. Now, with the last of Gensonne's three battlecruisers on site, they were finally ready to get this operation underway. "Send Captain Blakely my compliments," he instructed Imbar, "and tell him to haul his sorry carcass in pronto so he can start loading supplies and armaments. We head for Manticore in five days, and if he's not ready he'll be left behind."

"Aye, Admiral," Imbar said, and Gensonne could visualize the other's malicious grin. Imbar loved relaying that kind of order.

Gensonne keyed off the com, and with a scowl returned his attention to Llyn's report.

Seventeen warships. That was what the Volsung Mercenaries were bringing to the field: three battlecruisers, six cruisers, seven destroyers, and one troop carrier. The Manticorans, in contrast, had only thirteen warships with which to counter the attack.

Well, seventeen, really, if you wanted to be technical and add in the group guarding Gryphon. But they were way the hell over at Manticore-B. If the Volsungs did their job properly, that force could be left out of the equation. Llyn's spies hadn't been able to get a complete reading on the ship types in each of the two Manticore-A groups, but the earlier report had said the larger force had a single battlecruiser, and there was nothing in this latest intel to suggest that number had changed. The additional ships in the new intel had to be small, destroyers or corvettes.

Plus the fact that all the enthusiasm in the galaxy could mount impeller rings and graduate crewmen only so quickly. Even if Llyn's current count was off by a ship or two, the Volsungs should be facing no more than the same number of ships they themselves were bringing to the battle.

Still . . .

Gensonne murmured a ruminative curse. The wild card in this whole thing, and a wild card that Llyn either hadn't noticed or had deliberately downplayed, was this damn HMS *Casey*. The tables listed it as a standard light cruiser, but it was clear from the specs Llyn's spies had been able to dig out that there wasn't anything standard about it, certainly not for ships out here in the hinterlands. From the profile alone, he could see that the Manticorans had put in a modern grav plate habitation module, a high-efficiency radiator system, and had extended the length of their missile launchers. Possibly a railgun launch system; more likely just an absorption cylinder that would minimize the missiles' launch flares. Nothing really revolutionary, and nothing Gensonne couldn't handle.

Still, it was far more advanced than it should be, and better than most of the Volsungs' own mainly second-hand and surplused ships. The report didn't get into details about armament or defenses, but Gensonne had no doubt that *Casey*'s designers hadn't neglected to pack some serious firepower aboard.

And if King Edward had had the authority, the confidence, and the cash to turn his designers loose on *Casey*, he might well have used that same combination to speed up the de-mothballing of those other ships.

The smart thing would be to put off the operation until Gensonne had time to send his own people to Manticore. Get a real military assessment instead of having to rely on Llyn's paper-pushing guesswork. But getting a civilian spy ship way out there and back again with anything useful would take over a year, and Llyn wanted this done *now*.

Gensonne scowled. The ongoing mystery underlying this whole thing was what in blazes the Manticorans could possibly have that was worth this much effort. Llyn was paying the Volsungs a huge sum of money to take over three lumps of real estate on the bloody back end of nowhere. Gensonne had tried on numerous occasions to wangle that secret out of the smug little man, and every time Llyn had calmly and artfully dodged the question.

But that was all right. The Volsung Mercenaries weren't without resources of their own . . . and if Gensonne still didn't know the *why*, he now at least knew the *who*.

Llyn's employer, the man quietly funding this whole operation, was one of the top people in the multi-trillion, transstellar business juggernaut known as the Axelrod Corporation.

So the question now became why Axelrod would be interested in Manticore. Was it the treecats? Something else hidden in the forests of Sphinx or the wastes of Gryphon?

"Admiral?" Imbar's voice came from the com speaker.

Gensonne keyed the transmitter. "Yes?"

"Captain Blakely's compliments, Sir," Imbar said. "He confirms hauling carcass as ordered, and anticipates fourteen hours to zero-zero."

Gensonne checked his chrono. "Tell him that if he doesn't make it in twelve he might as well not bother," he warned.

"He anticipated that request," Imbar said, his voice going a little brittle. "He said to tell you that fourteen should do just fine if you can get the loaders to haul carcass at even half the speed he's doing it. If you can't, he'll just have to do it himself." The captain gave a little snort. "He added a 'Sir' to that, but I don't think he really meant it."

Gensonne smiled. Blakely was as arrogant and snarky an SOB as they came. But he was also a hell of a scrappy fighter, and Gensonne was willing to put up with the one if he could have the other. "Tell him he'll be losing one percent of his profit cut for every ten minutes after twelve hours he ties up."

"Yes, Sir, that should do it," Imbar said slyly. "I'll let him know."

"Do that," Gensonne said, his attention already back on the upcoming campaign. Standard military doctrine, of course, said that you went after the biggest ships first, taking them out as soon as you could clear away their screening vessels.

But in this case, it might well be smart to seek out *Casey* earlier rather than later and make sure it was out of the fight. If it *was* the Manticorans' modern showcase, its destruction might help convince them to sue for terms more promptly.

Which could be useful. Standard rules of war dictated that a planet was supposed to surrender once someone else controlled the space around it, a convention designed to avoid the wholesale slaughter of civilians in prolonged combat. Taking out *Casey* would give the Volsungs that control all the faster, and once Gensonne had King Edward's formal surrender document, any forces that remained at large would be legally bound to stand down.

Gensonne liked quick surrenders. It saved on men and equipment, and it boosted profits.

And if *Casey* wasn't, in fact, anything special?

He shrugged. It wasn't like the ship wouldn't have to be destroyed eventually anyway.

"Admiral, I have a response from Captain Blakely," Imbar once again interrupted. "He sends his compliments, and says he'll see you in hell."

Gensonne smiled. "Tell him it's a date," he said. "I'll be the one wearing white."

IV

The midwatch was technically the first watch of the ship's day, though whether it felt like the earliest or the latest was largely a function of how a given crewmember's biological clock operated. Some of *Casey's* officers and crew actively hated it, while others were less passionate on the subject but not any happier with the duty.

Travis had no such animosities toward midwatch assignments. On the contrary, he rather enjoyed them. Midwatch was the quietest period of ship's day, with the bulk of the crew asleep back in the hab module, only essential operations running, and minimal routine maintenance scheduled.

It was the best time of day, in short, to just be quiet and think.

He certainly had plenty to think about. For the past six weeks most of his waking hours had been devoted to learning everything he could about *Casey*, her armaments, her capabilities, and her crew. Lieutenant Commander Alfred Woodburn, the ship's tactical officer, had ridden him hard, but unlike some of the officers back on *Phoenix*, Woodburn was eminently fair and always seemed more interested in teaching Travis the ropes than in making himself look superior or his student look stupid.

Travis sent his gaze slowly around the bridge, at the men and women strapped into their stations, casually alert even in the quiet of absolutely nothing happening. *Casey* wasn't exactly home—Travis wasn't sure if any place would ever truly be home for him—but the ship and her crew had all the little quirks that he'd always imagined would exist in a home.

There were a few irritating personalities aboard, and Travis had had his share of small clashes with some of them. But for the most part, the crew seemed to be compatible with each other.

The commissioned complement had even more of that same pseudo-family feeling. On the bridge, Commodore Heissman typically dispensed with the formalities that Captain Castillo had always maintained aboard *Phoenix*, addressing his senior officers by their first names or even nicknames, some of which Travis still hadn't puzzled out. There was an air of easy camaraderie, the kind that Travis had read about in military-themed books and had experienced to some degree back at OCS.

Still, that familiarity and camaraderie went only so far. Heissman and the other senior officers still addressed Travis formally as *Lieutenant* or *Mr. Long*, and he was of course expected to reciprocate with that same formality. Hopefully, it was just a matter of Travis being on probation, that somewhere along the line he would be accepted as a full-fledged member of *Casey*'s family.

Unless *Phoenix*'s same political underpinnings were roiling quietly and undetectably beneath the surface. If so, he might as well get used to being *Casey*'s ugly duckling.

"XO on the bridge," Lieutenant Rusk called from the sensor station.

Travis looked up from his board to see Commander Belokas float onto the bridge. "Ma'am," he greeted her, reflexively reaching for his restraints before he could stop himself. Regulations said that when a senior officer entered the bridge all crew members were to immediately rise to attention, a standing order Captain Castillo had enforced aboard *Phoenix*. Commodore Heissman and Commander Belokas dispensed with that particular formality, and Travis was still getting used to it.

Briefly, he wondered if the officers and crew of *Invincible* had to float upright in zero-gee every time Admiral Locatelli came into any compartment, not just the bridge. He suspected they probably did.

"What can we do for you, Ma'am?" he asked as Belokas drifted across the bridge, her gaze moving back and forth between the various status monitors.

"I was wondering if there was anything new on that flicker we got from the northwest sector sixteen hours ago," she said.

"I don't believe so, Ma'am," Travis said, frowning as he pulled up the log. There hadn't been any mention of activity on the watch report he'd read when he'd arrived on duty an hour ago.

No wonder. The flicker Belokas was referring to was the barest bloop, something that would never even have been noticed if the rest of the universe hadn't been so quiet and *Casey*'s crew so bored. The duty officer had put it down to a sensor echo; the sensor officer, after a thorough examination of his equipment, had suggested it was probably a hyper ghost, a phenomenon that shipboard instrumentation was unfortunately not well-equipped to pinpoint or identify. For that, a large-scale orbiting sensor array was necessary, and Manticore wasn't likely to be buying one of those monstrosities anytime soon.

But if the frown on Belokas's face was any indication, she wasn't happy with either explanation. An odd reaction, really, given that such ghosts weren't exactly unheard of out here. "There's been nothing new, Ma'am," Travis told her. "Do you want us to run another sensor diagnostic?"

For a few seconds Belokas didn't answer, but merely continued her drift toward the command station. Travis watched her approach, his heartbeat picking up a bit. He was still somewhat new to this whole officer-in-charge thing, and he already knew how lousy he was at reading Belokas's expression and body language. Should he have run such a diagnostic already? Was she holding her peace merely because she wanted to be close enough to chew him out quietly, without the rest of the bridge crew listening in?

"More diagnostics won't tell us anything new," she said at last, catching hold of the hand grip beside his station and bringing herself to a halt. "Let's try something else. Run me a simulation of what a soft translation about fifteen light-minutes outside the hyper limit would look like."

"Yes, Ma'am," Travis said, and swiveled around to his console. That possibility had already been considered, he'd seen from the report. But between the diagnostics and the hyper-ghost hypothesis, that scenario had apparently been dropped. Certainly there was no record of anyone having done a simulation or even a data-curve profile.

Fortunately, it was a fairly easy job, with most of the necessary templates already stored on the ship's computer. A couple of minutes, and he was ready. "Here we go," he said, starting the run. "I set it to cover the full range of thirteen to eighteen light-minutes. If that doesn't work, I can extend it outward—"

"Hyper footprint!" Rusk called.

For a fraction of a second Travis thought the sensor officer was talking about the simulation. Then his brain caught up with him. "Acknowledged," he said, swiveling again and checking the sensor display. It was a translation, all right, a big, fat, noisy one.

And it was in the northwest sector, right on the same vector where the sensor bloop had registered. "We have anything on her?" he asked.

"She's reasonably big," Rusk said, frowning at his displays. "Low-power wedge, low acceleration. Probably a freighter, possibly a passenger liner. There's something funny about her wedge, too—some sort of nonrhythmic fluctuation. Could be she's having reactor problems."

Travis looked at Belokas, wondering if she would formally relieve him and take command. Ships didn't show up at Manticore every day, after all.

But she was just gazing silently at the displays. Waiting, apparently, for the officer of the watch to respond to the situation.

Travis squared his shoulders. "Send a request for identification and status, and inform the rest of Janus that we have a visitor," he ordered. "Then send an alert to System Command." He squinted at the tactical. "What is she, about ten light-minutes out?"

"Yes, Sir, just a shade under," Rusk confirmed. "So about twenty minutes until we get a reply."

"Unless she *is* having problems, in which case she's probably already screaming for help," Belokas said. She tapped her cheek thoughtfully. "Where's Aegis at the moment?"

Aegis, the callsign for Admiral Locatelli's Green One force. "The far side of Manticore," Travis said. "About twenty-two light minutes away from us, maybe thirteen or fourteen from the bogey. Shall I send an alert directly to Admiral Locatelli?"

"That would be a good idea," Belokas confirmed. "If there's trouble, we're definitely closest. But depending on what's going on, he may want to reconfigure Aegis while we head out there." Her lips compressed briefly. "And while you do all that, I also recommend calling Commodore Heissman to the bridge."

❀ ❀ ❀

"—and I think the reactor's mag bottle is also starting to fail," Captain Olver's frantic voice boomed over *Odin*'s com speaker. "My engineer says it could go at any time."

Gensonne listened closely, trying to ignore the annoying flutter in the carefully mistuned old-fashioned radio that Olver was using to supplement his com laser, hoping the other would remember his instructions to keep his voice pleading but not whiny. People hated whiny, even upstanding naval types willing to risk their lives for those in danger. Making *Naglfar* look stoic and sympathetic would encourage the Manticorans listening to his distress call to charge to the rescue with a minimum of delay and, hopefully, a minimum of prudence.

"Repeating: this is the personnel transport *Leviathan*, heading for the Haven Sector with three thousand passengers," Olver continued. "The same power surge that damaged our forward alpha nodes and the fusion bottle's also compromised our life-support system—we're trying to fix it, but it's not looking good, and I don't know how long before it fails completely. If you have any ships in the area, for the love of God, please get them out here. We're making as many gees as we can, but I don't know how much longer before we'll have to shut down the wedge completely, and we're a hell of a long way from anywhere. Whatever ships you've got—freighters, liners, ore ships—anything we can pack our people into—please send them. For the love of God, please."

The plea broke off as one of Olver's crew came up with his own anxiously delivered and almost off-mike report on the supposed fusion bottle failure, and Gensonne keyed off the speaker. They were still a good distance out from the inner system, but it looked like the nearest Manticoran force was about ten light-minutes away, which meant a twenty-minute turnaround for any conversation.

The Manticorans' response should be interesting. In the meantime, Gensonne had plenty of other matters with which to occupy himself. "What's the status of the main force?" he called across the bridge.

"We've temporarily lost contact, Admiral," Imbar called back. "They're definitely still behind us, but they're hard to spot with their wedges down."

Gensonne grunted, looking across the relevant display screens. Being difficult to spot was the whole idea, of course. But knowing exactly where to look should make the task a lot simpler.

Though perhaps he was being too harsh on Imbar and the sensor team. The fourteen ships of the advance and rear forces had translated into n-space together a few hours ago, coming in softly and quietly about forty light-minutes out from Manticore-A, where they ought to have been well out of range of RMN sensors. The enormous passive arrays typical of more populous star systems would certainly have picked them up, but shipboard sensors' range was always far more limited. The invaders had sorted themselves into Gensonne's six-ship advance force and *Thor*'s eight-ship main force, then headed toward the inner system in two waves spaced about an hour apart. A couple of hours of acceleration by both groups to build up some respectable speed, and then all fourteen ships had dropped their wedges to standby as they coasted inward. Even knowing where to look, the distant ships should barely even reflect Manticore-A's distant light.

Now, after hours of tedium, things were finally about to heat up. Far ahead, *Naglfar* had translated into the system—not with the same undetectable entry as the rest of the Volsung ships, but with a big, noisy translation that should have grabbed the attention of every RMN ship in the region. That sloppy entrance, along with Olver's frantic plea for help, should get the Manticoran ships falling all over themselves scrambling to come to his aid.

It would no doubt be highly entertaining to see how a Manticoran boarding party would react to finding out that a shipload of supposedly helpless civilians was actually five battalions of crack Volsung shock troops. Sadly, Gensonne would miss out on that picture. If all went according to plan, the Manticorans' first encounter with those troops wouldn't be in deep space, but at the Royal Palace in Landing City.

By then, of course, the surprise would be long gone. Still, the purpose of this exercise was capture and occupation, not entertainment. And once the RMN had been eliminated, Volsung control of the Manticoran centers of power would be a mere formality.

"Got a bearing on *Naglfar*, Admiral," Imbar called. "We're on a good intercept course. We should pass it in about ninety-seven minutes."

Gensonne checked the tac display. Ninety-seven minutes was shorter than he'd planned, but within acceptable parameters. "Have Olver increase acceleration to ninety-five gees," he instructed Imbar. He could always have *Naglfar* cut back later if Gensonne needed to fine-tune the intercept. "Any movement from the Manticorans yet?"

"No, Sir," Imbar said. "But Bogey One should just be hearing Olver's distress call now."

"Keep an eye on them," Gensonne ordered. "Once we know their jump-off time and acceleration, I want a quick plot of their zero-zero intercept. We need to make sure we're far enough ahead of *Naglfar* that they won't be able to turn tail and run once they spot us."

Though the other little surprise Gensonne had planned should help alleviate that problem. If the destroyers *Umbriel* and *Miranda* had translated in on schedule at their own spot around the edge of the hyper limit, there was a good chance their timing and vector would help cut off any retreat the Manticorans might attempt.

"Yes, Sir," Imbar said. "We're also picking up a second group of wedges, bearing oh-two-one by oh-one-eight. From the signature there seem to be significantly more ships there than in the first group. That probably makes them the main Bogey Two force."

"Distance?"

"Just under fourteen light-minutes."

Gensonne nodded in satisfaction. Llyn's most recent intel had suggested the two task forces would be positioned more or less this way relative to Manticore and Sphinx, and Gensonne had relied on that data in mapping out his attack plan. But there'd been no way to know for sure how the Manticorans would be arrayed until the Volsungs actually entered the system.

Now, with the defenders' positions confirmed, the plan was officially a lock. Assuming the Manticorans bought into Olver's story, Bogey One would rush to *Naglfar*'s rescue and be quickly destroyed by *Odin* and the rest of the advance force. If Bogey Two followed and moved to engage, its ships should arrive just in time to face the entire Volsung force as *Thor* and the rest of the rear group caught up with Gensonne's first wave.

If Bogey One opted instead to avoid battle and run for home, the end result would still be the same, just a few hours later. Either way, Manticore was as good as taken.

Llyn would be pleased. More to the point, Llyn's boss over at Axelrod would be paying a nice contractual bonus.

Smiling tightly, Gensonne settled back and waited for the Manticorans to take the bait.

⚜ ⚜ ⚜

"We're making as many gees as we can," the tense voice came from the bridge speaker, "but I don't know how much longer before we'll have to shut down the wedge completely, and we're a hell of a long way from anywhere. Whatever ships you've got—freighters, liners, ore ships—anything we can pack our people into—please send them. For the love of God, please."

Heissman gestured, and the com officer keyed the volume back down. "XO?" the commodore invited, looking at Belokas.

"All ships showing ready," Belokas reported.

"What's your estimate on how many passengers we can take?"

Belokas huffed out a breath. "Between all four of us, I don't think we can take more than five hundred. And *that's* if we pack them to the deckheads. Not exactly luxury travel."

"Still beats suffocating in the cold," Woodburn said with a grunt.

"That it does," Heissman agreed. "Send a copy of their distress call to Aegis with a request for aid. They're farther out, but they've got a lot more room."

"Assuming *Leviathan* can hold its bottle together long enough for Locatelli to reach them," Belokas warned.

"Nothing we can do about that," Woodburn said.

"So we *are* going to head out there?" Travis asked.

All eyes turned to him. "You have something, Lieutenant?" Heissman asked.

"Something *solid*?" Woodburn added. "Because hunches don't—"

He broke off at a small gesture from Heissman. "Continue," the commodore said.

Travis braced himself. "There's just something about this that feels wrong, Sir," he said, hoping the words didn't sound as lame to the others as they did to him. Especially since Woodburn had already warned him that no one was interested in his hunches. "The timing, the vector—same bearing as the hyper ghost—the fact that they came *here* instead of trying for somewhere else—"

"Their wedge *is* showing signs of stress," Heissman reminded him.

"And all indications are that it's a merchant or passenger liner, not a warship."

"Sir, zero-zero intercept course is plotted and ready," the helm reported.

"Feed to the other ships, and let's make some gravs," Heissman said. He looked at Travis. "And order all crews to Readiness Two," he added. "Just in case."

❊ ❊ ❊

"They're coming," Imbar announced. "Vector . . . too early to tell for sure, but it looks like they're lining up for a zero-zero intercept with *Naglfar*."

"Excellent," Gensonne said with a warm glow of satisfaction. The Manticorans had fallen for it. "Do we have a fix on *Umbriel* and *Miranda*?"

"Not yet," Imbar said. "But we're monitoring the area where they should be. Assuming they made it in all right, they should be lighting off their wedges sometime in the next couple of hours to fine-tune their own intercept with Bogey One."

Gensonne nodded. Having the two destroyers arrive just in time to catch the Manticorans in a cross-fire would be helpful, but it was hardly vital to his plan. If they missed out on this first skirmish, they would be able to switch to a similar attack role when the Volsungs came up against Bogey Two.

And if they also managed to miss out on that one, they would still be useful as scouts, sweeping the area ahead of the Volsung fleet toward Manticore proper after the two defending forces had been disposed of.

One way or another, Gensonne promised himself, every ship in the assault force would earn its pay today.

❊ ❊ ❊

Janus was still two hours away from its projected zero-zero rendezvous with *Leviathan*, and was making yet another course correction as the damaged liner once again adjusted her own acceleration, when *Gorgon* signaled the news that two more wedges had appeared in the distance.

"Shapira says it's pure luck she spotted them in the first place," Belokas said, hovering close beside Heissman's station as they gazed together at the unexpected and, to Travis's mind, unsettling data the destroyer had sent across. "Given that our wedges were all turned that direction, and all our crews busy with the course change, I tend to agree with her."

"Captain Shapira has a bad habit of ascribing to luck things which properly belong to training and vigilance," Heissman said thoughtfully as he gazed at the tactical. "Make sure we log a commendation for her and her bridge crew for this one. What do you make of it?"

"They're definitely smaller than *Leviathan*," Belokas said. "Could be small freighters. Definitely not ore ships or anything else that's supposed to be running around out there."

"Or they could be small warships," Woodburn added. "Destroyers or light cruisers. Especially—there! Now, isn't *that* interesting?"

Travis felt his eyes narrow. As suddenly as they'd appeared, the mysterious wedges had vanished. As if the ships had finished with whatever course change or acceleration they'd come out of hiding for and then dropped back into the covering blackness of interplanetary space.

Woodburn was obviously thinking the same thing. "They're hiding, all right," he said grimly. "You'll also notice that they saved their maneuvers for a period when we were doing some adjustments of our own and were theoretically at our least attentive. With all due respect, Commodore, this is starting to look less like a rescue mission and more like an invasion."

"Agreed," Heissman said. "Mr. Long, what did you come up with on our battle inventory?"

"Not as good as it should be, Sir," Travis said.

And instantly regretted the words. The fact that Janus wasn't running at full strength was the fault of the politicians in Parliament, not RMN Command. But his thoughtless comment could easily be construed as criticism of that leadership.

Or, worse, as a criticism of his own commander. Neither was acceptable, especially not on that commander's own bridge.

Fortunately, Heissman didn't seem to take it that way. "No argument here, Lieutenant," he said, a bit dryly. "Continue."

"*Without* the editorial comments," Belokas added more severely.

"Yes, Ma'am," Travis said, wincing. "My apologies. Our missile count is down to eighteen, but both fore and aft lasers are fully functional, as are the broadside energy torpedo launchers. One of our autocannon is a little iffy—cooling problems; the techs are working on it. We also have nineteen countermissiles, and all four of the launchers read green."

"What about the other ships?" Belokas asked.

"*Gorgon* has eight missiles and *Hercules* and *Gemini* each have four," Travis said. "Their point-defenses are about in the same shape and with the same capacity as ours."

"How many of those missiles are practice rounds?" Heissman asked.

"None, Sir," Travis said, frowning. "I didn't think I should count those."

"They still *look* like real missiles, even if they can't go bang," Heissman pointed out. "What's the count?"

"We have four, *Gorgon* has two, *Hercules* one, *Gemini* two," Travis said. But if the missiles had no warheads . . . ?

The confusion must have shown on his face, because both Heissman and Woodburn favored him with small smiles. "Never underestimate the power of a bald-faced bluff, Mr. Long," Heissman said. "At worst, a dummy missile can make an enemy waste rounds from their point-defenses. At best, its wedge can shred a hull with the best of them."

The smile vanished. "So basically, we're underarmed, undercrewed, and even with Aegis pulling all the gees they can we're a fair ways from any reinforcement. Recommendations?"

"The safe move would be to break off," Woodburn said reluctantly. "Our limping passenger liner could be anything up to and including a battlecruiser, and by the time we have accurate sensor data it'll be too late to get away."

He gestured. "And then we've got those two ships playing hide-and-seek out there. We're lucky to see two visiting ships a month; and now we've suddenly got *three* of them on the same day? *And* three ships which seem to be coordinating movements?"

"So you're recommending we alert Command and break with an eye toward a rendezvous with Aegis?" Heissman asked calmly.

"I said that would be the safe move," Woodburn corrected, just as calmly. "But we're not out here to play safe. We're out here to look for trouble, and when we find that trouble to assess and deal with it."

"So your actual recommendation is that we fly into the mouth of the beast?" Belokas asked.

"Right square into it," Woodburn confirmed. "But I also recommend we have *Gorgon* start drifting a little behind us and the corvettes. Not so fast or far that our friends out there take notice and wonder what we're up to, but far enough for her to run communications between us once we raise our sidewalls." His lips compressed briefly. "Hopefully, she'll be able to stay clear long enough to send back a full record of whatever's about to happen."

Travis swallowed. The implication was painfully clear. Woodburn didn't expect *Casey* or the two corvettes to survive the approaching encounter.

But that, too, was why Janus was out here.

"XO?" Heissman invited.

"I agree with Commander Woodburn's assessment and proposed action, Sir," Belokas said, her voice formal.

"Very good," Heissman said, his tone matching hers. "Alert all ships as to the situation, and have them stand ready for further orders. Albert, draw up a proposed timeline for detaching *Gorgon* and shifting us into combat formation. XO, we'll stay at Readiness Two, but warn all ships that we could go to Readiness One at any time. If we've got any spare warheads aboard, have the crews start swapping them into the practice missiles."

"Yes, Sir." Woodburn nudged Travis. "Come on, Lieutenant. We have work to do." He pushed off the hand grip and floated toward his station.

Travis followed, long practice enabling him to stay close to his superior without bumping into him. "A question, Sir?" he asked.

"Why *Gorgon* instead of one of the corvettes?"

Travis felt his lip twitch. "Yes, Sir," he admitted. "*Gorgon* has more missiles, more armor, and better sidewalls. If we're heading into a fight, we could use her up here with us."

"She also has aft autocannon," Woodburn reminded him. "If it comes down to the last surviving ship of Janus Force making a run for it, we need to make sure it's the ship with the best chance of making it through a barrage of up-the-kilt missiles."

Travis nodded, an odd thought flicking through his mind. *Casey* also had aft autocannon, and a better chance of survival even than

Gorgon. If the most critical priority was to gain information on the intruder and then run, the strictly logical answer was for *Casey* to take the rear position instead. Depending on what kind of warship was lurking behind the crippled-liner masquerade, having *Casey* in the battle probably wouldn't make that much of a difference in the outcome anyway.

He wondered if the option had even entered Heissman's mind. Or Belokas's, or Woodburn's. Probably not. They were in command, and they would of course take *Casey* into the thick of whatever was about to happen.

Yet Travis *had* thought of that option.

Did that mean he was a coward?

He stole a glance at Woodburn's profile. There was a tension around the other's eyes . . . and only then did it dawn on Travis that probably none of *Casey*'s senior officers, from Heissman on down, had ever been in actual combat. The Star Kingdom had been at peace for a long time, out here in its backwater isolation, and it was entirely possible that no one in power had ever seriously expected that to change. Certainly the faction of Parliament dedicated to gutting the fleet operated under that assumption.

Maybe *Leviathan* really was a damaged liner. Maybe there was a perfectly reasonable explanation for those other two here-then-gone wedges. Maybe this was just a bizarre coincidence that all of them would get together and laugh about over a drink someday.

But if it wasn't, then they were all about to see how the RMN handled a real, nonsimulated battle.

Back on *Phoenix*, Travis had wondered whether a taste of warfare would shake up some of the Star Kingdom's complacency. Now, it looked like they were going to find out.

※ ※ ※

It was time.

Gensonne ran his eyes over *Odin*'s bridge displays one final time. He and *Tyr* were in their combat stack, *Odin* a thousand kilometers above the other battlecruiser, where the constraints of wedge and sidewalls gave both ships optimal fields of fire for their missiles and autocannon. The two heavy cruisers, *Copperhead* and *Adder*, were in their own stack a thousand kilometers ahead and slightly above and beneath the two battlecruisers, positioned so their countermissiles could protect both of the larger warships. Fifteen hundred kilometers ahead of the cruisers and another thousand to starboard, the destroyer *Ganymede* guarded the starboard flank.

Ideally, Gensonne would have liked to have *Phobos* mirror-image *Ganymede* on the formation's portside flank. But with communications through sidewalls tricky at best, it was more important for *Phobos* to hang far back in com-relay position. In the heat of battle a communications blackout, even a brief one, could spell disaster. The only way to assure that didn't happen was to dedicate one of his ships to bounce signals back and forth through the unobstructed gaps at the other ships' kilts.

Besides, his full force was hardly necessary to complete the task at hand. In a pinch, *Odin* and one of Gensonne's cruisers could easily take out the four undersized Bogey One ships the Volsungs were closing on. Probably without even scratching their paint.

Just the same, Gensonne would indeed throw the full weight of his force against the Manticorans. After all, the only thing better than a painless victory was a *fast* painless victory.

He keyed his com. "Admiral to all ships," he called into the microphone. "Stand by battle stations. Relay status data now."

For a moment nothing happened. Then, in proper order, the status board indicators began to wink on. *Odin* showed green; *Tyr* showed green; *Copperhead*—

Gensonne felt his eyes narrow. Floating in the sea of soothing green were a pair of red lights. "Captain Imbar?"

"It's their ventral autocannon," Imbar called from the com station. "Starboard sensor miscalibration. They're working on it."

Gensonne mouthed a curse as he looked back at the status board, where more green was filling in around *Copperhead*'s red lights. Should he give *Copperhead* a few more minutes? The Manticoran force was in deceleration mode, their kilts to the incoming Volsungs as they aimed for a zero-zero at the distant *Naglfar* far behind him. If Gensonne signaled *Naglfar* to raise its acceleration a bit, the Manticorans would presumably respond by increasing their deceleration rate, which would postpone the rapidly approaching moment when the enemy's sensors would finally pick up the warships coasting stealthily toward them.

Gensonne straightened up, feeling the uniform collar peeking out from above his vac suit's helmet ring pull briefly against his neck with the movement. Ridiculous. Even if every one of *Copperhead*'s lights went red he still had overwhelming superiority.

Besides, the far larger Bogey Two was also burning its way toward them across the Manticoran system. Postponing the Bogey One skirmish would mean less time to reorganize and rearm before Bogey Two showed up.

Bogey One was nearly in range.

Time for them to die.

"Tell *Copperhead* to keep working until they get it right," he growled to Imbar. Keying his mike again, he straightened a little more. "All ships: stand by to light up wedges."

※ ※ ※

Heissman had sent Belokas and Woodburn off the bridge for a short break, and Travis was strapped into the tac station when the moment everyone aboard *Casey* had been waiting for finally came.

Only it wasn't the single ship they were expecting. It was far, far worse.

"New contact!" Rusk snapped from the sensor board, the words cutting across the low-level conversation murmuring across the bridge. "I make it six ships on intercept vector at two hundred fifteen gees. Missile range, approximately sixteen minutes."

"All ships, increase deceleration to two kilometers per second squared and go to Readiness One," Heissman called into his mike, the calm of his voice in sharp contrast to the sudden pounding of Travis's heart. "Mr. Long?" he added.

Surreptitiously, Travis touched the helmet of his vac suit, fastened securely beside his station. Knowing it was there made him feel marginally safer. Marginally. "Six ships confirmed for Bogey Three," he said, his eyes flicking back and forth between the displays and the computer's analysis of the incoming data. One of the many things Woodburn had beaten into him over the past few weeks was that you never simply took the computer's word for anything when you could do your own assessment and analysis. "From wedge strength I'm guessing two battlecruisers, two heavy cruisers, and two light cruisers or destroyers. One of the latter is hanging back in com position."

"Which pretty much confirms they're a war fleet," Woodburn's voice came over Travis's shoulder.

Travis looked up to see the tac officer float up behind him, the other's hard gaze flicking coolly across the displays. "Yes, Sir," Travis agreed, reaching for his restraints.

To his surprise, Woodburn waved him to stay where he was. "Any read on origination or class?" Heissman asked.

"No, Sir," Woodburn said as he settled into a hovering position beside Travis. "But the over/under configuration of the battlecruisers and cruisers might indicate Solarian training and military doctrine."

"Which doesn't actually tell us where they came from," Belokas pointed out as she floated rapidly across the bridge toward her station. "A lot of militaries use Solly doctrine."

"Maybe they'll be kind enough to tell us," Heissman suggested. "Everyone watch and listen." Reaching over, he keyed the com. "Unidentified ships, this is Commodore Rudolph Heissman, Royal Manticoran Navy. Kindly identify yourselves and state your business in Manticoran space."

There was a short pause, not much longer than the fifteen seconds that the signal would take to make the round trip. Clearly, the other commander had been expecting the call and already knew what he was going to say. "Greetings, Commodore Heissman," a deep voice boomed from the bridge speakers.

Travis looked at the com display. The face now filling the screen was light-skinned, the color of a man who seldom ventured out into the sun, with blue eyes and a mouth that had a sardonic twist to it. From the shape and angles of its creases, Travis guessed that *sardonic* was the mouth's most common mode. Above the face was a slightly balding carpet of pure blond hair cut in short military style. Below the face, a couple of centimeters of high-collared tunic could be seen above his vac suit.

"Black collar line, blue-gray knitted collar," Woodburn murmured. Travis nodded, already keying the parameters into the computer for an archive search.

"My name and origin are unimportant," the man continued, "but for convenience you may address me as Admiral Tamerlane. My business is, I regret to say, the destruction of you and your task force. I am, however, willing to discuss terms of surrender. If you're interested in pursuing that offer, you may indicate that by striking your wedges and preparing to be boarded."

He tilted his head slightly, and as he did so one of the muted insignia on his collar came into better view. A curved comet with a star at its inner edge, Travis decided, and added it to the search criteria. "This is, naturally, a limited time offer," Tamerlane continued. "I read you as coming into missile range in just under eighteen minutes; somewhat less, of course, if you break off your pointless attempt to escape and turn to offer battle. I'll await your answer." He reached off-screen and his image vanished.

"Confident s.o.b.," Heissman commented. "Anyone recognize him or his accent?"

The bridge remained silent, and out of the corners of his eyes Travis saw shaking heads. "Mr. Long?" Heissman asked.

"The uniform could be Solarian," Travis affirmed, scanning the search results. "But a lot of Core World navies wear something similar. What we could see of the insignia looked more like something the Tahzeeb Navy uses."

"So they're probably mercenaries," Belokas said.

"Probably," Woodburn agreed. "Not sure what calling himself Tamerlane means. The original was an Old Earth conqueror who ran roughshod over a good chunk of the planet a little over two thousand years ago."

"Tamerlane was also considered a military genius," Heissman said. "I wonder which of those two aspects he's trying to reference."

"Either way, he's definitely the megalomaniac type," Belokas said. "Confident, but probably not so confident that we can goad him into telling us what he has planned for Manticore after he runs us over."

"Certainly not until he's sure we can't send anything useful back to System Command or Aegis," Heissman agreed. "Speaking of Aegis, what's their current ETA?"

"They're still nearly two hours away," Belokas said. "We could postpone the battle a bit by pushing our compensators right up to the red line, but it wouldn't be enough for them to get here before we have to fight."

"What about Bogey Two?" Heissman asked.

"Nothing since their last course adjustment," Woodburn said. "Depending on where in the plot cone they are, they'll probably reach sensor range within the next ten to twenty minutes."

"So no allies, but probably more opponents," Heissman said. "In that case, I see no point in delaying the inevitable." He keyed his com. "All ships, this is the Commodore. We've been challenged to a fight, and I intend to give them the biggest damn fight they've ever been in. *Gorgon*, maintain current course and acceleration—your job is to get the records of what's about to happen back to Manticore. *Hercules* and *Gemini*, stand by for a coordinated one-eighty pitch turn on my mark."

Travis frowned. "A *pitch* turn?" he asked quietly. Most turns he'd seen had been of the yaw variety, where the ship rotated along its vertical axis, instead of a pitch flip that sent the ship head over heels and briefly put the stronger but more sensor-opaque stress bands between the ship and the incoming threat.

"A pitch turn," Woodburn confirmed, an edge of grim humor to his voice. "We can launch a salvo of missiles just before our wedge drops far enough to clear their line of sight, which will keep them from spotting the booster flares. By the time we've turned all the way over the missiles will be clear and ready to light off their wedges once Commodore Heissman decides which target he wants to go after first."

Travis nodded. *Casey* herself had electromagnetic launchers that didn't betray themselves with such telltales, but both *Hercules* and *Gemini* had the standard boosters on their missiles, vital for getting the weapons far enough from the ship that they could safely light up their wedges. If Janus could launch without Tamerlane spotting the missiles it would give the Manticorans at least a momentary advantage.

"Pitch turn: *mark*," Heissman called. "Stand by two missiles from each corvette and four from us, again on my mark."

Travis looked over at the tac display. *Casey* and the two corvettes were turning in unison, their loss of acceleration sending *Gorgon* toward the edge of the field even as the invading formation seemed to leap forward.

And the enemy would unfortunately have plenty of time to work on closing the remaining distance. Pitch turn or yaw turn, either type of one-eighty took a good two minutes to complete.

"Missiles on my mark," Heissman said softly, his eyes on the tac.

"Missiles ready," Belokas confirmed. "Target?"

Heissman watched the tac another moment, then turned to Woodburn. "Suggestions, Alfred?"

"I'd go with all eight on one of the cruisers," Woodburn said. "The way they're deployed strongly suggests the battlecruisers have opted for extra missiles instead of carrying their own countermissile loads, which would mean they're relying on the cruisers to screen for them. If we can kill one of them right out of the box, we may have a shot at doing some damage to one of the big boys."

"I'm sure Admiral Locatelli would appreciate us softening them up a bit for him," Belokas said dryly. "I'll go with Alfred on this one."

Heissman looked at Travis. "Mr. Long?"

Travis looked at the tac display. Three small ships against six . . . "I'd throw four at each cruiser, Sir."

"Reason?"

"If those are mercenaries out there, they may be running a nonuniform mix of ship types and classes," Travis said. "Watching their defenses might give us some clues as to what types of ships they have and how to more effectively attack them. By attacking two at once, we'll get that data a bit faster."

"Alfred?" Heissman invited.

"We'd still do better to saturate one of them," Woodburn said. "Frankly, Sir, we're not going to get a lot of shots off in the time we have. We should concentrate on doing as much damage as possible."

"You may be right," Heissman agreed. "But Mr. Long is also right. Information is what we need most, both for ourselves and for Admiral Locatelli. I think it's worth the risk." He keyed his com. "*Hercules* and *Gemini*: one missile from each of you at each of the leading cruisers. We'll throw an additional two at each one."

He favored Travis with a small smile. "Let's see how well Admiral Tamerlane can dance."

❧ ❧ ❧

The three nearer Manticoran ships finished their turn—a pitch turn, interestingly enough—and with that, their throats were open to attack. "Stand by missiles," Gensonne called. The first salvo would go to *Casey*, he decided. *Odin's* telemetry could only control six missiles at once, and while normally he would have preferred to hit the Manticoran cruiser with something a little more crushing, at this point it would be more useful to see what kind of defenses they could bring against a slightly less overwhelming attack. "Fire salvo: one through six, targeting—"

"Missiles!" Imbar snapped.

Of course missiles, was Gensonne's first reflexive thought. He'd already said to stand by missiles.

Then his brain caught up, and he jerked his head around to the sensor display.

There were missiles out there, all right: eight of them, creeping toward him with wedges down and only the relative velocities between them and the Volsungs providing them any movement at all. He opened his mouth to demand that Imbar tell him where they'd come from and why they weren't running under power—

And then, abruptly, all eight missiles lit up their wedges and leaped forward toward the Volsung force.

"Where the *hell* did they come from?" Imbar snarled. "They're not supposed to have electromagnetic launchers."

"It was that damn pitch turn," Gensonne said as he finally got it, throwing a glance at the countdown timer. One hundred and three seconds until impact. "They fired while our view of their booster flares was blocked."

Imbar grunted. "Cute."

"Very," Gensonne said darkly. "But don't worry about it. We can play cute, too."

Only for the next hundred seconds or so, he couldn't. Forty seconds from now, sixty seconds before the incoming missiles' projected impact, *Copperhead* and *Adder* would launch a salvo of countermissiles into the path of the incoming weapons. Forty-five seconds after that, all six Volsung ships would open up with their autocannon in an effort to stop any missiles that made it through the countermissile gauntlet.

The frustrating hell of it was that for most of the missiles' run it would be impossible to tell which ship or ships they were targeting. Still, if Heissman had any brains he would be aiming this first salvo at one or both of the cruisers. A properly competent flag officer should have deduced from the Volsungs' configuration that the cruisers were the ones carrying the countermissiles, and were therefore the ones that needed to be taken out before the Manticorans could have a reasonable shot at *Odin* or *Tyr*.

Well, let them try. The cruisers were carrying full point-defense loads, and if Heissman wanted to waste his missiles battering against their defenses he was more than welcome to do so.

Except . . .

With a curse, he spun around to the status board. There, still glowing red amid the field of green, were the lights marking *Copperhead*'s troubled ventral autocannon.

And if one of the Manticoran missiles happened to come in from the side with the bad sensor . . .

"All ships: cease acceleration on my mark," he snarled, turning back to the tac. The two standard responses to a situation like this would be for *Copperhead* to either yaw to starboard to adjust for the miscalibration or else pitch up or down to interpose his wedge between the ship and the incoming missiles. Unfortunately, if the rest of the force was under acceleration at the time, both countermoves would instantly break the Volsungs' formation. The only way to maintain their relative positions would be for all six ships to kill acceleration and coast.

Of course, that would also give the Bogey One ships a breather from the doom arrowing in on them. Still, it was hard to imagine what they could do with those extra few minutes. The rear ship, the one Heissman was clearly hoping would get clear with data from the battle, would gain a little distance, but it was already too little too late.

As for the other three ships, they would have to do another one-eighty if they hoped to do any more running themselves. Any such move would be relatively slow and instantly telegraphed.

No, Heissman's force wasn't going anywhere. Gensonne could afford the time to do this right. "All ships, cease acceleration: *mark*. Imbar?"

"All ships coasting," Imbar reported. "Formation maintained."

Gensonne nodded, peering at the tac display. *Copperhead* was already taking advantage of the lull and was starting its starboard yaw.

Hell with that. If they were going to be forced to coast anyway, there was no reason for *Copperhead* to waste any of its point-defense weaponry. "Von Belling, belay your yaw," he ordered into his mike. "Pitch wedge to the incoming fire."

"I can handle it," von Belling's voice came from the speaker.

"I said *pitch wedge*," Gensonne snapped.

"Aye, aye, *Sir*," von Belling said with thinly disguised disgust. "Pitching wedge."

On the tactical, *Copperhead* changed from its yaw turn to a vertical pitch, dropping its bow to present its roof to the incoming missiles. Gensonne watched, splitting his attention between the cruiser and the incoming missiles. If von Belling's momentary bitching had left the maneuver too late, the admiral promised himself darkly, he'd better hope the Manticoran missiles got to him before Gensonne himself did.

Fortunately, it wasn't going to come to that. *Copperhead* turned in plenty of time, and as *Odin's* autocannon roared into action Gensonne watched the incoming salvo split into two groups, one set of four targeting each of the cruisers. The ones aimed at *Copperhead* disintegrated harmlessly against its roof, while *Adder's* countermissiles and autocannon made equally quick work of the other group. "Stand by for acceleration," Gensonne ordered. *Copperhead* was starting its reverse pivot again, and as soon as it was back in position the Volsungs could resume their full-acceleration pursuit of the Manticorans.

Meanwhile, there was no reason Gensonne had to wait until for acceleration before he took the battle back to Heissman. "Missiles ready?" he called.

"Missiles ready," Imbar confirmed.

"Six at the light cruiser," Gensonne said. "Fire."

※ ※ ※

"All missiles destroyed," Rusk reported. "No hits."

"Acknowledged," Heissman said. "Alfred? What have we learned?"

"Their point-defense seems comparable to ours," Woodburn said, peering closely at the computer analysis. "Countermissiles on the cruisers, autocannon on everyone else. Looks like pretty high quality of both. Their ECM is also good—looks like they got a soft kill on at least one of the missiles, possibly two. They also don't seem shy about spending ammo."

"Or missiles, either," Rusk said tightly. "Missile trace, two: thirty-five hundred gees, estimated impact time one hundred fifty-three seconds. Make that four missiles, same impact projection . . . make it six. Missile trace, six, impact one hundred forty-eight seconds."

Travis winced. Six missiles, with all four of the Manticoran ships at only eighty percent of point-defense capacity.

Woodburn was clearly thinking along the same lines. "Commodore, I don't think we're ready to take on that many birds."

"Agreed," Heissman said. "But we also need to pull some data on their capabilities."

"So we're going to take them on?" Belokas asked.

"We're going to split the difference," Heissman corrected. "Start a portside yaw turn—not a big or fast one, just a few degrees. I want to cut the starboard sidewall across the missile formation, letting just one or two of them past the leading edge and trusting the countermissiles to take those out. That way we get a closer look at the missiles and their yield without risking having too many of them coming in for us to block."

Travis stole a glance at Woodburn, waiting for the tac officer to point out the obvious risk: that if the incoming missiles' sidewall penetrators functioned like they were supposed to, taking four or five on *Casey's* sidewalls could be a quick path to disaster. Most of the time that kind of maneuver was a decent enough gamble, given the notorious unreliability of such weapons. But anytime you had that many threats things could get tricky.

Especially if Tamerlane's ships were carrying more advanced sidewall penetrators that *weren't* so finicky.

But Woodburn remained silent. As Travis had known he would. The commodore had already agreed that *Casey's* mission was to gather information that would be crucial in helping Locatelli defeat this inexplicable invasion.

The missiles crept closer. Travis watched the tac display as Belokas fine-tuned *Casey's* position, a vague idea starting to form at the back of his mind. If he'd seen what he thought he'd seen during the first Janus salvo . . .

He swiveled around to his plotter and ran the numbers and geometry. It would work, he decided. It would be tricky and require some fancy timing, but it might just work.

There was a throbbing hum from the launchers' capacitors as *Casey* sent a salvo of countermissiles blazing out into space . . . and it occurred to him that if Heissman's trick didn't work, there was a good chance he would never know it. At the speed the missiles were traveling, they would reach the edge of the countermissiles' range barely two tenths of a second before reaching *Casey* itself. If the defenses failed to stop the attack, or the sidewall was breached—

There was a muted double flash on the tac as two of the missiles slammed into the countermissiles and were destroyed. Travis's eyes and brain had just registered that fact when the deck abruptly jerked beneath him and the tense silence of the bridge was ripped apart by the wailing of emergency alarms.

He spun to the status board. None of the four missiles that had slammed into the starboard sidewall had penetrated, but two of them had detonated a microsecond before impact, and the resulting blast had overloaded and possibly destroyed the forward generator.

"Sidewall generator two is down!" Belokas shouted her own confirmation across the wailing alarm. "Generator four undamaged, taking up the slack."

"Casualties," com officer Kebiro added tensely. "Seven down, condition unknown. Corpsmen on the way; crews assessing damage."

Travis mouthed a useless curse. Each of the two generators on each side of the ship was designed to be able to maintain the entire sidewall. But as the old saying went, two could live as cheaply as one, but only for half as long. *Casey*'s starboard sidewall was still up, but it was running now at half power. Another double tap like that one, and it could go completely.

And the cruisers and battlecruisers out there were showing no signs of running out of missiles to tap them with.

The alarm cut off. "Alfred?" Heissman asked, as calm as ever.

"Their missiles seem comparable to ours," Woodburn said, his own voice more strained. "Slightly better ECM, I think, but our countermissiles handled them just fine."

"Which again suggests mercenaries rather than some system's official fleet," Heissman said. "Certainly not any fleet connected with the Solarian League. Solly ships wouldn't be using second- or third-generation equipment."

"That's the good news," Woodburn said. His voice was subtly louder, Travis noted distantly, as if he was leaning over Travis's shoulder. "The bad news is that their missiles are as good as ours and they probably have a hell of a lot more of them."

"I wonder what they're waiting for," Rusk murmured. "This is the perfect time to launch a second wave."

"Probably taking a moment to analyze their data," Belokas said. "I imagine they're as eager to assess our strengths and weaknesses as we are to find theirs, and trying not to spend any more missiles than they have to. They'll certainly want to know everything they can about us before they tackle Aegis."

"And since we can't stop them from doing that," Heissman said calmly, "it looks like our best-hope scenario is still to slow them down long enough for *Gorgon* to escape with as much data as we can collect, while inflicting the maximum damage possible."

"Between us and the corvettes we still have twenty missiles, plus seven practice ones," Belokas said. "If we throw everything we've got, we should at least be able to take down one of those cruisers."

"We can't control nearly that many at once," Woodburn reminded her.

"As long as Tamerlane's ships aren't accelerating, that may not matter," Belokas pointed out. "They'll still have to defend, and even if all we can accomplish is to drain their point defenses it'll be worth it."

"Or we may be able to do a bit better," Woodburn said. "Mr. Long has an idea."

Travis twisted his head to look up at the other. "Sir?"

Woodburn pointed at the simulation Travis had been running. "Tell them," he ordered.

Travis felt his throat tighten. Suddenly, he was back on *Phoenix*'s bridge, offering half-baked advice to Captain Castillo.

But Heissman wasn't Castillo. And if the trick worked . . .

"I think the upper cruiser's ventral autocannon is having trouble," he said. "If it is, then—"

"How could you possibly know that?" Belokas interrupted, frowning at him. "They never even fired them."

"Because he was starting to turn to starboard when he shifted to rolling wedge instead," Travis said. "That looked to me like he was getting ready to favor that side when he changed his mind." He felt his lip twitch. "I had some experience with balky autocannon back on *Phoenix*, and that definitely looked like a sensor miscalibration problem."

"Alfred?" Heissman asked.

"He could be right," Woodburn said. "I just checked, and that aborted yaw is definitely there."

"Assume you're right," Heissman said. "Then what?"

"We start by assuming Tamerlane's as smart as he thinks he is," Travis said. "If so, he'll have seen his cruiser's brief yaw and guess that we also saw it and came to the correct conclusion. If we did, he'll expect us to try to take advantage of the weakness by throwing a salvo of missiles at it."

"At which point he'll again have to either use an iffy point-defense system or else roll wedge," Woodburn said, reaching over Travis's shoulder to key the simulation over to the Commodore's station. "If he does the latter, we may be able to catch him by surprise."

For a couple of heartbeats Heissman gazed at the display. Then, his lip twitched in a small smile. "Yes, I see. It's definitely a long shot. But long shots are where you go when you've got no other bets."

He gave a brisk nod. "Set up the shot."

※ ※ ※

"Analysis complete, Admiral," Imbar announced as he hovered over Tac Officer Clymes's shoulder. "Similar countermissiles as ours, with about a thirteen-hundred-klick range, and similar autocannon loads."

Gensonne scowled. So the Manticorans' countermissiles had a shade less range than the equipment aboard *Copperhead* and *Adder*.

And *Casey* was supposedly the most advanced ship of the Manticoran fleet. If Llyn had been right about that, then the weaponry aboard the larger Bogey Two ships burning space toward him would be even more subpar.

Yes, it could have been worse. But it could also have been a whole lot better. He'd tried like the fires of hell to talk Llyn into providing him with more cutting-edge equipment, but the damn little clerk had turned down every request. The Volsungs didn't need anything better, he'd insisted soothingly, and furthermore the Solarian League would rain down on all of them if they ever got wind of it.

Which Gensonne knew was a bald-faced lie. The Axelrod Corporation was way too powerful to worry about offending whatever bureaucrats were in charge of enforcing such regulations. Llyn simply didn't want a bunch of free-lance mercenaries running around with really advanced equipment.

But that would change. When Llyn saw how quickly and efficiently Gensonne delivered Manticore, Axelrod would surely want the Volsungs on board for whatever project was next on their list.

And Llyn could bet his rear that the subject of advanced weaponry *would* come up again.

"Salvo ready, Sir," Imbar said.

"Acknowledged," Gensonne said. The question now was whether they'd wrung out every bit of data Heissman and *Casey* could provide. If so, it was time to end the charade and finish them off. If not, a little additional restraint might still be called for.

"Missiles," Clymes called into his musings. "Looks like two from each of the corvettes."

Gensonne swiveled toward the sensor display. Sure enough, both of the smaller ships were showing the unmistakable signs of booster flares. A waste of time; but then, what else did they have to do? "Six missiles at the cruiser," he ordered. "Fire when ready." On the display, the missiles cleared the corvettes' wedges and lit up their own.

Two missiles from each corvette . . . but from *Casey*, nothing.

He frowned. Could the damage his attack had inflicted on the cruiser's sidewall have bled over into its launchers or control systems? Llyn had said that *Casey* was Manticoran-designed. Had the builders unintentionally incorporated a fatal flaw into its architecture? "Damage report on *Casey*," he ordered.

"Their starboard sidewall is at half power," Imbar reported, sounding puzzled. "We already went through this—"

"More flares," Clymes cut in. "One more from each corvette."

"Still nothing from *Casey*?"

"No, Sir."

Which made no sense, unless the cruiser had genuinely lost the ability to launch its missiles. Definitely a tidbit worth knowing, especially if similar flaws had been incorporated into the Manticorans' other ship designs.

And really, it didn't much matter which of the Manticorans were shooting and which ones weren't. What mattered was that they were trying the same saturation attack they'd tried before, and it was pretty obvious where that attack was aimed. Heissman was apparently the observant type, and von Belling's half-completed yaw turn earlier had tipped off the Manticorans as to where *Copperhead*'s weakness lay.

Which, again, was hardly a problem. "Order *Copperhead* to pitch wedge," he instructed Imbar. "*Adder* will prepare countermissiles; all other ships, stand by autocannon."

He listened as the acknowledgments came in, his eyes on the six wedges cutting through space toward his force at thirty-five hundred gees acceleration. A minute fifteen out, with probably forty seconds before they would either tighten their angle toward *Copperhead* or widen it to target both *Copperhead* and *Adder*. At that point, Heissman would show whether he'd truly observed *Copperhead*'s weakness or was a one-trick pony who was throwing missiles at his opponent simply because that was all he knew how to do.

Which would be pathetic, but hardly unexpected. Manticore had been at peace a long time. Far longer than was healthy for them. War was what kept men strong and smart. Peace turned them into useless drones, where the species-cleansing consequences of survival of the fittest no longer operated.

Could that be why Llyn had chosen Manticore as his target? Could it be that Axelrod was looking for undeveloped real estate and figured that no one would notice or care if a couple of fat, lazy backwater planets underwent a sudden regime change?

It sounded like a colossal waste of money. Still, Axelrod had money to burn. If they wanted to spend some of their spare cash to set up their own little kingdom, more power to them.

Copperhead had finished its pitch, its roof once again presenting its impenetrable barrier to the incoming missiles. The missiles were still holding formation, with no indication as to where they were heading. Whatever Heissman's plan, though, he must surely have accepted the inevitability of his own destruction. Best guess was that his goal was to simply keep throwing missiles in hopes of draining the Volsungs of as many resources as he could . . .

Gensonne looked at the sensor display, feeling his eyes narrow. The Manticorans had launched six missiles—Clymes had confirmed that. And six missile wedges were indeed showing on all of the bridge's displays.

But according to the sensors, all six missiles were running a little hot.

Why were they running hot?

On the tactical, a spray of countermissiles erupted from *Adder*'s throat, blossoming into a cone of protection that would shield both itself and the battlecruisers riding a thousand kilometers behind it. Gensonne watched as the cone stretched out toward the incoming missiles—

And felt a sudden jolt of horrified adrenaline flood through him.

One cone. Not the two cones this configuration was supposed to provide to shield the battlecruisers. Not with *Copperhead* turned roof-forward protecting itself from those Manticoran missiles.

Still nothing new from the sensors. Still nothing new on the missiles' track. But Gensonne was a warrior, with the instincts a warrior needed to survive. And his gut was screaming at him now with a certainty that all the ambiguous data in the universe couldn't counter.

Copperhead wasn't Heissman's target. *Odin* was.

"Full autocannon!" he snapped, his eyes darting to the tactical, wanting to order an emergency turn and knowing full well that it was too late. Six missiles showing . . . only his gut was telling him that wasn't the full number bearing down on them. Somehow, *Casey* had managed to launch its own contribution to the salvo, slipping them in behind and among the corvettes' missiles with just the right timing and geometry to keep them hidden until they could light off their wedges.

Odin's four autocannon were hammering out their furious roar, filling the space in front of the ship with shards of metal. Gensonne watched in helpless fury as the incoming missiles swung wide of *Copperhead*'s wedge, passed safely through the very edge of *Adder*'s countermissile defensive zone, and dove straight through *Odin*'s open throat—

And with a thundering roar the ship exploded into a chaos of screaming alarms.

❧ ❧ ❧

"Got him!" Rusk shouted, his voice hovering midway between triumph and disbelief. "One of them made it through."

"Damage?" Heissman asked.

"Assessing now," Woodburn said. "Lots of debris, but with something the size of a battlecruiser that could be mostly superficial."

"Missile trace," Belokas called. "Six on the way."

"Countermissiles and autocannon standing by," Woodburn confirmed.

"Assessment's coming a little cleaner," Rusk said. "Looks like they took damage to their bow, probably enough to knock out their telemetry system. If we're lucky, it'll have neutralized at least one of their launchers and maybe their forward laser."

"Excellent," Heissman said. "Fire four more missiles—let's see if we can get in before the upper cruiser realizes what happened and turns back to defense position."

"Aye, Sir," Travis said, checking the tracks of Tamerlane's incoming missiles and feeling a flicker of grim satisfaction. They were still almost certainly going to die, but at least they'd managed to bloody Tamerlane's nose.

The vibration of the autocannon rumbled through the bridge. "All missiles destroyed," Woodburn announced. "Four hard kills, two soft. Our missiles are still on target."

Travis was gazing at the enemy formation, trying to anticipate what Tamerlane would do next, when two new wedges flared into view at the edge of the display.

The mysterious ships that they'd spotted earlier had arrived.

❧ ❧ ❧

"Telemetry transmitters out," a strained voice came from the bridge speaker, barely audible above a cacophony of shouts and curses. "Number one laser's offline, number two's iffy, and One and Three autocannon are fried."

"Record indicates there were ten missiles in that salvo," Imbar snarled over the noise. "How the *hell* were there *ten* damn missiles?"

"Because *Casey's* got a railgun launcher, that's how," Gensonne snarled back, a red haze of fury clouding his vision. "That's how they launched an extra four missiles without our seeing them."

Imbar swore viciously. "That's why they looked too hot."

"You think?" Gensonne bit out. And that damn bloody trick had now cost *Odin* nearly half its forward armament.

"Four more missiles on the way," Clymes warned. "*Copperhead* is turning back . . . *Copperhead's* on it."

"About time," Gensonne muttered under his breath. He ran his eyes over the growing damage report, then looked up at the tactical.

Copperhead's countermissiles had just taken care of *Casey's* latest salvo when a pair of new wedges suddenly appeared at the edge of the tactical, leaping forward as they drove in from the battlefield's flank toward Bogey One.

The two outriding destroyers, *Umbriel* and *Miranda*, had finally arrived.

"Admiral?" Imbar called.

"I see them," Gensonne told him, his lips curling back in a snarling smile. "Order them to fire missiles. Hell, order *all* ships to fire."

He straightened his shoulders. They had enough data. They had more than enough data.

Time for Heissman and his ships to die.

"Target the ship at the rear first," Gensonne said. "Then destroy the rest."

❁ ❁ ❁

And in that single, awful microsecond, everything changed.

"Missile trace!" Rusk called out grimly. "Four from Bogey Two— look to be targeting *Gorgon*. Bogey Three ships are also firing with . . . missile trace ten on the way."

"He's learned everything he can and decided it's time to end it," Heissman commented. "Time for us to do the same."

He hit his com key. "*Hercules*, *Gemini*: split tail. Repeat, split tail. Good luck."

Travis winced. The split tail was the officially designated last-ditch maneuver for this kind of situation. The two corvettes were to pitch wedges toward Tamerlane's main force and accelerate away in different directions, with each ship's resulting vector taking it above or beneath the enemy force, hopefully before any of the opposing ships could rotate fast enough and far enough to fire a last shot up the escapee's kilt.

It was a risky tactic at best, given the range of modern missiles and lasers. But with a second threat now on Janus's flank, it was even worse. The geometry made it impossible for the ships to position their wedges in such a way as to block against missiles coming from both directions at once.

Worse, for *Casey* at least, the sidewall facing Bogey Two was the one already running on a single generator. Another solid hit there and the barrier could go completely, leaving that entire flank open to unprotected attack.

On the tactical, *Hercules* and *Gemini* were pitching in opposite directions, the first corvette aiming to go over Tamerlane's force, the second aiming to go under it. Far to their rear, Travis saw that *Gorgon* was rolling her wedge toward the two ships of Bogey Two, her kilt still open to Tamerlane's main force.

Leaving *Casey* to face the enemy alone.

"Commodore?" Belokas prompted tautly.

"Hold vector," Heissman said, his eyes shifting back and forth between the two sets of missiles converging on his force. "I want to fire off one last salvo of countermissiles, see if we can clear a couple of Bogey Three's missiles off *Gorgon's* tail."

"We've also got two missiles coming in on our starboard flank," Woodburn warned. "If we cut things too fine, we could lose it all."

"Understood," Heissman said. "Stand by countermissiles . . . fire. Pitch ninety degrees negative and kill acceleration."

Out of the corner of his eye Travis saw all heads turn. "Pitch ninety degrees negative and kill acceleration, aye," the helmsman said. "Pitching ninety degrees negative; acceleration at zero."

"Kill acceleration?" Belokas asked quietly.

"Kill acceleration," Heissman confirmed. "We're going to go straight through the center of their formation." His lip twitched. "The distraction may give the corvettes a better chance of escape."

There was a moment of silence, and Travis heard Woodburn murmur something under his breath. "Understood, Sir," Belokas said briskly.

"Starboard missiles coming in hot," Rusk warned. "Not sure the sidewall can take them."

"So let's try something crazy," Heissman said. "As soon as the missiles reach energy torpedo range, flicker the sidewall and fire two bursts along the missiles' vectors, then raise the sidewall again. Maybe we can take out at least one of them before it hits."

Travis felt his stomach tighten. Energy torpedoes, bursts of contained plasma bled straight off the reactor, were devastating at short ranges. But they hadn't exactly been designed as missile killers.

Woodburn knew that, too. "It's a long shot," he warned. "Especially since we might not get the sidewall up in time. We could miss completely and end up with both missiles coming right in on us."

"Granted," Heissman agreed. "But the option is to trust a half-power sidewall to keep them out on its own." He smiled faintly. "And so far, our long shots have been paying out pretty well."

"True," Woodburn said, returning the commodore's smile. "Very good, Sir. Energy torpedoes standing by."

On the tactical, the image that was *Gorgon* suddenly flared and vanished. "*Gorgon's* gone, Sir," Rusk said grimly. "Lower enemy cruiser swiveling to target *Gemini*."

"Computer standing ready to flicker sidewall and fire energy torpedoes," Woodburn added.

"Acknowledged," Heissman said. "Hand off to computer."

"Hand off to computer, aye," Woodburn confirmed. "Here we go . . ."

Travis felt the slight vibration of distant heavy relays as *Casey* blasted a barrage of torpedoes into space. They were amazingly fast weapons, nearly as fast as the beams from shipboard X-ray lasers. There was a second vibration as the second salvo followed the first—

"Sidewall back up," Woodburn called. Travis held his breath . . .

The hope and crossed fingers were in vain. An instant later, *Casey* gave a violent and all-too-well-remembered jerk.

The missiles had been stopped, but the second starboard sidewall generator had been overloaded and destroyed.

"Damage?" Heissman called as the alarms once again blared across the bridge.

"Generator gone," Belokas reported. "Secondary damage to that area. Casualties reported; no details yet."

Travis felt a tightening in his chest. Starboard sidewall gone, fewer than half their missiles left, and heading on a ballistic trajectory straight into the center of an enemy formation.

Worse, at the distances they would be passing the other ships, they would be well within beam range. Knife-fight range . . . and with *Casey's* throat, kilt, and starboard flank open, Tamerlane's only decision would be which of his ships would get the honor of finishing her off.

He frowned at the tactical, his fingers keying his board. Tamerlane had already shown he was smart and reasonably cautious. He would assume *Casey* had lasers fore and aft, and would therefore most likely choose to send his attack in from starboard, where there were no defenses except the energy torpedoes and a much bigger cross-section of ship to target.

Casey was down to eight real missiles, but they still had four practice missiles. And with the electromagnetic launch system instead of solid boosters they ought to be able to just goose one of those missiles from a launch tube without instantly sending it blasting away.

And if they could . . .

He cleared his throat. "Commodore Heissman? I have an idea."

❋ ❋ ❋

"Because I've got the shot and you don't," Captain Blakely said with his usual irritating air of pedantic superiority. "You want Heissman shredded, fine. But you're the one in charge of this little operation, and you can't just go running off formation whenever you feel like it. Not with Bogey Two about to come barreling down our throats. You need to be standing right out front where you can be the admiral." He paused, a slight smirk flicking across his face. "And where you can be ready to take that first shot."

Gensonne glared at the com display, wanting with all his soul to slap the other down.

But unfortunately, he was right. *Casey* was on a flat trajectory that would take it across the Volsung array, as fat and easy a target as anyone could ever hope for. But *Tyr* was in position to chase it down and deliver that death blow, and *Odin* wasn't.

Equally important, *Tyr* still had its chase armament in good working condition. *Odin* didn't.

"Fine," he growled. "Just watch yourself. You're going to be well within range of his energy torpedoes, and you'd look even stupider than you do now as a glowing ball of hot gas."

"You want to come over here and hold my hand?" Blakely countered. "I know how to stick a pig. Plus I'll be using bow target locks, he'll be using broadside ones, and that's a minimum quarter-second advantage, maybe even half a second. And *that* assumes he's even got target locks left after what we did to his sidewall."

He gestured impatiently. "You concentrate on taking out Bogey Two and making sure Llyn pays on time when we're done. I'll take care of Heissman and the Manticorans' precious *Casey*."

"Fine," Gensonne growled again. "Just make it fast. We're going to be pushing our timing as it is to get the main force here before Bogey Two arrives. I want you back in the stack before that happens."

"I'll be back before you know it," Blakely said soothingly. "If you get bored, have Imbar bring you a book."

Cursing under his breath, Gensonne keyed off the display. For another moment he scowled at the empty screen, then turned back to the tactical. Again, Blakely was right—the sensors and target locks for energy torpedo systems were by their very nature slower than those of a spinal laser. Heissman would probably try to move his ship within the wedge to throw off *Tyr*'s targeting, but provided Blakely fired within a half-second of the instant the cruiser came into view, he should have no problem gutting the ship before they could fire back.

So Blakely wanted to rub Gensonne's nose in the fact that he'd taken out the punk-sized ship that had slapped *Odin* across the head? Fine. Gensonne was bigger than that. He could see the full picture. That was why he was an admiral, and Blakely was just a captain.

And if Blakely had ambitions that direction?

Gensonne smiled tightly. For his sake, he'd better not.

※ ※ ※

Three quarters of a second.

Travis had run the numbers. So had Woodburn, and Heissman, and probably everyone else on the bridge. And those cold numbers led to the equally cold conclusion that *Casey* was doomed.

The enemy battlecruiser had finished her rotation, her forward spinal laser lined up on the spot where *Casey* would be passing through the formation ninety seconds from now. She would be at point-blank distance, barely a thousand kilometers away, an insanely short range in these days of long-range missiles and high-powered X-ray lasers.

The captain of that ship would certainly recognize the risks. But he'd undoubtedly run the numbers, too. The instant his bow cleared the edge of *Casey*'s wedge, his targeting sensors would pinpoint *Casey*'s location, send the data to the ship's spinal laser, and fire. It would all be automated, with no human hand required, and if the battlecruiser was running modern electronics the whole operation would take between a quarter-and a half-second.

It would be the battlecruiser's single shot, given the laser's recharge time. But with a nearly two-second window of opportunity, that half-second would be all they needed.

Casey's return fire had also been keyed in and automated, and would also fire at the best speed possible. But the reality of energy torpedo sensors and response times meant that her counterattack would take nearly half a second longer than the battlecruiser's.

A half-second longer, in other words, than *Casey* had to live.

Three-quarters of a second.

Travis knew what an X-ray laser could do to a ship. If the battlecruiser's beam hit *Casey*, it would slice straight through the hull and interior compartments, gutting the cruiser like a fish. If it happened to hit the fusion bottle, the end would come for everyone aboard in a single massive fireball. If it didn't, the crew would die marginally more slowly: some as the air was sucked out of broken work zones into space, others as they floated helplessly into eternity wrapped in their vac suits.

And all that stood between them and that fate was Travis's crazy idea. Travis's idea, and Heissman's willingness to try it.

Three-quarters of a second.

"Ten seconds," Woodburn announced.

Travis took one final look at his displays, automatically starting his own mental countdown. Ten kilometers to *Casey's* aft, held loosely in place twenty kilometers out from her starboard side by a tractor beam, was one of the practice missiles, waiting for the automated order that would light up its wedge and send it leaping through space. With the enemy battlecruiser a thousand kilometers away, Travis's mind automatically calculated, it would take the missile seven-and-a-half seconds to reach it. Under the present circumstances, an unreachable eternity.

Fortunately, that wasn't where the missile needed to go.

Travis's looked back at the tactical, marveling at how he was even able to calculate timings with his adrenaline-pumped time sense racing like a missile on sprint mode. His mental countdown ran to zero—

On the tactical, the battlecruiser appeared around the edge of *Casey's* roof, free and open to fire. A quarter-second, Travis had estimated before her spinal laser tore through the helpless cruiser.

And off *Casey's* starboard flank, the practice missile lit up its wedge and leaped forward.

Not heading away from the cruiser or toward the battlecruiser, but tracing out a path along *Casey's* hull.

Missiles had just two acceleration rates: a long-range mode of thirty-five hundred gravities, and a sprint mode of ten thousand. Those settings couldn't be changed, at least not by any equipment *Casey* had aboard, and even at the slower acceleration the missile wouldn't be pacing *Casey* for long.

But it didn't have to. With a wedge size of ten kilometers, and with *Casey* herself just under three hundred seventy meters long, the missile's wedge could block the enemy laser from the moment its leading edge passed *Casey's* bow to the moment when its trailing edge traveled beyond the cruiser's stern.

For a crucial three-quarters of a second.

Sometime in that heartbeat the battlecruiser undoubtedly took its single shot. Travis never knew for sure—the missile's wedge completely blocked *Casey's* view of what was happening on the other side. Then the missile was past, and momentum had carried the battlecruiser halfway through the open area between *Casey's* stress bands.

And with a final, massive barrage of energy torpedoes, Casey went for the kill.

❋ ❋ ❋

Gensonne stared at his displays, his mouth hanging open, his brain fighting to disbelieve what he was seeing. It was impossible. The numbers had proved that. *Tyr* couldn't possibly have missed its shot, and the Manticorans couldn't possibly have fired first.

But the numbers had lied. Somehow, they'd lied.

And as Gensonne watched in utter horror, *Tyr* disintegrated.

The bowcap went first, the hull metal peeling away like so much scrap paper as the first globe of superheated plasma tore through it. Even as that blast burned itself out, the second slammed into the battlecruiser, tearing deeper into the hull. The forward impeller ring went with that one, and *Tyr's* wedge vanished in a tangle of dissipating gravitational forces. Gensonne watched the next torpedo hit, and the next, and the next, daring to hope that the twin reactors clustered in the battlecruiser's aft section might escape the carnage.

They didn't. The final torpedo slashed through the shattered ship—

And *Tyr* became an expanding ball of fire, torn metal, and broken bodies.

For a long moment no one on *Odin's* bridge spoke. Gensonne shifted his eyes toward *Casey*, still coasting its way through the formation.

Or rather, what was left of the formation.

"Admiral?" Imbar spoke up, his voice hushed. "*Casey's* coming up on *Phobos*. Do you want them to take a shot?"

Yes, Gensonne wanted to scream. *Yes, take the shot. Kill them all.*

But he couldn't give that order. Whatever black magic Heissman had used on *Tyr*, there was no reason he couldn't use it against *Phobos*, too. Gensonne didn't dare risk a second ship when he didn't have the faintest idea how *Casey* had killed the first. "No," he said, the word a strangled lump of useless fury in his throat. "Order *Phobos* to roll wedge, and let them go."

He stretched his neck against his tunic. Besides, the main fleet was still back there, right in the direction *Casey* was heading, ready to light up their wedges and move in to support what remained of the advance force. They would deal with *Casey*, and then they would all deal with Bogey Two.

He looked back at the expanding dust cloud that had been *Tyr*. "See you in hell," he murmured. "I'll be the one wearing white."

❅ ❅ ❅

Travis saw just enough before *Casey*'s floor cut off their view to know that the battlecruiser was doomed. He felt himself tensing as they sped toward the com ship at the far rear of the Bogey Three formation, wondering if *Casey* still had one battle yet to face.

But the loss of his battlecruiser had apparently left Tamerlane shaken. *Casey* sped past the aft ship, catching only a glimpse of her rolled wedge.

It would be too much to say that there was a collective sigh of relief. But Travis could feel a definite lowering of tension.

Belokas broke the silence first. "What now, Sir?" she asked.

"I don't know," Heissman said thoughtfully. "The manual has a surprising dearth of information on what to do when you're behind an enemy formation. Probably because it doesn't happen very often."

"I suppose we could always improvise," Woodburn offered.

"That we could," Heissman said in that same thoughtful tone. "Let's give it a try, shall we? We'll get a little more distance to make sure we're out of aft laser range, then see what we can come up with."

Epilogue

"I wanted you to know," Heissman said, gazing up from his desk with an unreadable expression on his face, "that I put in for a Conspicuous Gallantry Medal for you."

"Thank you, Sir," Travis said, feeling an odd warming inside him.

Though like every other emotion that he'd felt over the two weeks since the battle, the warmth was stained with darkness.

He was relieved he'd survived, of course, and equally relieved that so many others in Green One and Two had done likewise.

But too many hadn't. Far too many. The RMN had been gutted, ships and people lost in wholesale lots, and there had been times when it had looked like all was lost. It had only been through the grace of God, the fact that Tamerlane had clearly expected less resistance, and a level of courage and skill Travis would never have guessed the Navy even possessed that they'd pulled it off.

He'd assumed, reasonably enough, that with *Casey*'s escape from Tamerlane's force, her part in the battle was essentially over. Once Locatelli arrived, there should have been nothing for the Manticorans to do except use their newly-superior numbers to mop up the remnants of Tamerlane's force.

Only Tamerlane had been smarter than anyone had thought. It was only as Locatelli's ships approached the field of battle and prepared to engage that the other half of the invasion force, a group no one aboard *Casey* had even suspected was there, lit off their wedges and closed in.

Leaving *Casey* caught squarely between two enemy fleets.

That had nearly been the end right there. It had required luck and skill and some very fancy flying for Heissman to pull them out of harm's way.

It was only then that the Battle of Manticore really began.

And it was only afterward, when the last missile and laser had been fired and it was finally over, that the true and horrible cost of defending the realm became clear.

Given all that, even talking about awards felt painfully premature, if not flat-out obscenely morbid. But Admiral Locatelli was already jockeying to grab the lion's share of the credit for the victory, both in Parliament and with the media. It was only right that the rest of the heroes—the *true* heroes, in Travis's opinion—got some of the recognition before Locatelli made off with all of it.

"Don't get too excited," Heissman said sourly. "The request was denied."

The warm feeling vanished. "Sir?" Travis asked in confusion.

"Certain persons in authority," Heissman said, pushing through the words as if he were trudging through a set of snow banks, "are of the opinion that your ideas were mostly luck, and that their success relied on both that luck and on the overall competency of *Casey's* officers and crew."

"Yes, Sir," Travis said. "I mean . . . well, of course it was a ship-wide effort. Ideas aren't worth anything without teamwork and—"

"And teamwork alone isn't enough when you're facing impossible odds," Heissman cut him off brusquely. "Which I attempted to make clear. You'll still get the same Royal Unit Citation medal as everyone else aboard—they can't deny you that—but career-wise, I'm afraid you're going to be lost in the general shuffle." He stared hard at Travis's face. "I get the feeling you have an enemy or two in high places, Lieutenant."

Travis winced. What was he supposed to say to that? "I haven't deliberately invited any animosity, Sir," he said, choosing his words carefully.

"Deliberately or not, you've apparently succeeded," Heissman said. "I'm guessing the latest batch is coming from your time aboard *Phoenix*."

Travis felt his lip twitch. Yes; the late Ensign Fenton Locatelli, nephew of the now famous and highly acclaimed hero of Manticore. Even before the battle Admiral Locatelli probably had enough clout to deny Travis a minor award. Now, it was practically a foregone conclusion.

But there was nothing Travis could do about it. And even if there was, he wouldn't have bothered to try. Compared to the sacrifice so many men and women had made to protect their worlds, his own modest contributions seemed pretty small. "I do appreciate your efforts, though, Sir," he said. "If that's all—"

"Not quite," Heissman rumbled. "Let me start with the obvious. I know this sort of thing is a kick in the shin, but I wouldn't spend too much time worrying about it. There are plenty of political animals in the Fleet. But kilo for kilo, there are a lot more of the rest of us."

The rest of us meaning those who wanted to do their jobs to the best of their ability? Or was Heissman also including the drifters who really didn't care where they were as long as they pulled a steady pay voucher? Because there were certainly enough of those, too. "Yes, Sir," he said aloud.

"And I'm not including the loafers you're always writing up," Heissman continued. "That really bothers you, doesn't it? People who don't follow proper procedure?"

"Procedures are there for a purpose, Sir."

"Even when you can't see that purpose?"

"There's always a purpose, Sir," Travis said, a little stiffly. "Even if it isn't obvious."

"I appreciate your optimism in such things," Heissman said. "But I have to say it makes you something of an anomaly. Typically, someone as solid as you are on following procedure is mentally rigid in all other aspects of life. You, in contrast, not only can think outside the lines, but you sometimes go ahead and draw your own lines."

"Thank you, Sir," Travis said, wondering if that boiled down to a compliment or an indictment. "But I really didn't do anything all that extraordinary."

"People with a talent for something never think it's a big deal," Heissman said dryly. "The point I was going to make was that both of those characteristics are going to make you unpopular in certain circles. But you *will* be noticed, and appreciated, by the people who matter. For whatever that's worth."

"Thank you, Sir," Travis said. "Please understand in turn that I didn't join the RMN for glory or recognition. I joined to help protect the Star Kingdom." He hesitated. "And if necessary, to die for it."

"I know," Heissman said, his voice going a little darker. "Unfortunately, *that's* going to make you unpopular in certain quarters, too. Genuine, unashamed patriots are an embarrassment to the cynical and manipulative."

Some of the lines in his face smoothed out. "Which leads me to my final question. This whole 'travesty of this, travesty of that' sarcastic catchphrase that seems to follow you around. What's all that about, anyway?"

Travis sighed. "It started back in high school," he said reluctantly. "One of the teachers fancied himself a scholar and a wit, and liked to give his students nicknames. I was Travis Uriah Long, or Travis U. Long, which he thought sounded like Travis Oolong, which was a type of Old Earth tea. Hence, Travis Tea."

"Travesty," Heissman said with a nod, a small smile playing across his face. "And with your penchant for enforcing even minor regulations, the sarcastic direction was probably inevitable."

"Yes, Sir." Travis braced himself. "I'd appreciate it, Sir, if you didn't . . . pass it around too much."

"Not a problem," Heissman said. "Well. I've just been informed that *Casey*'s going to be another month in dock, so everyone's leave's been extended. But you may be called up for more testimony at any time, so don't stray too far from Landing City."

And then, to Travis's surprise, he rose to his feet. "Well done, Travis," the commodore said as they exchanged salutes. "I look forward to returning to *Casey* with you. *And* as soon as possible."

His eyes went a little distant. "Because I have a feeling Manticore's about to lose the nice, peaceful backwater status we've enjoyed for so long. I don't know how or why. I don't think anyone does. But I can guarantee this much: as of two weeks ago the RMN is no longer a joke and a political football. Someone out there has us in their sights . . .and we *are* going to figure out who."

His expression tightened. "You said you were willing to die for the Star Kingdom. You may very well get that chance."

The End

HMS *Phoenix* (DD-08)
Salamander-class Destroyer

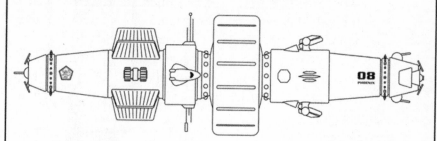

Specification

Mass: 43,750 tons
Hull Dimensions: 303 x 91 m
Acceleration: 213.4 G (2.093 kps²)
80% Accel: 170.7 G (1.674 kps²)
Armament: 2M (x6), 1L, 3AC

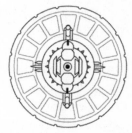

Internal Layout

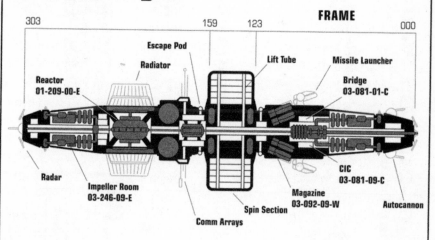

FRAME

303   159   123   000

Escape Pod
Radiator
Lift Tube
Missile Launcher

Reactor
01-209-00-E

Bridge
03-081-01-C

Radar

Impeller Room
03-246-09-E

CIC
03-081-09-C

Magazine
03-092-09-W

Autocannon

Spin Section

Comm Arrays

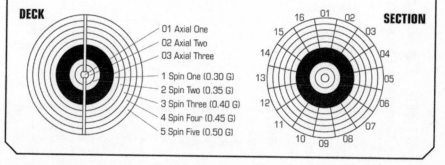

DECK

01 Axial One
02 Axial Two
03 Axial Three

1 Spin One (0.30 G)
2 Spin Two (0.35 G)
3 Spin Three (0.40 G)
4 Spin Four (0.45 G)
5 Spin Five (0.50 G)

SECTION

16 01 02
15   03
14   04
13   05
12   06
11   07
10 09 08

HMS *Casey* (CL-01) 1535 PD Refit
Casey-class Light Cruiser

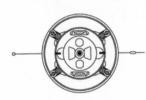

Specification

Mass: 73,000 tons
Hull Dimensions: 365 x 59 m
Acceleration: 261.3 G (2.563 kps²)
80% Accel: 209 G (2.05 kps²)
Armament: 4M/CM (x6), 2L, 4AC, 4 ET

Internal Layout

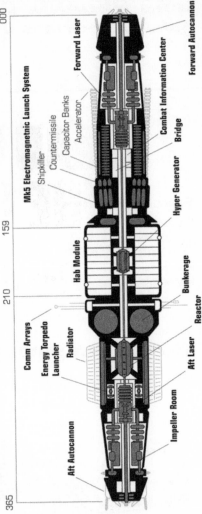

Comm Arrays
Energy Torpedo Launcher
Radiator
Aft Autocannon
Impeller Room
Aft Laser
Reactor
Bunkerage
Hab Module
Hyper Generator
Bridge
Combat Information Center
Forward Autocannon
Forward Laser
MK5 Electromagnetic Launch System
Shipkiller
Countermissile
Capacitor Banks
Accelerator

000
159
210
365

BEAUTY AND THE BEAST

David Weber

BEAUTY AND THE BEAST

"Lieutenant Harrington?"

Alfred Harrington turned. After the better part of two T-years, it no longer felt strange not to be addressed as "Gunny," but it didn't feel completely natural to be addressed as "Lieutenant," either. No doubt that would change. Everything changed, after all.

"Yes?" he said, raising one eyebrow as he looked at the man who'd addressed him.

He was a shrimpy little fellow. No more than a hundred and fifty-six centimeters—fifty-eight, at the outside—compared to Alfred's own two meters. Like a lot of Beowulf's population, he had the almond-shaped eyes of Old Earth's Asia, dark hair, and a complexion which reminded Alfred of Sphinxian sandal oak. And, on second impression, shrimpy or not, there was something about him that suggested he might be just about as *tough* as sandal oak. It wasn't really anything a man could put his finger on. Just something about the way he stood, or about the well-defined musculature, perhaps. Or about the eyes. Yes, it was the eyes, Alfred realized. He'd seen eyes like that before. They might have been differently shaped, or a different color, but he'd seen them.

"I'm Jacques Benton-Ramirez y Chou," the little fellow said.

"Gesundheit," Alfred said, before he could stop himself, then shook his head. "Sorry. I don't suppose a Navy officer ought to admit it, but I'm not at my best after a flight, I'm afraid. Besides," he smiled crookedly, "I doubt I'm the first one to make that particular bad joke."

171

"Here on Beowulf?" Benton-Ramirez y Chou cocked his head, looking up at Alfred's towering centimeters with the speculative eye of a logger considering a crown oak. "Actually, you probably are." He looked up at Alfred for another moment, then smiled. It was a slow smile, but just as crooked as Alfred's, and Alfred felt something inside warming as amusement gleamed in those eyes. "*Off* Beowulf, now, I think I may have heard it a time or two."

"Well," Alfred extended his right hand, reminding himself to mind his Sphinxian muscles and not absentmindedly crush the other's metacarpals, "I'll try to behave myself in the future, Mister Benton-Ramirez y Chou."

"Don't try too hard," Benton-Ramirez y Chou replied dryly, gripping the proffered hand with surprising strength. "I wouldn't want you to sprain any synapses."

Alfred's smile grew broader and he shook his head.

"I'll try to go easy on my poor, overworked mental processes," he assured the Beowulfer. "Of course, the air's thin enough here that I'm probably suffering from oxygen deprivation."

"Or altitude sickness," Benton-Ramirez y Chou offered affably, looking up at him.

"Possibly," Alfred agreed with a chuckle. "Possibly."

The smaller man grinned and released his hand, and Alfred felt that inner warmth grow stronger. It had been a while—much too *long* a while—since he'd felt something like that, and he stepped on it quickly, reflexively.

"Should I assume you were specifically looking for me and didn't just happen to read my nameplate and decide to strike up a conversation?" he asked.

"Guilty," Benton-Ramirez y Chou replied. "I was asked to meet you and see you squared away on campus."

"Oh?" Both of Alfred's eyebrows rose. "Nobody told me I rated an escort!"

"Well, consider it a military courtesy. It's not really 'Mister Benton-Ramirez y Chou;' it's 'Captain Benton-Ramirez y Chou.' Biological Survey Corps."

Alfred felt his shoulders square themselves automatically, despite the fact that the other man was in civilian dress, as he realized what he'd seen the first time he looked at the Beowulfer. The BSC, despite its civilian-sounding name, was one of the best special operations forces in the Solarian League. It was also quite small. There were rumors that not all of its operations accorded perfectly with official Solarian League policy, but it didn't seem to care very much about that. And it didn't hand out captain's insignia in cereal boxes, either.

"Pleased to meet you, Sir," he said more formally, and Benton-Ramirez y Chou shook his head.

"I'm a very new captain, you're due to make lieutenant (senior grade) in about five months, and that's the Osterman Cross ribbon on your chest, Lieutenant." There was very little humor in his voice now. "I don't think we need any 'sirs.'"

Alfred's lips tightened. A spike of anger flickered through him, made even brighter and sharper by the sincerity of the Beowulfer's tone. But that anger was irrational, and he knew it, so he made himself nod, instead.

"My family's got better connections than most with the medical establishment here on Beowulf," Benton-Ramirez y Chou continued. If he'd noticed anything about Alfred's expression, it didn't show. "Of course, here on Beowulf, just about *everybody*'s got at least some connection with BioSciences, but—I know you'll find this hard to believe, Lieutenant Harrington, but I *swear* it's true—there are actually people, real live Beowulfers, who don't have any association with medicine at all. We try to keep them locked in cellars deep enough, none of you outworlders will discover their shameful secret, though."

"I see." Alfred felt the lips which had tightened twitch in amusement. Then something clicked in his brain. Benton-Ramirez y Chou, was it? And "better connections" with the medical establishment? Well, he supposed that was one way to describe one of the two or three families which had been at the pinnacle of Beowulf bioscience for a mere nine hundred T-years or so. Just what in hell had sent a member of *that* family into the military? Or, for that matter, gotten him assigned to play nursemaid for an ex-enlisted Manticoran medical student?

"Your planet's shameful secret is safe with me, Captain," he said out loud.

"Thank you," Benton-Ramirez y Chou said with an air of great earnestness. "However, that connection and the fact that I've strayed from the normal family business into a rather different field of endeavor led certain people to conclude that I'd make a suitable escort to get you cleared through Customs and delivered to campus without your getting lost along the way."

"I see," Alfred said again, although he was oddly certain that Benton-Ramirez y Chou's explanation, while accurate, had not been complete. He didn't know why he was so positive of that, but he was accustomed to relying on his hunches, his ability to "read" people. After all, it had kept him alive on more than one occasion.

A fresh billow of darkness tried to blow through him, but he stepped on it firmly. It was easier than it had been. Possibly with enough practice he wouldn't even realize when he did it, and would that be a good thing or a bad one?

"Well, since I would truly hate to get lost in the urban jungles of downtown Grendel," he said, "I accept your offer of a local guide with gratitude, Captain. Let me grab my bags."

※ ※ ※

Much later that same day, Alfred sat on the small balcony attached to his apartment, looking out across the campus of Ignaz Semmelweis University of Beowulf at the massive pastel towers of the city of Grendel. The mellow, slanting rays of a setting sun gilded them in bronze and gold and shadow. Despite his joke about getting lost in urban jungles, Grendel really was an impressive sight for a boy who'd grown up in the Sphinxian bush. Landing, back on Manticore, was just as impressive in its own way, but Grendel was at least twice Landing's size, and far older. They were still areas in the heart of Grendel where historical buildings from the planet's colony days reared no more than forty or fifty stories from the ground, carefully maintained as historical relics. They deserved it after the better part of two thousand T-years, and they also reminded anyone who visited them that Beowulf was the oldest extrasolar star system to have been settled.

It was far warmer here than it would have been back on Sphinx, although not so warm as Manticore itself. He would have preferred something a little cooler, but he couldn't really complain. He'd grown up on a planet whose gravity was twenty-three percent greater than Beowulf's, so he felt light enough on his feet. And the air smelled good, seasoned with the greenery and flowering shrubs of ISU's beautifully landscaped grounds. He didn't like the birds, though. The Terrestrial imports weren't bad, and the local analogues were pleasing enough to the eye, but some of them had a peculiar, warbling whistle that reminded him of the stone ravens on Clematis. He didn't need that.

He sipped beer from the stein in his hand. Back home, he preferred his beer at room temperature, but room temperature on Sphinx was substantially lower than room temperature here on Beowulf. He'd gotten into the habit of drinking it chilled at OCS on Manticore, and this was clearly no place to start breaking such useful habits. And at least the beer was good. Not as good as *Sphinxian* beer, of course, but he'd already checked; Old Tilman was available as an import as soon as he got around to reprogramming the apartment kitchen. On the other hand, the wine list looked interesting, too. He was picky about his wines. His buddies in the Corps had ribbed him about that often enough, but he'd given as good as he got, and there were at least at least two dozen vintages on the list that he'd never even heard of. He looked forward to sampling them all; in the meantime, beer would do just fine.

He swallowed appreciatively while his mind ran back over the long day's activities.

Ignaz Semmelweis University's Beowulf campus was probably the most prestigious medical school in the explored galaxy. Competition for admission was always fierce, and Alfred suspected that at least some of his fellow students were going to resent his presence.

Beowulf was home to one of the Manticoran Wormhole Junction's secondary termini. The Solarian League in general wasn't especially fond of Manticore and its steadily expanding merchant marine, but the relationship between Beowulf and the Star Kingdom had been very close for centuries. There was a lot of intermarriage between Beowulf and Manticore, for that matter, and relations between the Beowulf System Defense Force and the Star Kingdom's military were cordial and based on mutual respect. The Star Empire had worked closely with the Biological Survey Corps on many occasions, as well, although that particular relationship was a bit more . . . fraught, given the nature of some of the BSC's operations. All of which helped to explain why the Royal Manticoran Navy was allocated a certain quota of students for ISU each year. Not everyone approved of that arrangement, and as surely as the sun would rise in the morning, someone was going to decide Alfred was here only because of that quota. Certainly an overgrown lummox from Sphinx who hadn't even bothered to complete his undergraduate degree before running off to join the Marines hadn't been able to make it on his merits as a student!

Actually, though, he could have. It might have been tight, given the University's scholastic standards, but he'd carried a perfect 4.0 GPA through the undergraduate studies and two years of premed the Navy had paid for, and he knew he'd aced the aptitude tests and ISU's written admission requirements. He hadn't done as well on the oral admissions interview, though. He'd known at the time that he wasn't earning top marks from two of the Beowulfers. That "hunch" ability of his had told him they weren't entirely satisfied with his explanation of why he wanted to specialize in neurosurgery. It wasn't that they'd disbelieved him, or that anything he'd said had been . . . objectionable. It was just that they hadn't thought he was being completely open with them.

Because he hadn't been.

His grip on the stein tightened, and he felt his brown eyes going bleak and hard as he looked out across the beautiful campus at the sun-washed towers of Grendel. He saw something else entirely in that moment. He saw Clematis. He saw the fires rolling through the city of Hope. He heard the explosions and the screams. He saw again what neural disruptors could do, and suddenly the beer tasted foul in his mouth and his stomach muscles tightened with remembered nausea. And with that terrible, burning rage. That sense of exalted purpose. The poisonous, soul-killing joy.

He closed his eyes and set the stein gently on the table at his elbow. He felt the remembered emotions guttering out through his nerves, felt his pulse settling back towards normal, and drew a deep, deep breath. He held it in his lungs, forcing himself towards stillness once more. And then, when the demons had retreated, he opened his eyes once again.

That was a bad one, he thought. *Probably because I'm tired. But that's okay. It's getting better. And I can't really complain too much. At least I got out alive, didn't I?*

His mouth quirked humorlessly and he inhaled again. He was probably bullshitting himself by blaming it on fatigue, but he really was tired. And maybe the universe really would look better again in the morning.

He pushed himself up out of the chair, gave Grendel one more look, then headed for bed.

❄ ❄ ❄

"So, Lieutenant Harrington, I take it you're settled in?"

"Yes, Sir. Thank you, Sir."

"Good."

Captain Howard Young, the Manticoran military attaché, was some sort of distant connection to the North Hollows, according to Alfred's briefing before he'd left for Grendel. He didn't look especially happy to see a towering Sphinxian ex-Marine on his com display, but at least he wasn't holding his nose the way some of the more aristocratically advantaged members of the Navy's officer corps seemed wont to do.

"Good," Young repeated. His right hand toyed with an antique paperweight on his desk, and he seemed to be feeling for the exact words he wanted. That struck Alfred as being just a little odd, since Young had screened him for the official purpose of welcoming him to Beowulf. Of course, he couldn't think of any reason for a captain of the list to worry about "welcoming" a mere lieutenant who'd been assigned to Beowulf to attend school, either, so he simply waited patiently. Patience was something he'd learned early, hunting on Sphinx, although he'd required a different variety of it since *leaving* Sphinx.

"Ah, something was called to my attention yesterday, Lieutenant," Young said finally. "A security matter." His eyes narrowed suddenly, looking out at the display into Alfred's.

"Yes, Sir." Alfred's voice was flatter than it had been, and his jaw muscles tightened. The intelligence pukes back home had cautioned him repeatedly about the need to keep his mouth shut. In fact, they'd reminded him so often he'd felt an almost overwhelming urge to pinch a few heads like zits. He understood, he wasn't an idiot, and he'd given his word, so why the hell couldn't they just shut up and leave him alone?

His hands clenched into fists outside the field of view of the com's pickup, and he felt his jaw muscles tense.

You're overreacting . . . again, he told himself harshly. *Young's probably just dotting all the "i"s and crossing all the "t"s. Or maybe he's protecting his own posterior—couldn't have the out-of-control jarhead shooting his mouth off on his watch, now could he?*

"I was thoroughly advised about that matter before leaving the Star Kingdom, Sir," he said levelly.

"Oh, good." Young seemed to relax, then he shook his head. "Sorry, Lieutenant. I didn't mean to harp on it. Unfortunately, my Admiralty counterpart didn't get all the little boxes checked in his dispatch to me. He told me *I* wasn't supposed to bring it up, but he hadn't specifically indicated that he'd told *you* about that. Under the circumstances, I thought I'd better check and save us both some grief if he hadn't gotten around to that."

"I understand, Sir." Alfred felt himself relaxing in turn and drew a deep breath. "It's not something I'd be likely to talk about a lot, anyway, though."

Young started to speak, then stopped, shook his head, and visibly changed what he'd been about to say.

"Well, I hope you understand that the embassy will be happy to see to anything we can do for you while you're on Beowulf. I don't think we have any other officers over there on campus at the moment, do we?"

"Not to the best of my knowledge, Sir. No."

"I didn't think so." Young smiled much more naturally. "I've been left adrift among civilians a time or two myself, Lieutenant. If you get the feeling that you need to talk to another uniform while you're here—just to retain your sanity, you understand—drop by. We've even got a couple of Marines on the staff, and we play a pretty mean game of poker."

"Thank you, Sir." Alfred smiled back. "I'll bear that in mind. I'm not completely without military contacts here on Beowulf, either, though."

"You're not?" Young raised an eyebrow.

"No, Sir. And to be honest, that little matter you've just reminded me about makes me wonder how much of a coincidence that really was."

"Why?"

"Because I had a greeter at the landing pad. A fellow named Benton-Ramirez y Chou. He said he was a captain in the BSC."

"*Jacques* Benton-Ramirez y Chou?" Young's eyes had narrowed again.

"Yes, Sir." Alfred shrugged ever so slightly. As a mere junior-grade lieutenant and a medical officer with no access to sensitive information (*aside from Clematis*, a corner of his mind said coldly), he wasn't required to file the "contact reports" whenever he encountered a foreign national, thank God. That didn't mean it wasn't a good idea to go ahead and mention it when it happened, though. It came under the heading of dotting more of those "i"s and crossing more of those "t"s, he supposed. "He said it was a courtesy to help me get settled here at the University. And he mentioned his 'connection' to the Beowulfan medical community."

"Well, that's true enough!" Young's expression was thoughtful. "It's probably a good thing you mentioned it, Lieutenant, but I doubt there was anything . . . official behind it. Benton-Ramirez y Chou is a naturally inquisitive sort, and he's got a reputation as something of a social gadfly. He may have picked up a few rumors, but it's unlikely anybody on Beowulf would be actively digging. On the other hand, his family is not only prominent but quite active in Abolitionist circles, so don't take that for granted where he's concerned. If he 'happens' to run into you again, let us know about it, right?"

"Yes, Sir. I will."

"Good man." Young smiled again. "And now, since I know you're due for orientation today, I'll let you go. Good luck, Lieutenant."

❈ ❈ ❈

"Watch where you're going!"

The voice was sharp, irritated, and carried a very familiar accent. Alfred turned toward the impact, looking for whoever had just run into him, and found himself looking at a fair-haired, slightly built young man, a good quarter meter shorter than him, who was probably about his own age, assuming they were both first-generation prolong. The other man was expensively and ultra-stylishly dressed. He also had an exquisitely coiffed civilian haircut, blue eyes, and an angry expression.

"I beg your pardon?" Alfred said. "Were you speaking to me?"

He deliberately emphasized his Sphinxian accent, although he knew he probably shouldn't be squirting any extra hydrogen into this particular fire. He couldn't help himself though. The stranger's upper-class, private-school, *aristocratic* Manticoran accent, coupled with that irritated expression, simply rubbed him the wrong way.

"There *are* other people in the hall, you know!" the stranger snapped.

"Why, I believe you're right!" Alfred marveled, looking around the crowded precincts of Benton Hall carefully before returning his attention to the other man. "Amazing. The place is so big I hadn't noticed. Thanks for pointing it out."

The stranger seemed to swell with outrage. Alfred could see him almost literally quivering in anger, and he didn't really need any "hunches" to read the fury rolling off of the fellow in waves.

"Some of the people in this hall *deserve* to be here," the other man said in a cutting, icy tone.

"Well I'm sure they won't mind your being here, too," Alfred replied. "By the way, why *are* you here?"

"Listen, you—!"

Alfred raised his eyebrows and shifted his balance. It was a small thing, but deliberate, and the other man chopped himself off in midsentence as the tall, powerfully built Sphinxian leaned over him ever so slightly.

He glared up at Alfred for another moment or two, then made a disgusted sound, turned on his heel and stamped away. Alfred watched him go, wondering what his problem had been.

Obviously, his problem was you, Alfred, he told himself sardonically. *And you didn't go out of your way to make it any better, did you? That's you all over again, isn't it?*

He drew a deep breath, forcing himself to center, remembering a time—it seemed long, long ago—when he would simply have let the little pipsqueak's ire bounce off. He'd like to be that way again, but it wasn't going to happen. So he'd just have to learn to deal with it.

He turned back to the queue wending its way steadily forward and reminded himself to work on that.

❈ ❈ ❈

"Sorry about that, Allison," Franz Iliescu said as he slid into the empty chair. He tried to make it come out ruefully, already regretting the anger he'd allowed himself to show. Not that the overgrown moron hadn't deserved it. But it had still been childish of him, and beneath his dignity, when it came down to it.

"What was that all about?" the beautiful young woman sitting across the table from him asked. "I was too far away to hear anything, but it didn't look as if the two of you were exactly bosom buddies!"

"Not hardly!" Iliescu snorted and spared one glance back over his shoulder at the towering figure in Royal Manticoran Navy uniform. The idiot had to flaunt it right here on campus, didn't he? "To be honest, it's the first time I've actually met him. And I didn't enjoy the experience any more than I'd expected to, either."

"Really?" She tilted her head, considering him thoughtfully. "Personally, I've found that expectations have a way of turning into self-fulfilling prophecies sometimes."

Iliescu's face tightened for just a moment, but then he gave himself a shake and inhaled a deep, calming breath.

"You may have a point," he acknowledged. His companion looked absurdly young for a graduate student, even in a prolong society, but that was probably because she'd received the second-generation therapies. They could be administered at a much earlier starting point, and he reminded himself that the person behind that youthful façade was within a T-year or two of his own age. "I have to admit I did let my . . . preconceptions, let's say, color my initial reaction. In this case, though, I think I can honestly say the two of us would never have cared very much for each other under any circumstances."

"Maybe not." She sipped delicately from her steaming cup of tea, then grimaced. The Benton Hall canteen didn't make the very best tea on Beowulf. She rather wished she hadn't agreed to meet Iliescu here . . . and not just because of the quality of the beverage service. But since she had, she might as well make conversation before she could find a way to slip diplomatically away.

"Why did you have such low expectations to begin with?" she asked.

"Because he's a moron," Iliescu said. "Look at him! Wearing that uniform at Registration! Doesn't he realize this is a *civilian* school? Just seeing him in it makes me feel embarrassed as a Manticoran."

"You have something against uniforms?"

"No, not in their place," he replied. "But this isn't the proper place for it. Oh, I realize somebody has to join the Navy or the Marines, and it's not as if there were anything *shameful* about it, I suppose. But ISU is supposed to be for people who are serious about helping other people—about *healing* other people—not for people who sign up to kill them in job lots! And I've heard stories about this guy. Ugly stories."

"What kind of 'ugly stories'?" Something dangerous glinted in her dark brown eyes, but Iliescu seemed unaware of it.

"Not the kind that make good dinner conversation," he said. "Nobody back home wanted to talk about it very much, which suggests a lot to me. Whatever it was, they hushed it up pretty quickly, but apparently he got a lot of people killed in the process of whatever it was. The Crown can't be too happy about whatever he did, anyway. Sure, the Queen pinned the medal on him, but the ceremony was all very hush-hush and family-only, and the citation's sealed. Obviously *somebody* didn't want the newsies getting hold of it!"

"Really?" She looked back across the enormous room as the lieutenant in the black and gold uniform disappeared through a door on its other side.

"Really. And then he used the medal to get himself admitted to ISU," Iliescu growled. He took a quick, angry sip from his own teacup. "He took advantage of the Navy's quota, *that's* how he got here. I hate that entire system. If you can't cut it on your own, then you shouldn't be here. And you sure as hell shouldn't be bouncing better students—people who're going to be *doctors*, not part of the business of killing other people—just because of a uniform with a piece of ribbon on the front. It's a damned entitlement system, just because they served in the damned military. *Anybody* could do that, and it's not like they didn't already have a benefits package better than any mere civilian's. Or that they didn't volunteer for the job in the first place, for that matter! No one *made* them do it, so why should that give them an edge over other people just because those other people *don't* want to butcher other human beings?"

His companion made a noncommittal sound, wondering if Iliescu had been denied admission personally the first time he'd applied or if someone else had failed to gain it. At least she understood now why he'd started so thoroughly on the wrong foot with the enormous lieutenant.

Well, I suppose it's possible he really did use the quota system to get in, she reflected, *but anyone who can make Franz that mad that quickly can't possibly be all bad!*

※ ※ ※

"So, tell me, Lieutenant Harrington. What makes you want to specialize in neurosurgery?"

Dr. Penelope Mwo-chi leaned back in her chair behind her desk, considering Alfred across it. This interview was one hell of a lot more important than most, and Ignaz Semmelweis University had some quaint and interesting customs, including personal face-to-face interviews and meetings between students and their teachers. It didn't seem very efficient compared to electronic meetings, but Alfred wasn't going to argue with the system which had turned out the galaxy's premier doctors for rather longer than the Star Kingdom had existed. Besides, those "hunches" of his didn't work through an electronic interface, and it was evident to him that Dr. Mwo-chi's question was rather more serious and pointed than her tone might have suggested.

"I think it's a challenging field," he said, after a moment, "and I like challenges. But I also think it's an *important* field, maybe even more important than ever now that prolong's becoming generally available. My primary interest isn't really in geriatrics or prophylactic care, but people are going to be living even longer, and we really don't know what a couple of centuries of additional life are going to do to neural pathways and synapses. Everything may work just as fine as the prolong therapists think it will, but it may not, too. I'm less sanguine than some people are about synthetic substitutes if it doesn't, although I do think it's a promising area to consider. For myself, though, I'm more interested in repair and reconstruction, especially after trauma, and I'm convinced we can improve prostheses to work better and interface more smoothly with the organic nervous system."

"I see." Mwo-chi tipped her chair a bit farther back, steepling her fingers under her chin. Despite her surname, she had blond hair and blue eyes, and now those eyes studied Alfred's expression very carefully. "That's a very satisfactory answer, Lieutenant. Why don't I think it's a *complete* answer?"

Alfred stiffened slightly in his own chair, looking back at her. There was something deep and important—to her, at least—behind that question. He could tell that much, but not why it was important. He considered prevaricating, but he didn't want to. He didn't want to give her her "complete answer," either, but that was more because *he* didn't want to go there, not because there was anything shameful about it. Except that he *did* feel ashamed, not to mention guilty. Yet Mwo-chi was the real reason he'd wanted to attend ISU in the first place. There might be one neurosurgeon in the galaxy who was better qualified than she was, but he knew damned well there weren't two of them. And the results of this interview would determine whether or not she accepted him as one of her personal students.

"I've . . . seen the consequences of combat wounds, Doctor," he said finally. "Some of them happened to people I . . . cared about." He made himself look directly into her eyes. "That's one reason I'm interested in reconstruction and improving prostheses, working on the organic-electronic interface."

"But those aren't the only things you're interested in, are they, Lieutenant?" she asked gently.

"No," he admitted. He closed his eyes for a moment, then looked back at her. "I've seen what neural disruptors do, too," he said very, very quietly.

Mwo-chi's nostrils flared and the muscles in her cheeks seemed to tense. Then she shook her head.

"Lieutenant," she said almost compassionately, "neural disruptors don't leave us anything to repair. That's why they call them 'disruptors.' The damage is at the cellular level, and I'm sure you already know how little that leaves us to work with. That's why the classic treatment for damaged limbs for the last seventy T-years has been amputation and regeneration. And for those who can't regen—or where we can't amputate and regrow—the only option is nerve transplants, for those who can accept them, or complete artifical nerve networks. We've made a lot of progress with nerve nets, especially in the last hundred years or so, and what we can do now is one *hell* of a lot better than what we used to be able to accomplish, but they're still a long, long way from replacing the organic originals. There's loss of function, whatever we do, and serious loss of sensation, as well, and some people simply never learn to adapt to them, however hard they try. But replacement is the only therapy we've been able to come up with, and given the amount of brain damage disruptors often inflict, assuming they don't simply crash the entire autonomic nervous system, even that's effective—or as effective as it *can* be, at any rate—in no more than twenty or thirty percent of all cases."

"I know the numbers, Doctor."

Alfred's reply came out more harshly than he'd intended, but he'd been half afraid of that response. It was the main reason he hadn't been more forthcoming with the University interview board. What he wanted to accomplish was at best quixotic and at worst a colossal waste of time and effort. He'd been afraid the board would reject his application in favor of someone whose work might actually lead to positive, concrete results.

"I know the numbers," he repeated in a voice that was closer to normal, "but I don't see any reason we ought to accept them as set in stone and unchangeable. Once upon a time, we didn't know how to vaccinate against cancer, either. Or how to create prolong. Or, if you go back far enough, how to prevent infection or childbed fever! Semmelweis ended up in an asylum, Doctor, because nobody believed what he was saying or that he could accomplish something so miraculous as preventing women from dying after childbirth just by washing his hands and his instruments. That didn't make him wrong, though."

"I see you know some history," Mwo-chi observed. She swung her chair gently from side to side, and the skin around her eyes crinkled in what might have been a smile. "But much as I admire the man this school's named for, you might also want to reflect upon the fact that Ignaz Semmelweis wasn't the least arrogant man ever to practice medicine. He didn't exactly endear himself to his colleagues by the way he went about presenting and implementing his conclusions. Or expressing his opinion of the colleagues in question, for that matter. He was right, and eventually the entire medical profession realized, but that didn't make him effective during his own lifetime. Not outside of the hospitals in which he himself worked, at any rate."

"I don't want to change the universe, Doctor," Alfred said. "I wouldn't object if that happened, you understand, but it's not what I want and not what I think is going to happen. I just want to be able to help. To undo some of the damage I've—" he changed his verb selection in midsentence "—seen. I'm not expecting any magic bullets, but it's something that's worth doing. Something worth *trying*."

"And you're willing to risk wasting the next three T-years of your life by investing them in something that almost certainly isn't going to work in the end?"

"It's *my* life," he replied. "Do I want to 'waste' it? Of course not! But no one who graduates from ISU's College of Neurosurgery is going to be a waste of time, Dr. Mwo-chi. Maybe I won't be able to find a way to repair disruptor damage, just like everybody keeps telling me I won't. That doesn't mean I can't change a lot of lives for the better anyway."

"But what you really want to do is learn how to repair the jellied, useless tissue disruptors leave behind, isn't it?" she challenged.

He looked into her eyes, seeing the city of Hope again behind his own, hearing the screams, seeing the bodies go down, smelling the smoke. Penelope Mwo-chi accepted very few applicants as her personal students, and even fewer as her assistants. The fact that he'd gotten this far said a lot, and might owe more to that piece of ribbon on his chest than he wanted to admit, but she wasn't going to waste one of those handful of slots on someone who honestly thought he might be able to find a way to repair that "jellied" tissue she'd just described. He knew that, yet he couldn't lie, and there was something behind the challenge she'd just issued. Something that wasn't cut and dried, that hadn't rejected his application . . . yet, at least. And so he met her gaze steadily across her desk and nodded.

"Yes, Doctor," he said. "It is."

She looked back at him for another moment, then let her chair come back upright, laid her hands flat on her desk, and nodded sharply.

"Good," she said softly. "Very good, Lieutenant Harrington." His surprise must have shown, because she smiled. It was a slow smile, but a warm one, and he found himself smiling back. "You're probably a lunatic, Lieutenant," she told him, "but medicine *needs* lunatics. And it needs dreams . . . and the lunatics who won't give up on them. I've been doing a little research of my own over the past decade or so, as it happens, and some of it relates directly to disruptor damage. I don't have any magical fixes or any breakthrough results, but I have made some progress, and if that's what you're really interested in, I think I have a research assistantship with your name written all over it."

❀ ❀ ❀

"There seems to be more to your friend Lieutenant Harrington than meets the eye, Franz," Allison said with more than a slight edge of gentle malice. The Manticoran looked at her, and she smiled. "Hadn't you heard? Dr. Mwo-chi's chosen him as one of her research assistants."

Iliescu's expression tightened. He started to shoot something back—something short and sharp, she suspected—then stopped himself. Instead, he inhaled deeply and then shrugged.

"Dr. Mwo-chi's entitled to choose anyone she wants," he said. "You may be right—there may be more to him than I think. I'm certainly not going to accuse Dr. Mwo-chi of picking anyone as an assistant if she didn't think he was qualified! That doesn't change my opinion about quota systems, though. It doesn't mean he deserved to get here in the first place, and it doesn't mean he didn't bounce someone who did deserve it. As for myself," he shrugged again, "I'm just as happy we're going to be an entirely different fields. ISU's big enough I won't have to run into him unless I'm just plain unlucky."

"You're right about that," she replied. "The university *is* big enough you can usually avoid people who tick you off. Oh, my! Look at the time! I'm going to be late to class if I don't hurry."

She turned and walked away, wondering what it was she'd thought she'd seen in Franz Iliescu when he first arrived on campus. He'd seemed personable enough then, and quite charming in his own way. He'd clearly fancied himself as a ladies' man, but he was prepared to take no for an answer with remarkably good grace when his interest wasn't reciprocated. And, in fairness, he was well informed, had good taste in music, and had proved a pleasant bed companion, as well.

Yet under all of those undeniable good points, there was a sharp-edged personality. The sort that tended to leave relationships bleeding in the end. It wasn't that he wasn't a very good student who, someday, was going to turn into a very good doctor . . . as a technician, at any rate. She didn't understand why he'd chosen obstetrics, given what she'd seen of him so far, but he was certainly smart enough if he could just get outside those preconceptions and that prickly personality of his.

She'd almost opted for maternal-fetal medicine herself, but she'd decided in the end that the focus was too narrow. A *wonderful* focus, yes, but more . . . limited than what she wanted to do with her life. Instead, she'd chosen gene therapy and surgery, despite the fact that it had been a family specialization for generations. She suspected sometimes that was why she'd been so inclined to choose against it, because she knew she had a naturally contrary streak. In fact, it was about a kilometer wide, and it had turned her into the closest thing to a rebel the family had experienced since her Great-Aunt Jacqueline had dropped out of college, changed her name, and emigrated to Old Earth. She didn't really mean to be "difficult," as her mother was wont to put it, but neither did she intend to just roll over and accept the dictates of tradition and other people's expectations. It was *her* life, when it came down to it. She had to be the one to decide what she did with it, whether the rest of Beowulf approved or not. And besides that, it was so *boring*, so limiting, to allow herself to be hammered into someone else's role just because that was what was *expected* of someone in her family. In fact, she'd almost followed her brother's example and avoided medicine entirely. Now *that* would have caused her parents to suffer a good old-fashioned fit of apoplexy!

In the end, she hadn't been able to do it, though. Maybe there really was something to her mother's insistence that it was "in the blood," although that always seemed particularly unscientific from someone who was herself one of Beowulf's dozen leading geneticists. But when it came down to it, Allison simply hadn't been able to turn away. The wonders of the human body, and especially of the marvelous, unending complexity and splendor of its genetic blueprint, had been too much. The lure of giving her life to their study had overcome her frustration at being shoved into a predictable niche. It struck her as especially unfair that she should find the human genome so fascinating that she couldn't resist giving in to her mother's endless gentle (and not-so-gentle) pushing and prodding. But that interest of hers in maternal and fetal might be part of what had initially attracted her to Iliescu. She was going to spend a lot of time working with expectant parents, after all, and whatever she thought of him as a person, he was clearly going to be a superior obstetric technician. Surely they should have had *something* in common!

Whatever had drawn her originally, however, it was wearing off quickly, and she found herself wondering about the towering Manticoran naval lieutenant he'd taken in such profound dislike. Anyone he disliked was probably worth knowing more about, after all. And there was something about Harrington. He certainly stood out on campus, and not just because of the uniform he habitually wore. He was much, much taller than the vast majority of Beowulfers, whereas Allison was *shorter* than most of them. In fact, he was a good half-meter taller than *she* was! No one would ever call him handsome, either, although he was at least passably good-looking.

Perhaps it was the way he moved? Someone that large shouldn't move . . . gracefully, yet he did. Part of that might be the difference in gravities, yet that couldn't be all of it, and she found herself wondering about his genetic profile. The Star Kingdom of Manticore had acquired more than its share of genies, after all. All of its planets boasted gravities heavier than Beowulf's, but Sphinx's was heaviest of all, and Harrington didn't have the stocky, over-muscled build of an unmodified human growing up in a gravity field thirty-five percent heavier than the one in which humanity had evolved. So clearly there was some modification in his family history, and she wondered which one it had been? Not Quellhollow; he didn't have the coloration for that. Meyerdahl was a possibility, of course, but so were the Kismet and Cantrell modifications. Not that it mattered, except that it piqued her professional curiosity.

She thought about it as she sauntered towards the class whose immediacy she had somewhat mendaciously exaggerated to Iliescu, then grinned. Her brother had teased her more than once over her curiosity. He had a passion for ancient literature, especially pre-space, Old Earth writers. One of his favorite authors was a fellow named Kipling, and he'd called her "Ricky" when she was a child. When she'd asked him why, she'd told him that he reminded her of two of his favorite Kipling characters, someone called "the Elephant Child" with his "'satiable curiosity" and someone else called "Rikki-Tikki-Tavi," whose motto had been "Run and find out." She hadn't known whether to be amused or insulted, so he'd given her copies of the original stories, and she'd decided in the end that he had a point. A very *good* point, as it happened.

※ ※ ※

Alfred Harrington moved quickly across the quadrangle. He'd always been good at memorizing maps and knowing exactly where he was, and that talent had served him well here on ISU's huge campus. Despite which, he was probably going to be late to his appointment with Dr. Patterson. He and Dr. Mwo-chi had run over on their scheduled lab, partly because they were still in the familiarization phase, and she'd promised to protect him if Dr. Patterson turned ugly. Given that Patterson had a reputation for being one of the kindliest, most cheerful professors on campus, he was unlikely to stand in *too* much need of protection, but he really liked Patterson. And—

"*Ohhh!*"

Alfred threw out one arm for balance as the small, black-haired, unreasonably good-looking young woman appeared out of nowhere. She seemed to literally materialize from behind a carefully shaped bank of flowering bushes, directly into his path. His reflexes were much quicker than those of an unmodified human who'd grown up in a single gravity, but they weren't fast enough to stop him in time, and he ran into her hard enough to send her bouncing backward with the impact.

❊ ❊ ❊

Allison found herself stumbling back with a squawk of dismay that was completely genuine. She hadn't realized how quickly he was moving, and she hadn't allowed for the sheer size and physical power of him. He was a third again her own height, with the dense muscle, heavy bone, and solid gristle of his home world. He must have weighed more than twice as much as she did, and it dawned on her as she felt her balance going that it might have been wiser to find a different way to "accidentally" encounter him.

Then his hand darted out. She'd never seen anyone move that quickly before, and the fingers that closed on her shoulder could have been forged of iron. They were gentle, but they were also completely unyielding, and she felt her incipient tumble being braked to a halt without any apparent effort at all.

"Excuse me," he said, so earnestly she felt a pang—brief, but a pang—of guilt over having arranged the collision. "I usually watch where I'm going better than that!"

"Don't be silly." She gave herself a shake and used her right hand to rake hair out of her eyes as he released her shoulder. "It was more my fault than yours," she went on with complete honesty. "I know how that butterfly bush blocks the sightlines for anyone headed for Priestly Hall. If I didn't want someone to run into me, I should've stopped and looked both ways before I stepped into the open around it."

"Are you all right?" he asked.

"I think I'm fine, Lieutenant . . . Harrington." She was careful to read the name off the plate on the front of his uniform tunic and smiled at him. "Obviously, you're from Manticore. How do you do?" She held out her hand. "I'm Allison Chou."

It wasn't her full name, but he didn't have to know that . . . yet, at any rate. And it was the one on her admission file here at the university. It had irritated her parents, and especially her mother, no end when she decided on that, but names were personal things here on Beowulf. No one could really object, and while she suspected she wasn't fooling very many of her classmates, she could at least pretend Chou was her complete surname.

"Pleased to meet you Ms. Chou." He took her hand, and once again she realized he was deliberately restricting the power of his grip. It was just as strong as she'd thought it was, but it was also gentle, and a strange sort of tingle seemed to flow into her own hand out of it. "Alfred Harrington. And, yes, I am from the Star Kingdom—from Sphinx, as a matter of fact."

"I thought I recognized the accent," she said, trying to understand that sensation. She'd never felt anything quite like it. "You're a student here?"

"Yes." He nodded. He released her hand, and she took it back almost reluctantly. "Neurosurgery. And you?"

"Genetics." She shrugged, wiggling her fingers unobtrusively. "Something of a tradition here on Beowulf, I'm afraid."

"Sounds interesting to me," he replied. "Of course," he smiled a bit crookedly, "a lot of us Manticorans, especially the ones from Sphinx, have a certain . . . vested interest in that field, you might say."

"I suppose you do," she agreed.

She gazed up at him, wondering why his voice seemed to carry a peculiar overtone. She couldn't quite put her finger on what it was, but it was almost . . . furry feeling. Like something silky soft stroking over her skin. It clearly wasn't anything he was doing on purpose, yet there was something . . . intimate about it, as if the tingle her hand had felt was spreading to other portions of her anatomy. Whatever it was, it wasn't anything she'd expected to feel. And there was something else with it. Something . . . darker, sadder. It was ridiculous, of course, and she knew it, and yet what she felt at that moment was a simultaneous need to purr and to burst into tears.

"So you'll be here on Beowulf for a while?" she heard herself say, and he nodded.

"At least two or three T-years. It's not that far back to Sphinx through the Junction, though. I can grab one of the daytrips home to visit anytime I've got a couple of days free, so it's not exactly like being in exile."

"No, I can see that."

She was beginning to feel a little foolish. There was something so *nice* about just standing here, talking to him, and that was ridiculous. First, because she didn't even know him. Second, because to be brutally honest, she'd been energetically pursued (and, on occasion, caught) by men a lot better looking than he was. Third, because she had no idea where that edge of darkness was coming from, and it scared her. And fourth, because it was pretty obvious that whatever *she* might be feeling, he wasn't feeling it at all.

"Well," she said, "you were clearly in a hurry before I ran into you, so I'd probably better let you get on to wherever it was you were going."

She stepped back out of the way, and he looked down at her. He hesitated a moment, then nodded.

"You're right, I'd better get moving," he said, and she had the strangest feeling that it wasn't what he'd started to say. "Maybe we'll run into each other again—a little less literally, next time."

"Maybe we will," she agreed, nodding back to him, then watched him walk away with that long, graceful stride.

Well, that *was weird enough*, she thought, watching him go, trying to remember anything like what had just happened. She'd met plenty of attractive men in her life, and been drawn to more than one of them. She *was* Beowulfan, after all, and she knew, without false modesty or conceit, far more attractive herself than most. But she'd never felt so . . . comfortable with someone so quickly.

She ambled across to one of the shaded benches and settled on it, her expression pensive. She didn't know Lieutenant Harrington from Adam's housecat, as her brother might have put it, and the entire experience had been more than a little disturbing. A lot of people thought of her as impulsive, and she was willing to admit there was some truth to that, yet she'd never encountered anything quite like this. It was as if there was some sort of link, some kind of connection, between the two of them despite the fact that they'd never even met, and that was just plain stupid. Things like that didn't happen outside really bad novels. Besides, that darkness . . . Now that the moment had passed, she tasted it far more clearly, like iron on her tongue, and she shivered. It was as if it hadn't been *her* darkness at all, as if it had been someone else's entirely, and that frightened her.

She blinked as she realized what she'd just thought. *Frightened* her? All right, it was strange, perhaps, but *frightening?* That was ludicrous. And, she decided, straightening her spine, she wasn't going to put up with it, either. Not that she knew exactly what she was going to *do* about it just yet. That was going to take some thinking, and it was obvious to her that there was rather more to Lieutenant Harrington than met the eye—where *she* was concerned, at any rate. And that meant she'd darned well better not be rushing into anything, Rikki-Tikki-Tavi or no Rikki-Tikki-Tavi. No, it was time to be subtle, to consider carefully . . . to be nosy. And what was the point in having family connections if you never used them?

※ ※ ※

"To what do I owe the honor?" Jacques Benton-Ramirez y Chou inquired as he pulled out his sister's chair. She settled into it, and he walked around the table to his own. He sat, eyebrows politely raised, and she smiled at him.

They looked very much alike, which was hardly surprising, given that they were fraternal twins. Of course, he was also five T-years—almost six, actually—older than she was, but that wasn't as rare on Beowulf as it was on some other worlds, where birth rates were less tightly regulated. He was slightly taller than she was, too, but no one who saw them together would ever have mistaken them for anything other than the twins they were.

"Why do you always assume I have an ulterior motive when I ask you to have lunch with me?" Allison inquired.

"Years and years of experience, mostly," he replied dryly, and she grinned.

"I never could put anything over on you, could I, Jacques?"

"Not for lack of trying, though."

"A girl has to practice on *someone*," she pointed out.

"I'm so happy to have been of use to you," he said with exquisite courtesy. "But you still haven't told me what this is about." He waved one hand gently around the expensive restaurant. "Mind, I've always liked the food at Madoka's, but this was rather short notice even for you."

"My schedule's tighter this semester." She shrugged. "I've got smaller holes to fit things into."

"And my own superiors' desire that I might perhaps accommodate *my* schedule to theirs figures into your plans exactly how?"

"Oh, be serious, Jacques!" She shook her head. "You've been twisting your schedule into a pretzel any time it suited your purposes for as long as I can remember. Don't tell me your 'superiors' think they're going to change *that!*"

He considered her thoughtfully. She had a point, although not as strong a one as she might have thought. A lot of that pretzel she was talking about was more apparent than real. It would please his superiors—and him—no end if they could convince someone with a working IQ that he was simply a child of one of Beowulf's elite families, amusing himself by dabbling with a military career and not taking it any more seriously along the way than he had to. He doubted they were going to fool too many of the people who really mattered, but it was always worth a try, and even people who knew better couldn't afford to ignore official appearances. If all the rest of the galaxy perceived him as a dilettante, they'd have to act as if *they* did, as well . . . or else explain why they didn't. Encouraging that perception was the reason he'd probably be leaving the military—officially, at least—in a very few more years, as well, and the thought didn't make him very happy. He'd seen and done some ugly things in the BSC, but he'd been part of some pretty damned *satisfying* things, too. He was going to miss going out with the teams, meeting the challenges they met in the field.

"Well, while I'm certainly not prepared to agree that there's any truth whatsoever in your aspersions upon my character," he said now, "I am here, and you indicated you had something to talk about. So . . . ?"

He arched his eyebrows again, and she began to answer, then paused as the waiter materialized at his elbow like a puff of smoke. Madoka's was among the top ten or twenty restaurants (depending on who was doing the rating) in Grendel, and the quality of its human waitstaff was part of the reason why. The twins gave the attentive waiter and his photographic memory their orders, then waited while he poured beverages and disappeared once more.

"You were saying?" Jacques prompted as soon as he had.

"Curiosity, mostly," she said. "Of course, I could have asked you about it over the com, but I haven't seen you in almost a month, so it seemed like an opportunity to kill two birds with one stone."

He nodded, smiling at her, aware that what she'd just said was nothing but the truth. The two of them were connected on a level deeper than was common even among twins, complicated by the fact that she was not simply his twin but his baby sister. There was always that itch neither of them could quite scratch when they were apart. They'd grown used to it, over the years, and it scarcely bothered them anymore, but they always felt the relief as the itch disappeared when they sat down across the table from each other like this.

"What kind of curiosity?" he inquired.

"It's about one of my fellow students, actually." She shrugged. "He's in neurosurgery, not genetics, so we haven't actually met. But I've run into someone who doesn't think much of him, and I'm wondering if there's any basis for it besides the someone in question's own swollen ego."

"And you couldn't just go and find out for yourself?" he asked politely. "I hadn't realized you'd become quite so ancient and feeble since the last time I saw you."

"Certainly I could go and find out for myself." She made a face at him across the table, yet he seemed to sense a certain evasiveness behind the expression. "I seem to recall, however, that one of my overprotective older brothers warned me a few years back about my social recklessness. I can't quite remember which one of them it was, though."

Jacques laughed, but she had a point. And maybe he *was* being overprotective, at that. But Allison had always been the one who chafed the most severely at being a Benton-Ramirez y Chou. She understood—and often resented—her family's prominence, the way its members were "expected" to go into public service or politics as well as—or even in addition to—medical careers. But she also had an almost feline refusal to be driven into anything by anyone, and she had a matching streak of impulsiveness. There was nothing careless or lazy or foolish about her, but she was a bundle of energy, capable of cheerfully multitasking in enough directions to drive anyone close to her insane, and the notion of taking precautions simply because her family was not universally beloved was alien to her. And, he acknowledged, not without a fair degree of reason. The Benton-Ramirez y Chous were widely venerated on Beowulf. It was probably one of the things Allison most disliked about *being* a Benton-Ramirez y Chou, he thought, because all a Benton-Ramirez y Chou had to do to be venerated on Beowulf was to breathe. Allison found that oppressive, irritating, and *unearned*, and he often wondered how she was going to cope with it once she left the university. But for the most part, she was absolutely right; the vast majority of Beowulfers she met were going to go out of their way to defer to her. Aside from the inevitable small number of deranged individuals to be found in any society, they certainly weren't going to *threaten* her in any way!

But not everyone in the galaxy was a Beowulfer, and there were better reasons than usual at the moment for her to exercise a little of that caution she hated so much. He had to admit that most of those reasons had to do with him, too, which gave his concern an edge of guilt.

"So who's the object of your curiosity, Alley?" he asked.

"He's from Sphinx," she said. "A great big tall fellow and a Navy officer. A lieutenant, I think, although I'm not sure. He's got one gold thingy on his collar, anyway." She tossed her head. "I get confused trying to figure out naval ranks even when they're *Beowulfan*, though. Why don't they use the same ones everyone else uses?"

"The Manties or the System Defense Force?" he asked with an amused smile.

"Either. Both!"

"Because navy pukes are senior to the rest of us and they don't have any intention of letting us forget it, mostly," he told her, sparring for time. He hadn't really expected her to ask him about Harrington, and he wasn't at all sure he wanted to encourage any interest in him she might be feeling. Not that he had anything against Harrington, of course. Quite the contrary, in fact. But he wasn't exactly invisible . . . or the safest person someone's sister—especially *his* sister—might be spending time with.

"Well, his name is Harrington," she said. "Since you made such a fuss about who I spend time with, and since he happens to be from off-world, I thought I'd ask you to . . . I don't know, check up on him, for me."

"And how much attention do you pay when I 'check up' on people for you?" he challenged, then grinned. "I told you that jackass Iliescue was going to piss you off, didn't I?"

"He's not as bad as you said he was," she replied. He only grinned at her some more, and she shrugged. "Okay, he's bad enough," she admitted. "He's just not as bad as *you* said he was."

"Oh, I see. Thank you for explaining that to me."

"You're welcome. And now, *are* you going to check out Lieutenant Harrington for me? Or should I just go ahead, walk up to him, and introduce myself? I'm perfectly willing to do just that, you understand."

"I'm sure you are." He considered her for another moment, and then it was his turn to shrug. "As a matter of fact, I already know quite a bit about him."

"You do?"

She was unfolding her napkin as she spoke, draping it across her lap, and she seemed to be paying the simple activity more attention than it really needed, he thought.

"Yes, I do. In fact, I made it a point to meet him when he landed, and I walked him through Customs to the university."

She looked up from her lap, her eyes suddenly intent, and he sighed. He knew that expression. He'd rather hoped she might decide he was hinting her away from Harrington, but clearly that wasn't going to happen. And the truth was that everything he knew about the Sphinxian was to the other man's credit, although he suspected Harrington didn't see it that way.

"Why?" she asked simply.

"Because Lieutenant Harrington is a very . . . interesting fellow," he replied. "Interesting to a fellow like me, I mean."

She pursed her lips slightly. Unlike quite a few other members of the family, she had a very clear notion of what Jacques' duties with the Biological Survey Corps had involved upon occasion. Even she knew only a part of it, of course, and he intended to keep it that way. But she knew enough to know that being interesting to a "fellow like him" could be a very bad thing.

"I don't know anything negative about him, Alley," he said quickly. "In fact, from everything I do know, he sounds like a very good man. But he's landed in the middle of some things that have . . . complications."

"What kind of 'complications'?"

"The kind I can't tell you about." He grimaced. "Not *won't* tell you about, Alley—*can't*. It's all very classified and hush-hush, and we don't know all the implications over at BSC yet."

"What *can* you tell me?" she asked, and his eyes narrowed.

He knew his sister well, better than he knew any other human being, and he recognized the edge of steel behind the question. What he didn't know was why he was hearing it. Obviously, her curiosity about Alfred Harrington was less casual than she'd tried to imply, yet there was a trace element of uncertainty in her, one he was unaccustomed to hearing or seeing. A part of him—a very *strong* part of him—was suddenly tempted to end this conversation now, immediately. There were currents here that he didn't want to get into, and the truth was that Harrington had made enemies of his own. Those enemies *probably* weren't foolish enough to try to do anything about their enmity, especially here on Beowulf, of all the planets in the galaxy, but there was no guarantee of that. And if his own activities were mixed into their calculations . . .

But this was his sister.

"He enlisted in the Manticoran Marines when he was eighteen," he said, his voice suddenly crisper than she was accustomed to hearing from him. "He did well. By the time he was twenty-three, he'd made platoon sergeant, and the Corps was considering offering him a commission. Then there was . . . an incident. It had nothing directly to do with the Marines. He found himself in a situation, a very *ugly* situation, that was none of his making. He did something about it. A lot of people died, he was badly wounded himself, and when the Manties found out about it, they gave him the Osterman Cross." He met her eyes across the table. "That's their second-highest award for valor, Alley, and it can only be earned in combat."

Their gazes held for a moment, then he shrugged.

"The Osterman Cross can also be awarded only to enlisted or noncommissioned personnel, and it's almost always accompanied by the offer of a commission. That offer is frequently turned down, and the Manties are smart enough to accept that without prejudice when it is. They know how important that kind of noncom is, and they're just *delighted* to hang onto one of them instead of insisting on 'up or out' the way the SLN does, but the offer is always made. And it was made in Lieutenant Harrington's case, but he had a rather unusual request. He asked for a transfer to the Navy and for medical school, as well." Jacques shrugged again. "That's not as strange as it might sound, since the Navy provides all of the Marines' medical support in the Star Kingdom, but it *was* unusual, especially for someone who'd obviously performed so well in a combat arm. Under the circumstances, and considering what he'd done, though, it was granted, and that's why he's here."

"What did he do to win the medal?" she asked quietly.

"That's part of what I can't tell you. It's classified, Alley. The Manties classified it when they gave him the citation."

She regarded him very levelly, thinking about what he'd said . . . and what he hadn't. He knew lots of things that were classified, sometimes when he wasn't supposed to, but she knew his sense of integrity. He'd probably already skirted perilously close to the limits of what he was allowed—what he would allow himself—to share with her. And as she thought about it, she felt herself remembering that darkness she'd sensed in Lieutenant Harrington and she shivered.

"Well," she said in a determinedly normal tone, "I can see that Franz was wrong—again—about whether or not Lieutenant Harrington deserved admission to ISU."

"I'd say that if anyone ever deserved a slot at the university, it was Harrington," Jacques agreed, then looked up as their appetizers arrived.

The waiter busied himself setting the salads and consommé before them and withdrew, and Allison picked up her fork, then glanced back up at her brother.

"Thank you," she said. "You've given me quite a bit to think about, Jacques."

※ ※ ※

"Here." Sojourner X handed the chip folio to Jacques Benton-Ramirez y Chou. "I hope this is going to help."

"Well, it probably can't hurt," Benton-Ramirez y Chou said, looking up at the towering, powerfully built ex-slave.

He'd pointed out to Sojourner once upon a time that the original Sojourner Truth had been a woman, not a man, but Sojourner didn't care. In fact, he'd already known, and he'd observed that "sojourner" was a genderless noun that worked equally well for a woman's name or a man's. Besides, he'd identified closely with the original inspiration of his name. That observation had sounded a bit strange coming from a hulking, craggy-faced, heavy-featured giant, but Benton-Ramirez y Chou had realized as soon as he thought it that that was an example of prejudice on his own part, based solely on outward appearances and stereotypes.

The realization had sent a spark of self-anger through him. If anyone on Beowulf should have been immunized against that sort of bias it was a member of his family. His direct ancestors had been instrumental in outlawing the weaponization of genetics—and opposing Leonard Detweiler's "superman" manipulation of the human genome—in the Beowulf Biosciences Code following the nightmare creations of Old Earth's Final War. They'd fought hard and successfully to get genetic weapons classified as weapons of mass destruction under the terms of the Eridani Edict, they'd spearheaded the effort to get the trade in genetically modified slaves outlawed (officially, at least) in the Solarian League, and they'd led the fight to draft the Cherwell Convention equating the slave trade with piracy . . . and imposing the same sentence for both. Beowulf had been solidly behind them in all of those fights, and Benton-Ramirez y Chou's birth planet was undoubtedly home to the largest population of liberated slaves anywhere in the galaxy. They repaid their new home world with the sort of patriotism which shamed many native-born Beowulfers (or ought to have), and many of his own Biological Survey Corps colleagues were either ex-slaves like Sojourner or the children of slaves. And yet, despite all of that, he'd fallen prey to an automatic, subconscious assumption that someone who looked as brutish as a Manpower heavy laborer model was probably of less than average intelligence. The truth was that Sojourner held the equivalent of two postdoctoral degrees, one in physics and one in chemistry, and lectured in both subjects at Warshawski University.

"It may not hurt, but it won't do any *good* if nobody acts on it," Sojourner pointed out now, his deep voice grim. "And it's got a limited shelf life, Jacques. Three more months, and the bastards will pull up stakes, shoot anybody not worth taking along through the head, and relocate."

"I know," Benton-Ramirez y Chou said more soberly. "I'll do my damnedest, Sojourner—you know that. But there are still a lot of official inquiries rattling around the League after that business on Haswell. Something about a dozen or so fine, upstanding Gendarmes who perished at the hands of 'assailants unknown' in the course of that raid on the slave depot that wasn't supposed to be there. Can't imagine why anyone would think *we'd* had anything to do with such a heinous act!"

His sorrowful tone was rather marred by his wolfish grin. But then the grin faded, and he twitched an unhappy shrug.

"Unfortunately, the truth is that anyone with two synapses to rub together has a pretty shrewd idea who was actually behind that one, Sojurner. And they probably have a pretty damned good idea where I—I mean, where *someone*—came up with the original intel. Given all that, it's going to be hard to convince even the Boss to okay the kind of strike we'd need here, assuming the data tells us what I think it will. And under the circumstances, he may have to go upstairs and get official approval from the Board of Directors. You know how long *that'll* take."

Sojourner scowled. On his face, the expression looked more than a little terrifying, and Benton-Ramirez y Chou sensed the genuine anger behind it. He knew that anger wasn't directed at him, but the waves of hatred radiating off the ex-slave made him feel as if he were leaning into a strong wind.

"Then maybe we need to call on someone more *un*official," the professor said harshly, and Benton-Ramirez y Chou inhaled.

"I can't be hearing this," he cautioned Sojourner. "Not yet, anyway," he added, and Sojourner's eyes narrowed.

Benton-Ramirez y Chou bit his tongue, cursing himself for adding the qualifier. If any of his superiors were forced to take official cognizance of the fact that he was talking to *anyone* with connections to the Audubon Ballroom, the consequences would be immediate and drastic. Many of them already knew he was, of course, but that wasn't the same as knowing it on the record, and the Ballroom was a very sore topic between Beowulf and the bureaucrats in Old Chicago who ran the Solarian League. He was pretty sure Giuseppe Adamson, the current Permanent Senior Undersecretary of the Interior, had at least circumstantial evidence that the BSC was not only in contact with the Ballroom, but had actively run operations with Ballroom assistance.

He might even have that sort of evidence about a planet named Haswell, and that could get decidedly dicey for the individuals involved in that particular op, one of whom had been then-Lieutenant Jacques Benton-Ramirez y Chou. The League took a dim view of League citizens who shot Solarian Gendarmes, even if the Gendarmes in question *had* been moonlighting as security goons in a Manpower slave depot on a planet where genetic slavery was officially illegal.

Well, you knew shit happens even before you signed up, he told himself. *And we* need *the . . . extra capabilities the Ballroom offers. If you hadn't thought it was worth the risk, you shouldn't have volunteered for the op. And don't pretend you didn't think it was entirely worthwhile afterward!*

Unfortunately, the Ballroom wasn't a neat, hierarchical organization. It was more of an umbrella, a collection of allied but independent chapters and groups, and it took people who could rely on the empowerment of hatred to pit themselves against the crushing power and enfluence of something like Manpower, Incorporated, and its corrupt corporate and political allies in the League. Even if the Ballroom's coordinating council had tried to rein in the more extreme members of their organization, there was no way it could have done it . . . and precious little evidence it wanted to. Given what most of the Ballroom's recruits had endured—or seen people they loved endure—it would have been foolish to expect them not to strike back as ferociously as they possibly could. Nor should it have surprised anyone that all too often for less embittered people's taste those reprisals took the form of the wholesale massacre of Manpower personnel and their business associates. Or that the Ballroom was none too fastidious about collateral damage when it struck at Manpower and its slavers. Many of the Ballroom's members and sympathizers, like Sojourner X himself, understood the downside of providing Manpower and its mouthpieces with atrocity fodder, but it would have required a direct act of God to actually stop it.

"I'll pass it along this afternoon," he assured his hulking friend, tapping the pocket into which he'd tucked the folio. "And I'll do everything I can to get them to move on it, but I'd be lying if I said I thought there was more than a fifty-fifty chance we'll be able to accomplish anything. If your three-month time estimate is right, we'd have less than six weeks to get the operation authorized, organized, and launched, and that'd be cutting it close even under more normal circumstances, much less this soon after Haswell. I'll try, Sojourner, but I won't promise what I don't know I can deliver."

Sojourner looked down at him for several moments, then nodded abruptly, once.

"The best you can do is the best you can do," he said. He laid one hand on the smaller man's shoulder and squeezed briefly. "I know you'll do everything you can, Jacques. Take care."

"And you," Benton-Ramirez y Chou said, and watched him walk away.

❊ ❊ ❊

"Why don't we just go ahead and shoot the little son-of-a-bitch?" Giuseppe Ardmore demanded.

He and Tobin Manischewitz sat at the desk in the cheap hotel room gazing down at the display of the computer on top of it. They could see Sojourner X ambling aimlessly away down the landscaped paths of Rosalind Franklin Park, but their attention was focused on the much smaller man he'd been speaking to. They knew where to find Sojourner again if they needed to, and he was less important than the man he'd met, anyway. As they watched, the object of their scrutiny seated himself on one of the benches, gazing out over the lake as if he had not a care in the universe.

"The bastard's caused us more headaches than any other three people I can think of," Ardmore continued, "and it's not like there's never any crime even here on oh-so-perfect Beowulf. Put a pulser dart through his brain, take his wallet and his chrono, leave them with a mugging by 'parties unknown,' and be done with it!"

"I can't say the notion isn't tempting," Manischewitz acknowledged, but he also shook his head sourly. "In fact, it'd tickle me pink, to be honest. Unfortunately, whatever we might be able to sell to the general public, BSC and the System Bureau of Investigation will know perfectly well what happened, whether they're ever able to prove it or not. That's why Upstairs seems to've decided he's just a little too prominent for us to get away with popping him right here on Beowulf. He may be only a pipsqueak captain in the BSC, but his family makes him a very *special* pipsqueak captain. If we knock off a Benton-Ramirez y Chou on Beowulf, hell wouldn't hold the Beowulfers' reaction. Hell, if he gets run down by a ground car crossing against the signal at least half of Beowulf will think we put a hit out on him!"

"So what?" Ardmore scowled. "They hate our guts anyway!"

"Look, nobody's going to scream too loud if we knock off one or two—even a dozen—other BSC officers. Oh, they'll be pissed, and we'll probably get whacked a time or two for it as soon as they get the chance, but for the most part, they'd put it down to the cost of doing business. The sort of thing that happens when they piss off someone like Manpower. But if we take down a Benton-Ramirez y Chou, especially here in Beowulf itself, that's a whole different game. That family *is* Beowulf, Giuseppe. I think our esteemed superiors are afraid a deliberate assassination directed against one of them is likely to provoke retaliation at a somewhat higher level, and none of them want to be the object of the lesson BSC and Beowulf in general might decide to deliver. Not unless there's one hell of a potential return involved, anyway! For that matter, I have to admit that killing him could have exactly the reverse of the effect we want. It could just as easily drive the Board of Directors into adopting the policy he's been pushing for and opening a direct connection to the Ballroom."

"Then why are we even bothering to watch him?" Ardmore waved a disgusted hand at the display, where Benton-Ramirez y Chou was leaning back on the bench with his legs crossed. "We didn't stop 'Sojourner' from passing along the info. We're not going to kill Benton-Ramirez y Chou. We're not going to kill 'Sojourner.' So just what the hell *are* we going to do? I mean, all due respect for Upstairs and everything," he didn't *sound* very respectful, Manischewitz observed, "but this is a colossal waste of time if we're not going to *do* anything!"

It was highly probable, Manischewitz reflected, that a lot of Ardmore's frustration stemmed from the fact that both of them knew things would not go well for them if they fell afoul of the Beowulfan authorities. Their cover as licensed employees of Black Mountain Security, one of Old Earth's biggest private security and investigative agencies, wouldn't stand any serious scrutiny, despite the fact that it was completely genuine. The Black Mountain executive who'd "hired" them to provide them with the credentials which did so much to facilitate their journeys about the Solarian League would disavow them in a heartbeat if Beowulf turned up a link between them and their real employers. And that was assuming their ostensible employer even knew they'd been grabbed. Beowulf had an almost fanatical respect for the individual rights of its citizens; it was rather less fastidious about the legal rights of *non*-citizens in the employ of Manpower, Incorporated.

"I don't know that we're 'not going to do anything,' Giuseppe," Manischewitz said after a moment. "Sure, Upstairs isn't crazy about escalating any potential retaliation to upper management, but I think someone's getting more worked up about our friend Benton-Ramirez y Chou for some reason, so maybe they are going to authorize a move against him. In fact, I'm starting to think there's a pretty fair chance of it, if it can be handled anonymously enough. Not even Beowulf's going to launch the overkill kind of response Upstairs is probably afraid of if they don't have pretty damned solid proof of who needs killing from their perspective. Just floundering around popping people in the executive suite in general could easily draw too much official attention from the League. I'm pretty sure Adamson and the rest of Interior's senior people are pissed off enough with Beowulf as it is. If they know Beowulf's going after the *right* targets after something like a Beton Ramirez y Chou hit, they'll probably just swallow it. The last thing they'd want is for Beowulf to dump proof of a Manpower op here on League territory in Beowulf. No telling what kind of other crap might make its way into the 'faxes if that happens. So, yeah, if they can come up with something Beowulf can't prove, they might just decide to let us take him down after all.

"Problem is, we don't really know a lot about his conduits, or how tied in he is to the Ballroom in general. I'm pretty damn sure 'Sojourner' isn't his *only* contact, though. And we don't know how far up he actually reaches in the system government or even the System Defense Force. We know Brigadier Tyson and Hamilton-Mitostakis think very highly of him, but not everyone in the SDF thinks all that highly of BSC's 'hotdogs,' and we don't know how Tyson's superiors regard him. We sure as hell don't know what kind of contacts he may have on the civilian side, either! I'd be ready to bet he's got quite a few of them, though, given his family connections. I don't think anyone's going to authorize just taking him out without being able to answer some of those questions. We need to know a lot more about what he's been up to and how to tie up loose ends before Upstairs'll risk the kind of retaliation killing him's likely to provoke, no matter how deniable they think they could make it."

"And how are we going to manage that?" Ardmore snorted. "We've had exactly zero luck getting any of our bugs inside BSC, and their security's even tighter on the Board of Directors' side. We were lucky we picked up in time to catch him and 'Sojourner' making the drop, but we could spend *years* trying to get a handle on everything he's 'up to' right this minute. And by the time we had it, he'd be years along in making even more trouble for us!"

"Maybe we could convince him to tell us about it himself," Manischewitz suggested softly.

"Lots of luck!" Ardmore snorted again, even harder. "I've tried to get info out of one of those Survey Corps bastards before. They're tough, they're better immunized against interrogation drugs than the frigging Solarian Navy, and every one of them has a suicide switch. Even if Upstairs let us grab him, and even if we could do it without that emergency beacon implanted in his shoulder bringing the local cops and the SBI—or the damned BSC—down on top of us, we'd never get anything out of him."

"You see?" Manischewitz' smile was not a pleasant thing to see. "That's why I'm in charge. You think in such direct, simple, brutal terms, Giuseppe. Assuming I can convince Upstairs to go along with us, I have a much more subtle idea in mind." His smile turned even colder. "One Captain Benton-Ramirez y Chou won't like one little bit."

❅ ❅ ❅

"Lord, that's a sick weapon," Alfred Harrington said, looking at the neural disruptor on the laboratory worktable. He felt a surge of remembered nausea, and he was actually a little surprised his hand didn't shake when he reached out to touch it.

"It is that," Penelope Mwo-chi agreed. She stood a couple of meters back from the table, arms folded in front of her, and her face was grim.

"I've never understood why anyone would develop the damned thing in the first place, Doctor," Alfred admitted. He turned it over and noted with a feeling of relief that there was no powerpack. "It's effective enough against unarmored opponents as a close-quarters weapon, but battle armor stops it dead, and over seventy-five or a hundred meters, it starts losing effectiveness fast even against unarmored targets. By the time you get to a hundred and fifty, you might as well be shining a flashlight at someone!"

"Agreed." Mwo-chi cocked her head. "That's right, you did say you'd seen what one of these did. Can I ask where?"

"I . . . can't say," Alfred replied. He looked up at her. "Sorry. I can't talk about it."

"I see." Mwo-chi considered him for a moment, and her nostrils flared. "I'll hazard a guess, though," she said. "I'll bet you it wasn't in the hands of any regular military force, was it?"

"No. No, it wasn't." Alfred frowned, and Mwo-chi chuckled harshly.

"Of course not, and not just because it's outlawed by the Deneb Accords, either. Like you just said, it's not very effective at any kind of range. At close range, sure. Anybody it doesn't kill outright will certainly be incapacitated and—what's that term you uniformed people use? 'Combat ineffective,' isn't it?"

"Yes." Alfred's voice was flat, and Mwo-chi shook her head quickly.

"That wasn't a slam at you, Alfred," she said almost gently. "Or at any of your people. But however lethal it may be at close range against unarmored opponents, it's a lot less . . . flexible than an old-fashioned chemical-powered assault rifle, far less a pulse rifle or a tribarrel."

"The crew-served version's got more range," Alfred said grimly. "I've seen one of them take somebody down at *three* hundred meters. But you're right—by the time you can get that kind of range out of it, you're talking about something half again the size of a heavy tribarrel that'll kill a battle-armored infantryman at ten times that range, with an energy signature a blind man couldn't miss. That's why I've never been able to figure out why anyone persevered with its development long enough to turn it into even a practical close-range weapon."

"That's because it wasn't originally developed as a weapon at all." Mwo-chi's voice was as grim as Alfred's had been. He looked back up from the neural disruptor in surprise, and she shook her head. "It was developed from something called a neural whip . . . on Mesa." Alfred's eyes narrowed, and she nodded. "By Manpower. I've got one of the damned things around here, and I'll show you my notes on its development history later, but basically they wanted an effective *discipline* tool, and they got one. After they'd realized how effective it was in that role, they started wondering how it would work as a ranged 'crowd control' weapon." She bared her teeth mirthlessly. "Give each slave a dose or two of the whip and then kill a couple of them in front of the others with the disruptor. Some forms of death are worse than others, and I imagine quite a few people who'd be willing to risk a pulser dart or a blade would think two or three times before challenging a neural disruptor. Especially if she knew it was going to be set on area effect and that everyone within ten or twelve meters of her would suffer the exact same thing she would."

Alfred's jaw tightened hard as pieces snapped into place. Clematis hovered in the back of his mind once more, ugly with smoke and screams . . . and understanding.

She's right, a tiny voice told him. *She's exactly right about how people would react. If I'd known*, guessed, *they'd had those damned things waiting for us, I'd never have—*

He cut the thought off ruthlessly. It was hard, but he managed, and drew a deep breath, swelling his lungs with oxygen. And if this abomination was, indeed, a product of Manpower and its genetic slavers, finding them on Clematis made perfect sense.

"Can I ask why you have this thing sitting here, Doctor?" he said, tapping the disruptor with a forefinger.

"For the same reason I've got that whip locked up in a safe—to remind myself what I hate, Alfred." She stepped closer, never unfolding her arms, and looked down at it. "Mesa's like Beowulf's dark twin. It's almost as if they're determined to deliberately turn themselves into our polar opposite in every way they can. And the hell of it is that we find ourselves doing exactly the same thing where *they're* concerned. I'm as guilty of that as the next woman, I suppose, but deep inside, I know it was a Mesan neurologist who came up with this thing. I can actually recognize the neural stimulator they took as the core of it, and that came from Beowulf, too. That's why I've been quietly looking for ways to reverse or repair the damage it does for so long, and I keep this here to remind me of what it is I hate." She lifted her eyes, meeting Alfred's gaze. "So don't think I don't understand whatever it is you can't talk about. And I guess I might as well admit I've been looking for an assistant crazy enough to join my efforts for a long time. Welcome aboard, Crazy Al."

❀ ❀ ❀

Allison Chou sat in the environment-controlled gazebo on the ISU quadrangle with her eyes theoretically focused on her computer display. Practice was somewhat different from theory, however. In point of fact, her eyes weren't focused on anything at all and her mind was someplace else entirely.

Three weeks had passed since she'd lunched with her brother, and she was no closer to deciding what to do than she'd been when she finished the dessert course. That wasn't like her. She wasn't actually the scatter-brained, reckless, impulsive person her parents had occasionally accused her of being, but it was true that she seldom hesitated or spent a lot of time second guessing herself. She trusted her instincts, and while she might be wrong upon occasion, she was practically never uncertain.

This time, she most certainly was.

A flash of space-black and gold flickered at the corner of her unfocused vision. She looked up quickly, and her lips tightened. She'd had more than a few liaisons, and at least two genuinely passionate relationships, but she'd never felt anything like what she felt as she watched Lieutenant Harrington's tall, athletic figure striding across the quadrangle. He moved so smoothly, so confidently, and her nostrils flared as if she could scent some elusive fragrance. But it wasn't anything she could *smell*; it was what she'd *felt*, and for the first time in her fearless life she was truly afraid of another human being.

No, be fair, she told herself. *You're not afraid of him; you're afraid of what you're* feeling, *because you don't understand it.*

And that was nothing but the truth.

She'd never felt so strongly drawn to a man, or to any other person. Even now, with him at least sixty meters away and not even looking in her direction, she felt that same, soft, warm *purring* sensation deep inside. It wasn't simply sexual attraction, although it was simultaneously one of the most erotic things she'd ever felt, and it wasn't appreciation of masculine beauty or awe of his brilliant intellect. He wasn't all that handsome, and while for all she knew he might well *be* brilliant, she'd scarcely even spoken to him, so he certainly hadn't had much of an opportunity to impress her with his intellectual accomplishments! It was just . . . *nice*, although that was a ridiculously anemic word for what she was feeling. It was as if she'd found something she hadn't realized she'd lost, encountered an old friend she'd never known she knew. As if she'd finally discovered what she needed to *complete* herself. The sheer intensity of it, for all its warmth and gentleness, would have been almost enough to frighten her all by itself. She would have wondered how much of that she was imagining, how much she was making up out of whole cloth, and how long anything so ephemeral, so impossible for her to define even to herself, could possibly endure.

But it wasn't alone, and that was what truly frightened her. There was that darkness, that sense of pain, like a promise of anguish—or anger—hidden just beyond the horizon. It was like a brooding shadow looming over everything else, and she didn't know what it was or where it had come from or what it might mean. Was it something coming from him, something inside him, hidden under everything else like poison at the heart of some delectable confection? Or was it something inside *her*, something she'd never realized was there which roused itself when he was near? Or some sort of premonition, some subliminal warning she was sending to herself on the basis of clues her conscious mind hadn't grasped yet? Or was it even real at all? Something she was simply imagining, just as she was imagining all the rest of it? And what right did a young man whom she didn't even know, someone from an entirely different star nation, have turning her calm, orderly life topsy-turvy without even so much as looking in her direction?

She sighed, shook herself, and made herself focus once again on the display. She was behind on her assigned reading, and Doctor McLeish wasn't going to take "I was mooning over a young man I don't even know" as an excuse.

※ ※ ※

Alfred Harrington never even glanced in the gazebo's direction, but he knew she was there. He always knew where she was—or in what direction, anyway—and that worried him. It worried him a lot.

He continued on his way, never breaking stride, never hesitating, never indicating any awareness of her presence at all, yet it was as if he could feel her inside his own skin with him. The strength of the attraction was astounding, and it frightened him, because he couldn't explain it.

Or is it really because you think you've actually seen something like it before?

Nonsense! He snorted dismissively, but the thought wouldn't quite go away, however hard he tried to banish it, for he'd grown up on Sphinx, and he was a Harrington.

Maybe you're a Harrington, boy-oh, but you're no frigging treecat! And neither is she. And you've got no business at all thinking this way about a woman you don't even know!

All of which was perfectly true . . . and didn't do one damned thing about his problem.

He reached his dormitory, rode the grav shaft to his floor, let himself into his apartment, and crossed to the balcony. He picked up the compact electronic binoculars and looked through them, and his mouth tightened as he saw her sitting in the gazebo, still studying her computer display.

He set the binoculars down, feeling as if he'd become some sort of Peeping Tom or voyeur, and dropped into a chair. He leaned forward, bracing his elbows on his knees, and scrubbed his face with both hands before he straightened up and inhaled deeply.

This was ridiculous. Unfortunately, being ridiculous didn't seem to be keeping it from happening, and he had no damned idea what to do about it. He'd been strongly attracted to a few women in his time, but never like this. Never with the sense that he was looking at the person who was meant to be his other half. The person without whom he could never quite be whole. It was like some incredibly sappy, turgidly written, really *bad* romance novel—the sort his sister Clarissa had loved to read when she was thirteen. "His *other half*"? Where did he get off feeling something like that about someone he'd spoken to exactly once in his life? He didn't believe in "love at first sight," and he never had, and—he told himself firmly—he didn't *now*, either. Whatever this was, it wasn't that . . . even if he had no damned idea in the world what it *was*.

Don't be so sure of that, the small voice he was doing his best not to listen to said. *You've always had those "hunches" of yours, haven't you? You've always been so smug about your ability to "read" other people. Used it to win quite a few poker games over the years, too, haven't you? And your family's been hanging around with 'cats for over three T-centuries, hasn't it? What if there's a reason so many*

Harringtons have been adopted over the years? What if there's something "different" about you?

Nonsense. So he was good at picking up hints from body language, and reading the subliminal clues everybody gave out! And maybe he had usually known when somebody in his unit was in trouble, needed a friendly ear—or an arse-chewing—to get him back on track. That didn't mean he had some kind of "extrasensory perception," and even if *he* did, *she* wasn't a Harrington, or a Sphinxian, or even a Manticoran!

And that, he finally admitted to himself, was a huge part of the problem.

He sighed and rubbed his face again, his expression grim. If he *was* . . . different, if it turned out he did have some . . . special ability, what right could he possibly have to use it on someone else? Did she feel anything at all for him? She certainly hadn't shown it, if she did. But *if* she did, was it because of something he'd done—done *to* her? He didn't feel like an evil wizard going around casting spells on people. He didn't *want* to be, either, and even if she did feel something about him, he wanted her to feel that about *him*, not about some mysterious aura he might be emanating!

He smiled crookedly as he realized just how twisted and convoluted that last thought had been, yet that made none of it untrue or irrelevant. And the smile disappeared quickly as he thought about the other side of it.

He was damaged goods. He wasn't the person he'd always thought he was, and sometimes it felt as if the veneer concealing the monster within from the rest of the world was growing thinner and more transparent. Clematis had shown *him* the monster, though. That was why he'd run away from the Corps, away from the sweet seduction of the killing.

He looked down at his hands as if they belonged to a stranger, and the remembered hot, intoxicating taste of blood pulsed through him again. It was a sickness, an infection, and he was afraid of it. More afraid than he'd ever been of anything in his life. A man with that monster hidden at his heart had no business getting close to others, for he was unclean . . . and he was dangerous.

He inhaled again, then climbed out of the chair and headed for his kitchen. At least someone with his metabolism could seek the solace of food without falling prey to terminal obesity.

⚜ ⚜ ⚜

"Well?" Giuseppe Ardmore demanded, and Tobin Manischewitz shook his head.

"You're not a schoolgirl, and this isn't your first party, Giuseppe," he said severely, but Ardmore only snorted.

"Maybe not, but that doesn't mean I'm not looking forward to it. If it's been okayed, at least."

Manischewitz shook his head again. That last sentence had been an afterthought, and not a terribly sincere one. Not that either he or Ardmore would have dreamed of moving without authorization; their employers had a nasty way of making examples out of people who did that.

And you are *the one who came up with the idea, so it's sort of hypocritical to hold Giuseppe's . . . enthusiasm against him. So why does it bother you so much*?

"Why is this so personal with you?" he asked out loud.

"Who said it was personal?" Ardmore shot back.

"The fact that you're so busy looking forward to it," Manischewitz replied, realizing in that moment exactly why the other's enthusiasm worried him so. "I don't much care for the entire Benton-Ramirez y Chou clan myself, but you're acting like you've got a New Texas mosquito trapped in your vac helmet. If we screw this one up—if we give the Beowulfers even a hint of a chance of IDing us before we dump the body and get off-world again—we're going to be so damned dead a DNA sniffer couldn't find us, and I don't like it when somebody on an op this risky gets his head too far up his arse because he's looking for personal payback. So what is it with you and this guy?"

"I don't like him, all right?" Ardmore said after a moment. "He and his family have been busting our chops for centuries now, and I don't like it. I don't like that smug, superior attitude of his—like he's so much smarter and better than any of the rest of us—either. He's being a pain in our arse, and he's gonna be a bigger one if we don't do something about it, and I'm not going to pretend it won't be especially satisfying to squash any Benton-Ramirez y Chou—and especially *this* one—like a bug."

"No, it's more than that." Manischewitz settled into one of the apartment's chairs, his eyes hard. "You've got a personal reason to want this particular guy's balls, and I want to know what it is. *Now*, Giuseppe."

Ardmore glared at him, but Manischewitz only leaned back, waiting. He didn't object to a little personal motivation if it could help get the job done, but too *much* motivation—or motivation that was *too* personal—was a good way to screw the pooch. And any unfortunate little failures here on Beowulf were likely to have fatal consequences for the people involved in them.

"All right," Ardmore said finally, with a scowl. "Three years ago, in New Denver, I had a little . . . run, in with the frigging BSC."

"In *New Denver*?" Manischewitz' eyes narrowed. "*The* New Denver? On Old Earth?"

"No, the one in Andromeda! Of *course* the one on Old Earth!"

"What the hell were you doing on Old Earth?!"

Manischewitz was shaken. He and Ardmore had worked together on several occasions over the last ten or fifteen T-years before they'd been more or less permanently teamed a couple of years earlier, but never in the Sol System. For that matter, their employers normally went far, far out of their way to avoid staging the sort of operations he got handed on the mother world. Genetic slavery thrived in the underbelly of the League, hidden in the sewers of corruption that most soft, protected Core Worlders never saw or knew about, and Manpower took pains to avoid anything that might cause it to intrude into the light where they *might* see it.

"If Upstairs had wanted you to know about it, they probably would've *told* you about it, don't you think?" Ardmore shot back. Then he shook his head. "Look, you want to know why it's personal with Benton-Ramirez y Chou? I'll tell you! We were in New Denver to take out Fairmont-Solbakken."

"You were going to assassinate *Aurèle* Fairmont-Solbakken?" Manischewitz demanded. This just kept getting worse and worse! Aurèle Fairmont-Solbakken was the senior member of the Beowulf delegation to the Solarian League's Assembly.

"Of course," Ardmore said impatiently. "The Beowulfers had just gotten the bureaucrats to sign off on permanently stationing a Frontier Fleet detachment in Lytton, and somebody Upstairs was pissed off as hell about it."

Manischewitz had to think for a moment before he could place the

Lytton System, then he remembered. It was a small, dirt-poor, nominally independent star system within a few light years of the Sasebo System . . . one terminus of the Erewhon Junction. Had—?

"Are you saying they were trying to set up a base in Lytton?"

"Of course they were!" Ardmore snorted. "The Erewhonese are skittish as hell where anything about the slave trade's concerned. Probably has something to do with being stuck off in a corner close to the Havenites and the Manties. Hell, for all I know they've got 'principles'! All I know is that Upstairs figured that a quiet little cargo transfer point in Lytton would let them take advantage of the Erewhonese Junction without having any . . . product on board when they went through Erewhonese Customs. They could head out through hyper, drop off a cargo at some out-of-the-way spot like Silesia, head home by way of the Manticore Junction clean as a whistle, come through from Erewhon, pick up a fresh cargo at Lytton, and deliver it to a whole sector's worth of customers far enough out from the Core that nobody was going to ask any questions. Then turn around and head back the other way, rinse and repeat. Hell, they could even pick up extra change shipping *legal* cargo over the Erewhon-Manticore leg! Until the Beowulfers shoved their oar in, anyway. And apparently Fairmont-Solbakken leaned on the permanent undersecretaries pretty damned hard. I always figured there was a little blackmail involved in the horsetrading, but I could've been wrong about that. What I know for certain, though, is that the Navy put a destroyer detachment in Lytton and kept it there. So Upstairs decided to 'send a message' to Beowulf, and my team and I were supposed to deliver it."

"Obviously it didn't get delivered after all," Manischewitz observed.

"No, not so you'd notice," Ardmore agreed in a hard voice. "Matter of fact, it didn't go so well for my team. There were eleven of us, including my partner Gerlach and me; I'm the only one who got out alive. Somehow, the Beowulfers figured out what was coming and they dropped a BSC special-ops team on us right in the middle of New Denver. I was out on surveillance when they hit; when I came back, it was like the rest of them had never existed. I don't know whether all of them were killed before their forensics people tidied up or if some of them got hauled back to a safe house somewhere on Old Earth and pumped dry first. I just know they were all *gone*, and that that little bastard Benton-Ramirez y Chou, who'd 'just happened' to be vacationing in New Denver when Fairmont-Solbakken arrived, was nowhere to be found after. So, yeah, it's kind of personal for me, Tobin. You got a problem with that?"

"I've got no problem at all, as long as you remember that I'm the senior guy on *this* team and you don't let the personal part of it get in the way of getting the job done. And as long as you remember that the whole object here is to *not* kill him. Yet, at least."

"Oh, yeah, I'll remember that." Ardmore's smile was ugly. "Because, you know what? I don't think it's gonna work. I think he's gonna try to get cute, instead, and when he does, both of them get dead. And that'll suit me just *fine*, Tobin. Just *fine*."

❦ ❦ ❦

Allison Chou breathed deeply and steadily, the soles of her running shoes crunching crisply on the gravel as she headed for the final bend in the trail before she headed back. She loved Rosalind Franklin Park, and especially its jogging trails. The park had been laid out the better part of two thousand T-years ago, and the great-great-grandchildren of the original Old Earth oaks, which had been planted by the long-dead landscapers, were as much as two meters in diameter now, spreading their massive branches to cover the trails in deep, green shade. It was almost like running at the bottom of one of the parks' koi ponds, and the bursts of sunlight when she passed through a break in the foliage were as brilliant as they were dazzling. And on top of all of its other attractions, the Watson and Crick Boulevard entrance was less than two blocks from her off-campus apartment. It was her favorite place to run, and running was one of her favorite occupations when she had hard things to think about.

Face it, she told herself severely, *you're going to have to deal with this. It's probably just a loose screw rattling around inside your skull. You always did have a vivid imagination, you know! God only knows what's caused you to fixate on this this way, but the only way you're ever going to put it to rest is to talk to him. Spend a little time actually with him instead of just sitting around wondering about him. You don't have to walk up to him with bedroom eyes, hit him over the head with a club and drag him off. You just need to . . . explore this, figure out what the hell is going on, and then either act on it or forget about it.*

She shook her head and rolled her eyes. Sure. That was all she had to do. It made perfect sense—or as much sense as anything *could* make, under the circumstances. The only problems were that she'd never heard of circumstances like these, they weren't getting better, and they didn't scare her any less.

She stopped rolling her eyes and closed them briefly, then opened them again. It was still there. It was fainter, but she was certain she could still have raised her hand and pointed unerringly in Alfred Harrington's direction. And the fact that it was fainter actually worried her more, because Rosalind Franklin Park lay on the far side of her apartment from campus. Which meant—if she wasn't simply losing her mind and imagining the entire thing—that whatever it was she felt was distance-sensitive. The closer she got to campus, the stronger that sense of direction became, like a stray chunk of asteroid rock drifting into a planetary gravity well.

Oh, there's a marvelous *simile!* she told herself. *Sums it up in a nutshell, doesn't it? Sure, that dark thing you feel scares you, but the* real *scare factor is that you may not be in charge of your own feelings anymore. It's like something is sucking you in, against your will, making you think about a total stranger this way. That's not just evidence you may be unhinged; it suggests some kind of . . . emotional dependency.*

She reached the final bend in the trail and started back, trying not to grimace as that sense of someone else's presence changed bearing like some kind of homing beacon. Enough was enough, she decided. When she finished this morning's run, it was time to shower, change, head over to campus and invite Lieutenant Harrington to share a cup of tea with her. At least she'd have the chance to sit down across the table from him and find out whether or not she'd been imagining all of this.

And what do you do if it turns out you haven't *been?* she asked herself, but herself offered no answer to the question.

❆ ❆ ❆

Alfred Harrington leaned back in the recliner on his apartment balcony, heels propped somewhat inelegantly on the balcony railing, a glass of Alessandra Farms 1819 on the table at his elbow. The *gewürztraminer*-style wine had been a pleasant surprise (for everything except his credit account) when he discovered it. It went well with the spicy Beowulfan smoked sausage and the wedge of sharp cheddar on the plate beside the glass, and Alessandra aged it in barrels of native Beowulfan red-spine oak, lightly charred on the inside to give it a pleasing smokiness to underscore the hint of peach and lychee.

His eyes—and most of his attention—were on the reader in his lap as he ran through his notes from his last lab session with Dr. Mwo-chi. A tiny corner of his awareness was somewhere else, of course. It was tracking that other presence like a compass needle, invariably pointing to wherever it was. He was doing his best to ignore it, however, and this time he was actually succeeding, after a fashion at least. It helped that Dr. Mwo-chi was still very much in the process of bringing him up to speed on her existing research, and the more familiar with her work he became, the more impressed he was. Not that anything she'd come up with yet offered the solution both of them were seeking, but deep inside he knew it was unlikely they ever *would* find "the solution" to the catastrophic damage neural disruptors wreaked on their victims. Maybe the best answer anyone would ever come up with would be to further improve synthetic nerves, but surely there had to be some way to convince the human body to regenerate just the destroyed nervous tissue?

Sure *there is, Alfred.* He reached for his wine glass again. *There must be, since you want there to be one so badly, right?*

The problem was that while modern medicine could regrow whole limbs for people—aside from that unfortunate but large minority of the human race for whom regeneration simply didn't work—it couldn't regenerate just specific parts of the limb in question. There was no switch to grow "only" nervous tissue or muscle tissue or bone; it was an all-or-nothing process. That was why an otherwise sound leg whose nerves had been reduced to mush by a neural disruptor, for example, had to be amputated above the highest point of neural damage and regenerated from scratch, as it were. That was clearly the best solution for a problem like that, but what did a doctor do when it was the spinal cord which had been disrupted? Nerve transplants were the obvious solution, and they'd been used effectively for less-critical portions of the nervous system. Even with the best surgical technique, though, there was always some loss of function, and what could be tolerated in an arm or a leg could not be tolerated in the spinal cord. Synthetics were another approach, and one that recommended itself for limb damage in those who couldn't regenerate at all, but they, too, were a far from satisfactory substitute for the original nerve, and all of the problems with peripheral portions of the system became much more pronounced dealing with the spinal cord.

And worst of all, a weapons-grade neural disruptor was not a finely focused weapon. It attacked nervous tissue over a wide area. Indeed, its effect actually ran *along* its victim's nervous system, which meant a hit on a leg could damage the spinal cord—often severely, even without totally disrupting it—as high as the thoracic cord's T10 nerve. A trunk hit higher than the hip was almost invariably fatal, and even hits which didn't kill could inflict massive brain injury.

If it only left us something to work with! But it's deliberately designed to go after the axons and rip them out by the root. There's nothing left to regenerate, whether spontaneously or under regen therapy. But there has to be a way to—

His reader went flying over the balcony rail, his wine glass shattered as it hit the floor, and Alfred Harrington catapulted up out of his chair. For a split second he stood staring out across the campus. Then he wheeled away from the balcony, charging across his apartment, pausing only to open the thumbprinted personal safe in his closet, scoop out its contents, and grab a light windbreaker.

Three seconds later, two of his neighbors found themselves unceremoniously bowled off their feet as two meters of Sphinxian muscle and gristle bulldozed their way into the grav shaft.

❀ ❀ ❀

Allison climbed off her old-fashioned, muscle-powered bicycle. She really didn't need the exercise after her morning's run, but it was her favored mode of transportation around her neighborhood, and it was always easier to fold the bike and rack it than to bother with an air car or a taxi. Besides, early spring was the very best season in Grendel, and she intended to enjoy it while it lasted.

She entered the unlock code, then hit the button to fold the bike's ultra-lightweight memory composites into a handy, briefcase-sized package. It began collapsing in on itself obediently, and she checked her chrono. She'd felt more than a little odd checking Lieutenant Harrington's schedule like some sort of creepy stalker, but she'd done it. And according to the file she'd convinced the registrar's computers to access for her, he didn't have any classes until fourteen hundred. That meant he should be free, and she didn't have to check where he was. She could feel his direction just fine—always assuming she truly hadn't lost her mind, of course—and according to her internal tracking device, he was almost certainly in his apartment. The number of which, she—like the creepy stalker she was certain she wasn't—had also obtained from the registrar.

You do have his com combination, too, you know, she reminded herself. *You could just* screen *him like a normal human being instead of turning up on his doorstep like a creepy stalker.* She grimaced as the last two words made their way through her mind yet again, but that description of her behavior was suggesting itself to her with increasing frequency of late. Especially when the dreams she'd been having started getting more and more explicit. *Of course, how would you go about beginning the screen conversation with him? "Hello, Lieutenant Harrington. I don't want you to feel nervous or anything, but I've been obsessing over you for the last few weeks, and I think you're really hot. I'm not a stalker or anything! Honest! But I really want to jump your bones, so— Hello?" That's funny. Wonder where he went?*

She snorted, amused despite herself, but this was a conversation she had to have face-to-face, if only to be sure that—

An agonizing, immaterial fist slammed into her from behind. Her eyes flared wide, but that was all she could do. The stun gun knocked out all other muscular control, and she went down, unable to catch herself in any way before she hit the pavement with shocking force. Pain exploded through her, and she tasted blood as her lower lip split.

Panic came on the heels of the pain, and then hands were rolling her gently over.

"Is she all right?" she heard someone ask. "That looked like a really nasty fall!"

"It was," another voice responded in tones of deep concern. She'd never heard it before in her life, but it belonged to the hands which had rolled her onto her back. She tried to focus, but even her eye muscles seemed to be ignoring her and everything was a misty blur. The second voice's hands pressed a tissue to her bleeding lip.

"I think she's had some sort of a seizure," the voice said, "but I've already screened for an—Ah! There it is now!"

Something grounded beside her in a soft whine of counter-grav, and then there were more hands. They picked her up, laid her on something. She felt straps being fastened across her inert body. Then she was moving again, sliding into some kind of vehicle. Doors closed, shutting off the outer world, and yet another voice spoke.

"Put her the rest of the way out," it said, and panic was an icy dagger in her throat as something pricked her arm and the world slid away.

❧ ❧ ❧

Alfred Harrington skidded to a stop at the university's Edgar Anderson Avenue gate. He looked around frantically, but he already knew she wasn't there. She was somewhere else, moving steadily away from him, and an almost paralyzing wave of terror flooded through him.

"Did you just see a young woman?" he demanded, reaching out and physically grabbing a Beowulfer of about his own age. "Right here—just a minute ago!"

"Hey! What do you think you're—!" the other man began, then gasped in pain as Alfred shook him. Gently, all things considered, but more than hard enough to leave bruises.

"Did—you—*see*—her?" Alfred grated.

"Yeah. Yeah, I did!" the Beowulfer said, looking at him the way any normal person would have regarded in obvious maniac. "Hey, ease up! What's your problem?"

"Where did she go?" Alfred snapped.

"*I* don't know! If she's the one you're looking for, she had some kind of turn or seizure or something. Fell right there." The Beowulfer waved at the sidewalk. "But some guy was already helping her by the time I realized she'd fallen. Already called an ambulance and everything."

"Ambulance?" A fresh and different fear stabbed at him as he thought of all the things that could have caused an apparently healthy young woman to collapse, yet somehow he knew that wasn't what had happened. He didn't know *how* he knew, but he knew. "What kind of ambulance? University Hospital, EMC, or from one of the other hospitals?"

"I don't know!" His unhappy informant said yet again. "Just an *ambulance*, man! White paint job, blue flashing light, siren—you know!"

"Which way did it go?"

"It went *up!* That's what counter-grav does. I didn't *worry* about which way it was headed, okay?"

Alfred suppressed a sudden desire to rip the other man's head off. Instead, he released him and began punching up a city map on his uni-link.

Ignaz Semmelweis University Hospital's ambulances wore the blue and white colors of the school. Most of the other hospitals—and God knew there were enough of them in Grendel—also painted their emergency vehicles in distinctive color combinations. Plain white was Grendel City Emergency Medical Services, but that couldn't be right either. Grendel EMC always transported to the *nearest* hospital unless they needed the services of a full-up trauma center . . . and ISU Hospital *was* a trauma center. In fact, it was Grendel's *primary* trauma center. So if she'd had some kind of seizure and they'd transported her to a hospital, then he ought to be sensing her presence *behind* him, not in front of him and moving steadily farther away.

"You're crazy, you know that, man?!" the Beowulfer he'd manhandled said, once he was safely out of arm's reach. Alfred was vaguely aware that the other man was glaring at him, but he had no time to worry about that. For that matter, it was entirely possible the Beowulfer was right. It *was* crazy to be so certain she was in trouble—and that he knew the direction in which to look for her—when there was absolutely no evidence to prove that she was.

His uni-link showed him the map he'd been looking for and he scrolled quickly across it. There wasn't a single hospital on a direct line towards her receding presence. Assuming he was really sensing her presence, of course.

He punched in the campus hospital's com combination and waited as patiently as he could for an answer.

"Campus Medical Admissions," the man on the tiny display said to him. "How may I help you?"

"Have you had an admission in the last five minutes?" Alfred asked as calmly as he could. "A young woman. She collapsed at the Edgar Anderson gate."

"A young woman?" The man on the display looked down, eyes moving as if he were reading something. Then he looked back up and shook his head. "We haven't had *any* emergency admissions in the last ten minutes."

"None at all?" Alfred pressed, and the other man shook his head. Alfred's jaw clenched, and he cut the connection.

What the *hell* did he do now? In his own mind—such as it was and what remained of it—he was certain she'd been abducted, but he had exactly zero evidence to prove it . . . and even less of a motive to *explain* it. He'd sound like a lunatic claiming that he'd "felt" a complete stranger being kidnapped on a public sidewalk in Grendel on a busy weekday morning. "And why would someone have kidnapped the young lady, sir?" He could almost hear the question, see the sharpening interest in the official eyes as someone wondered if the oversized foreigner had burned out a circuit or two. Probably better to invite him down to the precinct office while they got to the bottom of it. And while they were doing that . . . .

He drew a deep breath, nostrils flaring, and used his uni-link to screen for a cab.

⚜ ⚜ ⚜

Jacques Benton-Ramirez y Chou growled a modestly foul obscenity as his com chimed. He'd just climbed into the shower after an all-night training exercise, and he was tempted to just let it ring. But it was Allison's call tone, and he decided that he owed his twin sister an answer, at least. Of course, if she wanted anything *more* than that, she was just going to have to wait.

The water turned off automatically as he opened the stall door, and he grabbed a towel and knotted it around his waist. His family wasn't big on nudity taboos, but Allison might be calling him from a public place and there were proprieties to observe. Of course, he could have simply accepted the call audio-only, but he wasn't averse to letting his sister see him dripping wet. If she was going to haul him out of the shower, he could at least try to make her feel a little guilty about having done it.

He reached the bedside com and pressed the acceptance key, then frowned slightly. He'd accepted the call without limiting it, but it came up audio-only from her end, anyway. And the privacy mode was engaged; only someone whose com possessed the encryption key could have made any sense at all out of anything which might be said.

"What can I do for you, Alley?"

"You can listen very carefully."

The voice from the blank com display was computer synthesized .
. . and badly. It was the sort of synthesis any listener was supposed to
realize instantly wasn't an actual human being, and Jacques Benton-
Ramirez y Chou's heart seemed to stop beating.

"Who is this?" he asked.

No stranger listening to him would have believed the intensity of
the fear coursing through him, but the members of his team would
have recognized that soft, relaxed note and been reaching for their
weapons before he was done speaking.

"I'm not anyone you'd better piss off if you ever want to see the lady
this com's registered to again," the synthesized voice replied. "The fact
that I have it should suggest to you that I also have its owner."

Benton-Ramirez y Chou stood very still, his face expressionless,
knowing the person at the other end of the link could see him whether
or not he could see the man—or woman—behind that voice.

"I'm listening," he said.

"Some people are very unhappy with you, Captain Benton-
Ramirez y Chou. They don't like you, and they don't like your family,
and they'd really, really like to *hurt* your family, because they figure
you wouldn't like *that* any more than they like *you*. But they're willing
to be reasonable. All you have to do is give them what they want and
you'll probably get your sister back without any *serious* damage. Of
course, I could be wrong about that. But even if I'm wrong about that,
I can guarantee you won't like what finally ends up dumped on a
corner somewhere—or possibly *several* corners, in bits and pieces—if
you *don't* give them what they want."

An icicle ran down Benton-Ramirez y Chou's spine. If there was
one thing he knew, it was that whoever had Allison would never return
her alive, whatever he did. They might keep her alive as long as he did
whatever it was they wanted him to do, but when the time came—
when they had everything they wanted, or when there was nothing
left for him to give them or do for them—they *would* kill her. The
penalty for kidnapping on Beowulf was the same as the penalty for
first-degree murder, and that didn't even consider his connections to
the BSC and the SBI. They would kill her to dispose of any witnesses,
and they would kill her because they knew how badly it would hurt
him and his family.

Of course, he'd probably already be dead by then, as well, he thought harshly, because they couldn't afford to leave *him* as a witness, either. That wouldn't affect the thinking of whoever was hiding behind that voice, though.

"What is it you want?" he asked.

"I think of this in the nature of a first date," the voice replied. "We'll start with something small, just to see whether or not you understand how to follow instructions. I want a roster of the Biological Survey Corps personnel operating out of your embassies and consulates in the systems of Posnan, Breslau, Sachsen, Saginaw, Hillman, Terrance, Tumult, and Carlton."

Benton-Ramirez y Chou felt his teeth grind together. That list represented every sector capital in the Silesian Confederacy, which was steadily becoming a hotbed of genetic slavery transfers and sales points despite everything the Royal Manticoran Navy and the Imperial Andermani Navy could do about it. It was a region to which the BSC had been paying special attention for the last few T-years, because the situation was going to get nothing but worse. At least some Manties were beginning to realize what the People's Republic of Haven's military buildup was really all about, and it was inevitable that tensions between the Star Kingdom and the PRH were going to worsen. They were already pretty damned bad, given how enthusiastically Manticore had greeted Havenite emigres (and especially professionals fleeing the provisions of Haven's Technical Conservation Act). They'd grown steadily worse in the sixty-four T-years since the TCA was enacted, but when the SKM in general realized the "alarmists" were right—that the People's Navy's buildup wasn't just a "public works" job program, whatever the Legislaturalists had to say about it—the Manties would have no choice but to begin recalling more and more of their naval units in the face of that threat, and when that happened . . .

"What makes you think I have the reach to get you that kind of information?"

"Oh, come now, Captain! We all know what an ingenious sort you are. You have all sorts of contacts, and I'm sure a skilled BSC officer such as yourself is well-versed in all the ways to break into theoretically secure databases."

"That kind of information's not going to be in any one database I can reach." Benton-Ramirez y Chou shook his head. "I might be able to get to some of it, but not all of it. Not without tripping security fences right and left, anyway."

"Then you have a problem, Captain. Or perhaps I should say your *sister* has a problem."

"How do I even know she's still alive?" Benton-Ramirez y Chou asked harshly.

"You have a point. Just a moment."

Perhaps forty-five seconds passed. Then—

"Jacques?" It was Allison's voice, shaky and trying to hide its fear. "Are you there, Jacques?"

"I'm here, Alley!"

"They told me to tell you there's a reason you should listen to them," his sister said. "They—"

Her voice broke off in a high, shrill shriek that went on and on. It couldn't possibly have lasted as long as it seemed to, and then it ended with knifelike suddenness.

"Pity," the synthesized voice said as Jacques Benton-Ramirez y Chou stared at the blank com, his rigid face pale. "Passed out sooner than I expected her to. Oh well, there's always tomorrow, isn't there, Captain? I think you'd better go ahead and get me that information, don't you? I'm sure *she'll* think so, anyway."

He paused, and Benton-Ramirez y Chou could hear his own breathing. Then—

"We'll be in touch for a progress report soon, Captain," the voice said, and the connection went dead.

� ✿ ✿

Alfred Harrington forced himself to sit back in the hovering taxi, eyes closed, concentrating on the tenuous connection he was certain now that he wasn't imagining.

He had no idea what it was or how it had happened, but it was real. He could point directly to where she was, and when he focused as hard—and as desperately—as he did now, there was more. It wasn't clear, it wasn't sharp, but it was deep and powerful. Her presence had stopped moving, and he was actually sensing her emotions.

And the more he sensed, the more desperate he became.

She was *terrified*, with the gut-wrenching sort of terror that could come only to someone who was strong, who knew her own capabilities . . . and knew the horrifying reality of complete helplessness. And then, only minutes ago, had come something far, far worse—a frantic, silent scream for help she knew could not come that went on and on until it finally chopped off and all he could sense was the direction from which it had come.

His mind seethed with possibilities, questions, terrified speculation, but he forced all of them into the back of his brain, locked them down under the icy discipline of the Marine platoon sergeant he once had been, and forced himself to think coldly and logically.

He had absolutely no information about her captors, nothing upon which he could base an action plan, try to formulate a strategy or tactics. He had no idea how to contact any member of her family, and they would probably have thought he was a lunatic if he'd been able to reach them. Worse, they might conclude that he was the one responsible for her disappearance. The same was true where Beowulf law enforcement was concerned. If they checked, they could certainly determine that the "ambulance" which had picked her up had never delivered her to any of Grendel's hospitals, but that alone wouldn't be enough to convince them that a complete stranger like Alfred Harrington knew where to start looking for her. Hell, *he* wouldn't have believed it! His own immediate response would have been to take someone making such claims into custody on the grounds that he probably knew more about it than he was telling, but his knowledge had nothing to do with mysterious emotional links between complete strangers.

All of which meant he was almost certainly the only person who knew she was in trouble, and he was definitely the only one in a position to take any immediate action.

And immediate *action is what she needs*, he thought coldly. *I don't know what they're doing to her, but I know it's ugly. She's frightened, she's hurt, she's alone, and for all I know they're going to kill her in the next five minutes.*

Despite his iron self-control, his mind shied like a terrified horse from that thought. He didn't even know her, hadn't exchanged more than a couple of dozen words with her, certainly couldn't claim any relationship with her . . . and the thought of *losing* her was more frightening than anything he'd ever experienced in his life.

All right. That just means you're going to have to be at least halfway smart about this, he told himself.

The taxi waited with the patience of its artificial intelligence while he punched up more maps on his uni-link. The AI didn't mind hovering in one spot all day long as long as the meter kept running, and unlike a human pilot, it had no sense of curiosity to interrupt him with irritating questions.

He studied the display, orienting himself with the ease of long experience, superimposing the vector of his immaterial homing beacon onto the map.

They'd left Grendel behind over a hundred kilometers ago, heading out across rolling woodland dotted with the homes of people who preferred the attractions of a more sylvan existence to those of the city, and that told him at least a few things about whoever had kidnapped her.

Personally, Alfred would have opted for hiding her somewhere in Grendel itself. The city was enormous, with literally millions of people packed into it. Once they'd gotten away clean and gone to ground, which they certainly seemed to have done, they could have hidden for days—weeks—against that teeming background of humanity with very little chance that the authorities would be able to find them, unless they did something stupid to draw attention to themselves. The countryside *seemed* to offer more hiding places, but as someone who'd grown up in the Sphinx bush, he knew how much of an illusion that actually was. Traffic was easier to spot where there was so much less of it, buildings and encampments stood out sharply, and people had a greater tendency to notice strange air cars or strange people in the neighborhood, as well.

But the people who'd taken her had chosen the countryside. Unless he wanted to assume this was purely personal, a case of someone kidnapping her and dragging her off to his own home ground which simply happened to be in the country, that meant they wanted space, the ability to see people coming at long distances. It was always possible that "purely personal" was exactly what it was— that burst of terror could easily have come from someone who'd realized she was in the hands of a sadist or a serial killer—but it didn't fit the profile. Her abduction had been too smooth, too *professional*. The apparent seizure or collapse, the Good Samaritan and the waiting ambulance, all suggested careful planning by a *group*, not by a deranged individual. They wanted something, either from her or from someone who cared about her, and they intended to get it. Money was the first possibility that came to mind, although getting away with any ransom after the funds had been transferred would be problematical. He had no reason to believe her family was especially wealthy, either, and he took a moment to swear at himself for not having found out more about her. He should have at least found out who she was related to, damn it! But it would have felt too much like voyeurism, a confirmation that he was turning into the sort of obsessive stalker he'd been half-afraid he was becoming. All he knew about her was her last name—Chou—and that was scarcely an uncommon one here on Beowulf!

It was more likely they wanted something else, anyway, he told himself. Something that wouldn't leave traceable electronic footprints like a funds transfer. Information of some sort? That was certainly possible. Information techs didn't have to be wealthy or important themselves to have access to data that could be literally priceless to the right person. And information handed over on a data chip wouldn't have to pass through any of the galaxy's banking systems to be useful, either. He couldn't rule out a cash ransom, but the more he considered it, the more plausible the information theft motive looked.

Of course, what they wanted might be simple revenge for something, in which case they might well have—indeed, probably *did* have—no intention of ever returning her alive.

A fresh spike of fear threatened his cold detachment at that thought, but he forced it back. He couldn't afford it.

No. They were professionals, and that meant they probably wouldn't kill her immediately. But they'd brought her out here to make certain no one could get into striking range of their base undetected. They might also be out here because they wanted seclusion, but seclusion could be found in an urban environment, as well, if someone had a deep enough cellar. Most likely, they'd set up a military-style— or what they *believed* was a military-style—perimeter around their HQ, and that could be very, very bad. It was highly unlikely that anyone who could engineer this so smoothly would delude himself into believing he could have the firepower to stand off what the Beowulfan law enforcement agencies could bring to bear once they knew where he was. So his perimeter defense would be designed to buy *time*. Time for him to execute whatever bug-out plan he was counting on to get his arse out of the frying pan before it fell into the fire. And that bug-out plan was just as likely to include killing his captive before he ran for it as it was to include taking her with him.

All right. The first step was to find her. There was no point thinking about approaches or tactics until he'd managed that much, and at least he was pretty sure he knew how to do it.

He switched the map to a topological display, considering the terrain with a Marine's eye, and looked along the line between him and her. Distance was much harder to estimate than direction, especially when he had no previous experience with ESP, but there were a couple of places along that line that looked probable. He just had to figure out which one of them she was actually in.

"Come to a heading of zero-three-five degrees," he told the AI. "Head in that direction until I tell you to stop."

"Of course, sir," the AI replied cheerfully. "Would you like me to open an entertainment channel for you while we travel?"

"No," he said flatly.

"As you wish, sir. Ajax Cabs of Grendel appreciates your business. I hope you enjoy the flight."

❀ ❀ ❀

Jacques Benton-Ramirez y Chou finished dressing and sealed his tunic with a hand which should have resembled a castanet but didn't. His eyes were bleak, hard, and something entirely too much like panic gibbered just below the surface of his tightly focused thoughts.

It was Manpower. It had to be, given the information they wanted, and that meant his sister—his *twin*—was in the hands of people who routinely used rape and torture as "training tools" and couldn't care less how many mutilated bodies they left in their wake. Worse, they were people who had deeply personal, as well as professional, reasons to hate him and, by extension, his family. It was entirely too likely that whoever had hurt Allison to make the point of his helplessness to him had *enjoyed* doing it. That they would do it again, with or without the intention of driving him to do their bidding. And it was certain that in the end, they *would* kill her.

But what did he do about it?

The first thing he did was to stay as far away from the members of his own team as he possibly could. It was possible Manpower hadn't IDed any of the other members of that team, but it was unlikely. And if they did know the team members, they'd have any of them they'd identified under surveillance. They had to know his natural response would have been to reach out to the people he trusted most in the world to help get Allison back, and the instant they saw any of those people doing anything out of the ordinary, they would assume that was exactly what he'd done. At which point, Allison would almost certainly die.

But that didn't mean he couldn't contact *anyone* in the BSC. He'd just have to be insanely careful about who and how.

He left his apartment, locked the door behind him, and headed for the parking garage. No doubt he was under surveillance at that very moment, but the very information they'd demanded from him gave him a perfectly logical reason to head for the Biological Survey Corps' headquarters at Camp Oswald Avery three hundred kilometers outside Grendel. The sort of detailed information they wanted couldn't be remote accessed without all sorts of challenges and authorizations. From his workstation *inside* Oswald Avery, over the camp's secure server network, it would be quite another matter.

But so would his ability to communicate without worrying about any eavesdroppers.

※ ※ ※

"Damn, I hate it when they pass out that fast," Giuseppe Ardmore remarked, tossing the neural whip into the air, flipping it end for end and catching it again.

Allison Benton-Ramirez y Chou was still unconscious, drooping in the chair to which she had been strapped, and Ardmore smiled as he watched her breathe. She wasn't blindfolded or hooded, which would have told her brother a great deal about how likely she was ever to leave this room alive. *She* might not realize that, but she sure as hell knew now that she was in deep, deep shit and sinking fast.

He caught her hair in his free hand, pulling her head back to study her critically. She was a beautiful bitch, he'd give her that, and maybe before it was all over, he'd have the opportunity to take advantage of that, too. But for now—

"Do you really think he's going to roll over for us?" he asked, never lifting his hungry eyes from her face.

Tobin Manischewitz regarded the other man without any particular expression, yet Ardmore's attitude disturbed him. The original concept for the operation had been his, but Ardmore was making it too personal. Manischewitz wasn't going to be a hypocrite and pretend he hadn't known exactly what sort of ugliness his plan entailed, but for him, it was simply the cost of doing business. A man didn't go to work for someone like Manpower if he had much in the way of scruples, and Manischewitz had never claimed he did. He'd always known Ardmore had a vicious streak, as well—it was one of the things which had made him so effective when it came to "wet work"—but it looked like the man had a deeper and uglier vein of sadism to go with it than he'd thought.

In some ways, that suited Manischewitz just fine. Ms. Benton-Ramirez y Chou wasn't going to survive the operation, no matter what happened, and her brother's love for her was both well known and evident. If anything was going to shake his professionalism, get under his skin and cause him to make mistakes, it would be his burning fear of what would be happening to her. Manischewitz's own estimate was that Benton-Ramirez y Chou would give them what they demanded as long as it wasn't core information about BSC strategies and human intelligence sources. He *might* hand over the humint names, but that would be a far harder call for him, especially since whatever his emotions told him, the professional part of his brain must know how little chance there was of his ever seeing his sister alive again, whatever he gave up for her. But he'd give them what they asked for as long as he could convince himself that it wouldn't be *critical*, wouldn't cost the lives of people who'd put those lives on the line for him . . . and as long as he could convince himself there was still a chance of finding his sister and somehow getting her back.

There wasn't a chance in hell of that, and sooner or later he'd realize it, but in the meantime, letting Ardmore demonstrate what was happening to his sister—or what *would* happen to her if he failed to cooperate, at least—was the best way to push him off balance and keep him there. For a threat to be credible, however, it must be demonstrated to be real, and he would be more than happy to let Ardmore do the demonstrating.

Unless, of course, Ardmore's . . . enthusiasm was likely to lead him to kill the girl too soon. Worried or not, Benton-Ramirez y Chou wasn't going to continue committing treason if he wasn't convinced his sister was still alive to suffer if he didn't.

"I think if he wants to have any chance at all of ever getting her back alive, he'll geek to at least the first couple of demands," he replied after a moment. "I doubt we'll be able to string him along forever, though. Once he realizes he's not getting her back, he'll pull the plug." He shrugged. "I'm not sure what he'll do at that point. He could try something really stupid if he thinks he's figured out where she is, but that's not going to happen. Why?"

"Because I don't think he is," Ardmore said, and licked his lips slowly, his expression ugly. "I think no matter how hard I work at convincing him to be reasonable, he's not gonna cough up the information more than maybe once. And I'll lay you odds he's not gonna give us *accurate* info even the first time. I'm looking forward to that." He released Allison's hair with a flick of his fingers that bounced her head limply, and looked at Manischewitz with eyes that glittered hungrily. "I'm *really* looking forward to it. 'Cause when he sees what happens to his darling little sister in glorious HD, *I* think what he's gonna do is put a pulser dart through his own brain."

Manischewitz nodded slowly. That was his own estimate of Benton-Ramirez y Chou's ultimate response when he hit the limit of what he could—or would—deliver and realized how agonizingly his sister had died because he had. Still, the Beowulfer *was* a tough little bastard; it was possible he'd refuse to kill himself and dedicate what remained of his life to the pursuit of vengeance, instead. Manischewitz had taken that possibility into consideration when he planned the op, which was why Benton-Ramirez y Chou was scheduled to die on his final information delivery. A nice, nasty little bomb hidden in the dead drop and remote-detonated would see to that, without anyone ever being stupid enough to take the chance of letting Benton-Ramirez y Chou into range of a live human being.

"Just don't get carried away," he told Ardmore. The other man's expression tightened, and Manischewitz shook his head. "He's going to need a little more convincing even after he coughs up the first data dump, so don't worry. You'll get your chance to 'convince him.' But if we push too hard, too fast on the very first date, he's likely to balk or try something desperate the next time. These things have to be handled properly, Giuseppe. And"—he looked directly into Ardmore's eyes—"if I were you, I'd be careful how much time I spent on camera with her myself. You know what cyber forensics can do with visual data, no matter how carefully we camouflage things."

"Don't worry." Ardmore smiled and stroked the neural whip as if it were some treasured pet. "All he'll see is her and the end of *this*." He stroked the whip again. "And I'll make sure he gets a really nice close-up of her eyes."

⚜ ⚜ ⚜

"Christ, Jacques!" Colonel Sean Hamilton-Mitsotakis stared at the small, slender man standing in his office. "*Allison?* Right here in Grendel?"

"Why not?" Benton-Ramirez y Chou asked harshly. "God never promised me a cloak of invulnerability for my family. I should've remembered that. I should've *made* her take more precautions! But I didn't, and whatever happens to her is *my* fault."

"Don't be stupid!" Hamilton-Mitsotakis snapped, shaking himself back on balance. "You did warn her, and unlike some of the other members of your family, Allison always had a pretty damned good idea of what you do. And you know as well as I do what kind of escalation this represents. They've never tried something like this right here on Beowulf any more than we've ever mounted an op against one of the Manpower families on Mesa, and you know why."

"Well, they've sure as hell changed their operational parameters this time, haven't they, Sir?" Benton-Ramirez y Chou retorted, and Hamilton-Mitsotakis nodded.

"Yes, they have, and there's going to be hell to pay for it, I promise you that," he said harshly. Hamilton-Mitsotakis was the CO of the BSC's Special Actions Group. That meant, among other things, that he was the man who assigned assassination targets and planned the operations to carry them out, and Benton-Ramirez y Chou knew all about the folder of high-level Manpower executives and shareholders tucked away in the colonel's files.

"In the meantime, though," Hamilton-Mitsotakis continued, "we've got to get her back. I assume since you're talking to me that you've got at least something in mind?"

"Not very damned much," Benton-Ramirez y Chou admitted bleakly. "They're using her com to make sure I know they've really got her, and because there's no way a trace could lead back to anyone besides Alley. But they've disabled the locator function—trust me, I already checked—and they're bouncing it through at least a couple of hundred intermediaries before they get to me. Not to mention the fact that Allison has the best privacyware on the market." He grimaced. "In fact, I helped her pick it out. There's no way anyone's tracing that signal, and that means they could be anywhere on the frigging planet. For that matter, they could be *off*-planet; the delay with all the intermediate relays could be hiding the signal lag."

Hamilton-Mitsotakis nodded. Beowulfers took their civil liberties seriously, and the system constitution had established hard, definitive limitations on electronic surveillance from the very beginning of the colony. Citizens had an absolute right to the best privacyware—not just encryption software, but software to disable locator functions and tracking techniques—without government-mandated back doors and workarounds. In general, the colonel approved of that state of affairs, but it could be a pain in the arse for law enforcement . . . or for the Biological Survey Corps on the very rare occasions when it operated on Beowulf itself.

Which opened another can of worms.

"I don't suppose you've cleared a waiver of Prescott-Chatwell?" he asked.

"No, Sir, I haven't." Benton-Ramirez y Chou looked at him levelly. "Is that going to be a problem?"

Prescott-Chatwell was the law which specifically prohibited the BSC, which was *not* a domestic police agency, from mounting ops in the Beowulf System, and violation of it was punishable by up to thirty T-years in prison. It could be waived under special cirumstances, but that required a signoff at the level of the Planetary Board of Directors. Getting that sort of signoff was a time-consuming business, and time, unfortunately, was something Allison Benton-Ramirez y Chou didn't have a lot of.

Now Hamilton-Mitsotakis looked into Allison's brother's eyes for a long, still heartbeat or two and then smiled slowly.

"Problem? Why should I have a problem? As far as I'm concerned, given the information these bastards want you to hand over, this is obviously a direct attack on the BSC. As such, it's clearly my responsibility to respond immediately in order to contain the damage. There'll be plenty of time to sort out any minor jurisdictional issues once the immediate threat's been contained."

There was a moment of silence, then he shook himself.

"So if we can't track them, what do we do?" he asked.

"All I can think of for right now is to play for time, Sir," Benton-Ramirez y Chou admitted flatly. "I think they're going to want a physical drop, because they'll be too afraid of what I might piggyback onto an electronic transfer. I doubt they'll be foolish enough to arrange the delivery anywhere near their actual base, but the problem with a physical drop is that somebody has to pick it up. Our best bet—and it's not much of one—is to set up surveillance of the drop and follow whoever collects the data. It'll probably be a drone, somebody who doesn't know squat, but eventually that information has to reach them if it's going to do them any good. All we can hope is that Alley survives long enough for us to follow the breadcrumbs to somebody I can . . . convince to tell me where she is."

He met his superior's gaze levelly, and his eyes were bleak and cold. Cold with the promise that anyone who knew where his sister was *would* tell him in the end; bleak with the knowledge of how little likelihood there was that he'd ever have the chance to find her.

※ ※ ※

Alfred Harrington climbed out of the taxi and closed the hatch behind him.

He'd had it deposit him four and a half kilometers west of his destination, on the far side of a ridgeline from the people he was interested in. Hopefully, they wouldn't notice it, although he couldn't be positive they hadn't already picked him up. It all depended on the sensor systems they might have installed, and given the fact that they clearly wanted as small and unobtrusive a footprint as they could get, they were probably relying solely on passives. That would tend to limit the amount of reach and definition they had, but there was no point pretending that if they'd been watching, they wouldn't have seen the taxi fly over them, then swing to the northwest and—hopefully—disappear. The AI had been willing to come in to his present position at what passed for low altitude, but before he actually told it to land, it would never have agreed to violate the minimum hard floor of two hundred meters mandated by Beowulf's safety regulations. He was lucky it was prepared to wait for his return . . . and it had agreed to that only because he'd left a signed, thumbprinted authorization for it to keep the meter running against his card. At this rate, he was going to owe the cab company a solid month's worth of his lieutenant's pay.

It was possible he'd be making use of that taxi again. That was the plan—such as it was, and what there was of it, at any rate—although he wouldn't have cared to bet anything important on the likelihood. The best he could hope for was that before he'd cut back to the south, his approach had circled wide enough that the ridgeline had cut off any of the bad guys' sensors' line of sight to the taxi's actual approach and landing. And that by keeping it on the ground, he could prevent it from doing what it would normally have it done: lift straight up on counter-grav before heading back to Grendel for another fare. Even if he'd gotten in undetected, that would have been a flare-lit tipoff to any half-awake lookout.

This is insane, he told himself almost calmly as he made his way through the dense, unfamiliar Beowulfan trees. He might not know the names of the local species, but he'd spent enough years hunting and hiking in Sphinx's forests and the dark-bellied clouds were sweeping in from the east. He could smell the approaching rain, and a steadily freshening wind tossed the limbs overhead and filled the woods with the sighing song of dancing leaves and branches as they were flung about. A sense of motion and energy and life filled the air about him, and the scents of leaf mold, bark, and damp earth filled his nostrils. For the first time since his arrival in Grendel, he was actually in his element again, and in other circumstances he would have enjoyed the hike.

Not under these.

That other presence—Allison—was in front of him. He'd located her by the simple expedient of flying almost due north from the city, directly on his bearing to her, until suddenly that unerring sense of her presence was behind him again. The taxi had just crossed what appeared to be a nice-looking, remote hunting lodge, and as it had circled away to the west, he'd felt the bearing shift. There was no question in his mind. As preposterous as it sounded, he was certain Allison Chou was in that hunting lodge.

And if she is, what are you going to do about it, hotshot? he asked himself harshly. *You're not a cop. You're not even a* Marine *anymore. And even if you were, you're not a Beowulfer. You've got exactly no authority or jurisdiction on this planet, idiot! And even if that weren't the case, what're you going to do? Just* shoot *the first poor bastard you see?*

He grimaced, but he also reminded himself of the Marine Corps' motto: "Can Do!" And of the mantra of every Marine noncom who'd ever lived: improvise, adapt, and overcome. If there'd ever been a time and place for both of them, that time and place were here and now. And it wasn't like he'd never had to do it before.

A flicker of fear went through him with that thought, and he felt his hands begin to shake. He stopped in the dense shadow of a towering, vaguely oaklike tree and held those hands up in front of him, clenching them into hard-knuckled fists.

Stop that! This isn't Clematis!

Maybe it wasn't, but he was the same man he'd been on Clematis, and that was what really frightened him. That he *was* the same man, with the same monster deep inside, eager to get out.

He stood there for long, dragging seconds, trapped between the memory of what had been and the fear of what might be again, and panic pulsed at the base of his throat. He couldn't. He couldn't let it out again. He just *couldn't.*

But then his head snapped up, his eyes wide. She was aware once more, and she was frightened—terrified. And then a dreadful, jagged bolt of anguish ripped into him. Not his—*hers!* The mere echo of it went through him like a vibro blade, and his teeth clenched. His hesitation disappeared.

There was a time for monsters, he thought.

❊ ❊ ❊

Tobin Manischewitz heard the scream through the closed door and shook his head. He supposed it was unreasonable to expect anything else, and Ardmore did have a point about the need to record something suitably motivating for Captain Benton-Ramirez y Chou. But there was no need to start in on the girl this early.

No need except that it's how he gets his kicks, anyway, he thought.

Another scream, this one shriller and higher than the last, came through the door, and he grimaced. He thought about opening the door and telling the other man to lay off, but he didn't think about it very hard. In the end, it was no skin off his nose what happened to her before they disposed of her once and for all, and there was no point pissing Ardmore off any sooner than he had to. But he wasn't going to get any work done with that racket going on next door, so he gathered up his computer and headed down the stairs.

Yet another scream followed him.

※ ※ ※

Jacques Benton-Ramirez y Chou sat in the small, anonymous office. He knew all of the thirteen men and women assembled in the ready room on the far side of the borrowed office's door, completing the final checks on their gear. None of them were members of his own team, but he'd worked with several of them before, and all of them were good, solid people. Good, solid people who wouldn't have been noticed by anyone who was watching his own teammates as they drew ammunition and climbed into their armored skinsuits.

It was unlikely he was going to have anything for them to do, but if he did—if the bastards who had Allison gave him even a hint of where to find them—he was prepared to drop the entire world in on their heads, and screw Prescott-Chatwell's provisions. The only chance they'd have would be to go in quick and dirty, rushing the Manpower thugs who had to be behind this. The odds were frighteningly high that Allison would be killed in that kind of confused firefight, but her chances would be infinitely better than if the people who had her were given even a few minutes to kill her or turn her into a human shield.

Now all he could do was sit here, waiting for the synthesized voice to contact him over his com and tell him where to take the data he'd been ordered to steal.

※ ※ ※

Alfred Harrington reached the fringe of the cleared area around the hunting lodge and made himself pause. It was hard—one of the hardest things he'd ever done—and the waves of terror, the jagged bursts of agony, coming to him over that impossible link battered at him. He didn't know if she would have been able to sense his proximity the way he sensed hers even under normal circumstances; the possibility that she could sense him *now*, through the maelstrom of her fear and her pain, had to be vanishingly small. She couldn't know where he was, yet her frantic, silent plea reached out to him, gripped him like fiery pincers. He *had* to get her out of there! Yet if he simply charged in, he would succeed only in getting both of them killed. He knew that, but he also knew he might be running out of time. They were hurting her deliberately—terribly—yet he had no idea *why*.

The one thing he clung to was that the entire operation had been far too elaborate if all they'd wanted was to kill her. A pulser dart from a passing air car would have sufficed for that. It was entirely possible they wanted, for whatever sick reason, to take their time, make sure she suffered enough to satisfy them first, and that thought dried his mouth with a terror he'd never felt for himself. Either way, they were unlikely to kill her immediately, though. He couldn't *know* that, but the cold focus he'd forced upon his thoughts told him it was more likely than any other outcome . . . and that if he simply went crashing in in some sort of berserk charge, they *would* kill her.

The good news was that since he'd been planning on spending the day in his apartment, catching up on Dr. Mwo-chi's notes, he'd been in civvies, not uniform, so at least anyone who saw him wasn't going to automatically assume he represented some official law enforcement or military agency. That *probably* meant they were unlikely to just shoot him and be done with it instead of trying to fob the nosy neighbor off with some cover story. Presumably they'd be prefectly ready to kill him if it looked like they *couldn't* fob him off, but he ought to have at least a few seconds before they started trying to.

The better news was that even though he was no longer officially a Marine, some habits died hard. That was why he'd paused to collect the contents of his closet safe, and he reached inside his windbreaker to touch the butt of the pulser in the holster under his left armpit. Bewoulf's laws on weapons and the use of deadly force were less . . . understanding than the Star Kingdom's, which was why it had stayed safely locked up in his safe since he'd arrived at ISU. Beowulfers weren't totally unreasonable about guns the way some people—Old Earth came to mind—were, however, and he *was* a military officer, even if he was on-planet as a medical student. That created a certain gray area . . . and under the circumstances, he wasn't all that worried about a misdemeanor weapons charge even if the matter ever came up.

The holster was an old friend, a civilian rig his father had presented to him on his sixteenth birthday and he'd used ever since, but the pulser was pure military. He and his company's armorer had tweaked and tuned the long, barrelled, three-millimeter Descorso to suit his personal preferences, though, including after-market Shapiro grips, a Simpson & Wong 216 holosight, and an action smoother than glass, and two spare magazines rode the leather under his right arm. The Descorso might not have been with him as long as the holster, but it had been with him long enough, and so had the Marine-issue vibro blade mag-locked horizontally across the back of his belt. They were tools he knew how to use only too well, but they were also all he had, and he had no idea what he might face in the next few minutes.

He did have a little information, though. As soon as he'd located the lodge, he'd punched up a query on his uni-link, and he'd been lucky. It had been built as a commercial operation and it was the better part of three hundred T-years old, but it had been on the market for almost a full local year until someone purchased it barely three months ago, and as soon as he'd called up the deed and checked the record of the transaction, Alfred had realized the buyer had been a front. The sale had been registered by a shell corporation which no longer existed and had almost certainly been set up for the sole purpose of making the buy. That struck him as pretty solid evidence that Allison's abductors were indeed professionals, not simply some psycho stalker, and he tried to tell himself that was a good sign.

The actual transaction record had been interesting, if not terribly informative, but the original real-estate listing for the lodge hadn't been cleared from the realtor's site. It was still there, including a profile that showed a floor plan for the main lodge, specified its construction standards, and included a virtual tour of the house and the grounds, extolling a whole raft of recent renovations to the rather elderly buildings. The tour had obviously been intended for a sales tool, and it wasn't remotely close to anything he would have called a complete intel packet, yet at least it meant he had a firm notion of the physical layout of what he was going to be dealing with.

He'd also had the taxi AI bring up the sight-seeing features built into its windows and view screen and downloaded the magnified imagery of the terrain they'd overflown on their entire flight from Grendel to his uni-link, which meant he'd gotten at least some aerial shots of the lodge as they passed over it. It wasn't much—certainly not the kind of information military-grade sensors could have pulled up— but it had confirmed there was a commercial-style air-van in the vehicle park for the main lodge. He didn't have a very good angle on it, but it looked like the same sort of body that was used by almost all ambulances here on Beowulf, and if it wasn't painted white, it was easy enough to use smart paint and reprogram it to a different color combination when you were done playing dress-up.

He'd made himself spend several minutes looking at the plat from the sales site and from the Registrar of Deeds' office, as well, and comparing both of them to his own overhead imagery and the topographical maps available over the net from the planetary geographical base. The maps seemed to be very good, as good as anything the Sphinx Forestry Service could have provided back home. That was why he'd come in from the west. Not only had the maps suggested the ridgeline would offer the taxi at least partial concealment on its approach, but his overheads showed that the perimeter of the cleared area around the lodge pinched in closest to the main building from this direction. Even better, a ravine—it looked like it was probably a seasonal watercourse—snaked through the trees and out across the clearing, passing within no more than seventy meters of the lodge, and the maps indicated it was well over a meter deep—more than two meters, in places—for its entire length.

Now he looked out across that clearing, confirming his impression of the terrain. There was a small utility building between the ravine and the lodge. According to the real-estate site, it housed the lodge's power receptor, tied into Beowulf's orbital power stations. The entry on the site had had very little to say about the receptor, although it had waxed almost lyrical about the many ways in which the lodge's internal systems had been renovated and updated. That suggested one possibility, at least, and it also came closest to affording him cover for that final seventy meters. It wasn't much, but when the situation offered so little, it was up to a man to manufacture his own edge.

Another of those frantic, agonized bursts sizzled through him with the knowledge of someone else's pain and terror, and his nostrils flared. Enough! It was time to stop thinking and start doing.

※ ※ ※

The lights flickered.

It was so quick, so fleeting, Tobin Manischewitz might not have noticed under other circumstances. Under these circumstances, his nerves were cranked up to maximum sensitivity and his head came up abruptly. He looked around the sunny office on the lodge's ground floor, although he wasn't certain what he was looking for. At least it was far enough away from Ardmore to muffle the sounds as he . . . amused himself, and it offered a nice view of the mountain range rising misty-blue with distance to the north. It did not, however, offer him any clue as to why the power had just hiccuped, and he started to get out of his chair, then paused as the door opened and Riley Brandão, his third in command, poked his head into the room.

"What?" Manischewitz asked before the other man could speak.

"The frigging power receptor's down," Brandão said sourly.

"What happened?" Manischewitz sat up straighter, his eyes narrowing. The sudden failure of normally reliable bits and pieces of technology at critical moments in operations always sounded internal alarms.

"Looks like it's the tracking unit," Brandão replied. "The diagnostic panel in the kitchen says we've stopped tracking the assigned satellite. anyway. Sawney's gone out to check." He grimaced. "I *told* you we should've had the damned thing replaced when we bought the place. Piece of crap's older'n *I* am!"

Manischewitz resisted the temptation to roll his eyes. Brandão took an irritating relish in "I-told-you-so's" and he could be relied upon to find any potential fault with any plan, order, or piece of equipment well ahead of time, thus providing himself with endless opportunity to utter the fateful phrase. The fact that almost none of his gloomy prognostications ever came to pass didn't faze him one bit. Instead, he seized upon the thankfully few occasions on which he'd been right, and Manischewitz was torn between hoping it really was something as minor as the tracking unit and hoping it was something else entirely just so Brandão couldn't look at him triumphantly.

Unfortunately, Brandão was almost certainly right, he reflected gloomily. The power receptor *was* an ancient unit, and the one moving part most likely to fail was the tracking unit that moved it from powersat to powersat as the satellites moved across the heavens.

"How's the auxiliary?" he asked, and Brandão shrugged.

"Kicked in automatically," he admitted. "It's carrying the entire load with a thirty-percent reserve."

Manischewitz nodded. Brandão's current post was in the kitchen, monitoring the camera system they'd installed to watch the grounds. He'd tried a motion-sensor net first, but that had been a diaster, given the amount (and size) of the local wildlife, so they'd fallen back on visual imagery instead. He wasn't happy about the change, but as Ardmore had pointed out, their real security depended on not having anyone come looking in the first place. It wasn't like they were going to have the personnel or the firepower to fight off a full-bore commando raid, after all.

They'd put the primary monitoring post in the kitchen because it had been simpler to piggyback it onto the lodge's existing environmental and services monitor, and that had been located in the kitchen by some previous owner. There were drawbacks to the arrangement, since the kitchen had only one set of windows and the greenhouses on that side of the lodge blocked anything someone might have seen out of them. Still, it worked, and it meant Brandão had been in the right place to check the other systems when the receptor went down.

And at least the auxiliary power system, unlike the power receptor, was practically brand new. It was also rated to keep the entire lodge up and running for a minimum of one planetary week, so there was no immediate problem. Even assuming they couldn't repair whatever was wrong with the receptor out of their own resources—which was unlikely, given the skill set of his team—they had several days before they had to worry about getting a repair crew out here.

"Hopefully it's just a reset," he said now. "If it's more than that, send Sawney in to tell me how bad it is when he gets back."

"Gotcha."

Brandão nodded and closed the door behind him, and Manischewitz turned back to his paperwork.

※ ※ ※

Sawney Sugimoto grumbled under his breath as he trudged across to the power receptor.

He didn't often agree with Brandão, but this time the asshole had been right; the damn thing should've been replaced before they bought the place. Not that it was surprising it hadn't been. Power receptors were like roofs; people didn't worry about them . . . until they broke or started leaking. And to be fair, receptors were pretty damned rugged, built to designs that were mostly at least two or three hundred years old and about as reliable as hardware got. He just hoped it was something fairly simple, because if the tracking unit was shot they'd have to pull the entire thing, and he had a pretty fair notion who was likely to get stuck with the grunt work on *that* one. Just like he had a pretty good idea how he'd just happened to be chosen to go check out the problem in the first place. Just like Brandão to pick him for the job! Could he have chosen Mönch, or Grazioli, or Zepeda? No, he'd had to pick Sugimoto, even if he'd been—no, *because* he'd been—the outside man farthest away from the receptor. Of course, *Mönch* was an old buddy of his, wasn't he? Couldn't have Mönch getting his arse up out of his comfortable chaise lounge and actually doing some *work*, could he? Especially not if he could send Sugimoto to do it instead. It was the kind of petty, pain-in-the-arse, I'll-get-even trick Brandão specialized in, and one of these days. . . .

He reached the receptor shed and leaned his pulse rifle against the wall beside the door as he punched in the lock combination. None of the previous owners had ever bothered to change the combination from the default 1-2-3-4 setting, and frankly, Sugimoto couldn't imagine any reason why they would have. Or why they'd bothered to put a lock on the door in the first place, for that matter! Power receptors weren't exactly cheap, but stolen units weren't likely to bring in big credits, and they were big, heavy, and hard to move. Why anybody would—

The door opened, and Sawney Sugimoto's eyes widened in astonishment. There was a hole in the shed's back wall—a *big* hole, one that went almost all the way from ceiling to floor. It was almost two meters wide, as if someone had carved the wall's tough composite with a vibro bl—

A hand reached out from one side and caught the front of his tunic. It yanked him into the shed, spun him around as if he'd weighed less than nothing, and an arm like a bar of iron went across his throat from behind. He reacted automatically, driving his right heel back, reaching for the forearm across his throat with his right hand while his left shot back behind him, fingers clawing for the eyes of whoever that forearm belonged to.

A wrecking ball hammered his right calf as his assailant drove a booted foot into it, smashing down from above, just below the knee. Something popped in the joint with a white-hot explosion of pain, and what would have been a scream turned into a high-pitched, nasal whine as the forearm cut off his breath. His scrabbling left hand found nothing, and then he froze as a hand the size of a small shovel fastened on the back of his head. He recognized that hold, and his assailant's obvious strength was terrifying. A couple of kilos of pressure, and his cervical vertebrae would snap like a dry stick.

"That's better," a deep, quiet, terrifyingly calm voice said behind him. "Now lose the gunbelt with your left hand. And keep the right hand right where I can see it. I'd hate to have to break your neck before we have a chance to get to know each other."

✖ ✖ ✖

"Tracking unit's back online," Riley Brandão said, poking his head back into Manischewitz' office. "Everything green on the diagnostic board."

Brandão sounded moderately disappointed, Manischewitz noted, but he nobly forbore to comment on it. Instead, he simply nodded.

"Talk to Sawney at shift change. Find out what he had to do to get it back up and see if we really do need to go ahead and replace it. I don't want anybody out here in the next couple of weeks if we can help it, though."

"Gotcha," Brandão said again and withdrew once more.

✖ ✖ ✖

Alfred Harrington listened to the hum of the tracking unit, moving the receptor back into alignment after he'd removed the old-fashioned screwdriver he'd used to jam it, while he regarded his unconscious captive through bleak, hard eyes. He still knew entirely too little about what the hell was going on, yet he knew a lot more than the he'd known ten minutes ago. He wished there was time to gather still more information, but there wasn't. His prisoner hadn't wanted to cooperate, and Alfred wasn't about to put any childlike faith in the accuracy of what he'd said, but the other man had changed his mind about keeping his mouth shut when Alfred levered his left arm up behind his back until his shoulder joint separated. The Deneb Accords would have had a little something to say to Gunny Harrington about methods of interrogation if his prisoner had been a member of any recognized military organization. Not that that thought bothered him at the moment . . . and not that he was dealing with any recognized military organization.

The pulse rifle his prisoner had been carrying was a powerful, high-capacity-magazine military weapon, however. That alone would have been enough to convince Alfred that the current owners of the lodge weren't the innocent and law-abiding civilians they obviously wanted people to think they were. The pulser holstered at the man's belt would have been another indication in the same direction. And although he hadn't admitted it in so many words, even when Alfred twisted that dislocated shoulder, what he *had* admitted made it fairly clear who Alfred was dealing with.

Manpower. His nostrils flared, and he felt the monster stir, testing its chains as he remembered Clematis. Manpower, again. What could Manpower want with Allison Chou? What could possibly make her important enough for Manpower to risk an operation *here*? The entire galaxy knew about the searing mutual hatred between Beowulf and Mesa, and Manpower's operatives could have very few illusions about what would happen to them at the hands of the Beowulfan court system . . . assuming they got as *far* as the court system.

Unfortunately, he didn't have time to get more complete information out of his prisoner. They were bound to miss the man sooner or later, and probably sooner. The Manpower thug knew that as well as Alfred did, and he'd obviously been trying to play for time. He'd admitted that they'd grabbed Allison as part of some sort of extortion plot, although he'd also claimed he didn't know who the object of the extortion was. That was entirely possible—Alfred would have kept the operational details as closely held as he could if he'd been planning something like this—but it was also entirely possible the man had been lying. Trying to give up just enough information to satisfy Alfred's questions while he stalled until someone else came looking for him. That was why Alfred had given himself only ten minutes to ask questions. What he had at the end of that time was all he was going to get, and that was one reason he'd been as . . . insistent as he had.

His virtual tour of the lodge's layout had allowed him to catch his prisoner in two lies, and the pain he'd applied when he did had probably convinced the other man to be at least reasonably truthful. It had been hard to stop with mere pain. The monster was rousing again, and the repeated bursts of agony—and the sense of fading awareness—coming to him through whatever linked him to Allison had made it even harder. But now he had to decide what to do before he moved on, and he touched the hilt of the vibro blade. It had sliced through the synthetic composite of the shed wall like a knife through butter; a human throat would be far easier to cut.

Alfred's nostrils flared and his fingers tightened around the hilt. The need to remove the unconscious thug from the face of the galaxy quivered in those fingers, and the hot, sweet taste was back in his mouth, made hotter and sweeter still by his own sense of desperation as those thunderbolts of someone else's hopeless pain and terror ripped through him. It would be the easiest thing in the world to do, and anyone who gave his services to Manpower—anyone prepared to help kidnap and torture Allison Chou—had already paid for his own ticket to hell.

But Alfred Harrington *wasn't* a Manpower thug. He was—he *had* to be—better than that, because if he wasn't . . .

He snarled in frustration and reached for the roll of tape in the toolbox on the receptor shed's supply shelf.

❀ ❀ ❀

Giuseppe Ardmore made himself step back and switch off the neural whip. It was hard, and he licked his lips, savoring the rich, addictive delight of handing out pain. Of inflicting pain, especially on someone like this bitch. Benton-Ramirez y Chou's sister. Oh, that made it especially sweet as he remembered New Denver! But he had to be careful. Manischewitz would be pissed if he killed her too quickly. Ardmore could have lived with that—Manischewitz would get over it, in time—but *he* didn't want to kill her too quickly, either. He wanted to keep her alive for as long as he could, and he looked forward to using more traditional methods to help motivate her brother.

He clipped the neural whip to his belt and stepped over to the recording unit trained on the nearly naked young woman in the middle of the room. Watching the imagery and listening to the audio would be almost as good as doing it all over again, he thought, and it would be a very good idea to be sure he'd stayed out of the camera's field of view himself. Manischewitz was right about what could be teased out of even fragmentary images, although no one was likely to get much from a gloved hand wielding a neural whip. Best to be positive about that, though.

He gave his semiconscious victim another glance before he hit the replay button. He'd been very careful with the setting on the neural whip, making certain it was set just low enough to avoid any *permanent* damage to her nervous system, but her skin was mottled with dark, angry marks and her muscles continued to jerk and quiver uncontrollably wherever the whip had kissed. He'd made sure to record a full minute of that after he switched the whip off. Might as well give her brother proof of how high it had been set, after all.

❂ ❂ ❂

Alfred was grateful that the ravine had gotten him as far as the power receptor unseen, but there was no convenient fold in the ground between the receptor's shed and the main lodge building. He eased the door back open a crack, looking through it, and his jaw tightened. His prisoner hadn't lied about at least one thing, he thought, considering the man reclining on the chase lounge. The lounge was a good sixty meters from his present position, at an angle from the shortest line between the shed and the lodge, parked beside an outside table with a sun umbrella. The man in it didn't look to be the most alert sentry in the history of mankind—there was what looked suspiciously like a beer bottle on the table at his elbow, and Alfred knew what *he* would have had to say if one of his perimeter guards had decided to park his arse in the shade instead of staying alert and on the move—but he could scarcely miss seeing a two-meter-tall stranger sauntering across the lawn.

On the other hand, he *was* sitting down, wasn't he? Presumably the rest of his team knew him well enough to expect him to be doing just that. And the cushioned back of the chase lounge was higher than his head and the chase lounge itself faced away from the lodge. Not only that, but the clouds were closer, the temperature had dropped slightly, and the wind had picked up even farther, churning the trees around the lodge with a soft, multi-voiced roar and murmur like ocean surf. All of which suggested . . .

The Descorso was a comfortable, familiar weight in his hand. He gripped the shed's doorframe in his left hand, pressing his elbow lightly against the half-open door as he turned his forearm into a rock-steady rest. He laid the pulser's long barrel across that forearm, brought the sight's red dot down until it rested directly between the seated guard's eyes.

His own eyes were very calm, very still, and the monster purred within him. He inhaled, let half the air trickle back out of his lungs, and squeezed.

❦ ❦ ❦

Riley Brandão finished building his ham and cheese sandwich, snagged the open bottle of beer from the counter at his elbow, and settled back down in front of the surveillance system. Technically, he was supposed to stay glued to the display, watching it with steely-eyed attention as if the fate of the universe depended upon it. Actually, nobody could get anywhere near the lodge without passing through one of the outside men's field of view, and it was past lunchtime, so it was fortunate the universe had been able to get along without him for two or three minutes.

He chuckled at the thought and double-checked the household diagnostics panel, just to make sure the damned receptor hadn't stopped working all over again. It hadn't, although he questioned how much longer that would be true. Overaged piece of crap, that was what it was, and Manischewitz should have listened to him about it in the first place. He felt a mild glow of satisfaction at having his estimate of its decrepit condition confirmed, but he wondered idly why Sugimoto hadn't already reported back on what had caused the problem.

Probably still bitching about getting sent out to check it in the first place, he thought and snorted in amusement. He and Sugimoto didn't much like each other, and he was pretty sure the other man had figured out why Brandão had chosen him for the job. *Serves him right.* Brandão grinned. *Bastard thinks he's such a killer ladies' man? Right—sure he is! If he hadn't come sailing in with that stack of credits . . .*

He chewed a mouthful of ham and Swiss cheese and reminded himself that it was small-minded to dwell on past grievances. But that was all right with him. He was as small-minded as it got when it came to women, and Sugimoto had known that when he horned in. Good old Sawney still had plenty to make up for in Brandão's book, and he was sure ample opportunities to make Sugimoto's life miserable would present themselves. He swallowed and reached for his beer, reflecting on the grievance in question. That prick Ardmore had probably put Sugimoto up to it, for that matter. Of course, it was safer to get even with Sugimoto than with Ardmore, but someday he'd get around to—

As it happened, Riley Brandão was wrong about that.

He was just bringing the beer bottle to his lips when the kitchen door opened behind him. The lodge had been built with deliberately rustic and archaic internal features, and its doors were old-fashioned, manually operated things with actual knobs and hinges. Brandão's beer hovered in mid-air, just short of his mouth, and his eyebrows started to rise. He didn't know what he'd heard—or sensed—from behind him. Perhaps it was the latch turning, perhaps it was the squeak of the hinge or simply air moving as the door opened. Brandão didn't know, and he never found out.

Alfred Harrington pushed the door open with his toe, and the pulse rifle Sawney Sugimoto no longer required came down like a pile driver. Its butt smashed into to the back of Brandão's skull and crushed his occiput like an eggshell.

❈ ❈ ❈

Alfred stood half-crouched, head and ears cocked. His eyes never even flickered as the man he'd just killed slid bonelessly out of the chair to the floor. The corpse's head hit the floor with a thud, and blood pooled, spreading out across the tile, sending tendrils oozing like thick, crimson tentacles. There was no expression at all on Alfred's face as they spread, but his nostrils flared, and he made himself wait, listening for any sound, any movement.

There was none, and after a moment, he straightened. His virtual tour of the lodge had told him where the kitchen was, and Sugimoto had "volunteered" the information that the external sensor net—such as it was, and what there was of it—had been wired into the household systems monitoring station. He'd been far from certain about trusting *any* of Sugimoto's information, but a quick look around showed him it had been accurate . . . this far, at least. But there were at least eight more men in and around the lodge, and there was only one of him.

Perhaps there were, but he had one advantage they couldn't know about. He had his monster, and it quivered within him, red-fanged and ready, eager to be loosed. It was a dark thing, his monster—the thing which had driven him into the field of medicine, where it would never again be offered the freedom it had achieved on Clematis. He'd promised himself that, not because what he'd done on Clematis hadn't needed doing, but because of what it had threatened to do to *him*. What it had threatened to transform him *into*. And now, despite his promise, he had no choice but to turn to it once more.

He inhaled again, deeply, and closed his eyes for just one heartbeat. They were no longer actively hurting her, but she hovered weakly on the very brink of unconsciousness from what they'd already done. This close, the link between them clawed at him with talons of fire, and he knew exactly where she was. Above him and to the left. The virtual tour replayed itself in the back of a mind that was ice and steel over a roiling sea of lava, and his eyes opened once more. The exercise room, he thought. The third-floor, east end of the building. There were three ways he could get there from here, but two of them led through the main foyer and past several "public" rooms on the ground floor. The third was a little longer, but the back stairs led past what had been designated as staff bedrooms when the lodge was built. It seemed unlikely that anyone was simply sitting in his room in the middle of the day. He might be wrong about that, but he had to pick a route, and he turned towards the stairs.

❃ ❃ ❃

Allison Chou raised her head weakly. Red waves of agony washed through her, and her arms felt broken, aching with the strain of supporting her weight. She was barely conscious, but something . . . something had reached into her hopelessness and despair. She felt it. It was coming closer, and it was focused with deadly purpose upon *her* . . . and filled with a terrible, burning anger.

Her brain was barely working. She didn't have the least idea what these people wanted from Jacques, but she'd already realized they were going to kill her in the end. It was the only way it *could* end, and after the last two hours, part of her hoped that end would come soon. But it was only a *part* of her, and the rest reached out to that flame of hatred. Its searing fury ought to have terrified her, a tiny fragment of her mind reflected, but she'd learned what true terror was. And, even more than that, she knew that furnace flame's purpose. She rolled her eyes to one side, seeing the back of the man who had hurt her so terribly, and as she felt that seething tide of hatred come steadily closer, she smiled.

❃ ❃ ❃

Alfred went up the final flight of stairs with the pulse rifle at his shoulder, trained up the stairwell. He reached the top and stepped out into the third-floor hallway.

❃ ❃ ❃

Allison licked her lips. It had to be now, she thought. She couldn't be wrong about what she was feeling, and there was a pulser on the desk beside the HD her torturer was watching. He had the audio turned down, but she recognized the sound of her own screams, and her mind flinched away from the memory of what had wrung them from her. But that pulser was too close to his hand.

"Please," she managed to whisper. "*Please*, let me go."

He heard her, and he looked up, his smile evil and hungry as he realized she was conscious once more.

"Sure, honey. We'll let you go," he sneered, and she twisted weakly as he picked up the neural whip and stepped towards her once more. "We just can't let you go *yet*, though," he told her, and she moaned as he pressed the button and the whip began to hum once more, but every step towards her was one step *away* from the pulser. "First *you* have to do a little something for us." His eyes glittered. "Don't worry, I'm sure it will come to you."

"Please, *don't!*" she moaned through a sudden choking surge of terror, but he only laughed and raised the dully gleaming baton of the whip.

※ ※ ※

A sudden, sharper stab of fear went through Alfred. It wasn't his; it was *hers*, but he tasted a spike of panic all his own as he realized she was doing something. He didn't know what, but he'd felt the flare of her determination. She was . . . she was deliberately goading her tormentor!

He was in two worlds at once. In one, he raced down a hallway on feet which were preposterously quiet for a man of his size; in another, his throat closed with another's terror; and in both of them, the monster was awake and hungry.

※ ※ ※

Giuseppe Ardmore paused for a long, lingering moment, savoring the fear in her eyes, tasting the whimpers she couldn't suppress however hard she tried, watching her try to shrink away from him, letting her hear the hum of the whip and remember what it had already done to her. The power burned through him, sweeter and more addictive than any drug, and he cocked his wrist.

The door crashed open behind him, and he spun in disbelief as a complete stranger, at least twelve centimeters taller than he was, came through it with a pulse rifle in his hands.

※ ※ ※

It hit Alfred Harrington with an instant totality and clarity that he knew even then would live in his nightmares forever. Allison Chou stood in the center of the large, sunny room, surrounded by exercise equipment, with her hands held above her head by a tightly knotted rope. Her wrists were raw and oozing from the rope's bite, she was three-quarters naked, hanging heavily from those wrists, and he recognized the red, ugly marks stippled across her skin. He would have recognized them even without the hard, painful muscle spasms wracking her long after the marks had been inflicted.

Even without the neural whip in the hand of the big, fair-haired man between her and the door.

The pulse rifle was at Alfred's shoulder, but Allison's torturer was directly between the two of them. If he fired, the darts would rip straight through his target and hit *her*. He saw the shock, the total surprise, on the other man's face. Saw the panic which followed the surprise. But whatever else he might have been, his brain obviously worked quickly. His eyes widened as he, too, realized Alfred couldn't shoot without hitting Allison. He spun towards the door, simultaneously circling to be sure he remained between her and Alfred, and the neural whip shrilled as his thumb shoved the rheostat to lethal levels.

Alfred never hesitated. He took one long stride forward, and his eyes were ice. His left hand retained its grip on the pulse rifle's forestock, and his right hand brought the butt down from his shoulder, swinging it below his left.

Giuseppe Ardmore's scream was cut short as the rifle came up in a short, vicious arc that shattered his jaw. The impact was so powerful it lifted him from his feet, and he flew backward, losing his grip on the neural whip as he crashed to the floor. The pain was worse than anything he'd ever experienced. It exploded through him, smashing any vestige of rational thought, but pure survival instinct took over. His hands pushed at the floor, shoving as he scrambled away from the door on his back.

Alfred Harrington took two more long, quick strides. His eyes were cold, focused, and the pulse rifle rose in his hands again. He slammed one foot into the other man's chest, driving him flat on the floor once more. A hand clutched at his ankle; another rose in a useless gesture of self-defense . . . or an even more useless plea for mercy. But there was no mercy in Alfred Harrington. Not that day, not for that man. He was retribution, and he was justice . . . and he was death.

The butt of his pulse rifle came down on Giuseppe Ardmore's forehead like the hammer of Thor driven by all the power of his back and shoulders and hard, hating heart.

❈ ❈ ❈

Alfred glared down at the dead man, and all he felt in that moment was regret. Regret that he couldn't kill him all over again. The monster roared within him, seeking fresh victims, and Alfred's soul quivered with the need to feed it.

But then he closed his eyes. He made himself inhale and he turned away from that hunger to something infinitely more important.

❈ ❈ ❈

Allison felt her head wobbling as weakness, shock, fear, and pain washed over her, yet even as she hovered once more on the edge of darkness, she recognized him. She'd known—*known*, without question or doubt—who that flame of hatred had been. Who'd been coming for her. She had no idea *how* she'd known, but that didn't matter. What mattered was that she knew no power in heaven or hell could have *stopped* him from coming for her.

"Alfred," she whispered, and then his hands—those strong, deadly, *gentle* hands—were there. She felt them freeing her, felt them gathering her close, and behind them she felt *him*. She didn't even *know* him, yet she was the most precious thing in his universe, and she let herself sink into the cleansing furnace heat of his need for her.

❈ ❈ ❈

Alfred felt her droop in his arms. She weighed so little. How could someone so small be larger than all the rest of the universe put together?

His jaw tightened as he felt the uncontrollable residual muscle spasms lashing through her. He gathered her close, pressing his face against her sweat-soaked hair, feeling her cheek against his chest, and he wanted—needed—to hold her there forever. To soothe her until the spasms faded and the pain vanished. But he couldn't. There was too little time.

He set her gently in a chair. It was hard—hard to let go, and hard because her hands clung to him so tightly—but he did it. Then he stripped off his windbreaker and draped it around her. She looked so small inside its vastness, but it least it covered her, and he recovered the pulse rifle and slung it over his shoulder. Then he gathered her up once more, laid her gently across his other shoulder, drew his pulser with his right hand, and headed back down the stairs.

⚜ ⚜ ⚜

"Rinaldo, you asshole," Kuprian Grazioli growled as he trudged around the corner of the building, "you're *supposed* to be at least halfway awake! The next time I com you, you damned well better—!"

Grazioli's complaint chopped off as he realized why Rinaldo Mönch hadn't responded to his com request about the sound which had drawn Grazioli's attention. And he knew what that muted "Crack!" had been, as well. Lost as it had been in the sound of the wind in the trees, he'd half-thought he'd imagined it when it wasn't repeated again. Now he knew better.

He could see only the back of the chaise lounge, but that was all he needed to see. White stuffing had been blasted out of its back, just at head level for someone sitting in it. Whatever had done the blasting had obviously been traveling at a very high velocity, and the center of the tufted white flower of ruptured stuffing was a dark red, glistening rose.

He ran towards the chaise lounge and grabbed for his com again.

⚜ ⚜ ⚜

"*Tobin!*"

"What?" Tobin Manischewitz looked up from his paperwork as his name crackled from the com.

"Kuprian," the voice identified itself. "Rinaldo's dead! Somebody put a pulser dart between his eyes!"

"*What?!*" Manischewitz exploded out of his chair. "You're sure?"

"Of course I'm goddamned sure!" Grazioli shot back. "I'm standing here looking at what's left of his head! And I tried Riley before I tried you—he didn't answer."

Manischewitz' expression tightened. If Brandão hadn't answered, that meant whoever had killed Mönch was already *inside* the lodge. Not only that, he'd known enough to go for the security post in the kitchen first!

For just a moment, his brain refused to function. This couldn't have happened. It just wasn't possible! Even if Benton-Ramirez y Chou had gone straight to the authorities—even if he'd convinced the

BSC to back an operation right here on Beowulf despite Prescott-Chartwell—he couldn't have *found* them yet!

Could they have somehow traced the com signal after all? But that's crazy! We put our own com satellite into orbit and bounced the first signal off of it, and that's the best software in the galaxy. We bounced it through so many nodes God *couldn't've unraveled it yet. There's no way they could have back-traced it this quickly! Unless she had a tracer on her we didn't know about? But we checked. And even if she did—*

He shook himself. How they'd done it mattered far less than the fact that someone *had* done it. But if it was the SBI or the BSC, where the hell was the rest of the attack? No SBI SWAT team would have taken out one perimeter guard and then penetrated the lodge without backup! And while the BSC was capable of finesse, it also believed in overwhelming firepower delivered in a single, finely focused strike designed to paralyze its intended victims before they could even begin to think about responding. So what kind of—?

He stabbed the all-stations button on his com.

"Com check!" he barked, and made himself stand motionless as the startled members of his team responded.

They came up four men short: Brandão, Mönch, Sugimoto . . . And Ardmore.

Shit! The damned power receptor! Manischewitz thought. *Whoever this bastard is, he sucked one man out to check the receptor, took him, and made him talk. And then he walked right through our perimeter, killed Riley, and—*

Then the implications of Ardmore's silence hit him squarely between the eyes. If he'd taken out Giuseppe, then that meant he had to've—

His brain was still racing after that thought, his thumb already stabbing the all-stations button again, when Kuprian Grazioli came back up on the com.

"*Tobin!* Somebody's coming back out the—!"

Manischewitz heard a pulser whine over the com, and then Grazioli's shout chopped off with abrupt finality.

"Somebody's gotten inside the lodge and the bastard is headed back out!" he barked into the com. "Whoever it is, he's breaking for the west! Palacios, Tangevec, Mészáros—you three hold the perimeter.

He may try the ravine—if he does, kill his arse! The rest of you, head for the back veranda! We'll link up there!"

He went on talking as he jerked open a desk drawer and snatched his own pulser out of it.

"Whoever the bastard is, he's already taken out four of us—*five* with Grazioli—so watch your arses! I'm guessing he got through to Giuseppe before Grazioli found Mönch, so he probably has the woman with him. I want her back alive if we can get her, but the main thing is to make sure this son-of-a-bitch is *dead*. If that means losing her, too, that's just the way it is."

※ ※ ※

Alfred swore as the man standing beside the chaise lounge tumbled backward. The Descorso's dart had struck just above his upper lip and hydrostratic shock blasted a cloud of bone splinters, finely separated brain matter, and blood from the ruined back of his skull. But he'd been shouting into a com when Alfred fired, and Alfred's heart turned to ice as he heard someone else shouting from the wind-tossed woods to the north.

His only real chance had been to get in, find Allison, get her back out again, and reach the waiting taxi before the Manpower killers realized what had happened. Only he hadn't, and he had few illusions about the kind of men he faced.

He almost turned to make a break for the woods, but a burst of pulser fire ripped over his head in the long, rippling crack of the darts' supersonic passage. He snarled another curse and took the only option he had, sprinting not for the woods but to the south, circling to put the power receptor's shed between him and that rifleman to the north.It covered him for a few, precious moments; then another burst shrieked past him. He jinked and swerved as he ran, then flung himself down into the ravine.

A third burst ripped into the inside of the ravine's southern wall, pulverizing grass, dirt, and leaves, but the shooter could no longer see them. He had to be shooting blind, not that it was going to matter much in the end. They knew where he'd gone into the ravine, and that bastard to the north was closer to its western end than he was. They'd post that one to watch that end, send someone else to watch the *eastern* end, and then they'd systematically close in on him.

He slid Allison off his left shoulder as gently as he could and snatched the captured pulse rifle off his right shoulder. At least the man he'd taken it from had been carrying three spare magazines. That meant he was unlikely to run out of ammunition before they closed in and killed both of them.

He elbow-crawled up to the brink of the ravine and raised his head cautiously. The dry water course was almost two meters deep at this point, which was good, and he had wide fields of fire in all directions. Unfortunately, he could only cover one of them at a time, and yet another fusillade of pulser darts screamed overhead. These had come from a different direction, farther east than the other fire, and his eye caught a flicker of movement as the man who'd fired darted towards another of the lodge's outbuildings, closer to the ravine.

The pulse rifle was at his shoulder, like an old, familiar companion, and his right forefinger squeezed.

The running man seemed to trip in mid-air, then went down in the bone-breaking slide of eighty kilos of dead meat, and the monster snarled inside him. That was five of them. At least they'd by God know they'd been in a fight!

The thought flashed through him, and it was poison bitter on his tongue as he darted a glance over his shoulder at Allison before he turned back towards the enemy. It didn't matter how many of them he killed before they killed him, for he'd failed, and she was going to die anyway.

Stop that! Maybe you have, but she's not dead yet, and neither are you! Keep it that way, you stupid bastard! And—

"Alfred?"

His eyes widened as Allison called his name weakly.

"Yes, Allison. It's me." He was astounded by how gently his voice came out, but he dared not look back at her.

"You . . . came for me," she said.

"Of course I did." He considered lying to her, telling her everything was going to be fine, but he knew she would read the lie the instant he said it, and so he shook his head. "It's not looking too good just now, though."

She astonished him with a ghost of a laugh, but the laugh ended in a sob. A sob of hurt, he knew, but also of inner pain. The pain of knowing *he* was going to die, as well.

"Here!" He pulled the uni-link from his pocket and tossed it to her.

"Screen the cops and tell them to home on your signal. Maybe they'll get here in time."

He knew there was no hope in hell of that, but he was astounded by the sudden explosion of excitement which echoed through their link as she caught it in trembling fingers. He started to say something more, then whirled as a burst of fire came from the direction of the main lodge. He returned fire and heard someone shout in alarm, although he was certain he hadn't hit anyone. There were at least four or five of them coming from that direction, though. He was going to have to take his chances on what might still come from the woods, and he flung himself across to the south side of the ravine. He got there just in time to catch one of them rising to dart forward while the others covered him. Darts screamed everywhere, but they were firing blind, without a hard fix on his position, and he squeezed off a quick three-round burst.

The running man went down screaming, right leg blown off at mid-thigh, and Alfred ducked back, squirming several meters to his left while a storm of darts flayed his firing position. He waited, holding his own fire until he had a target.

"Jacques!" He heard Allison's voice behind him.

❁ ❁ ❁

Jacques Benton-Ramirez y Chou didn't recognize the com combination when the caller ID came up. It wasn't Allison's, but perhaps the people who had her were willing to use additional coms now that they'd made their point. He stabbed at the acceptance key, but someone else spoke before he could answer.

"Jacques!"

"*Alley?*"

He stiffened in his chair, wondering why they'd given her the com again, terrified it was so that he could listen to her scream once more. But then he heard a sound which could never be mistaken by anyone who had heard it before and bolted to his feet as the crack and scream of pulser fire came over the circuit.

"Jacques, it's me! Home on this com! We're in a ditch near a lodge of some kind and they're closing in on us! *Hurry*, Jacques!"

"*Alley!*"

There was no reply, but the connection was still open, and he heard more pulser fire. *Lots* of pulser fire.

"Sergeant Brockmann! Saddle up! *Move*, damn it!" he shouted, flinging himself through the office door and racing for the waiting assault shuttle.

❋ ❋ ❋

Alfred fired again—more to keep heads down than anything else—and started working his way farther to his left. They'd expect him to break back to the right . . . or he hoped so, anyway.

Something tugged at him and he looked over his shoulder just in time to see Allison pulling the pulser which had once belonged to Giuseppe Ardmore out of his belt. He looked at her, and she managed a shaky smile.

"You watch that side; I'll watch the other," she said.

"You know how to use one of those?"

"Not as well as you do, but my brother's taken me to the range a time or two. Besides," she gave him another one of those heartbreaking smiles, "I'm all the backup you've got."

"True." He actually felt himself smiling back, then he shook his head. "Keep your head down. Just pop up, take a look, then duck back down—and never put your head up in the same place twice!"

"Yes, Sir," she said and crawled towards the other side of the ravine.

It was absolutely insane, of course, but at that moment, as he watched her crawling towards a firing position with the pulser of her torturer in one hand, clutching his enormously too large windbreaker about her with the other, still shaking like a victim of old-fashioned palsy from the neural whip, he knew he'd never seen a more desirable woman in his life.

Not the time, *Alfred! Not the time!* a voice in the back of his brain told him, and no doubt it was right, but that didn't make it untrue.

He lifted his head just far enough to get his eyes back up above the lip of the ravine, saw something move from the corner of his eye, and waited patiently. The main lodge was flanked by half a dozen topiaries in the shapes of various species of Beowulfan wildlife, and he watched the shrubbery where that movement had vanished. A moment later, the greenery stirred again. A head poked cautiously up over it, and the immaculately groomed branches exploded in a spray of red as he put a pulser burst into them.

❋ ❋ ❋

Who the hell is *this guy?* Tobin Manischewitz thought furiously as Emiliano Min died. The corpse thudded to the ground less than three meters from Manischewitz, and his jaw clenched. The man behind that pulse rifle had already killed Gualberto Palacios and Häkon Grigoriv. With Min added, that made *eight* of Manischewitz's team, and nobody had even *seen* the bastard yet!

Aside from the ones he's already killed, anyway, he corrected himself.

He was down to eight men, including himself, and he didn't like the situation one bit. It was obvious he'd been right, that this character was some sort of lone wolf, because otherwise the SWAT teams who'd been waiting for him to get the woman out of the lodge would be swarming all over their arses. That didn't mean it was going to stay that way, though. The bastard had to have a com, and he had to've used it now that he had her out in the open. The question was how quickly he could reach someone and get them to believe him . . . and how quickly they could respond once they did. And the reason that question was important was that they'd managed to pin him down in the worst place imaginable because it gave him a direct line of fire to the vehicle park. There were three air cars and the "ambulance" in that parking area . . . and they couldn't bug out when someone that good with a rifle was waiting to kill them the instant they tried to.

God, this sucks! *Somehow I don't think he'd believe me if I told him all we want to do is leave. Hell, I* wouldn't believe it! *Let somebody in an air car get high enough to fire down into that frigging ditch? No way.*

Their only hope was to take him out before anyone could respond to his call for help, and at least they could count on a little grit in the official gears. It wasn't as if the SBI kept a SWAT team on full-time standby, and one of the reasons they'd bought the lodge in the first place was that it was outside the jurisdiction of any metro police force. The local yokels were more game wardens than cops. It was unlikely they'd be able to get themselves together in a hurry, and even if they did, they wouldn't have the heavy weapons and training of someone like the Grendel PD or the SBI. So they still had a little time, but not much of it.

"O'Connor, you and Schreiber cut back to the north. Get beyond his field of view, then swing across the ditch and link up with Tangevec and Mészáros. We need to rush this bastard from both directions, and we need to do it now! Zepeda, I need you, Yang, and Meakin with me. Keep your damned heads down, though!"

Acknowledgments came back, and he made himself wait despite the desperate sense of seconds ticking away into eternity. He'd seen too many men killed by impatience, and he wasn't going to rush himself into a fatal error against somebody who could shoot the way *this* son-of-a-bitch could.

❈ ❈ ❈

"There's more of them on this side than there were," Allison said. "At least one more. Maybe two."

Her voice was weak, frayed around the edges, and he knew she was hanging onto consciousness only by sheer, dogged determination and guts.

"They'll probably try a rush," he told her levelly. "One or two of them will get up to charge across the open space. The others will lay down covering fire. I want you to stay right where you are until you think they're ready to come at you. Then I want you to shift to your left or your right, pop up, take your best shot, and duck back down. *Don't* wait to see if you hit anyone! They'll probably go to ground when they hear the darts, even if you don't hit them, and you don't stay in one place long enough for the ones laying down the covering fire to find you. Understand?"

Allison looked over her shoulder at him, feeling the fiery concern under the icy focus of discipline and self-control. There was something else in there, too. Something that knew this was the sort of moment for which he'd been born. Something he hated. But overriding everything else was his desperate need for *her* to live, and she felt the strength of him flowing into her. The dark spots wavering across her vision faded, and she drew a deep breath, wondering what sort of bizarre, impossible connection let that happen.

"I understand," she said, and her voice was stronger, steadier than it had been a moment before.

❈ ❈ ❈

"We're in position, Tobin," Terjo O'Connor said tautly over Manischewitz' com.

"Okay, he can only look one direction at a time," Manischewitz replied. "On a three-count. Right?"

"Right."

Manischewitz drew a deep breath and eased himself up onto one knee behind the concealment of the same topiary which had done such an inadequate job of covering Min. Not that Manischewitz had any intention of poking *his* head up where it could be shot off. He and Yang were going to provide covering fire for Rudi Zepeda and Lazare Meakin.

At least for the first bound, he thought grimly. Then it was going to be his turn, whether he liked it or not.

"One," he said over the com. "Two. Three! *Go!*"

He threw himself to the side, staying low, and squeezed the trigger and his pulse rifle spat death at two hundred rounds per minute.

❄ ❄ ❄

Alfred saw the first movement a split second before the covering fire began. He ducked instantly, rolling to his right, then came up with the rifle already at his shoulder, and his eyes were cold.

Pulser darts shrieked overhead, but he had a brief flicker of time before the minds behind those rifles could recognize what their eyes had seen and redirect their fire. And in that instant, Alfred Harrington found his own target, exactly where he'd expected to see it. Lazare Meakin was still straightening, still getting his feet under him, when a three-round burst ripped through his torso. He hit the ground, trying to scream with lungs which had been blown into bloody vapor, and Alfred ducked back into the ravine just as Manischewitz and Yang swung their rifle muzzles towards him.

Rudi Zepeda took one look at what had happened to Meakin and flung himself flat in the minuscule protection provided by a dip in the ground. He'd made no more than four or five meters towards the ravine before he hit the ground, and he dragged his own pulse rifle around, hosing blind fire in Alfred's direction.

Ardmore's pulser whined behind him, and Alfred felt Allison's desperate determination. From the undertones rippling through their link, he doubted she'd hit anyone, but her stark determination to kill snarled through him, calling to his own killer side. And if it was different from the darkness inside him, it was no less strong.

Movement stirred before him again, and he ripped off another quick burst. This time he hit nothing, and the return fire blasted grit and dirt into his face. One of the darts cracked past so close his head rang, and he dropped down, half-stunned, pawing frantically at his eyes. He blinked on cleansing tears, shaking his head and and praying none of them had guessed how close they'd come. His vision cleared— mostly—and he lifted his eyes above the lip of the ravine again. It was like looking through a sheet of wavy crystoplast, and he blinked again and again. Something moved, and he snapped off a quick burst at the motion even as Allison fired again—and again—behind him. He heard a shriek from one of her targets and felt vengeful satisfaction boiling through her, but he knew their enemies were gradually working their way closer to the ravine from both directions, and he prayed that none of them had grenades.

※ ※ ※

Tobin Manischewitz's jaw tightened as Kazimierz Mészáros reported Terjo O'Connor's death. That burst of pulser darts had sawn off O'Connor's right leg like a hypervelocity chainsaw. He bled to death in minutes, and neither Mészáros nor O'Connor's partner, Schreiber, could have reached him to do anything about it even if they'd tried.

They were down to only six men now, but they were also within no more than forty or fifty meters of the ravine.

Only a few more minutes, he thought grimly, sending another long burst of darts screaming towards their objective as Yang dashed fifteen meters closer and flung himself back to the ground just in time. *Next time, I frigging well will bring grenades, no matter* what *the mission profile says, damn it! But we're almost there. Only a few more minutes, a couple of more rushes, and we'll have them.*

※ ※ ※

Something made Alfred look up.

He never knew what that something was, or why. Perhaps it was only instinct, because it couldn't have been anything he'd heard. At Mach six it was upon them long before the sound of its passage, but one glance told him what it was.

He threw himself back from this position, grabbing for Allison, dragging her down into the bottom of the ravine, and flung his body across hers as the universe came apart.

※ ※ ※

Tobin Manischewitz never had time to realize what was happening.

His calculations had never factored in the possibility of an all-up assault shuttle. The use of transatmospheric military craft in civilian airspace at speeds in excess of Mach two wasn't simply frowned upon;

it was profoundly illegal. Assault shuttles didn't have the strident transponders of civilian emergency vehicles to warn other traffic to scatter out of their flight paths. They didn't have the ability to override air-car flight computers to clear them out of the way, either. And they certainly didn't have authority to rip across civilian flight corridors in the middle of the day at better than six thousand kilometers per hour. Any hotshot military pilot foolish enough to try something like that was looking at a court-martial and serious prison time, not just demotion, reprimands, or fines.

Manischewitz knew all of that. So did the BSC. The problem was that the BSC didn't *care*.

※ ※ ※

The assault shuttle came shrieking in far ahead of its earthshaking sonic boom, and its targeting systems had hacked a direct feed from one of the Beowulf System Defense Force's tactical satellites. The SDF almost certainly would have given it to them anyway, but there'd been no time to go through channels, and the BSC always *had* been an . . . unconventional organization.

Jacques Benton-Ramirez y Chou occupied the gunner's station, and his dark brown eyes were chipped agate. He'd watched the vicious firefight through the satellite while the shuttle howled off the ground, accelerating so rapidly its nose and leading wing edges glowed white with heat while its crew rode the grav plates against the G forces which should have crushed them back into their flight couches. Nobody could possibly have reached his sister more rapidly than they could, but her location was over five hundred kilometers from from Camp Oswald Avery. That was seven minutes' flight—not even an assault shuttle could accelerate instantly to Mach six in atmosphere—and the satellite looking down on the location fix from the still-transmitting com had frozen his heart within him. He had no idea who was with her, but the satellite's exquisitely sensitive sensors had shown him only two people in that ravine with ten closing in on them, and seven minutes was an eternity in combat.

But somehow Allison and whoever was with her had managed to hang on. Not only to hang on, but to take steady toll of their enemies. And now, as the shuttle hurtled towards them like Juggernaut, he squeezed the trigger on the gunner's joystick.

Two pods blasted from the shuttle's weapons bay on meticulously plotted flight paths. They accelerated away at a rate which dwarfed even the shuttle's shrieking engines, and then they blew apart . . . directly above the men closing in on that ravine. Four thousand powered flechettes blasted straight down from each of them in precisely targeted oval patterns, each a hundred meters long and forty meters across, whose inner perimeters came within twenty-five meters of both sides of the ravine. Solid clouds of dust and semi-vaporized soil exploded upward from the beaten zone, and as the assault shuttle flashed overhead, banking hard to kill velocity and reverse course, there was no living thing beneath that rising pall of death.

❈ ❈ ❈

Allison Chou opened her eyes to a pastel ceiling and sunlight. Her gaze took in the bedside readouts, recognized the familiar aura of a hospital, and it was so quiet she could hear the soft, quiet beep of the heart monitor.

She lay very still for a moment, holding her breath, then exhaled in a deep, cleansing sigh of relief as she realized she didn't hurt anywhere. She closed her eyes again, lips trembling in gratitude, and then, to her own surprise, she smiled.

Your priorities need work, she told herself. *Not hurting is wonderful, but you might want to reflect on the fact that you're still* alive, *too*.

A throat cleared itself, and her eyes popped open again, her head turning to the left on the pillow. Matching eyes looked back at her, and she watched them blink, saw the tears in them, and reached for her brother's hand.

"Hi," she said. Her voice was huskier than usual, her throat sore and raspy, and she shivered as she remembered the screams which had made it that way. Jacques must have seen the shadow in her eyes, for his hand tightened on hers as he leaned forward to kiss her forehead.

"Hi, yourself," he said, and the huskiness in *his* voice had nothing to do with screams. He sat back a bit, lifting the back of her hand to touch his cheek, and shook his head. "Had me worried there, Alley."

"Me, too." Her lips trembled again for just a moment as they shaped a smile, then her eyes narrowed. "It was Manpower, wasn't it?"

"Yes." Jacques lowered her hand from his cheek, holding it on the edge of her hospital bed in both of his, and cleared his throat.

"Yes," he repeated, "it was."

"What did they want?"

"Information. They wanted me to turn over the identities of all of our people working out of the embassies and consulates in Silesia." Jacques' mouth twisted. "I'm sure they'd have gotten around to asking for more, eventually, but that was 'all' they asked for the first time around."

Allison's eyes widened. She'd guessed it had to be something like that, but surely Manpower must have realized Jacques couldn't— *wouldn't*—have given them that sort of information, no matter what they did to her. It would have destroyed him not to, but he would have known even better than she what Manpower would have done with that information, how many other lives it would have cost. And as she looked into his eyes, she saw the confirmation—saw his own anguished knowledge that he couldn't have done it even to save her.

"It wouldn't have mattered," she told him now, freeing her hand from his to stroke the side of his face. "It wouldn't have, Jacques." She shook her head, her eyes dark. "They were going to kill me anyway in the end."

"I know," he whispered, closing his eyes and turning his head to press his cheek more firmly against her palm. "I knew it from the beginning. Part of it was who we are, and part of it was to send a message." He managed a brief, quirky smile. "Apparently they were even more upset with me over something that happened on Old Earth than I thought they were." He inhaled deeply. "I always knew what I do could splash on the people I care about—even on you, Alley—but I never really *believed* it. Not until now."

"That's because what you do is so much worth doing," she told him. "And while we're kicking ourselves, I probably should've been just a bit more careful myself."

"Well," he said grimly, "I think I can assure you that Manpower's never going to come close to you again, Alley."

There was something hard, frightening, about his eyes, and Allison felt her eyebrows rise in question. He saw it, and laughed harshly.

"We got one of them alive—found him tied up with tape in a utility shed, I believe—and we've . . . spoken to him at some length. And because we have, we know who planned and authorized the entire operation. The person who actually planned it is already dead; some time in the next few T-months, the people—plural—who authorized it will *also* be dead. In at least two cases, that's going to require an operation on Mesa itself, so we'll probably start there—take out the hardest targets first—and then pick the others off later. But trust me, Alley. Manpower will get *our* message loud and clear."

"I don't want anybody to risk—" she began, thinking of the enormous dangers of mounting any sort of operation on Mesa, whose security services were among the most efficient—and brutal—in the explored galaxy. What had happened to her was bad enough already; if men and women of the BSC were killed "avenging her," it would be even worse.

"It doesn't matter what you want, Alley." Allison looked into Jacques's eyes and knew that flat, hard voice belonged not to her brother, but to Captain Benton-Ramirez y Chou, Biological Survey Corps. "And this isn't about getting even for what they did to you. Oh, there's some of that involved, don't think for a minute there isn't! But this whole thing started when they tried to assassinate Aurèle Fairmount-Solbakken on Old Earth. Our reaction there was purely defensive, but then they escalated, went after the Corps right here on Beowulf, and did it in a way guaranteed to underscore the fact that they *were* escalating. We don't like that, and we're going to make it very clear to them that it was a really, *really* bad idea. The sort of idea that gets the people who approve it dead, no matter how long it takes or how hard they are to reach."

"You really expect that to stop it?" She sounded skeptical, and she knew it, but he only showed his teeth in a thin, cold smile.

"Manpower isn't the Ballroom, Alley. They're not motivated by belief systems or the need to liberate the victims of genetic slavery. They don't think that way, because they're only in it for the money. They don't give a damn how many people they kill or maim or torture—just like you—in the process, of course, because people aren't human beings to them; they're only things to be used. Only disposable, replaceable, unimportant items on a spreadsheet somewhere. But they think in terms of doing things to *other* people. They think their wealth and their power and the Mesan security systems protect them from people who might think about doing the same sorts of things to them. We're going to have to hush the whole thing up, of course—if the rest of Beowulf found out about this, they'd probably demand an all-out military strike on Mesa, and you can just imagine how the rest of the League would feel about *that!* But *Manpower* knows about it, and they'll understand our response just fine. They think of themselves as 'businessmen,' Alley, and when they discover the cost of 'doing business' here on Beowulf, or against people like Fairmont-Salbakken or, yes, people like *you*, they'll decide it's too high."

Allison looked up at him, tasting the harsh iron in his voice, seeing the flint behind his eyes. Perhaps he was right. She *hoped* he was, anyway, and she felt a reflection of that same flint, that same iron, deep in her own soul. She'd always hated and despised genetic slavery. Now it was personal. Now she'd experienced at least a taste of what millions upon millions of genetic slaves had endured for centuries, and she *understood* the truth of their existence in a way no bloodless intellectual analysis could ever have shown her.

Jacques looked back at her for a long, still moment. Then he shook himself and smiled.

"That's enough doom and gloom for a while, Alley! Wait here. I'll be back in a sec."

"Wait here?" she thought as he climbed out of the chair and disappeared, closing the hospital room door behind him. She looked down at the flimsy hospital gown—some things never seemed to change—and shook her head. *Just where does he think I'm going to go? Until they get me some clothes, at least! Besides, he and I both know doctors too well to think anyone's going to release me just because I happen to feel fine. They're going to be running neurological tests and psych evaluations for days before anyone's willing to sign off on—*

The door opened again, and her thoughts broke off as a very tall man followed Jacques back into the room. Her eyes widened, and then she realized he'd been on the other side of that door all along. That she'd *known* he was, even as she spoke to her brother, and that she hadn't realized she knew only because it had been so natural, so inevitable, that he *had* to be there. She would have recognized his absence instantly; his presence was like the beat of her own heart, so central, so necessary to her own completion, that it called itself to her attention only when it *wasn't* there.

That's what it was all along, she realized. *That . . . incompletion.*

That sense that things were out of balance somehow. It was because he was too far away. Or maybe because neither of us knew what was going on, what was happening.

A distant part of her brain told her that she still had no idea what was happening, or why, but that didn't matter. It wasn't something which had to be understood; it was simply something which *was*, and she felt her face blossoming in a huge smile as that awareness flowed through them both.

"I don't believe the two of you have ever been formally introduced," Jacques said. "Alley, may I present Lieutenant Karl Alfred Harrington, Royal Manticoran Navy. Lieutenant Harrington, allow me to present my sister, Allison Carmena Elena Inéz Regina Benton-Ramirez y Chou."

He smiled devilishly as Allison darted a deadly look in his direction, but the smile softened quickly, and he reached up to lay one hand on the towering Sphinxian's shoulder.

"I don't pretend to understand everything Alfred's told me, Alley. I don't have to. I know what he *did*. That's more than enough for me, and I also know I'll never be able to repay him for doing it."

He looked into her eyes for a moment, and then he walked back out of the room, closing the door behind him once more.

"Good morning, Lieutenant Harrington," she said softly, holding out her hand—and her heart—to him. "Thank you for my life."

He took her hand in his as if it were the most precious thing in the entire universe and settled into the chair beside the bed. His eyes were dark, examining her face with an almost frightening intensity, as if he had to confirm that she was actually there. That she truly had survived. She shivered as she felt the searing power behind that regard, the *need*. It was the most powerful emotion she'd ever felt . . . and it was someone else's. Under other circumstances, in another time or another place, or from another *person*, that . . . hunger for her would have terrified her with the iron tang of its compulsiveness. Its *obsessiveness*.

But this wasn't another time or another place, and it certainly wasn't another person, and what would have terrified her under those other circumstances had no power to frighten under these, for she felt the same need within herself. She shivered not because it *frightened* her, but because it had become so central to who and what she was and it had taken her all unaware. It was so warm, so caring, so *gentle* and yet so ferociously strong. It made her want to laugh, to cry, to fling her arms around him and bury his face in kisses. It sang through her like the note of some enormous crystalline bell fit to set the universe singing, and it was simultaneously the most comforting and the most erotic thing she had ever experienced in her life.

She didn't know how long the two of them simply gazed at each other. It seemed to last forever, and yet it ended far too soon as he drew a deep breath and settled farther back in the chair, still holding her hand.

"Allison Carmena Elena Inéz Regina *Benton-Ramirez y Chou*," he said in that deep voice that sent little shivers of delight through her bones. "Excuse me, but I sort of thought your name was Allison *Chou*. It would've simplified things a lot if I'd known you were a Benton-Ramirez y Chou when this whole thing started. I could've called in the whole *world* to get someone from your family out of trouble! At least I'd've known to call your *brother*, anyway."

"Yes, that's my entire name, *Karl*," she said in a slightly dangerous tone. "It's also something I've spent most of my life running away from," she added in a softer voice, admitting something she would have admitted to very few.

"Why?" he asked simply.

"For the same reason they hung all those names on me in the first place. Because I want to be *me*, not just another Benton-Ramirez y Chou buried under all those tons of family history and tradition. Nobody on Beowulf would dream of forcing me to do anything I didn't want to do . . . and that won't stop them for an instant from doing it anyway. I don't want to be preprogrammed. I want to know— to *know*, Alfred—that the decisions I make are *my* decisions. And I don't want to be some kind of . . . of medical *royalty*. I want to be just Allison.

"I'm not like Jacques. It's never occurred to him for a moment to live up to the expectations people have of our family. Trust me, there are scores of people who were disappointed in him, who looked down their noses at him when he refused to go into medicine and settled for being an obscure, fairly junior military officer—and one who doesn't seem to take his duties all that seriously, for that matter. But that's because they don't really *know* him. They don't know what he's truly done with his life, what he still plans on doing with it, and having so many people underestimate him and take him lightly is part of what lets him do that so very well. But I don't want that. I want what I'm pretty sure the first Benton, and the first Ramirez, and the first Chou who took up medicine wanted. I just want to be a *doctor*, Alfred. That's all. Just to be a doctor doing what a doctor does, one patient at a time, because it fills her with joy and she knows it's what she chose to do and not what everyone *expected* her to do."

She stopped, suddenly and burningly aware that she had never once expressed that so clearly to anyone.

Including myself, she realized wonderingly. *I've never found the words for it before. Maybe because I've never really looked at it that clearly till I had to explain it to him. And I did have to explain it to him, even if I never have to explain it to another human being ever again. I had to tell* him.

"I can see that," he told her, and she realized he truly could. That he did, with a clarity no one else could have matched. He looked at her for another few moments, and then his eyes darkened and he looked away, as if unable to meet her gaze any longer.

"I can see that," he repeated in a low voice freighted with some emotion she couldn't quite identify, "because I'm running away, too."

She stared at him, and suddenly she knew with that emotion was. It was *shame.* And it was worse than that, for it was leavened with horror as well. It was that darkness within him, and it frightened him as dreadfully as the neural whip had terrified her, but—

"You're wrong," she told him softly. He froze, and she squeezed his hand. "I know what you're afraid of, and you're wrong."

Stillness hung between them for long, silent seconds. And then, finally, he looked back down at her, and she felt the roiling force of his emotions.

Neither of them, she realized in that moment, would ever be able to lie to the other. Whatever sang and danced between them, there could be no prevarication, no deceit in it. But the fact that they couldn't lie didn't necessarily mean that what they believed was the *truth,* either, and she felt the power of his rejection. Felt his need to strangle the monster before the monster destroyed him or, far worse, the people he cared about.

"I know what you're afraid of," she repeated, and squeezed his hand even more tightly, shaking it between them for emphasis. "I *know*. I don't know *how* I know, and I don't know why, but I do, and you're wrong."

"No," he half-whispered. "*You're* wrong. You weren't there. You didn't *see*."

"I didn't have to be there then," she said gently. "I was here now. I saw the man who came for me, who saved me, and I know *that* man better than I've ever known anyone else in my entire life. I know him better than I know myself, because I see and feel him whole and entire. Because—Oh, I don't have the *words* for it, Alfred, and neither do you, but you know what I mean!"

"Allison—"

His hand tightened on hers, and for the first time she felt its true strength in that viselike pressure. It hurt, but it was a *good* hurt, and she met his eyes unflinchingly, knowing what he was about to say.

"I got people killed," he told her, his voice frayed around the edges, his eyes bottomless as interstellar space. "So many people. And I killed so many others myself. It was . . . it was—God, I don't know how to *tell* anyone what it was like!"

He was trembling, and she laid her left hand atop the one which was crushing her right as she saw the ghosts in his eyes and felt what *he* was feeling as he faced them.

"I had to do it," he said. "I *had* to. If I hadn't, even more people would've died, and not just on Clematis. I didn't have a *choice*, and I knew it, and it was what I was trained to do. But I did it so *well*. I was like . . . like a *machine*, Allison. It was all ice and focus and purpose and I'd never been so *alive* in my life. And it was even worse than that. It was a need . . . a *hunger*. I knew exactly what I was doing every moment, and I never hesitated, never flinched, never once stopped to think about all the lives I was taking. At the end I was covered, literally *covered* with blood, and I probably shot at least a dozen people who were only trying to surrender before I could make myself stop."

His soul was in his eyes, strangled by the ghosts of his dead, and she recognized the anguish in it. She understood it, and she felt the tears in her own eyes.

"I don't know what happened on Clematis," she said quietly. "I never even heard of it before. But I know what's inside you, Alfred.

That's why you asked for a transfer to the Navy and medical school, isn't it?"

"I'm too good at killing people," he said very, very softly. "Too good at it. And if I let the monster out again, what will it do? What if I *become* the monster? What if that becomes who and what I *am?* I don't want to live with that. I *won't* live with that. And that's why I ran away from the Marines, why I'm hiding as a doctor instead of what I really am."

"What you are *is* a doctor." Her soft voice was as unyielding as battle steel. "You may be running *from* what happened on this Clematis, but what you're running *to* is what you were always meant to be. It's not just guilt, not just trying to find some safe way to sublimate your 'monster' and expiate your responsibility for all the people who died. Tell me you don't take joy in it! Tell me you don't know deep at the core of you that this is what you want more than any other possible life's work. *Tell* me that, Alfred, because you may be able to lie to yourself, but you can't lie to *me.*"

His lips trembled, and she shook her head.

"Jacques is a historian," she told him. "More than a historian—at least half our family thinks he's some kind of nut. He belongs to something called the Society for Creative Anachronism, and he's got an entire library stuffed with old books and stories that go clear back to pre-space Old Earth. He used to read to me for hours when I was a child, and one of those stories was about a girl who agreed to become a monster's prisoner to save her father. Only the monster wasn't a monster—not really. But he was under a curse, and he couldn't stop being one, couldn't transform himself back into the human being he was meant to be. Not until *she* realized the truth. That broke the spell, and I thought it was a wonderful story when I was a little girl, but I realize now that it went even deeper than that. *He* had to believe he was no longer a monster, no longer 'the beast' he'd allowed himself to become. He needed to care more about her than about anything else in the world and let go of the things that had twisted his outside appearance to match the torment inside him. And when she saw beneath that appearance, she allowed him to see it as well."

She shook her head, her eyes brimming with tears, and lifted his suddenly lax hand in both of hers. She cradled it against her tear-slick cheek and smiled at him.

"That's us, Alfred. It's *us*! Me, running away from home because I need to be myself, and you, terrified of your 'monster,' afraid you're becoming the beast. But you're not. Maybe the beast is inside there, but it isn't *you*. You *control* it, and it was the beast that let you save my life. And you didn't come for me because you wanted an excuse to kill other people. You came for me because what you are is a good, caring, decent, *gentle* man. I know that—I *see* that—and you know I do. You *know* it, Alfred, and you've been alone with the beast too long. Trust me. Oh, *trust* me, my love."

❀ ❀ ❀

Alfred Harrington gazed into those shining, tear-filled eyes, feeling her total certitude, her absolute belief, and something crumbled inside him as she called him "my love." Something he'd clung to for so long simply turned to smoke in his hands as he realized she was right. She was *right*. The monster—the beast—*was* part of him, but so was she, and he could turn away from the exaltation of the Angel of Death and find the monster's silver bullet in her. Not as some sort of talisman, some kind of magic charm, but as the one person in the entire universe who truly *knew* him for who and what he was . . . and was not.

He reached out a left hand which had never shaken even once in combat on Clematis or here on Beowulf, and its fingers trembled as he touched her face with feather gentleness and leaned towards her.

"I do, Alley," he whispered. "I do."

And their lips met at last.

THE BEST
LAID PLANS

David Weber

THE BEST LAID PLANS

"I don't really mind your going as far as the dam by yourself if it's all right with your mother, you pack a lunch, and you remember not to be late for dinner."

"Of course it's all right with Mom. I talked with her after breakfast, before she left for the office, and she said it sounded like a good idea to her. I wouldn't have asked you if she hadn't."

"Oh?" Her father cocked his head at her from the com screen a moment later, after the inevitable transmission delay. She could see the bulkead of his office aboard the space station *Hephaestus* behind him in the display, and his expression was just the tiniest bit skeptical "I seem to remember a few occasions when you neglected to make sure of that minor fact."

She concentrated on looking simultaneously as innocent as the new fallen snow and moderately martyred. He continued to gaze at her for several moments, then snorted.

"All right, Honor. Go! Have fun. And be careful!"

"Yes, Sir," she said obediently and waited for the display to clear. Then she shook her head. "And yada yada yada," she added under her breath, rolling her eyes. "I'm not exactly an *infant* anymore, Dad."

Fortunately, the link had already been closed. And even more fortunately, from Honor's perspective, her father hadn't specifically asked her if she'd asked her mother for permission. She could say with scrupulous honesty, as she just had, that she had discussed the possibility of the expedition with her mother over breakfast, and that her mother had expressed no opposition to the notion. Indeed, her female parental unit had been cheerfully in favor of it. Of course, Honor hadn't quite gotten around to informing her mother that she was thinking about making that trip *today*, but that didn't change the fact that Mom had clearly been agreeable to the notion in a general sort of way. And it wasn't *her* fault her mother was going to be tied up with patients straight through to lunch. Or that there were strict rules about not breaking into consult time or interfering with examinations, except in cases of emergency. And since no one could argue that this came under the heading "emergency," it was obvious she couldn't *possibly* justify screening her mother directly over something this minor.

Honor was aware that a true stickler might argue that she'd been guilty of misleading both of her parents to at least a tiny extent, but she *had* cleared it, and with just a little more luck, Dad would forget to ask Mom if she had authorized the trip for today.

Yeah, sure! And when was the last *time you had that much luck?* she asked herself sardonically. Actually, the odds were pretty good she'd find herself grounded for at least a week, but that would be a fair exchange. If her timing was right, the huge banks of purple mountain tulip above the dam should have come into full blossom during the last three or four days.

Honor hadn't mentioned their existence to either of her parents, because they just happened to be her mother's favorite from among all the flowers and blossoming trees of Sphinx . . . and tomorrow just happened to be her mother's birthday. She had a carefully worked-out plan that began with the double-chocolate cake (her mother's favorite flavor) and culminated with the original copy of the sixth-century Diaspora poet Dzau Syung-kai's collected works, which her Uncle Jacques had found on Beowulf, and enough of those mountain tulips for the enormous centerpiece she was constructing for the dining-room table would be the crowning touch.

She couldn't very well explain all of that if she wanted her birthday present to be a surprise, and even if she could have she was pretty sure her mother would never have let her go that far into the bush without "adult supervision." Neither of her parents believed in keeping their daughter wrapped up in cotton, and they seldom objected to her spending a day rambling around in the woods as long as she didn't stray too far from the house. Her father insisted that she take along a pistol when she did (a paternal decree to a then eleven-year-old daughter, which Honor suspected her mother, who'd grown up on *über*-civilized Beowulf, had taken some getting used to), but she'd been rigorously drilled in gun safety since her tenth birthday. Their definition of "too far from the house" (and especially her mother's) wasn't quite as flexible as she might have wished, however.

In fact, that was the reason she'd been creatively vague talking to her father. Honor never lied to her parents—even when she'd tried, her father had always been able to tell as easily as if her skull were made of glass and he'd been able to peer inside it, so she'd given up the effort early—but there was a difference between lying and . . . shaping the truth to best advantage, and this was a perfect example. There were two dams, both with their own populations of near-beavers, and she hadn't gone out of her way to tell Commander Harrington which of them she intended to visit. When he asked her about it, she was going to have to admit it had suited her purposes for both of her parents to assume she was talking about the one on Sand Bottom Creek, where she'd been conducting her school wildlife observation project for the last three months. And she was also going to have to admit that while she'd known neither of her parents would have any problem with her going by herself to Sand Bottom, they *would* have objected—strenuously—to her wandering off to Rock Aspen Creek. That was almost five kilometers deeper into the freehold . . . and the SFS had reported that peak bears were coming down out of the higher mountains early this fall.

Honor could understand why her parents might think that feeding the peak bears—especially if the meal in question happened to be their only daughter—wasn't the very best idea anyone ever had. On the other hand, she had no intention of doing anything of the sort. She'd grown up in the woods, hunting with her father and fishing the streams of her family's freehold or hang-gliding across it. She wouldn't go so far as to say she knew every nook and cranny—that would have been a bit much for a square of mountains and still-virgin forest twenty-five kilometers on a side—but she'd hiked and flown over most of those sixty-two thousand-plus hectares one time or another. And she knew Rock Aspen better than most, since it was one of her and her father's favorite places to fish. She knew how to keep her eye out for the nastier members of Sphinx's wildlife, too. That was something of a family tradition, after all, all the way back to Great-Great-Great-Great-Whatever-Grandma Stephanie. It was unfortunate that she couldn't hang-glide to Rock Aspen because of the tree cover (not to mention the quantity of tulips she planned to be bringing back), but her personal counter-grav would still take her up a tree in jig time, as Uncle Jacques liked to put it, if something wicked came her way.

And just in case something went wrong with Plan A, there was always Plan B, which was why she had claimed her Simpson & Wong from the gun safe. She didn't really expect to need it, but when the inevitable parental wrath descended upon her head, she would be in a position to point out that anything which had wanted to eat her would have had to comb the S&W's old-fashioned ten-millimeter slugs out of its teeth first. Her mother probably wouldn't be especially moved, but she expected her father would cut her a little slack if she could demonstrate she'd been suitably armed to deal with trouble. He'd probably prefer one of his pulse rifles to the S&W's old-fashioned nitro-powder, but he was also the one who'd taught her to shoot, and he knew what she could do with a rifle or a pistol. She'd just shot High Expert in the Twin Forks Youth League for the SFC and walked away with the Shelton Cup for the second year in a row, with a score of 600 out of a possible 600, and at a hundred meters, the S&W's 19.5-gram bullet, traveling at 840 meters per second, would deliver almost 7,000 joules of energy to any unfriendly critter she encountered. In fact, it would deliver over 3,000 joules all the way out to five hundred meters, although she didn't have any business shooting anything at that range "in self-defense." Besides, the S&W was her favorite shoulder gun, and not just because it had been her birthday gift from Uncle Jacques two years ago.

It had been almost as long as she was, at the time, although she'd put on one of the promised (or threatened) growth spurts since then. Now she was closing in on thirteen T-years old and already almost a hundred and seventy centimeters tall. That left her over thirty centimeters shorter than her father, but it meant she towered over her mother. Big enough to handle the S&W's buffered recoil, anyway.

Honor told herself that was a good thing and tried not to think about how . . . overgrown she was beginning to feel. No one was quite sure when so much altitude had crept into the family's genes, although the majority opinion was that they could look all the way back to Great-Great-Great-Great-Whatever-Granddad Karl. There seemed to be a few holes in that theory, as far as she was concerned, though. Certainly her grandfather had been tall—almost as tall as her dad, in fact—as had *his* parents, but most of the previous generations had been of little more than average height, so where had Grandad Karl's genes been *then*? Besides, there was her mom's genetic contribution to consider, and all of the Beowulf side of the family was on the short side.

Wherever all that height had come from, and however great a thing it might seem to the *male* members of the family, it was a pain in the backside for an all-but-thirteen-year-old girl who could confidently expect to break a hundred and eighty centimeters before she was done and had a brilliantly intelligent, exotically beautiful, sleekly graceful, *petite* mother. She loved her mom dearly, but why, oh why, couldn't the female Dr. Harrington have passed along some of that beauty to her daughter? Or at least offset the upsizing which had afflicted the family for so long?

She brushed the thought aside, texted an "I'm going out, Mom!" to her mother's account; pulled on her jacket; slung the S&W over her shoulder; checked her belt gun, bush knife and counter-grav; made sure the uni-link in her pocket was fully charged; hung her lunch-packed rucksack over the other shoulder; snagged her favorite fedora from the coat tree; and headed for the door.

❀ ❀ ❀

<*And how much trouble are you in with Songstress today?*> Sharp Nose asked amiably, turning on the branch to present his belly fur to the sun.

<*And why do you assume I must be in trouble with Songstress at all?*> Laughs Brightly inquired, looking down at his younger brother from the branch above him.

<*Because both of you are awake at the same time,*> Sharp Nose replied dryly. <*If you have not yet done anything to irritate her, I am sure you will get around to it soon.*>

Laughs Brightly flirted his tail, but he also bleeked a laugh of agreement. Bright Water Clan's newest memory singer was the daughter of their mother's sister, and she seemed to feel it was her familial duty to restrain Laughs Brightly's sense of humor.

Or attempt to, at any rate.

<You wrong me,> he told Sharp Nose after a moment. *<I have not done anything which could possibly upset her since I helped show Crooked Tail his golden ear supply was not as safely stored as he thought it was.>*

<That long?> Sharp Nose marveled. *<Why, that was almost a full hand of days ago!>*

<Not quite,> Laughs Brightly admitted modestly, *<but close.>*

<And has Crooked Tail thanked you for assisting him?>

<Not yet. I am sure he will once he has discovered all of the places where I hid it, though.>

Sharp Nose shook his head in one of the gestures the People had learned from the two-legs with whom they shared their world. Laughs Brightly was almost a full hand of turnings his elder, and much as Sharp Nose loved him, he had never understood how his prankster brother could be so popular with the rest of the clan. Crooked Tail, who was almost certain to become one of Bright Water's elders in the next few turnings, was not noted for his sense of humor. Yet even though every member of the clan knew exactly who had purloined his treasured supply of stored golden ear, no one—including him—had attempted to take Laughs Brightly's ears over it. No doubt that was because they knew he would return every single ear of grain the moment Crooked Tail asked him to. Which, of course, made it a matter of pride for Crooked Tail to find all of Laughs Brightly's hiding places personally. Exactly how Laughs Brightly had managed to steal away the other Person's entire supply without being caught at it was just one of those mysteries Laughs Brightly excelled at creating. Still, he had been scrupulous about leaving Crooked Tail the clues he needed to identify the one who had "borrowed" his grain.

<I do not know how you have survived this long, Brother,> Sharp Nose said now.

<Every clan needs someone like me,> Laughs Brightly replied tranquilly, his mind-voice rich with amusement. *<We keep the rest of you from becoming too set in your ways.>*

<You mean you keep all of us hovering in dread of what you are going to do to us next.>

<But that is exactly what I just said!>

<I am sure you think so, at any rate.>

Laughs Brightly laughed again, then leapt lightly down to his brother's lower branch and stretched out beside him.

<*You are becoming too fat and lazy for one of your youth, Sharp Nose. You should come with me today. The exercise would be good for you, and perhaps a day in my company will help teach you how to laugh!*>

<*And where are you headed?*> Sharp Nose asked a bit suspiciously. His brother was one of Bright Water Clan's most skilled scouts—another reason the rest of the clan put up with his supposed sense of humor, no doubt—and his idea of a leisurely jaunt through the net-wood could quickly exhaust anyone unwary enough to accept one of his invitations.

<*It is not that far,*> Laughs Brightly chided. <*Only as far as Thunder Mist. Bark Master and Wind of Memory have asked me to estimate how many swimmers the stream holds and to discover whether or not the green-needle and gray-bark pods have been stunted by the dry weather.*> His mind-voice turned a bit more serious. <*The task would go more quickly with another to help.*>

Sharp Nose twitched his whiskers at the idea that Thunder Mist was "not far" from the clan's central nesting place, but Laughs Brightly's mission was clearly an important one. They were well into leaf-turning. It would not be so very much longer before the first snows began to blow down from the mountains, and green-needle and gray-bark pods were an important—and tasty—part of the People's diet during the months of ice. And he had to admit that he was flattered by Laughs Brightly's invitation. Although Sharp Nose was respected as a hunter and a tracker, he was not one of those normally chosen for the sorts of tasks the clan's scouts usually undertook. He knew part of that was his youth, for he was barely half Laughs Brightly's age, and the opportunity to spend the day in his brother's company was an attractive thought. In many ways, for all its importance, Laughs Brightly's task was routine, but Sharp Nose could still learn a great deal under the tutelage of such a skilled scout. Besides, despite the difference in their ages, he and Laughs Brightly had always been close.

<*No doubt you will need me to help keep you from getting lost,*> he said after a moment, and heaved a great sigh as he rolled over and came to his feet. <*So I suppose I had better come and keep an eye on you.*>

❀ ❀ ❀

From comments her mother had made upon occasion, Honor supposed that someone who hadn't been born and raised on Sphinx might have found the morning chilly. For her, though, it was merely a bit brisk, and she walked with her jacket unsealed, enjoying the crisp, clean air. Dried leaves crackled underfoot as she made her way through the near-pine and red spruce, the sound sharper and louder than it really should have been thanks to the dry weather. It wasn't as bad as it had been upon occasion, though. Every four or five planetary years—twenty or twenty-five T-years—they had a *really* dry summer and fall, the sort that turned Sphinx's forests into tinder boxes. She couldn't remember a year like that, but her father could, and he'd been increasingly firm in his warnings about careless use of fire as the long, slow summer drew on. The predictions were that this winter would produce even more snow and snow pack than usual, though, and that should help next year. She didn't know about that; it would be only her third winter, and the first one didn't count, since she'd been born halfway through the first one and didn't remember it at all.

And it would also probably be her *last* winter at home. Her pace slackened for a moment, and she looked around and filled her lungs to the aching point with the cool Sphinxian air, the treasured scents and smells of the woods of the planet on which she had been born and raised. She would miss them—oh, how she would miss them!—but there was always a price to pay for dreams, and she'd known ever since she'd been a very little girl sitting in her father's lap what her dream was.

Honor didn't really know where it had come from. Part of it was probably her father's example, although she had no temptation to become a physician as both he and her mother had. Besides, he'd been only the third member of her family to serve in the Royal Navy, and the only one in the last three or four generations. He hadn't started in the Navy, either, although he'd never explained to her exactly why he'd transferred into it from the Royal Marines. She'd asked—once, when she'd been much younger—but he hadn't told her. That was unusual, because he and her mother always answered her questions. She was pretty sure that meant it had been something ugly, something he hadn't wanted to talk about with her until she was older. Or maybe even at all. Fathers could be like that. Especially, she suspected, with daughters, which was pretty silly, since he was the one who'd taught her how to dress out her own game when she'd been only ten T-years old and she'd been cleaning fish for at least two T-years before that. But she supposed there was a difference between skinning and butchering prong bucks or a Baxter Goose and killing another human being.

She'd found her father's medals two years ago and looked them up. That was how she'd found out that the Osterman Cross was the Star Kingdom's second highest decoration, that it could be earned only for "extraordinary heroism" in combat, and that it could be awarded only to enlisted personnel and noncommissioned officers. But she'd also discovered that the award was classified. Or if it wasn't *officially* classified, where, when, and how Platoon Sergeant Harrington, RMMC, had earned it wasn't part of the public record, at least, for some reason. Then there were the three wound stripes he'd been awarded. He hadn't gotten those as a Navy doctor, either, and if he hadn't wanted to discuss how he *had* earned them with his then-eleven-year-old daughter, he'd earned that right, as well. Someday, she knew, he would tell her about them, if only to be sure she truly understood the possible consequences of the career she'd already chosen. Until that day, she could wait.

Her mother seemed a bit more baffled by her plans than her father did, but she'd never tried to talk Honor out of them. A military career wasn't exactly high on the probable career tracks of upper-class Beowulfers like Allison Harrington, but unlike some star nations, Beowulf did regard it as an honorable profession. Uncle Jacques had served in the Biological Survey Corps, too, and despite its peculiar name, the BSC was one of the best special-forces organizations in the Solarian League. Whatever anyone else might think of the military, her mom had always been a firm supporter of both the BSC and her father's Navy career.

No, Allison's bafflement had far more to do with how early—and how firmly—Honor had made her decision. And the amount of planning she'd already put into it. They'd discussed it more than once, and her mom had suggested that perhaps she might have waited at least until she was, oh, nine or ten before deciding what to do with the entire rest of her life. Ambition was a good thing, and so was clear thinking, forethought, and planning, her mother had pointed out, but most people seemed to wait just a *bit* longer before diving into such decisions. That seemed pretty silly of them to Honor. If you knew what you wanted to do with your life, then you ought to start working on it as soon as possible. That was only sensible. The female Dr. Harrington had muttered something about "forces of nature," "stubbornness," and "statistical outliers" (not to mention an occasional "*just* like her father!"), but she'd finally conceded the point. Which had simply proven to Honor how much her mother loved her . . . and that she was smart enough to recognize when discretion was the better part of valor. Perhaps she still hoped Honor might grow out of it, but if she didn't, Allison would be just as supportive as her husband.

Honor treasured knowing that, even if she didn't know what had originally sparked her interest in naval history. Maybe it was the way the Star Kingdom's dependence on the commerce pouring through the Manticoran Wormhole Junction made the Navy such a vital part of its life and prosperity. Maybe she was just fascinated by the thought of distant suns and planets, different people and cultures. Or maybe it was all just a romantic fantasy that she'd grow out of quickly once she experienced the reality. All she knew was that she'd read and viewed every scrap of naval history—all the way back to when warships had floated in water back on Old Earth, before humanity ever ventured beyond atmosphere the first time—she could get her hands on for as long as she could remember. And she knew—*knew*—she wanted a starship's deck beneath her feet in the service of her king. It was . . . important to her in some way she'd never been able to articulate clearly, even to herself.

But she *would* miss mornings like this one, she thought, looking around her and trying to absorb the essence of Sphinx through her pores. This was where she came from, this was who she'd grown up being, the place that would always be there at the center of her memories. She knew that even some of her fellow Sphinxians, far less people who'd been born and raised on Manticore, probably thought of people like her and her family as backwoodsmen. Rubes who weren't quite civilized, or they wouldn't let twelve-year-olds wander around the woods packing guns. Most of them came from cities, however, and Honor regarded anyone doomed to that sort of existence with a kind of bemused tolerance, even pity. People who thought that way *shouldn't* be allowed to wander around the woods where they might get hurt. That meant they would never enjoy a morning like this, though, and the loss was theirs.

Oh, stop it! she told herself with a grin. *Yeah, you'll be headed off to the Academy in another four or five T-years. So what? It's only a few hours either way between Manticore and Sphinx, so it's not like you won't be able to get home for visits, now is it? And Daddy didn't exactly shake the dust of Sphinx forever from his feet when he joined the Marines, did he? Everybody grows up, and everybody has to decide where to go and what to do with their lives. At least you've already got a pretty good idea what you're going to do with yours.*

She gave herself a mental shake and checked the GPS on her uni-link. Her father had insisted that she learn to find her way around with only a compass—uni-links, he'd pointed out, could be broken or lost, as could compasses, now that he thought about it, so while she was at it, why didn't she notice which side of the trees the moss grew on, too?—but she personally had no objection to knowing *exactly* where she was. And where she was happened to be a full three kilometers short of her destination, so she'd better get a move on.

※ ※ ※

<The green-needle pods seem well grown to me, Laughs Brightly,> Sharp Nose observed.

<True, but there are many fewer of them than usual,> Laughs Brightly replied, sending his brother a mental picture of this same stretch of woodland from turnings past. *<And look there, on the far side of the stream. Do you see where that entire stretch of gray-bark trees has no pods at all?>*

Sharp Nose paused, the sensitive nose which had earned him his name pointed in the indicated direction. He cocked his head, looking very carefully, then twitched his whiskers.

<You are right,> he acknowledged. *<Why is it so, do you think?>*

<I am not certain.> Laughs Brightly's tail reached up to curl around a branch above his head and he swung himself up to a higher perch, gripping it with hand-feet and true-feet while one true-hand groomed his own whiskers. *<I discussed it with Bark Master and Wind of Memory yesterday, and Wind of Memory sang back through the memory songs. The wind has not been much out of the lowlands this green-leaf time, and there has been less rain. Perhaps that is the reason. But I think it more likely the People can thank the bark-borers and*

leaf-eaters for it. See, those gray-bark trees' leaves are the color of sickness. I think the bark-borers have wounded the trees, and the leaf-eaters have taken many of the pods before they fully ripened.>

<*That is not a good thing,*> Sharp Nose said somberly. <*The clan will miss those pods this ice time. Why do you think the bark-borers and leaf-eaters have done so much more damage this season?*>

<*I think there have been too few swift-darters to feed upon them,*> Laughs Brightly replied after a thoughtful pause. <*I have seen this before, in dry seasons—dry seasons that stop short of fire season. Without the rain in the middle of the season of green leaves, the swift-darters make fewer nests and hatch fewer young. When that happens, there are many more bark-borers and leaf-eaters during leaf-turning than at other times.*>

<*Will it pass with the snow and ice?*> Sharp Nose's mind-voice was more than a little anxious, and Laughs Brightly flirted his tail.

<*I think it likely that it will. The cold and ice will freeze the bark-borers and leaf-eaters, and if there is enough rain in mud time, the swift-darters will return in greater numbers to devour their eggs before they can hatch once more. But I fear that some of these gray-bark and green-needle trees are too badly hurt. I do not think they will survive ice time.*>

<*This is the real reason Bark Master and Wind of Memory sent you to scout Thunder Mist, is it not?*> Sharp Nose asked.

<*It is,*> Laughs Brightly acknowledged. <*Wind Seeker was here two hands of days ago, hunting bark-chewers, and it seemed to him there were too few pods. So I was sent to check, and it would seem he was correct.*>

The older treecat's mind-glow was somber as he clung to the branch, looking out across the foam-streaked rapids at the foot of the towering waterfall. The stream was not huge at this point, little more than a triple hand of People-lengths across as it raced down the narrow valley, but it ran deep and fast despite the unsual dryness of the season. Farther downstream it was broader and slower-flowing, especially when it reached the lake builders' dam and grew wide and very deep. The water there was rich with striped swimmers, many of them more than a People-length long, although catching them could be an . . . interesting challenge. The fishing was easier here in the shallower water of the rapids, where the sheer height of the falls raised the continual cloud of fine mist which had earned them their name. It was ironic, he thought, that in a turning of such marked dryness, when the swift-darters were so few, the wet breath of Thunder Mist had watered these damaged trees so well.

<Will this endanger the clan this ice time?> his brother asked him.

<I think not.> Laughs Brightly groomed his whiskers again. *<This area is more badly hurt than any other in our range. Now that we know that it will yield so many fewer pods, no doubt we will harvest here first, to save what we may from the leaf-eaters, but there are more than enough other gray-bark and green-needle trees beyond this part of our range which have not been hurt . . . yet, at least.>*

Sharp Nose would have been happier if Laughs Brightly had not added that final qualifier, yet he felt a sense of satisfaction at having aided, if only by bearing his brother company, in discovering something important to the clan's well-being.

<Look there,> Laughs Brightly said suddenly. *<Do you taste it?>*

Sharp Nose looked in the indicated direction, and his tail kinked as he saw the young two-leg walking quietly through the forest towards them.

<It is Dances on Clouds!> he said. *<What is she doing so far from her nesting place without her sire?>*

<Something she should not be doing,> Laughs Brightly said, his mind-voice richly amused. *<Taste her mind-glow more deeply, Sharp Nose. It reminds me very much of* your *mind-glow when you thought you were sneaking off without our sire or dam noticing.>*

<She should not be here,> Sharp Nose said crisply, doing his best to ignore his brother's amusement. *<It is not safe!>*

<That two-leg may be young,> Laughs Brightly replied, stretching comfortably along the limb to which he clung, *<but she is well able to look after herself.>* He laid his chin on his folded true-hands, his eyes half-slitted as he gazed at the approaching two-leg. *<I have seen her use that thunder-barker of hers before.>* His mind-glow carried an unmistakable edge of approval. *<A snow hunter—or even a death fang—that threatens her will not enjoy the experience!>*

<If she knows it is coming, perhaps,> Sharp Nose returned stubbornly. *<But she is a two-leg, Laughs Brightly! Not only is she mind-blind, her nose is but a poor thing, and all the People know that two-legs' ears are half deaf at the best of times.>*

<Indeed?> Laughs Brightly cocked his head at him. *<Then it is a very strange thing that death fangs and snow hunters have learned to fear them rather than the other way around, is it not?>*

<I have admitted that if she sees a danger she can deal with it with her thunder-barker. My fear is that she will not see it until too late.>

<Oh, I think she will see it,> Laughs Brightly said thoughtfully. *<I have not tasted her mind-glow in almost half a season, but there is much of the scout in her. Taste again, Sharp Nose. This is a two-leg who feels everything about her almost as one of the People would. And her mind-glow is stronger than it was when last I tasted her.>*

Sharp Nose glanced at him dubiously, then turned his attention back to the two-leg and reached out to touch her mind-glow. His ears rose slowly as the sheer strength of it washed over him, so powerful it was almost painful to sample it too closely. Yet Laughs Brightly was correct, he realized. That youngling was almost as well aware of the trees and mountainside about her as any scout.

<I had not realized her mind-glow had grown so strong,> he said to Laughs Brightly after a moment in a tone of profound respect. *<That is very strong indeed, even for one of Death Fang's Bane Clan!>*

<It is very like her father's,> Laughs Brightly replied. *<I remember him when he was her age. Very strong, he was! All the world knows that Death Fang's Bane's children have always had bright mind-glows, even for two-legs, and there is something very like the taste of Darkness Foe's mind-glow from the memory songs about Deep Roots and Dances on Clouds, in fact. It is not the* same, *only similar in . . . clarity, perhaps. They see much and they* feel *more, Sharp Nose. And I believe their mind-glows may well be stronger than any who have come before them.>*

Sharp Nose blinked in surprise, then looked back at the young two-leg. He had never really thought about it, but even if he had, it would probably not have occurred to him to think such a thing. Every kitten of Bright Water Clan grew up with the memory songs of Death Fang's Bane, of the bright, fearless taste of her mind-glow and the depth and richness of her bond with Climbs Quickly. It was one of the glories—and the deepest tragedies—of the clan, for with Death Fang's Bane's passing, Climbs Quickly had followed that glorious mind-glow into the darkness with her. She had lived a long life for a two-leg, but none of the People had realized then how short two-legs' lives truly were.

Yet now, as he sampled that approaching mind-glow more cautiously, he realized Laughs Brightly might actually be correct. It was as if the sun itself had come down below the golden-leaf and green-needle branches, blinding any eye that looked too closely upon it. Sharp Nose had never felt the least temptation to bond with one of the two-legs, even of Death Fang's Bane Clan, which was honored and loved by every clan of the People. Yet if he had ever felt the desire to reach out to that glory, bind himself to it forever, this mind-glow would have drawn him as a flame drew the night-flyers.

<She is truly Death Fang's Bane's daughter, however many the turnings between them, and not just because she, too, dances upon the clouds,> Laughs Brightly said quietly. *<I have tasted Death Fang's Bane many times in the memory songs, and this one . . . this one will be as strong, do as many things—or more—I believe.>*

<Have you ever considered bonding with one of the two-legs?> Sharp Nose asked, and Laughs Brightly bleeked softly in amusement.

<Not I, little brother! If I had, I would probably have leapt at the chance to bond with her father when he was but little older than she is now. Yes, their mind-glows blaze bright, but their lives are too short. There are too many wonders in this world still for me to see to bind myself to a two-leg, even one as youthful as this youngling, and miss so many of them! Besides, she is Deep Roots' daughter even more than she is Death Fang's Bane's. Like him, she is bound for other worlds, other suns, and I am a child of this *world, Sharp Nose. Scout though I may be, I do not wish to leave it.>*

Sharp Nose twitched the tip of his tail in slow agreement, considering what his brother had said. Death Fang's Bane's mind-glow burned bright still in Bright Water Clan's memory songs, but *this* had been her world. Though she had left it upon occasion—and Climbs Quickly had accompanied her when she did, returning with mind songs of the two-legs' other worlds—she had always returned, for it had been the treasure for which her heart had hungered. Yet not all of her descendents had shared that heart hunger. Still . . .

He looked at Laughs Brightly speculatively, and the older treecat turned his head to return his regard, ears cocked as he tasted his brother's question.

<How can you be so sure she is bound for other worlds?> Sharp Nose asked finally, and Laughs Brightly's ears twitched in surprise.

<How can you doubt that she is?> he returned. <Can you not taste the way in which she is saying goodbye even now?> He returned his gaze to the two-leg youngling. <It will not be tomorrow, or even the next day, but she is leaving, Sharp Nose, and she does not know if she will ever return. I tasted the same from her father.>

<I cannot taste it,> Sharp Nose admitted. <Perhaps her mind-glow is simply too bright. Still, Wind of Memory has said you have a stronger mind-voice than most males, and you are a scout.> All the People knew scouts became scouts because their mind-glows reached to sample the world about them so much more clearly than others could. <Perhaps that is why you taste more clearly than I.>

<It might be so,> Laughs Brightly mused. <Our line has been close to Death Fang's Bane's Clan for many hands of turnings, though, and I am older than you. Perhaps that is why I taste her more sharply.>

It was true that he and Laughs Brightly were directly descended from Climbs Quickly, Sharp Nose reflected, yet that was true of many of Bright Water's People after so many turnings. And he did not think that was the sole answer. All of the scouts and hunters of Bright Water Clan kept watch over Death Fang's Bane Clan. Even those to whom no Person ever bonded were . . . family, to be cherished and guarded when they ventured into the clan's range, and Dances on Clouds was no exception. Although none of the People had bonded with her, many had shared the soaring flights which had earned her her name among them. Like Death Fang's Bane herself, she was one with the wind, never happier than when she launched herself into flight and gave herself to it with all her heart and mind. Who could share that wondrous moment with her, taste her joy and delight, and not take her to his own heart?

Yet there was a dark side, as well, and Laughs Brightly had placed his true-hand squarely upon it. The shortness of their lives had always made Death Fang's Bane's children even more to be cherished, for their natural span was less than half that of one of the People, and in the memory songs it often seemed as if they were gone almost before they had arrived. That lent an added poignancy to guarding them when they walked the clan's range, yet for all the care with which the clan kept watch over "their" two-legs, he did not think any of the others could have tasted what Laughs Brightly tasted now. Or thought he tasted, at any rate.

<They are changeable, two-legs,> he pointed out. *<Deep Roots left turnings ago, before I was even born, yet he is here now and he is, indeed, deeply rooted to the world.>*

<He is, but at great price. I do not know what happened to him, but I tasted his mind-glow after it, and he was deeply wounded, Sharp Nose. The pain in him cried out to me. It made his mind-glow even stronger, yet he had not yet rooted himself here once again. That did not happen until he returned with Laugh Dancer. It was she who made him whole. Indeed, they are as deeply bonded in many ways as any of the People who mate. They do not see and taste as the People do, but they are not nearly so mind-blind as others of their kind, and their love for one another burns like a crown fire. I think, perhaps, if Deep Roots had not bonded to her so closely—>

Laughs Brightly broke off, and Sharp Nose's eyes narrowed as he caught the fringes of what his brother had left unsaid.

<But enough of lying here watching two-legs!> Laughs Brightly said more briskly. *<We have much yet to see before we return to the clan. Come—I will make a scout of you yet, Sharp Nose!>*

※ ※ ※

Honor wasn't sure what had drawn her attention to the treecats initially.

Their cream-and-gray coats provided excellent natural camouflage, and like all of their species, this pair was capable of holding still with the absolute, motionless patience of a predator. She'd considered addressing them as a matter of courtesy, after she'd noticed them watching her. There were those—including many people born right here on Sphinx, who should have known better—who continued to doubt the level of treecat intelligence, but Honor wasn't one of them. She'd read Stephanie Harrington's journal, and the diaries of a dozen other Harringtons who'd been adopted over the last three T-centuries. There was no question in her mind that 'cats were at least as smart as, if not smarter than, the majority of humans she'd ever met. At least some of them clearly understood Standard English far better than most people believed, and as far as she was concerned, that was the crowning proof of their intelligence. Stephanie Harrington's journal had made it clear how frustrating she and Lionheart had both found their inability to communicate fully, and Stephanie's hypothesis— that the 'cats had to be functional telepaths among their own kind—only made the fact that they had ultimately made the leap to comprehending a *spoken* language even more impressive.

But she couldn't be certain these two would have understood her, and they'd kept their distance, which meant they might have considered it rudeness, not courtesy, if she'd intruded upon them. Besides, these were their woods even more than they were hers. The Harrington Freehold was one of the minority of original freeholds which had been maintained completely intact, passed from generation to generation without a break ever since it was first granted to Richard and Marjorie Harrington all those T-years ago, but the 'cats had been here even before them. If they were gracious enough to share with the Harringtons, then they had every right to be the ones who initiated any contact.

There'd been a few times, especially when she'd been younger, when Honor had rather wistfully considered the possibility that *she* might be adopted by one of them. No one knew exactly what drew a 'cat to a human—or to a *particular* human—although more members of Honor's family had been adopted than of any other family on Sphinx. Whatever it was, though, humans didn't choose 'cats; 'cats chose *them*, and their standards were obviously picky.

The truth was that Honor had been surprised that *any* treecats *ever* bonded with humans when she'd discovered how long the 'cats lived in the wild. Humans had been slow to realize a treecat could reach well over a hundred and fifty T-years, and none of them had realized at first that bonded treecats virtually never survived their human partners' deaths. The thought of all the 'cats who had chosen humans, even after they *knew* how short-lived those humans were, how much of their own lives they would sacrifice, still brought tears to her eyes, and she wondered what could possibly have been strong enough to lead them to it.

At least prolong's changing that at last, she thought now. *I wonder if the 'cats have realized it, though? Daddy's only first-generation prolong, after all; have enough of us lived long enough for them even to notice the difference? Have they figured out that now the humans are going to be outliving them, instead? And if they have, how will that change their attitude towards adopting?*

She didn't have the least idea how to answer those questions, and they didn't much matter in her case, anyway. She'd had more contact with them than the vast majority of humans could ever hope to, and none of them had chosen her. They obviously *liked* her, and she could pick out at least a dozen of them—especially the ones who had gone hang-gliding with her—from their relatives, yet none of them had ever looked into her eyes the way Lionheart had looked into Stephanie's.

Just as well, she told herself now, standing still and watching the treecats flow away through the trees. *Treecats belong here, on Sphinx. It wouldn't be fair to take one of them off-world, and I don't know if one of them could even stand being separated from all the rest of his clan for T-years on end. Even if he could, how could I justify asking him to, anyway? Besides, if there's one thing guaranteed to screw up my plans, it would be a treecat!*

The Navy's official policy ever since Queen Adrienne had been that humans who were adopted by treecats were allowed to take those treecats with them aboard ship and at their duty stations. But Honor suspected the Navy was probably less than delighted at the prospect of dealing with a bonded pair, whatever the Regulations might say, which was an excellent reason for someone hoping for an appointment to the Academy not to add that to her baggage. It would be harder for the daughter of a yeoman to secure one of the precious appointments, anyway, although being the daughter of a yeoman named Commander Alfred Harrington probably wouldn't hurt. It might not help enough to get a treecat past the selection board, though, whatever *official* policy might be. Besides, she knew the Navy's practice where adoptions were concerned was to direct the human partner's career track into one which would keep her and her companion right here in the Manticore Binary System, on one of the space stations or on dirtside duty, where they could return readily to Sphinx at need. That might not be what the Regs stipulated, but that didn't change the policy. Nor should it, really. Honor might long for the Navy, but she was Sphinxian to the bone and she was a Harrington. The drive to protect treecats was in her DNA, so how could she possibly object to a policy that kept them safe and close to home, where they belonged?

Still, the discovery of that policy was the reason she'd abandoned any thought of 'cat adoption by the time she was eleven. Even if the opportunity had offered, she would have had to refuse it if she ever hoped to command one of His Majesty's starships and deploy to the distant stars she longed to see. The odds were monumentally against her ever securing that sort of command even without the encumberance of a 'cat, and she knew it, because there weren't that many commands to go around and the families with influence tended to monopolize the best ones. But if she was going to dream of a Navy career, she might as well dream of the one for which she truly hungered.

She waited until the last flicker of moving 'cat had vanished into the gentle stir of breeze-touched leaves, then drew a deep breath. The cool mist of Jessica Falls drifted to her under the trees, caressing her cheek almost like a farewell from the treecats, and she felt it in her lungs like some cleansing elixir. She stood a moment longer, gazing up at the falls' plunge down the ninety-meter cliff, letting the unending, rumbling thunder and the splash and gurgle of the rapids soak into her bones, then turned and headed downstream for the near-beaver dam and the mountain tulips she'd come to collect.

⚹ ⚹ ⚹

<*The trees' pods may be thinner than usual,*> Sharp Nose remarked as he and Climbs Quickly scampered through the net-wood, <*but the swimmers seem numerous to me!*>

<*That is because they are,*> Laughs Brightly replied. <*And I believe they are larger than in seasons past, as well.*> He paused, gazing down at the wide rings radiating across the still surface of the lake builders' water where one of the striped swimmers had risen to capture an incautious small flyer. <*I believe they have fed well because the swift darters have been so few. There are more of the small flyers for them to feed upon, and they have grown fat and sleek.*>

<*There is always something to feed upon such bounty,*> Sharp Nose agreed, and then felt a quick flicker of embarrassment as he tasted Laughs Brightly's silent chuckle. He hadn't meant to sound like a clan elder tutoring some newly weaned kitten!

<*You are correct about that,*> Laughs Brightly told him after a moment, his tone an apology for his amusement. <*Come, though. We should see how the lake builders are faring. After all, they are sometimes easier to catch than swimmers!*>

<*But not necessarily safer to catch,*> Sharp Nose pointed out, sending a mind picture of the lake builders' formidable teeth. A fully grown lake builder was actually larger and much heavier than a Person, and while they preferred to flee to some safe, underwater

hiding place when danger threatened, they could be formidable fighters if they were cornered.

<*The world promises no one safety, little brother,*> Laughs Brightly told him. <*The trick is to remember that most clearly when the danger seems farthest away.*>

Sharp Nose flicked his tail in agreement, and the two of them flowed onward through the net-wood. Fallen leaves drifted on the surface of the lake below them. There were more of them than there would normally have been at this time of year, another sign of the season's dryness, and some of the branches about them showed signs of death and brittleness.

<*The bark-borers have been busy here, as well,*> he pointed out, and tasted Laughs Brightly's unhappy agreement.

<*The gray ones like the taste of net-wood more than most. And they bore deeper than many of the others. Help me take note of which of the bridges are worst damaged, Sharp Nose. It will be well for the clan's hunters to know where to take the greatest care.*>

❀ ❀ ❀

Honor grimaced as she passed a red spruce, more than half of whose scaled, blue-green leaves had turned brown and yellow. She'd seen more and more of those, and she'd made a mental note to com the Forestry Service about it. There was plenty of sign of bark beetles and flat case borers, which was only to be expected, she supposed, after such a dry summer. The rock martins and hill swallows which would normally have preyed on them hatched far fewer fledglings in years like this one. Reproduction rates for both species of bird analogue were tied to a whole host of environmental and climatic factors, and they were always lower in particularly dry seasons. Probably because the insect species upon which they usually subsisted were likely to be in shorter supply, she thought. Unfortunately, whatever might have been the case elsewhere on Haley's Land, there seemed to be plenty of moisture along Rock Aspen Creek, and the insect population *here* was doing just fine. In fact, it had gotten considerably worse since her last visit, and she was seeing plenty of evidence of leaf cutter ants and leaf shearers, too.

It was all part of the natural cycle of the planet, and the SFS was scarcely likely to fog the area with insecticides, but the Rangers did like to keep track of data like this. And the flat case borers, especially, were some of the worst tree-killers in Sphinx's entire ecosystem.

I wonder if that's what those two 'cats were out here checking on? This is a fairly important part of their range in fall and winter. It'd make sense for them to keep an eye on it in a year like this one. I hope they're not going to end up short of food this winter!

She knew that happened sometimes, and it was always hard for anyone who cared about the 'cats. Treecats who turned up at one of the Forestry Service's stations in a distressed state could count on being fed and offered emergency medical care, but the SFS had decided centuries ago not to intervene in the wild except in cases of disaster relief. Hard winters didn't constitute "disaster" by the Forestry Service's definition unless they produced acute starvation, and intellectually, Honor understood why that was. Offering assistance too readily was likely to encourage both 'cat dependency on humans and the sort of overpopulation which led to genuine catastrophe. Not that understanding the policy would prevent her or her parents from providing meals to any 'cats who turned up at their front door. In fact, they could usually count on at least one treecat visitor every week or so during the winter. It was painfully obvious that word had gotten around long ago that the Harringtons were an easy touch who always had celery stashed away somewhere.

The creek broadened and deepened as she approached the near-beaver dam. The meter-long critters could top sixty kilos in weight, and the stumps of red spruce, near-pine, and mountain hickory gave clear evidence of just how efficient they were as loggers. Like the merely four-limbed Old Earth species for which they had been named, near-beavers tended to cut the timber for their dams and lodges in spring or summer and let it season until they needed it for building purposes in fall and winter. They could take down trees as much as thirty-six centimeters in diameter, although they usually settled for smaller prey, and—also like Old Earth beavers—they constructed "canals" to float bigger trunks and branches to where they needed them. In many ways, they were among Sphinx's most destructive life forms, given what even a small population of them could do to woodland. On the other hand, the water they impounded behind their dams played a critical part in maintaining healthy wetlands and watersheds. And they also helped the spread of picketwood.

For some reason, they never touched picketwood. It wasn't because of any sort of toxicity issue—the SFS had determined that long ago—but picketwood was a clever survivor which had worked out resistance modes for many of the diseases and parasites (including near-beavers) which attacked other Sphinxian flora. Apparently, it just plain didn't taste good as far as near-beavers were concerned, and their habit of eating everything else along the banks of their streams and ponds cleared space for it, which had to make treecats happy.

Pity it doesn't work the same way for the flat case borers, Honor thought now, picking her way through the near-beavers' lumberyard. *On the other hand, of course, if they were willing to bring down the picketwood, too, it would probably mean I could get in here with a hang glider, which would've saved me quite a hike!*

She spent a couple of minutes trying to convince herself that she really would have preferred to fly, rather than hiking. The effort didn't work out very well, though, and she snorted in amusement at herself.

She reached the upstream end of the near-beaver pond proper and smiled appreciatively as a leopard trout broke the surface, leaping half out of the water to take one of the insects buzzing above the pond's surface. It wasn't the biggest leopard trout she'd ever seen—they could go was much as eighty or ninety centimeters in length—but it was certainly well grown. There was going to be some excellent fishing up this way this fall.

She looked around, getting her bearings, and saw a distant flash of purple through the tree trunks. At least the bugs hadn't eaten the mountain tulip she'd come after! Now all she had to do was hike halfway around the lake, cut the blossoms she'd come for, and then hike back home again.

※ ※ ※

Sharp Nose froze suddenly, his head coming up in alarm.

<*Snow hunters!*> he exclaimed, and tasted Laughs Brightly's surprise echoing his own. His brother's concern wasn't as deep as his, though, and he found Laughs Brightly's calmness reassuring.

<*I did not expect to see them so far down this early in the season,*> Sharp Nose added after a moment, and Laughs Brightly flicked his ears in agreement, accepting the younger treecat's explanation for his surprise.

<*It does not happen often,*> he agreed. <*I suspect the hunting has not been as good for them as usual with the year's dryness, however. That may explain it, but best we see what we may see.*>

The two treecats moved cautiously closer. Snow hunters, like death fangs, were far too big and heavy to follow a Person up into the trees, and they were normally less territorial than death fangs. That did not mean that they would not happily eat any Person they could catch, though, and only death fangs were bigger than they were. At the moment, two of them stood shoulder-deep in the lake builders' pond, and as the brothers watched, one of them pounced, snatching a striped swimmer from the water and flipping its head to fling it ashore.

<*There is the reason they are here,*> Laughs Brightly said, and Sharp Nose tasted the suddenly stronger edge of caution in his brother's mind-glow. <*They have borne young out of season.*>

Sharp Nose nodded as he watched the pair of snow hunter cubs scuffling through the brush to where the wildly flopping striped swimmer had landed. They were very young, although already several times a Person's size, and their clumsiness was obvious, but there was nothing wrong with their jaws. The still-squirming swimmer came apart into two unequal-sized pieces as the cubs squabbled over it, and the one with the smaller piece squalled unhappily as it realized its sibling had done better than it had.

<*I think the fishing is not going to be as good as we had hoped it would,*> Laughs Brightly continued more glumly, and Sharp Nose could only agree once more. A single snow hunter could eat many times a Person's weight in swimmers in a single day; a pair of them, hunting to feed their young, could easily strip even a pond this size of its swimmers in short order.

And even if they did, their young were unlikely to survive through ice time, for they would not be able to sleep through the long cold.

Sharp Nose sat very still on the net-wood branch, looking down on the snow hunters, and felt a surge of sympathy for them. Snow hunters were but little brighter than death fangs, yet these two parents realized, at least dimly, how unlikely their cubs were to survive. He could taste it in the muddiness of their mind-glows. There were no thoughts to share as there would have been among the People, or to taste without sharing like the two-legs, but even snow hunters had feelings, and the fishing adults below him were angry at the approach of that dimly sensed loss to come.

<*It is sad, Laughs Brightly,*> he said quietly.

<If they are fortunate, if the snowfall is late, their young may live,> his brother replied.

<And how likely is that?>

<Not very,> Laughs Brightly acknowledged. <And if the hunting is as poor in the heights as I fear it is, other snow hunters will be following them. If that happens, they will be forced to fight for their range . . . and their young. For that matter, they may encounter death fangs.>

Sharp Nose's ears flattened at that thought. If anyone had ever been inclined to think of snow hunters as remotely like People, their willingness to eat the young of *other* snow hunters would quickly have changed his mind. And death fangs, of course, were prepared to eat *anything* they could catch. None of which even considered how quickly a pair of hunting snow hunters with young to feed could strip a clan's range of almost all its prey animals at a time of year when less and less of those prey animals were being born.

<The elders will not be happy to hear about this,> he observed.

<You are truly gifted with insight, little brother,> Laughs Brightly said dryly. <I cannot imagine what better neighbors the clan could desire!>

<Perhaps not,> Sharp Nose retorted. <I think, however, that it would not be amiss for us to warn Dances on Clouds to be cautious with snow hunters about.>

<Now that, Sharp Nose, is a very good idea, indeed,> Laughs Brightly agreed. <Of course, it would be far simpler if we could make her hear our mind-voices!>

<A Person cannot have everything.>

<Perhaps not, but that does not mean he cannot wish for it.>

Laughs Brightly's mind-voice was very dry, and Sharp Nose sensed him turning his attention elsewhere. For a moment, Sharp Nose could not understand what his brother was doing, but then he realized, and his tail kinked in surprise. Laughs Brightly was questing for Dances on Clouds' mind-glow.

That was ridiculous at such a range, even for a scout . . . but not as ridiculous as the fact that Laughs Brightly had found what he sought.

<She comes from that direction,> he said, one true-hand pointing upstream. <And she is already on the snow hunters' side of the lake builders' pond.>

<Then I think we should go to meet her,> Sharp Nose said, and leapt lightly from his net-wood branch to the next bridge over.

❈ ❈ ❈

Honor waded across one of the canals the near-beavers had constructed in seasons past. It was well into the process of collapsing upon itself, but it was still too wide for her to simply jump over and it behooved her to be careful. The water came no higher than mid-calf, well below the tops of her boots, but the bottom's thick layer of mud was slippery and she held her S&W balanced across her shoulder to keep it out of the way while she concentrated on not losing her balance. Falling flat on her face would be as humiliating as it would unpleasant.

Not that anyone would be here to see it, she reminded herself. *And if I manage to get home before Mom, I could probably be changed and clean by the time she—*

Her head snapped up as a sound ripped through the whisper of breeze and rustle of leaves like a bandsaw through plyboard. It came like ripping canvas, and she'd never heard anything like it in her life. Yet somehow, she knew what it was. She *felt* what it was, and she hurled herself up the canal's sloping bank towards it.

❈ ❈ ❈

<Sharp Nose!>

Laughs Brightly's mind voice was a scream of warning that came too late. His brother sprang onto the solid-looking net-wood branch . . . and half the branch collapsed into powder as he landed. The bark borers had eaten deep into it, riddling it with tunnels, and Sharp Nose's weight pulverized the surface under him. The claws which should have caught in the net-wood's bark found no purchase as the weakened, spongy wood disintegrated, and the younger treecat went tumbling into space.

His tail caught frantically at another branch as he plummeted past it, and for a moment Laughs Brightly thought he had saved himself. But it might have been better if he had simply let himself fall, for the bark borers had weakened that branch, as well. Sharp Nose's weight was just enough to break it loose from the main trunk, and it followed him down. He landed barely two People's lengths from the closer of the two snow hunter cubs, and the cub reared up in shock, squealing to its parents in alarm. And then the broken branch landed on top of him, and Laughs Brightly heard his own high-pitched squeal of pain as the impact fractured his mid-pelvis.

The adult snow hunters wheeled from their fishing as they heard their infant's panicked cry. The cub tumbled backward, away from Sharp Nose, but its parents were already lumbering out of the pond, headed for Laughs Brightly's brother. The instinct to defend their young would have been enough for that, but they were unlikely to pass up the opportunity to feed their cubs.

Laughs Brightly swarmed down the net-wood trunk, taking the time even in his frantic haste to be sure each branch would bear his weight. If he could reach Sharp Nose first, perhaps he could help him to safety in the net-wood. Perhaps—

<No, Laughs Brightly!> Sharp Nose cried. <I cannot use my hand-feet or climb! Do not come down!>

Laughs Brightly's mind-glow cried out in formless protest, but Sharp Nose was already moving, dragging his crippled body across the ground. He managed to reach a fallen gray-bark, downed by the lake builders and left to dry. It was more than half a Person's length in diameter, and he squirmed into the tangle of dry, dead branches and somehow found a space under the trunk just big enough to wedge himself into. Laughs Brightly could taste the lightning-like stabs of pain ripping through him as those broken bones shifted, but even through his anguish, Sharp Nose's voice came clearly.

<There is no reason we both should die,> he said as the first adult snow hunter began ripping a way through the gray bark's branches. <Stay where you are!>

Laughs Brightly knew his brother was right, but it didn't matter.

<No!> he shot back. <I will not leave you!>

<Do not!> Sharp Nose screamed. <Do not, Laughs Brightly!>

But it was too late. Laughs Brightly plummeted from the net-wood, snarling in desperate, hopeless fury, and landed squarely on the back of the snow hunter's neck.

❀ ❀ ❀

Honor was still seventy-five meters away when the treecat hurled himself out of the picketwood. Even in the aftermath of the near-beavers' lumber harvesting there was more than enough underbrush to keep her from seeing clearly, but she didn't have to see. She *knew* what was happening. Somehow, some way, she *knew*.

Her heart leapt into her throat as the small cream-and-gray defender landed squarely on the peak bear's neck. The huge creature was almost three meters long. It must weigh over five hundred kilos, and it howled its fury as the 'cat's razor-sharp claws slashed at it. But peak bears' hides were thick, their skins loose, riding on deep layers of fat no treecat's claws were long enough to penetrate. The 'cat could hurt and enrage the monstrous omnivore, but he couldn't possibly defeat it, and he knew it. Honor knew he knew it, because in that moment she *shared* that knowledge with him . . . just as she shared the knowledge that he would die trying.

The peak bear raged around in a circle, temporarily abandoning its quest to dig the other treecat—the injured treecat Honor *knew* was under the fallen red spruce—out of its futile burrow while it tried to reach the six-limbed fury ripping and tearing at its heavily furred pelt. Its mate galloped towards it with its species' clumsy-looking but deceptively fast gait, and Honor saw the gray flash of the attacking treecat as it somehow evaded the massive paws trying to rend it apart.

The peak bear squalled in as much frustration as pain and hurled itself down. It landed on its side, rolling, and Honor's heart tried to stop as she realized it was trying to crush the treecat under its enormous weight.

❈ ❈ ❈

Laughs Brightly heard Sharp Nose's despairing protest, but it scarcely registered. His world had narrowed to a boil of blood-red fury as he tore into his enormous foe. There was no room or space for anything else, and he twisted and dodged even as he ripped at the snow hunter's hide. Somehow he slithered through the deadly net of the snow hunter's claws, using his own claws as if the enormous creature were a tree he was scaling. He was too close to it for it to reach, and he heard it squalling in pain and rage as he swarmed from the back of its neck, under its chin, down between the its forelegs, then back up around its shoulder as if he were scaling a fur-barked tree.

There was no time to think about what he was doing. It was all react, improvise, move or die. Yet even through the madness and the confusion, it was as if he were somewhere else, watching. He could actually *see* the snow hunter, recognize the moment it decided to roll and crush him, and somehow he flung himself clear in the instant before the creature crashed to earth.

❦ ❦ ❦

Honor suddenly discovered her rifle was in her hands.

She couldn't remember how it had gotten there. Didn't remember snapping off the safety. Didn't remember bringing it to her shoulder. But somehow, there it was, and in that instant she discovered something about herself. Something she had never suspected.

She was calm. A sense of panic, of horror, hovered about her, frantic with concern for the treecats, but it couldn't touch her. It was a part of her, but it was apart *from* her, as well. Her hands were steady, her breathing almost normal, and her flashing thoughts were clear, clean, and icy cold.

She didn't see the treecat break clear before the peak bear landed, but somehow she knew—knew with that same certainty, that same absolute assurance—that he'd done it. And the icy precision of her brain moved her aim point from the peak bear he'd attacked. Her rifle tracked with machine-like precision, finding the *other* peak bear, the one who'd seen where the treecat landed and lunged towards him.

❦ ❦ ❦

Laughs Brightly cried out in pain as he landed.

He might have avoided the snow hunter's plunging weight, but he hadn't gotten away unscathed. One of the snow hunter's paws struck him a grazing blow, and he tasted anguish of his own as even that glancing blow broke ribs. It batted him out of the air, like a kitten playing with a green-needle pod, and he squalled again as he bounced off of an exposed boulder. He was badly hurt, his left forelimb numbed and useless—probably broken—but he clawed his way back to his feet and bared his fangs in a snarl of defiance . . . just in time to see the first snow hunter's mate open its jaws wide and lunge toward him.

❦ ❦ ❦

CRAACKKKKK!

The S&W surged against Honor's shoulder. She had an ideal, broadside target, she knew exactly what a peak bear's anatomy looked like, the glowing dot of the Brownfield Holographics sight had settled midway between the creature's shoulders and mid-pelvis, and she knew even before she squeezed the trigger that the shot was flawlessly placed. The 19.5-gram slug exploded through the hurtling peak bear's lungs and heart in a perfect kill shot, and suddenly the charging monster spun halfway around. It went to the ground in a boneless, slithering slide that slammed into the boulder the flying treecat had already encountered.

The remaining peak bear heaved itself to its feet, howling in fury, put its head down, and turned upon its fresh enemy. Facing a charging peak bear on the ground was not the sort of situation many hunters were likely to survive, and the picketwood overhead was too dense for her counter-grav to carry her clear in time, but Honor's coldly, meticulously whirring mind measured speeds and angles with icy precision. There was no way to avoid the thing, and so she stood her ground, instead. The S&W swung back and the glowing dot settled on the oncoming creature. She found the sight picture, saw the lowered head, realized there was an excellent chance that even the mighty S&W's slug might ricochet from the immensely thick bone of a peak bear's skull. She started to squeeze the trigger anyway, but something stopped her—just for half a heartbeat. Something she'd seen, recognized without realizing what it was. Some tiny, preliminary muscle shift, perhaps. *Something.* And then the peak bear raised its head, roaring as its gaping maw closed in on her, and her right hand squeezed without any conscious command from her.

CRAACKKKKK!

The bullet just missed the peak bear's lower jaw. It struck two centimeters to the right of the exact center of its chest, and the creature's roar turned into a high, shocked squeal. It staggered, continuing to drive forward but no longer under control. Momentum carried it, not purpose, and Honor Harrington stepped smoothly to one side, pivoting to keep her target in her field of fire as five hundred kilos of mortally wounded peak bear staggered past her. It went down, twitching, struggling to get its legs back under it so it could rise and kill her with its own dying strength. It snarled, spraying blood as it started to come back upright . . . and she put a second shot through its right ear from a range of five meters to be sure it didn't.

❦ ❦ ❦

<*Laughs Brightly!* Laughs Brightly!>

The mind-voice trickled into his awareness. It took him what seemed a very long time to recognize it, to realize Sharp Nose was still alive. Then he realized that since he was hearing it, *he* must still be alive, as well, and neither of those things was possible. The last thing he remembered was the anow hunter Dances on Clouds had killed, still rolling forward, tumbling towards him. He had tried to leap clear, but there had been no time. It had felt as if a golden-leaf tree had fallen onto him, and then there had been only darkness.

Now he managed to open his eyes and discovered that he was wrapped in a thin but tough and incredibly warm blanket. It was a two-leg blanket, made of one of their magical substances, and he realized his left forelimb had been straightened and immobilized by the length of branch fastened to it with some of the sticky-sided stuff two-legs used to tie everything in the world together. And then he realized that the blanket in which he was wrapped lay in a two-leg's lap, and looked up at the brown eyes of the two-leg to which it belonged.

❊ ❊ ❊

"—coordinates," Honor told the Sphinx Forestry Service ranger on the uni-link's display. "We're about a hundred and eighty meters north of the near-beaver dam below Jessica Falls on Rock Aspen Creek, and I need a 'cat-certified vet out here bad. I've got one 'cat with a broken forelimb and ribs who's been unconscious for at least ten minutes, and another one with a smashed mid-pelvis. I think that one has some internal injuries, too, so please hurry. And I guess you'd better send someone along to collect the cubs, too."

She realized her own voice sounded far too calm as she sat there between two dead adult peak bears with a pair of horribly injured treecats while a pair of orphaned peak bear cubs moaned disconsolately as they tried to understand what had happened.

"The vet's on her way," Ranger McIntyre told her. She knew him vaguely and remembered him from her wilderness survival course. He'd always been friendly enough, but he was hardly someone she knew well, yet she'd been astonished by how happy she'd been to see him when he receipted her call.

"You ought to see her air car in the next fifteen minutes," McIntyre continued. "But let me get this straight, Ms. Harrington. You're out there by yourself with two dead peak bears, is that right?"

"I know it's not peak bear season," she replied a bit defensively. "But I didn't have much choice, you know. They were going to kill the 'cats, and then they decided they might as well kill *me*, too!"

"Oh, I understand *that* part," he said. "What I don't understand is what you thought you were doing out there all alone in the first place.

I don't suppose you happened to tell your parents where you were going, young lady?"

"Of course I did!" she said virtuously. "Sort of," she added a bit more lamely when the ranger looked unimpressed. "I'd've been fine if the 'cats hadn't gotten into trouble!"

"I'm sure you would have," McIntyre said in a voice which implied exactly the opposite. Then he inhaled deeply and shook his head. "Although, now that I think about it, I don't see why I should be particularly surprised by such a boneheaded, stubborn, impulsive antic—especially from *you!*"

Honor's eyes widened. She couldn't think of a single thing she'd done in her entire life—well, up until today—to deserve that resigned tone from Ranger McIntyre. She hugged the injured treecat in her lap very gently—the other 'cat was too badly hurt for her to risk moving any more than she'd had to after she'd used her bush knife to cut away the log under which he'd hidden himself and covered him with her jacket—and stared into the display in confusion.

"Oh, don't look so innocent at me, young lady!" McIntyre snorted. "This is a tradition in your family!"

Honor blinked, and then her eyes went wider than ever as she realized what he was talking about. But that was ridiculous! She hadn't been adopted by either treecat—she didn't *want* to be adopted by either treecat! She'd only been doing what needed to be done, and it was—

She made the mistake of looking down.

Two grass-green eyes looked back up at her, brighter and deeper and simultaneously darker than any sea she had ever seen. She fell into them, as if they had no bottom, no end. And as she fell, she felt something—some*one*—reaching back to her. It was as clear, as sharp, as any voice she had ever heard, and yet she couldn't hear it. It was there, and it wasn't there. Imagined, and yet more real than anything else she had ever experienced. It was nothing at all like Stephanie Harrington's description from her journal . . . yet it was simultaneously perfectly and exactly the same.

But I can't be adopted, a little voice in the back of her brain wailed. *It'll mess up* everything! *All my plans. All my . . . .*

That voice faded into silence, inconsequential beside that other voice, the one she heard without hearing. The dream was still there, the plans and hopes, the determination, but she was going to have to make a few changes, because now the dream had to include *this,* for it was unthinkable that it could not.

Ranger McIntyre was still saying something over the com, but she was no longer listening. She was listening to something else, and her hand was gentle as she touched the treecat's—*her* treecat's—silken, tufted ears as if they were what they had just become . . . the most precious thing in her universe.

❧ ❧ ❧

<I thought you were certain you would never bond with a two-leg, Laughs Brightly,> Sharp Nose's mind voice was shadowed with pain and weaker than usual, yet amusement flickered in it. *<Plans, I think you said you had?>*

<One day you will be well again, Sharp Nose,> Laughs Brightly replied, *<and on that day, you will pay for all of this.>*

<It was not my *idea!>* Sharp Nose protested, his mind-glow as soft with unvoiced love for his brother as Laughs Brightly's was with love for him. *<I told you you should not attack a snow hunter! You were the foolish one who would not take my advice! And it was not* my *fault the net-wood broke.>*

<Perhaps not, but that will not save you in the end, little brother. I am the one who is supposed to play jokes on others; you and the world are not supposed to play jokes on me! *And do not tell me that you are not already gloating over how you will describe this entire afternoon to Songstress!>*

Sharp Nose bleeked a soft, pain-shadowed laugh and reached out to caress his brother's mind-glow gently. Laughs Brightly's mind-glow had always been strong; now it was brighter than sunlight on water, and it was growing stronger still by the moment.

<I am sorry your plans have been upset, elder brother,> he said softly, *<but I also think you were right about Dances on Clouds. She is Death Fang's Bane's daughter . . . and you are Climbs Quickly's son. They flew high, Laughs Brightly, but you—you will fly higher yet.>*

<I think you are right,> Laughs Brightly replied, ears twitching as he heard the whine of a rapidly approaching two-leg flying thing. He knew, without knowing exactly how he knew, that it was a healer, summoned by his person, yet that was unimportant, and he drew the bright, welcoming joy of her about him like a still softer and endlessly warmer blanket on a day of ice and snow.

<I think you are right,> he repeated, *<for there are many worlds, and Dances on Clouds means to see them all. That may take a long, long time, but she* will *do it, for this is a two-leg who does not know how to fail. So she will see them, and I will see them with her, and ours will be a memory song the People will never forget.>*

OBLIGATED SERVICE

Joelle Presby

OBLIGATED SERVICE

Grayson Midshipwoman Claire Bedlam Lecroix palm-locked the entrance to the GNS *Ephraim*'s third auxiliary repair bay behind her and stormed around her machinery looking for something to punch. The hard surfaces mocked her. She had to settle for nestling her just-delivered package on a counter and mashing her fists into the soft bundle several times.

The punches didn't give her anything like the satisfaction of beating the surface of the lap pool at Saganami Island. No one ever swam in Grayson's toxic oceans, but the Manties with their clean, safe planets had no such aversions. Claire had thrived in Manticore's upside-down society starting with a mental pretend game where she was an actress playing a male officer, and while she was in the role she'd even believed it didn't matter. In the reality of the *Ephraim*, Claire muttered to herself, "Yes, Aunt Jezzy, I know I should have known better. Yes, Lucy, dreams are catching. You warned me it would be hard to come back to reality."

She checked the door one more time, not wanting to have someone walk in while she talked herself down from the latest frustration. Then she smacked the bundle with a few more solid punches.

For the required physical training, Claire had avoided actual swimming classes lest Steadholder Burdette or, worse, Aunt Jezzy, hear of the indecently skintight swimsuits. Instead, taking Lucy's strong encouragement to heart she had signed up for one self-defense course after another. Those classes had taught her to fight back, and in the water, Claire had stayed afloat only by sheer violence, slapping and kicking against its unchangeable surface.

The *Ephraim* had no pool, and returning to her own culture was significantly less of a relief than Claire had imagined it would be just a year ago, when her Saganami Island class graduated. The Manticoran middies had started their first cruises, with plans for the ensign promotion parties at the end; *she* had reported to the *Ephraim* and managed maintenance projects while the ship failed inspection after inspection. Now she smashed the ensign uniforms that she might never get to wear. Then she drew a deep breath, shook herself, and undid the bundle again to check for telltale wrinkling in the uniform fabric.

The Grayson Space Navy uniforms, a gift of the Lady Wives of Steadholder Burdette in three complete skirted sets, hung smooth from Claire's shaking fists. Of course they did. The steadholder's ladies wouldn't know how to find a store that sold anything less than luxury clothing. And of course the gift assumed she'd be able to afford a tailor for the final bespoke finishes. The uniform board might have allowed the new skirt option in deference to the dignity of the female service member, but they weren't fools. The skirts were split for full freedom of movement and decency in a zero-grav environment, and the tail ends belled up to cuff into the tops of the uniform boots just like the trouser uniform variant. They were supposed to cuff, that is. These unhemmed skirt ends would fill a boot top and leave no room for the foot.

Perhaps the ladies assumed she had magically achieved Admiral Alexander-Harrington's height between this gift and their last present of her midshipman uniforms? They had little understanding of steaders' lives and even less knowledge of life in the Bedlam family. It wasn't actually unreasonable for them to expect a midshipwoman who was possibly almost an ensign to pay for hemming. Even Claire had expected herself to be an ensign by now—nearly a year and a half after Saganami Island class of 1920 graduation.

She took deep breaths again, trying to swallow her fury at her overdrawn bank account. Thank the Tester, she had checked the balance from her station-side bachelor officer quarters room instead of bouncing a payment at a seamstress shop's checkout line. She knew the shopkeepers saw the mottled skin from roughly treated childhood skin cancers and marked her immediately as unlikely to be able to repay any credit that might be extended to someone who wasn't a grasper.

The shop owners themselves could easily feature in Burdette street preacher sermons that warned good people against grasping after the false god of riches and rumors of prosperity, but people rarely considered that such insults could also be stuck to them. Graspers ended up alone and vulnerable in someplace like Birdies, not running a successful orbital-based business. And didn't graspers deserve it, since they'd hidden from their life's Test instead of facing it—unless, as Claire hoped, you could sometimes beg forgiveness to choose your own Test?

She briefly considered asking for a loan from one of her cousins at Birdies and crushed the thought. There would be no certainty she could pay them back any time soon. Besides, the rest of the family might realize she knew that the working girls were holding back on the family. Lucy could be counted on. She still held tight to the anger that had inspired her to leave Burdette Steading, but their mutual cousin Mary occasionally broke down and went back home.

Worse, Mary repented with disturbing regularity and confessed everyone else's sins along with her own. Everyone else usually meant just Lucy, but Claire didn't want to be looped in for those inevitable follow-on rounds of family recrimination.

If Aunt Jezzy had cause to entirely empty Claire's account like the transactions showed, there would be a reason, and it would be neither a cheap reason nor an entirely paid-for reason. At least not yet. Of course, her cousin Noah might have found the account and debited it directly himself. Claire gritted her teeth and tried to remind herself that the teenage head-of-household was due his privileges.

Noah had approved her authorization to work outside the home and signed all the renewals without a fuss. Who was she to hold his age against him?

Claire gently laid the uniforms out on the cleaner portions of the work counters and looked for a way to do the hemming herself. An industrial cutter made for materials far tougher than smart fabric made short work of the long tubes, and she gathered up the scraps.

The cut bits had quite a lot of stretch to them; she smiled at the idea of offering them to Lucy to use as a costume in one of her dance routines just to see the laughter in her eyes when she refused them. But Mary would miss the joke and want to do a team routine with Lucy, each with one well-covered ankle. The Birdies Club would bill it as a midshipwoman's uniform, and those boys in the audience would love it.

Claire stuffed the scraps firmly in the waste bin.

❄ ❄ ❄

Claire arrived breathless at the XO's wood-paneled outer office, answering the summons before the other two officers named in the page. The assistant tactical officer jogged in moments later. He glanced at her and away with a slight pinch to his lips.

"Have you done something wrong recently I should know about?"

She tried not to clench her teeth as she answered the real question. "I don't know what this is about, Sir."

Ambling in from the passageway, the Auxiliaries Officer shook out a handkerchief and wiped his forehead. His tailored gray-green suit matched his eyes and the fabric's undertone brought out the gleam of the silver sprinkling his dark hair. He had definitely been on his way off the ship, dressed in civilian clothes and looking to impress someone. *Ephraim* held the dubious honor of an extra engineering department billet, the AuxO, created by the Office of Personnel to repair if not prevent the ship's frequent maintenance issues. The AuxO winked at her and playfully punched the ATO on the shoulder.

"Claire's too straight-laced to cause trouble. I bet you the XO just needs something fixed."

She hoped his prediction was right. She ran through the mental list of potential Navy sins that might warrant XO-level censure: a few sign-offs behind on her qualification studies for ensign (okay, a lot behind), the package in her arms, and the drunk who had mistaken her for Lucy.

The inebriate had apologized to the duty officer yesterday once he'd sobered up, and her cousins carefully kept their blood relationship to her a secret, even from the AuxO who was one of their better tippers.

The sign-offs? Why would the XO start to care about that now?

It had to be the ensign uniforms. Claire risked a glance down that might draw attention to the officer insignia she hadn't earned yet and maybe never would. Could the XO blame her just for having received the package?

Actually, yes, she was pretty sure he could. They would treat it just like Midshipman Harris's care package from old schoolmates with the images of women undoubtedly in the same profession as Lucy and Mary.

The two male officers exchanged banter, oblivious to Claire's unease. The ATO even let himself smile, and if it faded a bit when his eyes tripped over her, he didn't let the opportunity pass to quiz the AuxO on the dress-up. Their back-and-forth revealed that he was to meet the mothers of a possible fiancée to show them around Blackbird Yard. He flashed a quick smile at Claire, and she returned it even though he was clearly just practicing for the upcoming visit.

The ATO's frown deepened, and Claire dropped the smile. Ever since his wives had made public their unhappiness at sharing a junior lieutenant's pay and objections to spreading the income with a third wife, his curt interactions with the single midshipwoman in the bevy of middies nominally under his training guidance had grown decidedly strained.

At the last wardroom officers-and-wives function, Claire had tried to make clear that she was only in the service to learn some skills to transfer to a job on Blackbird Yard just as soon as her obligation was met. A few comments from the XO's wives about Claire's looks not being good enough to attract an officer anyway might have helped, even if they had set her teeth on edge. If the ATO had had a touch less to drink he might not have responded that all women look the same in the dark or his whisper might have been pitched lower so the fully drunk Midshipman Harris could not have repeated it at full volume. The invitation to the next function had specified officers and wives, ensigns and above only. Exclusion was almost a relief.

For Claire's part, working surrounded by the men was almost restful compared to growing up on Burdette Steading with Grayson's toxic birthrate of three girls to every live boy. Dr. Allison Harrington, the famous Admiral Alexander-Harrington's lady mother, had found a cure, but that would be the salvation of the next generation. Nothing could bring Claire's many stillborn brothers back to life.

Grayson men might still expect Claire to be continually hunting for a husband, but they weren't constantly measuring and evaluating the way women did. Well, they were, Claire amended to herself, but that was different. A midshipman, midshipwoman, whatever, was supposed to be forever polishing up military knowledge and skills, after all.

Lucy and Mary, dancing at Birdies, were very nearly cut off from the family, yet they meticulously braided their hair and made up their faces before leaving the club in street clothes on their days off. Strangers on the street would chastise any woman who didn't care for her appearance. At least a woman had the one time Claire had gone without makeup.

She automatically shifted back against the bulkhead and tucked her chin down, coming to attention as the door to the XO's office opened. The laughing crinkles normally lingering at the corners of the XO's eyes were displaced today by a flat twitch on just the left side; both full officers straightened in response.

She tried a bright smile. It felt like showing her teeth. She licked her lips ready to attempt an opening bit of chitchat but clamped her mouth shut at an eye bulge and miniscule headshake from AuxO.

"What's that, Middy?" The XO said, pointing at her bundle.

She stumbled through a tortured explanation of the Burdette ladies sending uniforms from time to time. With the new uniform regulations for officers they had wanted to send her skirt sets, but, she admitted, they had ensign insignia.

The XO cut her off with a curt gesture. The ATO sucked in air, ready to lay into her, but his eyes flittered back and forth between Claire and the XO waiting for his cue.

The XO pointed at his private bathroom and said, "Go put them on."

The ATO deflated with a stunned series of blinks.

Claire returned with the two remaining new skirt sets folded inside a bundled midshipwoman uniform.

The lieutenants were hunched at the XO's desk signing forms with matching expressions of unhappiness while the XO paced.

A pair of bags sat just inside the cabin next to the entry hatch. The scuff of grease on the one side looked much like Claire's own bags. Her stomach dropped. The *Ephraim* was supposed to be leaving the yards tomorrow. Since a cabin hadn't been assigned to her yet, she'd brought her bags from the room on the station and put them in an empty locker in auxiliary repair bay three, and those, definitely her bags, had been brought to the XO office.

The two officers finished their work. The XO applied a stamp form of the CO's signature. Claire swallowed hard; something was very wrong here. The commanding officer, Captain Ayres, was just on leave, not incapacitated. The XO jabbed the send button and whatever it was transmitted without a chance of being called back for formal review by the CO.

Turning to Claire, the XO held out his hand. "Congratulations on your promotion, Ensign."

That just sent transmission had to be Claire's unearned promotion package on its way to the Office of Personnel. The ATO glared at the wall, but the AuxO gave her a tentative smile. She managed some kind of thank you that probably wasn't quite the right military response, quivering internally. The last time someone on the ship had been promoted to ensign there had been a formal ceremony and reception in the wardroom, and Captain Ayres had given a little speech about how hard the man had worked to earn the ensign pips.

The XO coughed and said, "You'll be reporting to the *Manasseh* tomorrow."

He added something very quickly about the CO's concerns about having a female officer onboard while in space. Captain Ayres had requested Claire be transferred to Blackbird Yard permanently, the XO explained. Since all such transfers required the officer be at least an ensign, the request was in now. The XO was sure it would be approved before that ship departed again, even with Commander Greentree over on the *Manasseh* not knowing how to relax and enjoy placing a ship in the yards from time to time.

An expression of pure envy passed over the ATO's face, and even the AuxO appeared faintly wistful. For a moment she wondered if they were jealous of her.

❦ ❦ ❦

Ensign Claire Bedlam Lecroix left her first ship without ceremony.

She stood alone with her bags on the Arrival's Concourse aboard Blackbird Alpha, the central control and personnel platform of the widely dispersed Blackbird Yard. Off to her left, the regular shuttle to Blackbird Bravo filled with a cheerful mix of commercial and Navy spacers on their way to the mass of eateries and entertainment venues in the B sections. Lucy and Mary shared a large enough place above Birdies in Section B3 to give Claire a bed, but she could be drummed out of the service if anyone saw and assumed the wrong thing.

Going back to the bachelor quarters probably wouldn't work since she'd checked out that morning and by now the payment would have bounced. The desk clerks didn't like the work of debiting future paychecks and could both refuse her a room and recommend the officer in charge consider placing a letter of instruction in her file for the failed payment. It was best to remain a number in their database to keep the clerks from thinking about her long enough to get angry. She lugged her bags down the corridor to the docking bay receiving shuttles from *Manasseh* and several others, praying that the ship would have an empty stateroom.

Claire waited for the shuttle and pressed moist hands against the heavy fabric of her skirts with nervous sweat trickling down her back. The industrially-cut and tape-hemmed ends of the billowing split skirts tucked into her uniform boots kept sticking and ripping at her ankles whenever she fidgeted. She admonished herself silently to stop dancing about like a waitress eager for tips and project presence like a Harrington.

She'd been an awful waitress for Aunt Jezzy's restaurant. This officer thing wasn't working out so well, either, but the pay was so much better. Claire repeated the mantra in her mind. Just one tour in the Navy. Do the payback for the cost of Saganami. Get out, and find some job in the space industries where they hired women. Today, all she had to do was find someplace to stay that wasn't a room over Birdies.

A reflection in the chrome bulkhead froze Claire's expression in a bug-eyed grimace. It wasn't. But yes, those were the pips of a full Captain, and that was Captain Matheson Ayres, Commanding Officer of the GNS *Ephraim*, standing beside and a bit behind her with his lips tilted in a bemused smile. Not for the first time, she wondered how he could be a full captain and only be commanding a destroyer.

Claire forced every muscle on her face into blank stillness as her mind twitched wildly. "Did I forget something aboard the *Ephraim*, Sir?" Inwardly, she winced. She hadn't been allowed to have anything on the *Ephraim*. If Captain Ayres realized she'd kept a locker in the chiefs' mess for lunches and spare uniform bits, it could cause the chiefs no end of grief.

Captain Ayres just laughed off the suggestion. He wasn't one for detailed considerations and analysis of things. Why should he be? His life must be rather straightforward. It was just the graspers like Claire who would continually try to upset the natural order. It must be something of a continual shock to him that she even kept bothering, but he was here now and this was another opportunity . . . She hit him with her best disarm-unruly-customers smile.

She tried to squelch the doubt that added a tremble to the corners of her smile. The inner voice whispered that ineptness with customers rather than skill with machinery was why Aunt Jezzy had kept the teenage Claire occupied with broken-down dishwashers instead of demanding customers.

She gamely fixed the corners of her lips and widened her eyes, trying to convince herself of the hope in her own words, "You must have changed your mind then, Sir. I won't be any trouble at all. I was checking the piping diagrams around medical, since AuxO told me about the cost of the women's berthing and lavatory ship alt—"

The captain's face was wrinkling up like he'd just smelled something awful. Claire stumbled a bit, but she pushed on with her pitch, "You know, Sir, and how it wouldn't be appropriate to have a junior officer use the visiting flag officer's lavatory."

This wasn't working, she realized midstream, but she couldn't just let it die.

Her treacherous mind insisted on replaying past errors even as she blustered on to describe how the ship could be modified in little ways to create a small, private space for one junior female officer to sleep.

Mistakes in customs and protocol with the *Ephraim*'s officers and their wives intermeshed with the memories of Aunt Jezzy keeping her firmly in the back of any restaurant, street cart, or stall, fixing the machinery and managing inventory. Only on rare occasions, like the complete absence of all servers on a shift or an overflowing customer glut, was Claire sent out to interact with customers and attempt to take orders, fill glasses, or bus tables. But never mind the past failures, she had to make the attempt to convince Captain Ayres to take her back— to meet the Test and all that—she had to try in spite of the extra human-imposed traps added to what the divine Tester assigned every man and woman.

Claire concluded finally with, "So, anyway, Sir, I've got the diagrams in my old files in Aux Three, and I figured out a way to make a lav in the supply closet behind medical and fit in a bedrack and locker. And it won't cost many austins at all. In fact, the savings from using that other distributor for our galley supplies that I showed you a couple of months ago would more than cover it." Claire renewed her flagging smile. Finish strong. That was important; Aunt Jezzy said so. "So, shall I take my things back onboard *Ephraim*? I wouldn't want to delay undocking."

Captain Ayres just rolled his eyes.

Looking over Claire's head, he said. "Hey Phin, I just wanted to come out here and apologize to you personally."

She looked quickly over her shoulder and felt heat pour from her face. A normal-looking master chief with somewhat scraggly hair and a slightly crooked nose stood a few steps away, but Captain Ayres hadn't been addressing him. *Ephraim*'s CO was talking to the commander—tall and well enough muscled for a recruiting poster— wearing the maroon and gold uniform of the Protector's Own. He held a bag with the GNS *Manasseh* ship's crest embroidered on it, three gold rings encircled his sleeves, giving lie to the fresh face and silky gloss of close-trimmed black hair, and the name plate on his chest read: "Greentree, Phineas."

Claire gulped. The simply gorgeous officer in the Mayhew colors of Protector Benjamin IX had to be *Manasseh*'s CO.

Captain Ayres accepted Greentree's salute.

"I hope you'll extend my apology to Elsabeta and Annette Marie. I know my Jennie was horrified when Personnel sent a—" At this, Ayres waved at Claire but mercifully left out whatever epithet he meant to affix to her. "I told the Station Commander here on Blackbird to keep her chaperoned and away from my boys. Willard did it for a while, but I hear that some of those foreign-headed men in the Protector's Own got to him. No offense, Phin, I know you aren't like those foreigners. They just happen to be wearing your uniform."

The master chief stilled in not quite parade rest and held the fixed gaze of a long-time military man who clearly intended to ignore a conversation between officers that, from the slight flare his eyelids, did not fit his view of military courtesy and customs.

Captain Ayres barely even paused for breath, "Pleased as punch to be a straightforward GSN officer myself these days."

Claire mentally ran through the lists of GSN and Protector's Own ships memorized while she was at Saganami Island. The *Manasseh*, like *Ephraim*, was definitely a normal Grayson Space Navy ship and not one of the elite squadron directly under Protector Benjamin Mayhew. That made Phineas Greentree one of those exceptional officers requested by the GSN from the Protector's Own to fill command slots.

Commander Greentree listened with a calm, controlled smile as Captain Ayres continued to apologize for Claire's transfer, or possibly for her existence. There had been a Grayson Midshipman Greentree at the Saganami Island Naval Academy a couple years behind her, and Claire gritted her teeth at being sent to yet another ship commanded by an officer with a family interest in preserving tradition.

The Bedlam family had been beaten with the stick of tradition too many times to have developed the reverence for it that imbued so many naval families. Egalitarianism in the service was a beautiful Saganami fantasy, but Aunt Jezzy had taught her better than to believe in fairytales.

Captain Ayres said often enough that women were not meant to serve in uniform. His family had been in service with Captain Hugh Yanakov himself on the founding voyage to colonize the Planet Grayson, so an Ayres could be counted on to know. Of course, *every* Grayson's lineage went back to that colony ship, and it had been run mostly by automated computers, with the colonists and crew in cryostasis for the trip. Claire hadn't argued. She'd learned not to.

Captain Ayres finally wound down with, "And don't take her blather just now too seriously. I had her watched closely. She never once coupled up with any of my boys, though a number of them did offer for her. Not the officers, of course, which might be what she's been holding out for, though some of them would have had some fun if she'd been willing. The girl's naive is all. You heard her describing building a love nest behind the infirmary on my ship just now, innocent as the dawn, thinking that anyone would want to allow a midshipwoman some out-of-the-way cubby for a sleep space where no one could keep a proper eye on her activities."

"Midshipwoman?" Commander Greentree glanced from Ayres to

Claire with a tight-lipped question, "Are you out of uniform, Ensign, or is it Midshipwoman?"

Claire was certain that she was scarlet by now. "I—uh—" She looked to Captain Ayres. He had the grace to flush.

Captain Ayres shrugged in a decidedly unmilitary way, waving his hands at Claire. "She kept asking, Phin. I wasn't going to allow her onboard or anything like that, but it was about the time that most of the middies get bumped up to ensign. That and the Office of Personnel was asking, too. They wanted a Letter of Instruction to file in her record as to why she wasn't made an ensign after the first T-year.

"I gotta tell you that I put together a draft of the letter. I figured that if all of us in the fleet just stood strong and didn't promote the poor girls that got pushed into this mess—Well, their families would have to take them back to do right by them. My XO had this idea, though, you see, if she were just to stay on Blackbird she could be laterally transferred to the yardbirds, but they don't take transfers for middies. Only officers.

"So—" Ayres shrugged. "I'm sorry again, Phin, I don't know what to tell you. You could strip the rank, I suppose."

"Your XO. Right." Commander Greentree's lips had thinned even more. "Sir."

Claire felt like throwing up. *Manasseh*'s CO looked almost as angry as the ATO had been.

"Did you at least do a board?" In one small mercy, Commander Greentree stopped looking quite so much like a vid star when he was furious, but Claire flinched at his lack of honorific for Captain Ayres. Then she remembered that the *Ephraim* CO's second wife was Jennie Greentree Ayres, so they were family, surely that meant it was all right.

Captain Ayres appeared not to notice the slight at all.

"A board? Of course not, it was just a paper promotion! I had no idea that she'd refuse to sign the transfer paperwork and push to get put on a ship."

Claire blinked trying to remember refusing to sign anything. She hadn't even made her initials on anything in the *Ephraim* XO's office that morning. What had the XO told him?

"Any sane woman," Captain Ayres continued, "would realize that we just can't allow our own women to run wild like the Manties do. But sometimes they get ideas, you know. Fun, when they're in your bed. Not so much when you try to command one."

Commander Greentree finally got Captain Ayres to wind down. Ayres repeated sheepish apologies for passing on his problems to a brother-in-law when he had intended to pass them off to Willard, the stuffed shirt running the Blackbird maintenance division, who properly deserved Claire since he was an advocate for the Protector's outlandish social engineering.

Ayres dipped his head in a final apology and walked off.

Commander Greentree turned to Claire. His quick up-down look focused a bit too much. She force-relaxed her jaw to keep from gritting her teeth or letting a change of facial expression escape. So maybe she was plain to the point of near-ugliness, and maybe the slight mottledness of the skin spoke of skin cancers caught late and treated without much concern for the aesthetic impact on the patient. She looked well enough for a not-so-wealthy steader from Burdette who had never had enough marital prospects to make it worth her family's while to mortgage their lives for beauty treatments.

Claire's new CO welcomed her with: "Why aren't you at least wearing makeup?"

Of course she was wearing makeup. It just wasn't very good. Claire was sure her smile had slipped into the mulish blankness that the Burdette Ladies often chastised her about. "No excuse, Sir."

Commander Greentree shot a glare at the departing back of his brother-in law. "At least get yourself over to base medical and have a skin treatment. Jennie is constantly writing Elsabeta about them, so I know they've got a spa dermatologist up here, for all that Jennie claims the service in the waiting room isn't what she's used to back on the Steading."

Claire opened her mouth to object, but Greentree talked right on over her. "Any way, we can't have the Manties thinking that we let our service members walk around with untreated service injuries so easily corrected. What did you do anyway, get sloppy at the engineering depot?"

Claire blushed furiously at that implication of negligence. She'd been four or maybe five the last time she'd had a skin cancer.

Greentree shook his head. "Nothing for it. You've learned. I see that. But get it fixed now. Wearing your mistakes on your face helps no one. You hear?"

"Aye, Sir." Claire could do that much. She gave up a half-formed line of explanation to spell out his mistaken assumptions, and instead she grasped for the glimmer of opportunity. "Sir, when should I report for my board?"

"What board?"

"For ensign."

Commander Greentree's nostril's flared. "You're wearing the rank. I assume your pay's already been adjusted. If not, my exec will see to the admin details. Regardless, the orders your Captain Ayres signed on his honor as a commissioned officer say you are reporting as an ensign. You'll just have to learn as you go along. Try not to fall on your face too often in front of your people. You'll be having requalification or," at this he grimaced again, "I suppose your first qualification boards for the watches. That will have to do." Almost under his breath, Commander Greentree muttered his brother-in-law's name like a curse and then added in a voice used to issuing commands, "Don't expect empty promotions from me."

Claire kept her face carefully still and boarded the shuttle to *Manasseh* as Commander Greentree waved her on with a final grimace. Master Chief Wallens joined her for the return flight. Without the two COs present, Claire introduced herself and asked who she should see on the ship about getting assigned a place to sleep. The master chief presented her with a stateroom assignment, ship patches for her uniforms, and a new ship's comp filled with study material and ship-system schematics. Claire barely held back the urge to hug him.

❈ ❈ ❈

On the relaxed ride up to the ship, Master Chief Wallens told Claire anecdotes about the crew and asked after her family and steading. Claire skipped over explaining about Jezzy and Noah and told him about Steadholder Burdette instead.

Claire gave the master chief points for not flinching at the oblique reference to the late Lord William Fitzclarence, Steadholder Burdette. That Lord Burdette, in the most extreme case of steadholder bad behavior in recent memory, had challenged Steadholder Harrington as Protector Benjamin's champion to a duel and lost. Fatally.

The new Steadholder Burdette, Nathan Fitzclarence, had chosen to send female midshipmen candidates to Saganami Island for his steading's Academy nominations as a peace offering to Protector Benjamin IX and, in a less direct way, to Steadholder and Admiral Harrington. He'd made it quite clear to the three women he'd nominated that he didn't expect actual graduation from Saganami. The Academy curriculum would be far more advanced than a women's finishing school, and of course they would be wanting to start families in short order. He took it as a personal favor that their fathers had allowed the attempt and that the girls were willing themselves. Claire, at Aunty Jezzy's advice, had not mentioned that with her father dead and most of the Bedlam women unmarried, her head-of-household was actually her younger cousin, Noah.

Lord Burdette had rationalized that one couldn't expect mere Graysons to be Harringtons after all. The Harrington woman was a marvel beyond her sex, an admiral in both the Grayson Space Navy and the Royal Manticoran Navy. Likely no other woman would ever be able to fill her slippers. She was even a steadholder. Lord Nathan had said the words with a reverence of one bred to honor the steadholder position. Even years later, he still seemed stunned to be holding that exalted position himself.

It was only at Saganami that Claire understood the duel. The single combat broadcast on live, planet-wide HD ending in the steadholder's shameful death had been a steading-wide embarrassment and not something explained to children. Better recordings existed, but in the way of students of war unaccustomed to actual carnage, the favorite at Saganami was the most gruesome. It showed a bad angle with not much audio except barely muttered curses by Lord Burdette directed at Steadholder Harrington. The vid wouldn't have caught the attention of midshipmen at all, except for the final seconds. Burdette's back obscured the view just long enough to fill the screen with a solid twelve inches of steel sheering through the wet meat of the man's neck from Harrington's killing blow.

. The other two Burdette midshipwomen dropped out of Saganami Island as soon as their families arranged other options for them. Claire vaguely remembered meeting one later with her husband, an older wife, and several children. Claire had stayed. She hadn't dared do otherwise.

The initial application was for a position that promised full Grayson Space Navy health pension and dependent aid benefits in exchange for arduous space duty. When Claire found herself nominated for an appointment to Saganami Island, with a position as an officer to follow if she could complete the course of study, Aunt Jezzy and the extended family had lost no time in sharing their feelings on whether or not it would be acceptable to demurely resign her position should the Academy prove too arduous for her gentle sensibilities. They were agreed to the woman. She could quit if she liked, but if she did, Claire could find some other family to come back to.

The Tester gave a steader family an opportunity like this but once every seventh generation or so. Had they realized just what Claire was applying for, they'd have sent . . . Well, maybe there wasn't anyone better in the family to send, but by All That Was Holy, she had better not blow this.

There hadn't been a Bedlam to attend, let alone finish, an advanced school as far back as they could remember. There may have been a Lecroix or two a few generations back, but Claire's father had died in an industrial accident when she was nine. Like most steader families, there just weren't that many men. When he'd died, his sisters were already married into other families.

The Bedlams weren't a good family anyway, and it didn't help that Claire was an only child. Her mother had, at least in Claire's memory, been attempting one fertility aid after another. At least three times that she knew about, something had actually worked, but her would-be brothers were all miscarried or stillborn. Some medicines, and fertility spas, and even technical surrogacy worked for those with the funds, but those sorts of benefits did not come with a farm technician's pay on Burdette Steading.

They came standard, Aunt Jezzy was quick to point out, with the Grayson Space Navy's pay and benefit package. One didn't even need to be in the elite Protector's Own. Everyone got it. The Bedlams spent some time poring over the details and admiring the wonder of it all. Even Noah had been drawn in by the excitement.

Claire had heard indirectly that her family had tried to push Noah to enlist in the GSN at eighteen, since he hadn't achieved a nomination for a Saganami Island appointment. He had balked. Claire didn't blame him, much. The GSN was work. Noah was nice enough in person, but he didn't care for doing more than he had to. And besides, Noah liked having his toes on the floor, as he put it, without all that vast nothingness between him and good solid earth. Claire was just as pleased to have gotten some space between herself and the heavy-metal poisons of nature.

※ ※ ※

On the *Manasseh*, the plaque on Claire's assigned stateroom had her name already engraved and thoroughly shellacked in a shiny, clear coating. Relief at finally seeing it lifted her shoulders. Then she read the next line down: Ensign Cecelie Rustin.

Claire flushed. She'd heard about that girl in the class that followed hers at Saganami Island. There were a ton of Grayson students, sure, but darn few of them were female. The boys seemed to think that every midshipwoman was somehow the same girl, responsible for every female's actions in ways no guy would hold himself accountable for another midshipman's behavior. Claire tried to remember which of the outlandish things she had been accused of condoning were perpetrated by Rustin. Cecelie Rustin had been a year behind her, Claire was at least sure of that.

She choked back bitter bile as she realized that Rustin would had to have proved herself fast to already be an ensign instead of a midshipwoman.

Claire calculated furiously. Even if Rustin had been one of those to figure out her first posting early and spend Saganami Island school breaks out with the ship, learning her systems, she couldn't possibly have been here even half as long as it had taken Claire to make ensign. Fury mixed with shame, and Claire pushed through the door into her new stateroom, nearly catching the bag porter in the doorway as it wobbled trying to follow her abrupt action.

Had Rustin been the one on the triathlon team that won all those awards that usually went to heavy-planeters? Or was she that study-mad one taking all the extra courses and forever asking professors questions that had nothing to do with the material on the exams?

The smug little Rustin was sitting hunched over a terminal with her back to the door when Claire barged in. It was definitely the studious one. Claire visually swept the space, looking for things to detach from their safety housings to make room for her luggage while she moved in.

With a broad smile that Claire immediately distrusted, the Rustin girl looked up and broke into an outright grin. Chattering a welcome, she fairly bounced up from her chair in a way that must have been entirely normal for her, because while Claire was wincing, waiting for the back of the overturned chair to hit the bare metal deck, Rustin's free hand flew back behind herself, caught the edge of the chair mid-fall and set it back upright without even turning around to look at it.

Claire matched the smile with habitual wariness and made noncommittal noises as Rustin flurried around verbally for several minutes about how delighted she was to have a new friend onboard, not that the guys weren't friends, of course, but women have a special bond—or at least that was what Commander Greentree said.

Claire felt her face tighten at the reference to their too-handsome CO, and Rustin paused. She looked a little disconcerted, as if she wasn't feeling that "special bond" just at the moment. But when Claire smoothed the edges of her mouth into a friendlier shape, Rustin relaxed and bounded verbally onward after on the briefest of pauses.

Claire decided that actual verbal responses were not apparently necessary and busied herself with figuring out which of the lockers weren't already claimed so that she could unpack, collapse her luggage, and find someplace out of the way to store it. Rustin responded to Claire's unfastening of the top of her luggage by opening up empty compartments and then showing the ones she'd already filled and offering to switch if Claire would rather have the use of those.

There was an embarrassed deferral to Claire's earlier graduation date here, and Claire's smile must have slipped because Rustin switched to a wildly ranging discourse on how everyone knew that ships in the yards didn't grant midshipwomen as much opportunity for studying operating ship's systems and continued on from there to a side discussion again about Commander Greentree. The logic was difficult to follow, but it seemed that at least Rustin believed that Commander Greentree had asked the Office of Personnel to send another female officer to his ship.

The theory that women needed to be in groups featured prominently along with the commander's marital experiences. Apparently since Commander Greentree's first wife, Elsabeta, was tremendously unhappy attempting to manage the social obligations of a rising officer. Greentree's marriage to a second wife, Annette Marie, had made a world of difference.

But, in what Claire was quickly coming to recognize as Rustin's habit of covering any possible misunderstanding with a pile of words, the other ensign insisted that of course the senior wife Elsabeta was due all proper dignity and social respect. Even though—this part was rather talked around—it certainly sounded to Claire as if Annette Marie had a flair for the social hobnobbing expected of a senior officer's wife while Elsabeta would just as soon stay home, possibly with a cat and a book. If anyone didn't like it, Elsabeta was perhaps more than willing to mix pulverized cat droppings into their tea should she be forced into hosting anything remotely like a ladies' tea.

Claire managed a few diffident questions. The cat droppings had not been invented by Rustin and had been verified or at least repeated to Rustin by no less than three officers' wives. Also, Rustin found all of the officers' wives, with the exception of Elsabeta Greentree, to be eminently avoidable and by varying degrees students of the social art of public evisceration.

Claire, having by this point fully cataloged the spontaneous blushes which warmed her roommate's creamy complexion and the tendency of bouncing blond curls to escape the hairstyle attempting to severely restrain them, felt confident she could accuse the *Manasseh* Wardroom Wives' Club of having selected one Ensign Cecelie Rustin as public enemy number one. The group had likely closed ranks against Rustin almost as soon they'd caught sight of her. Pure instinct to defend marriages strained by repeated separations would make them hate Rustin. These women had all the whores of all the worlds to worry about already, and, in her, they had a woman actually traveling with their men day in and day out. In retrospect, Claire was mildly annoyed that the *Ephraim* Wives' Club had been so accepting of her own presence.

As Claire put away the last of her uniforms, Rustin exclaimed in delight over the industrial tape she'd used to finish the hems of the uniform split skirts. Then the other young woman produced an elaborate sewing kit of the type Claire had seen in the hands of one of Steadholder Burdette's wives during her mandatory visits there.

These were the tools the idle rich could use to devote hours and hours to doing what a machine would do in seconds. True artisans would use them to create the one-of-a-kind creations worn by the most fashionable of steadholder wives. Now Rustin picked up the fabric shears, imprinted with the brand of Grayson's finest clothier, and transferred them from her left hand to her right to recut a mangled pair of split skirts.

Claire snatched the scissors out of her hands.

Those uniforms were too expensive. She could not watch a left-handed amateur seamstress using right-handed tools attempt to cut without even a pattern guide. Her new roommate took Claire's mutterings without rancor and readily admitted to destroying the last set. Rustin's moms had sent the sewing kit and two new uniforms for her to learn to do it properly.

Claire goggled at the idea that a family would have so much money as to be able to send two new uniforms but would still insist that Rustin do the hemming herself rather than just have them be professionally fitted.

Her roommate responded that it was important to learn to be independent, entirely unaware of the irony of an adult receiving clothing from her parents while claiming to be independent. Claire decided not to mention that her own financial transfers went in the other direction.

After unpacking, Claire struggled with the communications system on the ship as she tried to obey her new commanding officer's order to get a skin treatment. Rustin stepped right in and made the connection from her own console. As she punched in the com code, she explained that personal off-ship communication required a transfer fee, and while contacting medical was professional business, getting privacy in any of the ship's offices would be a nuisance.

Rustin laughed off the question of when the bill would arrive for Claire to pay her part. She said it was nothing and not worth the trouble of trying to break it out from the much more expensive, lengthy transmissions Rustin assured her she sent to her moms each week.

Her roommate stepped outside to give her privacy, and Claire gave the closed door a genuine smile. The other ensign really was actually and truly a nice, if clueless, person. She resolved to help her as much as she could even if it meant hemming all of the woman's uniforms.

Claire called the clinic and reached a bored dermatologist who had her dial up the camera's resolution and turn this way and that to show her full face and then hands when he caught a glimpse of the scarring on the back of her right hand. He sent a prescription directly off to the *Manasseh's* medical unit for her to pick up later. He muttered about butchers playing pediatrician but seemed to think her skin would be fine in a matter of weeks. When Claire tentatively asked about the cost, he looked confused.

❧ ❧ ❧

The introduction to Claire's new boss, a harried Lieutenant Loyd, went quickly and smoothly. He'd read the *Ephraim* AuxO's equipment failure reports and wanted to be sure *Manasseh* didn't miss the same maintenance and follow her sister ship into a prolonged repair period. He asked her some technical questions. They quickly revealed that he didn't actually understand radiation deformation of metals beyond knowing that it existed and that certain schedules of preventative maintenance could sometimes extend machinery service life. He was a tactical track officer, though, so Claire forgave him. At least he knew that machinery mattered and wanted there to be someone tracking it and making sure it lasted longer than just his own tour of duty.

The interview was conducted in the wardroom, with several of his peers popping in and out and making various observations or throwing challenging questions her way. At the end of it the executive officer came in and asked a couple of tactics questions.

Claire wasn't even sure why they mattered. She turned to her boss.

Lieutenant Loyd immediately told the exec that he would work with her to brush up on her tactical proficiency and run some sims for her now that she was on a fully functional *Joseph*-class ship. The exec snorted, pointing out that sims could be run just as easily in a yard as on a ship in space. He glared at Claire and told her that there would be no excuses for shirking her continued tactical education on this ship.

The exec slapped a comp on the table. It was scrolled all the way to the end of a formal midshipman's board for promotion to ensign and already signed by all the officers who had been dropping in and asking questions. The exec patted his pockets and then looked around with a pained expression. Claire produced a stylus from her pocket. The exec snatched it out of her hand scribbled the final signature and slapped his thumbprint down.

Loyd and the exec stood. Claire stumbled to her feet, copying the others from Saganami-trained instinct.

Commander Greentree's clear tenor came from just to her left, calling for the exec to hand him the ship's patch. Claire counted herself lucky that she wasn't an easy blusher. The man was too gorgeous.

According to Rustin, he had two wives. But on a commander's salary, he could certainly afford a third—if, that was, he actually wanted one and if his first two wives could tolerate her. The Burdette Ladies were sure to comment on that. Greentree, for his part, seemed not even to notice her jerking her face away from him to cut off her lingering inspection of his body. Letting a boss know you like him is a horrible idea, Claire reminded herself. Why couldn't he have been just a bit smelly like Captain Ayres or have dirty fingernails or something?

The wardroom filled quickly with the *Manasseh's* full officer complement while Claire concentrated on keeping her eyes off her CO. Rustin gave a little wave from the corner, giving two thumbs up paired with a giant grin. Not hopping up and down was probably surreptitious for the woman. Claire credited Rustin's Saganami Island training for that.

The Office of Personnel did not have a record of Claire's oath for assuming the rank of ensign back on GNS *Ephraim*, Commander Greentree informed Claire in a voice meant to carry to the whole wardroom. His wry smile gave away that he was fully aware of all that he wasn't saying. Blackbird Yard Public Affairs had not been able to locate a quality recording to send to Burdette Steading for the local news release. So, if she didn't object to the irregularity, he'd just as soon hold the ceremony again here on *Manasseh*. He had Rustin provide him with some of her midshipwoman insignia and motioned for Rustin to switch out Claire's collar and shoulder devices for the single silver collar pip of a midshipwoman.

Commander Greentree shooed Rustin back to her corner vantage point and cued up the spacer drafted to capture the proceedings to begin recording. The exec called the assembled officers to attention and read off the official orders from the Grayson Space Navy Office authorizing Midshipwoman Claire Bedlam Lecroix to wear the rank of Ensign and assume all the duties and responsibilities of a commissioned officer of the Grayson Space Navy at the recommendation of Commander Phineas Greentree, Commanding Officer *GNS Manasseh*.

The Ayres name was notably absent from the orders. Somehow Claire doubted that if Personnel had resent a copy of an old approval, they would have gone back and changed the requesting commanding officer's name to the current reporting senior.

Claire pulled her attention back as Commander Greentree administered her oath of office. She swore loyalty once again to Grayson, Protector Benjamin Mayhew IX, and the Office of the Protector. She would do her duty to God and her star nation and ever rise to meet the Tests set before her in the faithful performance of her duty. The words were so familiar that she had to focus to avoid embarrassing herself by switching up phrases with the common prayer for the Protectorate of Grayson or the Burdette Steading pledge of allegiance.

Commander Greentree smiled rather broadly at her. It wasn't fair. A man that lovely should know what he did to women and control himself better. Claire curled her toes inside her ship boots to distract herself from the whiff of aftershave as he leaned over to pin the two silver pips of an ensign to her collar and shoulder boards.

She looked around the room, trying not to think about how it would feel if a man were clasping a necklace instead of pinning on rank insignia. She should think herself lucky to be here. Really, she should.

So what if the Burdette Lady Steadholders worried that she was not going to find a man interested in even a third wife who was constantly away in the GSN? This was all a means to an end. She had a degree, after all, and a really quite amazing education at Saganami Island in the engineering of ship power systems and auxiliaries. Merchants used different systems. But, physics was physics. Claire resolved to continue studying for the technical-school certifications in those other merchant systems.

A Grayson in-system shipper might not want to hire her, but there were others who did business in Yeltsin's Star who wouldn't mind hiring a young woman. A life could be built on Blackbird Yard that way. And who knew, she might meet someone who'd want a wife who could travel with him and knock out some of the qualifications required by Grayson Transit Control, thus saving him the cost of hiring extra hands.

It was a cold plan, but Claire thought it might work. The GSN kept providing more and more training. The ship-combat simulations were completely useless for any long-term plans, but they'd been easy to avoid on the *Ephraim*. The *Manasseh* would not be much different. And even when Claire did have to waste time on them, ship-combat sims still beat washing dishes by hand when the restaurant had to wait to clear enough profit to buy the parts for fixing the dishwasher.

The ceremony drew to a close with a burst of applause prompted by the exec, and at his chivvying, the officers made their way around the room to congratulate Claire one by one and welcome her to the ship. The lieutenants and higher ranked officers asked after her pastimes at Saganami, course of study, and so on. They seemed to listen to each other's questions since they repeated questions only every fifth person or so.

The midshipmen and ensigns offered a simple "congrats" or sometimes "welcome aboard and congratulations."

Rustin gave her a hug. Claire held her awkwardly and scanned the room for disapproval. That's when she first saw the Royal Manticoran Navy exchange officer, a leering man with the broad frame that came of extreme athleticism in school followed by a few years of carb loading without the sport to burn the energy. As a Grayson, his rounded face might be just old enough to belong to a midshipman, but on the Mantie lieutenant commander it just meant he'd received the prolong life-extension treatment. She reexamined the Mantie and decided his expression couldn't have actually been ill intended since the rest of the wardroom hadn't reacted.

Commander Greentree poked the exec in the ribs with his elbow. Too many side conversations muffled the words, but it was clear that the CO was celebrating having a second female officer onboard and chiding his exec for doubting that she and Rustin would get along like sisters.

Claire didn't have sisters or brothers. That was relatively rare among Grayson steaders, but it was well-nigh unheard of among the wealthy steadholder families. Unless of course, there was something very shameful going on, like infidelity leading to divorce and disownment or maybe a tragic death, or several.

The next well wisher in line must have caught part of the CO's comments. He paired his congratulations with a question on how her siblings would react to the news.

"I'm an only child, Sir." Claire felt her smile freeze as she surrendered information about herself that she had managed to keep hidden on *Ephraim*.

The lieutenant gawked.

An uncomfortable silence spread around the room, until Rustin, who was still only a few steps away, spun around and injected a cheery, "Well, she's got me now, and I'm delighted."

The edge of battlesteel in Rustin's voice was entirely surprising. Did Rustin really think she could protect anyone else when it seemed as if Rustin herself had spread her own whole life out for these people to dissect and judge?

Claire pushed the confusion aside for now, focusing on the next potential attacker in line. There would be time in private later to try to figure out Rustin's motivations and decide whether or not her apparent friend was actually capable of sealing her own shoes.

Lieutenant Loyd was up next. The crease between his eyebrows seemed to imply that he hadn't missed the wardroom undercurrent of speculation on sordidness in Claire's family past. His slight smile could either be anticipation of skewering her with his question or an attempt to put her at ease.

Claire tensed. If it was the second, he needn't have bothered. Claire no longer believed that it was possible to be at ease in a public setting.

Lieutenant Loyd made a joke about killing the *Ephraim*'s tactics officer twice in the next fleet exercise in retaliation for failing in Claire's tactics training, which got their corner of the room chuckling again. It seemed that the *Manasseh* wardroom was proud of Lieutenant Loyd's prowess in the tactical simulations, and they didn't seem to think he was boasting beyond his ability to deliver.

The last questioner turned back and suggested that the group horse up Claire so that she could be the one to represent the *Manasseh* and take down the *Ephraim*.

That suggestion was greeted with howls of approval.

Claire flinched at little at the implication that her old ship was so far behind *Manasseh* that they thought they could send a just-passed ensign up against lieutenants and lieutenant commanders in the sims and fully expect to win. What did they do, *live* in the tactics simulators on this ship? Commander Greentree was a Protector's Own officer, sure, and those were known to be hard over on training time, but could it really make that much difference? Claire was pretty sure that Captain Ayres had made certain the lieutenants and lieutenant commanders did the fleet requirement of four hours in the simulators each week.

Lieutenant Loyd finished up his impromptu monologue on how Claire was going to shine as a tactician with a claim that she'd be the best ensign to come out of Owens Steading since Abigail Hearns.

Commander Greentree lost his recruiter vid star grin to a careful blankness. The master chief had reported back apparently.

Claire realized that she'd have to share another bombshell. "Actually, I come from Burdette Steading, Sir."

Several of the listening officers repeated the steading name for the ones in the back, and this time the entire wardroom stared at her, shocked.

The exec broke the silence from all the way across the room this time. "Wait a minute here, Ensign Lecroix. That was entirely left out of the officer's biography sent over from the *Ephraim*. You gotta tell us how you got a Saganami Island nomination out of Steadholder Burdette."

Claire swallowed, carefully marshalling her thoughts to try to explain without saying anything that would be horribly misinterpreted, either here in this company or back on Burdette Steading. The less said the better, but this group didn't seem interested in letting this one go without a full explanation. First, brush over the dueling death of Lord William Fitzclarence. No, be honest at least in your thoughts, she reminded herself. It must have been at least an attempted murder of Admiral Alexander-Harrington. She could see in the group's eyes that they were all thinking about how the last Steadholder Burdette had done his best to kill Admiral Harrington, the first and most impressive woman to wear a uniform in defense of Grayson.

"Um." Great, Claire, she told herself, brilliant start. "Lord Burdette was good enough to nominate me for a position, Sir."

She paused as some of the officers murmured to each other that this was Nathan Fitzclarence, the cousin who had inherited the steadholder position after William's duel.

Lieutenant Loyd watched Claire with his lips parted as if he were trying to find a way to ask more without taking her into another orbital minefield. She wished he'd just stop and let the subject change.

"What was he thinking?" The lieutenant finally asked, and Claire tried to shrink into the wall.

"Steadholder Owens sent Abigail Hearns the year before," she said. "The Protector seemed to approve . . ." Claire did blush now, and fiercely. "I really don't understand all the politics, Sir, but Lord Burdette was only interested in nominating girls that year. Our elder said, ah, not very nice things, but Lord Burdette said that we were to try, and when it got too much for our, um, sensibilities he'd see what he could do to help us marry properly. But that he had to show Cr—"

The CO coughed, loudly, and Claire realized she had almost said Crazy Benjie, the barroom nickname for the protector common under the *old* Steadholder Burdette.

"Ah, he said he had to show Protector Benjamin that Grayson women weren't meant to be like Steadholder Harrington."

A baffled silence followed, and even Rustin seemed completely speechless.

Lieutenant Loyd spoke first with: "I'm totally lost. You were sent to Saganami Island with directions to quit. So what happened?"

Claire just glared at him, entirely forgetting the last five years of carefully developed military courtesies. "It's a good job."

Loyd's jaw dropped again, but in a wide, open-mouthed smile. He turned to Commander Greentree and the exec. He called across the room, as if everyone hadn't already heard Claire's response, "It's a good job, Captain."

Claire contained her glare, barely, by keeping it focused on her amused lieutenant instead of her CO.

"A steader can't just quit a good job." Her intended soft reply rasped with anger, carrying clearly back across the room, and she strangled the volume back to a whisper in an attempt to control the thoughts spilling out. "I got people to keep fed, you—" She managed to not use the disparaging term for scions of steadholder families that came to mind.

Claire pleaded with her lieutenant, "Sir, I can't go dropping a good job just 'cause someone thinks it should be too hard."

Her bottled rage simmered as she thought: Hard? What did a steadholder's family know about hard jobs anyway?

Lieutenant Loyd just stood in front of her shaking, with laughter, interpreting her fury as just slightly off-color humor.

The next man had to take several minutes to finish guffawing before asking his question. Now all the questions were about Burdette. None of them noticed that she didn't find her situation funny. It didn't seem to matter what she said. They all thought it was a phenomenal joke.

Most of them now said things on the theme of "Can't keep a good steader down." Slowly Claire realized that most of the other officers thought that they were steaders themselves and identified with her for all that they had family influence that far exceeded anything a Bedlam might expect to gather. That family influence, from Claire's perspective, came from connections to steadholders, but if they all wanted to spontaneously adopt her, who was she to argue? Claire filed this all away to try to figure out later if they were all somehow mocking her in a way she just didn't understand yet.

Lieutenant Loyd planted himself next to her in the receiving line as the rest of the officers came around with their congratulations and questions. When she glanced at him from the corner of her eye, he only smiled again and announced that he needed to be the first to hear whatever other stories his new ensign had to tell, since he absolutely refused to hear them secondhand from another department head.

The lieutenant also shot down questions with quick regularity if they prompted Claire to wedge herself too far back against the wardroom bulkhead. She watched for warning signs in his unasked-for protection, but he didn't touch or crowd or emit any of the subtle markers of a man intending to control her. If anything, he was policing the rest of the wardroom, and Claire tried to force herself to calm down and regain a measure of composure.

The last of the officers wound through the line, with the Mantie bringing up the rear. He approached with a slightly odd gait, like he was trying to imitate a vid actor. He had a nice smile and hadn't seemed to follow the laughter that had infected the rest of the wardroom. He introduced himself as Lieutenant Commander Kevin Lockhart, but "Call me Kevin," and told Claire to meet him later if she wanted some watch signatures.

Rustin watched him leave with pursed lips.

❀ ❀ ❀

Claire pinned another invitation from the *Ephraim's* Wives' Club on her blotter, half listening and half ignoring Rustin as she chattered on about the latest thing to happen with her division. Her roommate had been even happier than usual, nearly bouncing off the walls for the last couple days since her division had gotten near-perfect marks on the laser-shooting qualification. Commander Greentree was pleased and in a good mood about it, which naturally transferred down to the entire wardroom and crew complement. The CO was pretty good about keeping his bad days from overly affecting his ship, but a commander's actions and inactions decided so much about daily life of a ship that there was no way for his personality not to affect them. Claire had considered using this time to try to float a leave-request chit to take two weeks off to attend a merchant life-support systems advanced technician's qualification cram session and certification exam. Actually, she had more than considered it; she had tried. The exec hadn't routed the chit, as far as she could tell, so she'd actually printed the thing and taken the papers herself to the CO during his office hours. He'd refused it. Request denied.

Claire stared at her screen trying not to cry . . . and failing. This was like the *Ephraim* all over again, except that there she actually expected it, so she hadn't relaxed and gotten gut-punched like this. Rustin was composing a letter to her little sister again, so it wasn't like she would actually notice that Claire wasn't paying attention or really responding. Claire kept her face averted and let the tears spill down her face.

To have something to pretend to be doing, Claire checked her own messages. The console still wasn't set up with a bank account number to send anything, but she could get them. Aunt Jezzy was asking for some more money this month to buy a bassinet or something for the newest grandniece. Somehow Aunt Jezzy had kept from Noah that Claire had a raise with her promotion, but in return Aunt Jezzy wanted access to take the extra money from time to time. Noah had spent what Aunt Jezzy had budgeted for the new child on a hover bike, so the family needed a bit more from Claire this month.

Aunt Jezzy advised Claire to see if it were true that Harrington Steading had a bank that allowed deposits in a woman's name alone. Denying Noah access to accounts to which he was the legal owner was fraud, of course, but it didn't feel like that since the accounts only existed at all because Claire was being paid for service in the GSN. Planet-wide Grayson law laid down by Protector Benjamin did allow female property ownership, but Burdette Steading law still made a woman's debts or property the responsibility of her protector. The not-quite-contradicting laws combined in ways Claire was pretty sure the Protector had never intended, and Noah jointly owned her accounts. Worse, her cousin had learned that he could debit the family bank accounts directly once he found them. Apparently Noah's latest surrogate father figure, a church deacon, had had something to do with teaching him that.

Claire blew her nose. She wished she were on the *Ephraim*.

Someone knocked on the door, and Rustin looked up, pausing her message to her sister.

Claire looked at the door, forgetting that would show her face to Rustin. Claire scrubbed her eyes quickly and started to stand, but Rustin waved her off toward their stateroom sink and answered the door herself.

She opened it only partway, though, blocking it with her body. Claire couldn't see past her, but she knew it was Lieutenant Loyd on the other side. She could clearly hear him talking to Rustin.

Claire washed her face quickly, even though the sound of the water would give away to Loyd that she was hiding behind her roommate.

Rustin tried to claim that Claire was unavailable without telling Lieutenant Loyd that Claire had been bawling.

Lieutenant Loyd wasn't having any of it.

He just overrode Rustin. Claire hadn't really expected her to be able to stop anyone, but it was sweet of her to try. That was Rustin, perpetually sweet, but not entirely effective. Claire was surprised he didn't simply force the door open or come in. Maybe he thought she was naked.

Instead, Lieutenant Loyd just ordered through the door, "Claire, meet me in CIC in five."

Rustin tried one more time to talk him out of it somehow, but Claire swallowed and answered herself with an "Aye, Sir." It sounded weepy, but she couldn't really help that.

Lieutenant Loyd must have left, because Rustin slipped right back in, shut the door firmly, and then turned into a dervish of motion. She straightened Claire's uniform, brushed off lint, and finally slapped a little plastic tube of eye drops into Claire's hands. The crystal liquid miraculously cleared the redness in a moment. Without that to draw attention, the puffiness seemed hardly noticeable.

Rustin gave Claire a quick hug and shoed her out the door to meet whatever new nastiness was about to enter her day. Senior officers never sought out ensigns in their staterooms for anything pleasant. Claire thought of her last watch qualification sign off with Lieutenant Commander Lockhart and shuddered.

※ ※ ※

Claire made her way down to CIC and belatedly realized that she'd forgotten her comp pad. Patting her front pocket, she found that Rustin had stuck it in there along with a stylus. The pointy bit of plastic to make notes on a computer screen had a designer brand name, making it one of Rustin's. Claire carefully fitted the stylus back in her pocket to keep from losing it, still walking fast. She slammed into Lieutenant Commander Lockhart just outside of CIC.

The impact was cushioned by Lockhart swaying a step back with her as if he had been just standing there waiting for her to step into him. He leaned in as Claire tried to step back. Chuckling, Lockhart held Claire in a bear hug, reached around, and grabbed her bottom and pinched.

Claire slammed her fist into his solar plexus.

Lockhart stumbled back, swearing at her, and promised to clear all the tactics sign-offs he'd given her.

Claire bit her lip and just backed away. If he decided to tell Commander Greentree, she wasn't sure what would happen, but it wouldn't be good.

Lockhart let a smile creep back on to his face and told her to come to his stateroom when she was ready to apologize. Then he turned smartly and marched away down the passageway humming a ditty popular in strip clubs that made Claire's ears burn.

Lieutenant Loyd stood inside the open hatch to CIC, white-lipped. Claire cringed, her stomach sinking as she wondered what he had decided to see. He blew out a long breath of air. "We need to go see the captain about that."

Claire felt nauseous. "I'm not going to do you either. No matter what you're going to tell the captain. I won't."

The lieutenant flushed with fury just as Claire had expected him to, but he didn't make any farther threats.

Claire backed against the bulkhead nervously searching for a protective audience. Claire didn't think Lieutenant Loyd would get grabby. He hadn't done anything like that yet. She backed a few steps just to be sure and tripped over an ankle-height junction box.

Lieutenant Loyd caught a flailing arm and pulled her upright, but then dropped her arm like it was arc welder-hot. He stepped away with his hands palm up.

"Ensign, that is so fucked up that I don't know where to start. This was supposed to be a counseling session where I told you that if you wanted this 'good job' you needed to start doing it instead of playing GSN dress-up." He narrowed his eyes. "Obviously, I have no idea what's going on with my own officers. So, we're going to fix that."

Claire crossed her arms and hugged herself, hunching her shoulders over. It hid her breasts a little, but not really enough. Claire tensed, waiting to find out what her outburst was going to do to her this time.

The lieutenant ducked back into CIC and with a quick word sent some petty officers scurrying down the passageway.

Claire hovered half in and half out, wanting to be around more people but reluctant to leave him before learning what he intended to do to her.

Master Chief Wallens took the corner at a quick lope and then slowed to wander into CIC as if he just happening to be strolling by.

Claire followed him in, and Lieutenant Loyd directed her to take a chair.

The master chief sat down next to Claire with a bit of space between the chairs but angled towards Lieutenant Loyd and flipped out his own comp and appeared to completely absorb himself in some kind of paperwork.

Lieutenant Loyd sat, scrubbed his forehead with his hands, and still rubbing his temples, started talking. "Okay, Ensign Lecroix, the sum total of this counseling session was supposed to be you standing at attention while I yelled at you about not doing the tactics sim sessions that I told you to do. And that the captain told you to do back when you got your promotion. You were supposed to leave here chastised, having promised to stop lazing around, and go spend the next four hours blowing up ships. And then you were supposed to spend half your days for the next couple weeks blowing things up, too, and by that time you'd probably manage to make the ship that gets blown up be something besides your own ship at least some of the time. But that happened." Lieutenant Loyd flipped a hand towards the passageway and flared his fingers. "Why didn't you just kick him in the balls?"

The master chief's sudden stillness revealed he was listening after all.

Claire bit her lip.

"This is the part where you say something, Ensign." Lieutenant Loyd chided quietly.

Claire hunched farther in her chair. She was sure her expression was mulish, but she'd never been good at controlling it when she felt like she was being attacked. "No excuse, Sir." She attempted the standard answer.

Lieutenant Loyd's response of "Fucking Academy" was not what she expected. He resumed rubbing his temples and sighed.

Claire glared at him and waited for him to try to drag another answer out of her. You couldn't win when something like this happened, but you could hold onto your pride and not lose.

Lieutenant Loyd looked back, occasionally blinking or glancing around enough to keep it from being a staring contest, but he didn't break the silence.

"You can't kick them." Claire whispered.

Lieutenant Loyd made an inquisitive noise but matched her volume.

"Look, it's—" Claire coughed and tried to return to a normal tone and keep the quaver out of her voice. "When someone does something like that," she looked at Master Chief Wallens warily as she continued waiting for him to exclaim or interrupt or demand details or proof or something. The master chief didn't show any response at all, so Claire continued, "When, that is, if it was some stranger I suppose it might work, but you'd have to kick pretty hard and not miss, and it's not the kind of thing you can practice. But strangers don't really do that. It's people you know who you have to see day after day. A punch they might laugh off and get over without feeling the need to make it into some kind of power thing. Because, well, if it becomes a power thing that's when it really gets bad." Claire clamped down before she spilled too much more. Those were Aunt Jezzy's secrets to tell anyway, not hers. She'd just been taught from it, was all.

Lieutenant Loyd shook his head. "Ensign Lecroix, we really need to work on your tactics."

Claire planted her elbows on the table in front of her and folded her hands. "No."

Lieutenant Loyd snorted and arched his eyebrows at her. "I wouldn't let you pull that shit normally. You should know that, but I'd like to think that this hasn't been a normal day for you. Would you say that was true?"

Claire swallowed unsure of what to do since he hadn't blown up at her defiance. The master chief feigned total absorption in his screen again. Turning back to Lieutenant Loyd, Claire said, "I apologize for what I said in the passageway."

Lieutenant Loyd just raised his eyebrows and waited.

Claire just looked at him in confusion and then flushing added, "Sir."

"Apology accepted," he answered immediately. "And I still want you to work on tactics."

Claire shook her head, "LT, I guess you mean well, but what's the point?"

"Oh, I don't know: the continuation of politics by other means, fighting and winning our star nation's wars, or maybe just because it happens to be your job and doing your job to the best of your ability is the right thing to do?"

Claire hunched again, swallowed, and closed her eyes. "When Lockhart reports me to Commander Greentree, and he's gonna, I'll be out. Maybe just off the ship, or maybe out of the whole GSN."

She shivered. "There's no reason to do this tactics stuff, and look, Sir, there never was. The best I could do was last long enough to get some solid engineering experience to transfer to civie jobs. Tactics doesn't do that."

"Wow, Saganami Island really failed you." Lieutenant Loyd breathed.

He straightened and went on. "Now here's some free officer continuing education for you. There're two kinds of counseling, right?"

Claire jerked a nod, stiffening to attention in her chair, "Yes, Sir."

"So right now we've got informal counseling right here while I try to find a way to get through your thick steader skull that I like you and want you to be a good officer, and even if I didn't, it wouldn't matter because the captain has decided that you are going to be turned into a good officer. You may have noticed, he's a Greentree. There's a fair number of them in the service. They're generally pretty hardcore, and he's hardcore even for a Greentree.

"Maybe you noticed the maroon trousers? Yep. He got himself into the Protector's Own because he wanted to study warfare under the likes of Alfredo Yu, Harriet Benson-Dessouix, and, oh yeah, Honor Alexander-Harrington. And they took him. Which says even more, because the Protector's Own only takes the very best.

"Anyway, onward to the next kind: formal counseling. That's what you use for the hard cases that you need to build a record for in case you need to kick them entirely out of the service. Its generally bad practice to discuss the flaws of senior officers with subordinates, but I'm junior to him too. So we'll call this part a bitch session of the JOPA, okay?"

Claire glanced over at Master Chief Wallens. He was still pretending to do routine paperwork, or maybe he was really doing paperwork and got called in to play chaperone for sketchy informal counseling sessions all the time. "Um, that's the Junior Officer Protection Association, Sir?"

"Exactly. Generally a load of bunk that gets claimed when somebody did something idiotic and wants to use peer pressure to keep from having his ass properly handed to him. But from time to time, captains get crazy. It has its uses. Like now.

"So let's just say that I happen to know that there's already a file on Mr. Lockhart and that the XO has been looking for a final nail for that coffin. I just gave it to him. Or rather you did, and I reported it. I used to feel sorry for him since his marriage on Manticore fell apart, and he seemed to think that Grayson girls would be nearly a different species from the Mantie women he tried dating. I thought he was grieving, not hunting. If we're entirely unlucky, he'll be on-board for another couple weeks. But it's more likely we'll pull into the next available station and dump him."

Claire felt a wave of relief . . . mingled with shock that she wasn't being punished for standing up for herself.

❈ ❈ ❈

By Lieutenant Loyd's metric, the *Manasseh* was entirely lucky. The XO stopped by Claire's stateroom later that evening, after she'd spent a long session in the simulator being repeatedly killed by various adversaries. The lieutenant had replayed each session in detail pointing out why she had died.

The XO had a similar recording as evidence against Lockhart. Lieutenant Loyd had been working a tactical session of his own and recording it while waiting for her to arrive, and it included some visual through the open door and all of the audio of her encounter with the Mantie exchange officer. The XO blushed and couldn't meet Claire's eyes when the fast-forwarded display showed the Mantie grinning at her impact and caught the pinch in clear detail. The XO just needed her thumbprint and signature that she was the person shown. Then he provided the contact information for Legal Assistance if Claire wanted to press assault charges.

Rustin was in the back of the stateroom engrossed in studying the approach for docking at the station. So Claire didn't hesitate to ask, "Sir, I hit a senior officer. Why aren't I the one being charged?"

The exec just shook his head. "I didn't hear that. What did you say?"

Claire said it again, and the exec again denied hearing her.

She started to repeat herself a third time and then stopped. Finally, she said, "What else is on the tape?"

The exec pushed a button and the rest played through. Lieutenant Loyd rose quickly and blocked the view before Lieutenant Commander Lockhart's muffled grunt and then very clearly audible solicitation. The exec shrugged. "He could try to file charges under the Articles of War, but no Grayson admiral would hear them, and no one else has jurisdiction. The commanding officer could make an issue of it, but he feels that you need all the time you can get in the tactical simulators and should not be distracted by petty charges any reasonable Admiralty Review Board would throw out."

Claire blinked. "You have a witness . . ." She trailed off, realizing Lieutenant Loyd had either left that out of his report or colluded with the exec.

The exec snorted as he walked away. He called over his shoulder, "Merchant-class Advanced Technician is a hack exam that you could have passed after your first year at Saganami. I'll approve your leave chits to go waste time prepping for a civilian career when you get competent in the tactics sims and stop signing yourself up for scams." Then she remembered the certification course she had been trying to take leave to attend. It wasn't a scam! Unless . . . she tried to remember if any of the glossy advertising had actually mentioned who gave the certification or accredited the training program. The whole thing seemed less important now.

Claire mulled over whether she could just have said something weeks earlier instead of ducking Lockhart's advances. More than the master chief on this ship seemed trustworthy.

She spent another afternoon and morning running sims while *Manasseh* prepared to dock at the poorly outfitted station orbiting Masada. A few days had passed since she'd had a chance to review maintenance logs or run spot checks. If being an officer meant 'fighting the ship' as Lieutenant Loyd and the exec insisted, she had to depend on other officers to remember to schedule their maintenance smartly and ensure the crew had the time, tools, and training to keep the *Manasseh* from dissolving in hyper from radiation corrosions. The materials were pretty fantastic, so actual structural integrity would likely never be an issue on a modern warship, she reflected wryly.

Rustin took the bridge watch for the docking. Claire paused her sim when the ship got close to watch on the screen in CIC where Rustin's boss, Lieutenant Knutson, had duty and would be watching to keep an eye on his division officer. She was distracted from the initial calls to the station by the duty officer's selection and practice targeting of the station and the other ships in orbit. The whole ship drilled on killing things out of sheer habit. Captain Ayres would have strenuously objected to his crew running targeting solutions on allies, especially since one of the Mantie cruisers would be taking charge of Lieutenant Commander Lockhart and saving *Manasseh* an extra trip to Manticore, but Commander Greentree obviously felt differently.

Lieutenant Knutson paused the tracking session and turned up the speakers as *Manasseh* neared the station and Rustin's voice repeated the standard docking orders with no response from the station. A steady green indicator showed com channels were clear, and the duty officer's quick scroll back to the previous watch's logs showed even a voice confirmation from a few minutes before turnover to the current shift.

The duty officer's eyelids flared and he grabbed the sides of his console a moment before the ship's hull moaned with a muted grinding noise, accompanied by a long shiver. Claire hopped out of her vibrating chair and found the decks and bulkhead trembling too-but not buzzing in the steady rhythm of equipment light-off. The whole ship jerked with starts and stops. The duty officer flicked through screens and spoke softly to other stations through his headset. Claire spun about, trying to identify what must be breaking and what watch station was utterly failing to shut down whatever machinery was in pain.

Knutson settled on a camera angle and whooped as he called several petty officers in the space to gather around a display. His targeting screen increased magnification on a streak of shiny bright metal along the station where arrays hung sideways from where the *Manasseh*'s hull had scraped against it.

He grinned. "That's going to leave a mark."

One of the petty officers shook his head. "I didn't hear a single response to our docking requests from the station."

The duty officer snorted. "Oh, they responded just fine before the watch turned over and Ensign Rustin took the conn for the approach. We'll hit them hard with that if they dare file a complaint. They try that silent treatment trick a lot when a woman's driving the ship and the station leaves a Masadan at their com instead of the Mantie supervisors. I hear Mantie skippers adjust their watches to have male officers do the approach here. After the last few days, though," he shrugged, "I guess the Captain didn't feel like coddling them."

The petty officer grinned in return and leaned over the duty officer to get a closer look at the damages to the station. "That'll teach the Masadans to listen to Momma."

Lieutenant Knutson nodded in agreement and predicted the firing of the port officer in charge of coordinating the ship's approach using his docking arms.

A *Joseph*-class wasn't really built to dock without the arms. It was technically possible, the duty officer acknowledged, grinning, but he hadn't heard of any other destroyer doing it outside of a sim.

Claire looked back at the damage to the station and wondered aloud about how bad the *Manasseh* had been hurt. No damage control alarms had sounded, so it couldn't be that bad.

With another chuckle, the duty officer called for damage reports but the gleam in his eye implied that he already knew what they'd be. The reports came in quickly; a purely cosmetic scratch ran half the length of *Manasseh*'s hull. Low-bidder station construction subcontracted with Masadan workmen was no match for Grayson battlesteel.

Back in the stateroom, Claire tried her best to explain to a mortified Cecelie Rustin that Commander Greentree had decided to make a statement. Claire hugged her roommate, trying to convince her it wasn't about her at all.

Cecelie just kept muttering, "But I scratched up the ship. My first time driving and I scratched it all up."

The Masadan station was about as dirty as one would expect from a group that felt cleaning was something that should be done for free, but then mostly kept the women who might have pitched in to do it off the station. Cecelie returned to the ship just hours into her shore leave, irate about food vendors refusing to sell to women. Claire shrugged it off when it happened to her, too. That happened in Burdette, from time to time. Some places just didn't want to serve women, but there were other places. Cecelie seemed to take it personally, the poor girl.

The *Manasseh* detached from the station without incident, with Claire driving this time. Thankfully her roommate wasn't the jealous type. The docking officer was very exquisitely polite and immediately responsive. Claire wondered a bit if a less-connected officer than Commander Greentree would have been able to browbeat the station commander for that incident instead of being cashiered himself for continuing to dock without appropriate communications with docking control. True, the idiot who had been their docking officer for the connection had never gotten back on the com to tell the *Manasseh* to break off the approach, but . . . She didn't think she would have tried it, even if it was delightful to hear her orders to the arms repeated back and see them followed with precision.

The next day, the rotation gave her a glorious full day between watches, and after her sim time she used it to review the logs for the noncritical systems typically lumped together as auxiliaries. Her scan revealed the ship's medic had missed the routine

Joelle Presby

maintenance on the nanotech customizer. She flagged it, reminding him to reschedule the job and get it done. Her fingers hesitated over the keyboard as she considered telling him the exact day to do the work, but sure it would irritate the generally competent spacer, she deleted the accompanying note.

Afterwards, as she hunted the logistics network for the fastest way to get the replacement parts, Claire reminded herself that equipment does not always break when it gets cleaned. It just did this time.

She tried to get an appointment with the exec through Lieutenant Loyd to apologize for the poor maintenance schedule, but her department head just rolled his eyes.

"Equipment breaks, Ensign."

"But, Sir, that's it exactly! I should have scheduled the maintenance to plan for that so we'd be right next to a parts depot when we did it."

"And should we avoid battles unless we are right next to depots, too?" Lieutenant Loyd rubbed a hand over his mouth, hiding a smile. "It's a warship, Ensign. It's supposed to get broken from time to time. If we're running it a bit harder than a commercial liner, that's a good thing."

He distracted her with a few suggestions on how to improve her survival rate in the battle simulations.

Within the week, a stomach virus from station crud swept through the ship's crew.

Lieutenant Loyd called her from his bed to groaningly tell her that next time, she was to micromanage the medic to within an inch of his life.

Fortunately, the parts came in quickly, and Claire fixed the nanite customizer with the medic watching nervously over her shoulder. A line of patients waited outside medical, and he hurried out to treat them as soon as the unit disgorged the first lot of medication.

The XO filled the rest of the morning with announcements for sections of the crew to report to medical for treatment.

The medic came to find her in CIC later that afternoon, and Claire's stomach dropped. "Please, please tell me the customizer didn't break down again."

"No, Ma'am. No, Ma'am." He glanced around with a slight flush and measured the distance to the petty officers at their watch stations.

Claire judged them within earshot but the medic relaxed his shoulders, perhaps deciding they were too busy to pay attention. "It's about Ensign Rustin, Ma'am."

Claire took off her headset to listen.

"At the sick call," he gestured towards medical, "I was asking everyone in line about the symptoms and," he lowered his voice to a whisper drawing the attention of several nearby petty officers, "she couldn't say if they were from the crud or the woman thing."

The tips of his ears moved from pink to red as Claire puzzled out that he meant menstruation. "Okay." She waited for some hint of why he was telling her this.

One of the closer petty officers was in Cecelie's gunnery division, and while he remained focused on his console, Claire noticed him push one side of his headset entirely off his ear.

The medic gnawed at his lip. "But she's in pain all the time."

"No way—a week a month, maybe a week and a half."

"You don't understand." He pleaded with his eyes. "She asked for me to stock menstrual nanites when she reported, and I said, 'No.'"

Claire blinked at him. "Why would you do that?"

"Well, I didn't think they were important. My sisters never mentioned needing any special pain meds. And you didn't ask for anything when you came onboard."

"What?" She processed the accusation, realizing that the medic was wanting her to somehow confirm or deny Rustin's medical history. "Doc, Get her the drugs."

"Oh, um, I did, Ma'am, and I'll keep them stocked." His ears returned to red. "Miss Lecroix, Ma'am, do you need any?"

She held back a giggle at the look of fear mingled with embarrassment in his expression. "No, I'm fine thank you." She smiled at him.

"But why?"

Claire shook her head at him. "People are different, Doc."

The crew took to calling Cecelie Rustin "Ensign Toughin" in response to the fast-spreading story that she regularly had all the symptoms they had just endured. The medic endured cheerful but ongoing harassment from Cecelie's division for withholding treatment from their much-liked officer, with Claire's division also joining in an unusual alliance of gunners and mechanics that left the doc promising to always maintain full stocks and to keep his maintenance perfectly on track.

Claire watched them with a suppressed smile. Her roommate was going to be fine after all; she was tougher than she looked. Claire marveled at how easily the *Manasseh*'s spacers adapted. If only Noah were as easy to teach as the medic. The demands of shipboard life quickly distracted her from that wistful thought.

Lieutenant Loyd started teaming Claire with other officers in the sims. She by far preferred fighting from the damage control console rather than taking the hot seat on tactical control. At that engineering watch station, she filled her screens with detailed system schematics and huddled with her division, plotting out ways to keep the ship fighting. Someone else in those team drills would make the attack and defense decisions, and when their mock ship took hits, Claire would take power, air, or whatever else was needed and reroute it to keep the ship able to fight and to escape to fight again.

Her department head still insisted she study fighting the ship from tactical control, but the XO's roster gave her the damage control central slot for the next fleet exercise when they got back to Yeltsin's Star.

In the fleet reports, *Ephraim* was having maintenance issues again and had returned to Blackbird. *Manasseh* would run the war exercise with their sister ships in Blackbird simulators instead of live action, so the *Ephraim* could take part.

※ ※ ※

The deafening clangor of General Quarters yanked Claire up out of a deep sleep. The throbbing alarm beat on as she rolled out of her bunk and grabbed for her skinsuit. She threw herself into it, her waking brain waiting for the final notes, which would inform the crew that this was only a drill.

They didn't come.

She closed the last seal, opened the stateroom door, and ran for Engineering. Spacers crowded the passageways as everyone else who'd been off watch charged towards their duty stations in an ordered rush. She slid through the Engineer hatch, noting every face was as tense as her own, yet there was no confusion, and everyone arrived within moments. She saw a lot of concern in their eyes, but no fear—yet, at least—as she took her own station and plugged in her earbud.

"All Hands, this is the Captain."

The voice came up quickly on all channels, and Claire felt a quick surge of relief at how normal he sounded. That relief didn't last long.

"We've just translated back into normal-space for our precision navigation drill," Commander Greentree went on. "We're just over thirty light-minutes from Uriel, and we haven't picked up the Blackbird nav beacons. We haven't gotten any response to our FTL transmissions, either. Now, I'm probably overreacting here." He chuckled easily. "But, the Protector would like us to take care of his ship, so we're staying at General Quarters until I know for certain what's going on. And when we find out it's all the fault of those idle layabouts at Blackbird, the first drink on-station will be on me! Carry on."

On the command channel, Claire heard Lieutenant Loyd report the *Manasseh*'s course set for an approach to Blackbird Alpha at full acceleration. Moments later, he announced drone launches, and her stomach clenched. Those birds were expensive; the CO would only authorize two if he wanted a look at Blackbird badly. Claire switched her display to mirror tactical control and saw her department head had countdowns for when each drone would begin reporting on Blackbird. The first sensor was set to skim past at max acceleration, and even at closest approach it would stay well clear of the yard complex, moons, and Uriel itself. The second would decelerate to provide detailed information but arrive nearly an hour after the first. Two of her techs switched their consoles to mirror the drone sensor operators' screens in CIC just as they had done before in drills to get early hints of where their tiger teams would be needed. Claire found and added the voice channel the two operators were using.

For just over two hours, they waited.

The operator for drone one yelped a startled curse over the com when that sensor's screen flashed red—Failure to lock onto navigational beacon: "Blackbird Alpha, Blackbird Bravo, Node 2A, Blackbird Charlie, Node 3A . . ." The screen text scrolled quickly as more beacons should have been in range, and weren't. Then that warning shifted to just the bottom quarter of the screen as a new warning appeared in yellow, listing automated beacons found and recognized. The sensor operator transmitted before Claire could make sense of the gibberish from the located beacons.

"Captain, this is drone one." The operator reported. "Blackbird orbital yards beacons have sustained major damage. Most navigational beacons not transmitting. Those still functional are reporting out-of-position errors. Some of them are way out of position with course momentums that make no sense. The not-transmitting ones—I'm not sure there was even anything there."

"Drone two, forty-eight minutes to sensor range." The second operator tagged onto the end of the first spacer's initial report.

A slight pause, and then Commander Greentree answered, "Very well. Continue reporting."

Too much darkness filled drone one's screen as the operator spent the three-quarters of an hour detailing missing and misplaced pieces of the yard shown as streaking specks on his display, with most of the detail coming from the automated collection.

The second drone, when it arrived, turned those pristine specks into horror. What should have been a precision clockwork of interweaving yard stations lapping the moon Blackbird roiled in a cloud of twisted alloy and fog-atomized debris tumbling in dirty orbits. Scans showed pieces escaping off towards Uriel or just away. Most was decaying, with moon impacts visible even to untrained eyes more used to repairing their own than assessing enemy combat damage.

Silence reigned for one long second. Then the operator for drone two began reporting in a flat, numb voice.

Claire let his damage descriptions flow through her right earbud, and on her left, flipped through the other channels. It couldn't have been an accident. The extreme destruction showed targeting of not just the shipyard facilities and military industry, but also habitat modules, navigation beacons, and the transit shuttles which might have collected survivors.

The external frequencies held a jumbled panic of emergency transponders and frantic transmissions between the civilian ships huddling around Grayson.

Manasseh's command net transformed into a mad hive of activity while Claire and her techs listened to the gory details spilling out of the speakers. This was a sneak attack with no hostiles left in the system. The yard's remains smeared the skies of Blackbird and Uriel.

With the attack more than six hours old and over before *Manasseh* had translated into the system, the ship had nothing to attack. If this were a battle, her engineering rating chief would send out repair teams with Claire leading the most critical ones. *Manasseh* didn't need that, but Blackbird Yard did.

Claire keyed in a message to Lieutenant Loyd tagged low priority. "Sir, Recommend manning shuttle one. My techs can do search and rescue."

Her text reappeared on screen as highest priority with the lieutenant's response. "Concur. Make it happen. Take the medic."

"Prepare the boat bay for launch." The XO's voice hummed over the command net, echoing slightly from the many speakers selected to the same channel. "Standby for immediate launch of shuttle one. Medic report to the boat bay for search and rescue."

Claire hopped out of her chair, tearing off the earbuds. "That's us! I'm taking repair team one. Double check your oxygen, we'll be doing a lot of space walks. Bring lights and heavy-duty cutters. Chief, we need every emergency life-support pack you can find. Let's go."

❈ ❈ ❈

Away from the *Manasseh*, the chaos of the disaster showed just bones of the many station segments jutting out of the misted life support gases and refrozen flowers of blasted alloys. Destruction like this would be unsurvivable on a ship. A station was no different.

The pilot shied away from the screen and turned to Claire.

"There." She jabbed a finger at the closest large piece of wreckage with an emergency beacon. "Match rotations with that if you can. We'll use tethers from the shuttle and see if we can find anyone. It looks big enough to have survivors."

Her techs cycled out the airlock with life-support packs flapping optimistically from their belts and clipped lines to the exterior of the shuttle. The piece of station proved to be completely depressurized. Claire directed them to cut through a wall she recognized from a station mural on the side of a popular restaurant. The diners and staff were slumped together penned by tables or against the wall that had become the floor with the acceleration the last of the nearby strikes had given this section.

The crumpled opposite side, which had once held a wide, welcoming entrance, pinched around the headwaiter's podium where the emergency transponder nestled discretely out the customers' sight. Likely installed to contact station security if the evening crowd ever got too rowdy, Claire thought as she checked the transponder. It was set to activate automatically on loss of station power to the restaurant. The manual switch had not been turned.

She keyed it on and added the brief optional text record intended to allow the business to silently notify security in the event of a robbery. "Depressurized portion of Section B2 investigated by GNS *Manasseh* shuttle team. No survivors found. Remains of twenty-three souls present." That should keep them from accidentally circling back and rechecking this piece before looking at all the others.

She couldn't just turn the transponder off. The families would want the remains.

Claire motioned for the team to follow her back out to the shuttle.

The pilot saw their gray faces and didn't ask, but he told them that while they were inside B2, *Manasseh*'s sensor techs had compiled a list of wreckage most likely to hold survivors.

The pilot laid a course to the next piece of debris.

Claire noticed it took them directly away from the part of the roiling mass that should have encapsulated Birdies in section B3. She called up a magnified view of the piece of space; it held only pulverized bits. Claire's tears blurred the carnage.

"Lecroix, This is *Manasseh* actual." Commander Greentree's voice rang from the speakers. "Report status, over."

She keyed to transmit, "Sir." She choked once and swallowed her horror, surprised to find her voice even and clear in spite of the wetness on her cheeks. "No survivors found. En route to second search location. Request *Manasseh* continue to coordinate search pattern and identify possible survivor locations."

"Well done. We'll keep sending you locations. Keep me informed. We have more shuttles and ships on their way."

The *Manasseh* directed them from one chunk of wreckage to another, and they went, found the bodies, and reported back on the way to the next one. Sometimes Claire's team found recognizable corpses, but never the air that might have sustained life. She made her techs leave the dead as they lay. The shuttle didn't have room to collect them.

"We can't slow down," Claire told the techs, clinging to the hope that there might still be someone to care how quickly they arrived. "The next one might have survivors." She tried to banish the doubt from her voice.

It almost worked. Her team responded with a list of possibilities. "Maybe an air pocket."

"Somebody in a suit. Lots of EVA work happens in these yards. Got to be somebody was in his suit when it hit."

"Yeah. Or even one of those facemask air things. Lots of people have those."

Claire nodded at them, glad to have their support and grateful the bodies would stay in their twisted metal crypts for a while longer. All the dead had started to look like Lucy or Mary if she looked too long, even the obviously male ones.

Her team settled for making choppy recordings to mark the bodies for later retrieval, placing the masses with remains in clear orbits, and proceeding on to the next hulk. Some hours later—twelve according to the shuttle's clock—*Manasseh* directed them back to the ship for a relief instead of providing the next set of coordinates.

On the short return flight, Claire's senior tech on the com updated the team on the bleak news from the other search-and-rescue operations. Four shuttles had hailed the *Manasseh* as soon as the ship broke com silence. The shuttles had been traveling between sections when the attack struck and had somehow avoided being holed by hypervelocity debris in the aftermath. The shuttles also had the crew from a shipbuilding slip who had been performing their own attempted rescue operation.

In their miracle, the crew of the building slip had launched its last ship the day before and wasn't slated to start the next build for a few weeks. Those still on station had been mostly moving their things out to go to the next job. As shipbuilders, they had suits, and it was easier to wear them than carry them. Their slip took only a single hit, which breached the hull in large enough holes to prevent quick repair, but caused little real damage. None of the other slips with their half-built warships fared as well. The hyper-capable ships, from the shuttle pilots' descriptions, had been a special target of the attackers, with only the weapons-production facilities receiving a higher density of fire.

That brought the survivor count to one forty-three, and gave *Manasseh* four more shuttles to continue the search.

The com crackled with unnecessary noise. "Hey! We got a live one out here." That had to be the shuttle with the shipbuilders.

Claire's heart jumped and she longed to turn the shuttle around. But the builders had saved themselves once already, and the CO would send in support if they needed it.

The XO responded this time. "Understand, Mr. Cuoio. Where have you found survivors? And do you need additional support? Over."

"Oh. Sorry. Yeah. It's on the moon. One of the bases on Blackbird's got somebody tapping out horse in the static. Uh, wait, your Navy guy says it is Morse. I don't know what it is, but somebody's alive if they are tapping, and there's a whole pile of stuff getting ready to rain down on the place. Do you have any guns?"

The Navy guy, who turned out to be a senior lieutenant, quickly confiscated the com to explain the situation. A large orbital wreck had obliterated an adjacent base but retained enough integrity to shield the sister base from streaming debris. A few larger bits looked to be impacting soon, and he asked for the other shuttles to be rerouted to move them into other impact paths. He did not, repeat not, believe it would be necessary for Blackbird to be fired on again.

"Roger, Lieutenant," the XO answered. "Shuttles on their way. Go ahead and land. We'll keep your skies clear enough to get you back off that moon."

Claire listened to Mr. Cuoio's delight as he listed of names of the survivors as they found them. She tried to remember all the yard workers she'd known from the *Ephraim* to see if any might match.

A fresh crew met them in the boat bay, all wet-faced but focused. The new crew swarmed around Claire's team to check systems and take the shuttle back out with a turnaround speed that almost certainly broke regulations. Commander Greentree stood just inside the doors to the bay and said not a word to slow them.

Instead, he asked Claire if she'd like to sit down. The boat bay control room held only the chair occupied by the tech cycling shuttles in and out. Greentree's normally slight wrinkles furrowed around blank eyes. She short-circuited the death notification as much as she was able.

"I saw the debris. I know. My cousins' club was in the B3 section of the Yard. They weren't planning any vacations, not that they had the money for that. So I know Lucy and Mary have to be dead."

Commander Greentree just closed his eyes. "I'm sorry for your loss." He started to ask something, then just shut his mouth silently.

Claire tilted her head. "You didn't know about my cousins? Then what was . . ." Realization dawned. "The *Ephraim*. They were behind schedule still."

"It was quick," said Commander Greentree. "It had to be. The warships in dock were directly targeted."

She nodded, tears finally beginning to come.

"Some of the crew would have to have been on leave or training," Greentree said.

Claire just looked at him, and his mouth tightened. Most of the training facilities were in the Blackbird Yards. "Or visiting home," he amended.

Her throat closed up on its own accord. She made her way to her stateroom, where Cecelie met her with some food and murmured condolences. Only then did she realize that Jennie Ayres had probably been living on Blackbird, as Captain Ayres liked her to do while the ship was in the yards. Claire fished a cream-colored elegant paper invitation from the *Ephraim*'s Wives' Club from the pile in her desk. They had rented the Blackbird Officers' Club for a special-occasion ladies' luncheon. Today. Claire's legs folded beneath her.

Not just Lucy and Mary were gone. Nearly every single member of the *Ephraim* and their wives were frozen corpses or pulverized remains waiting for a shuttle to have the time to identify the dead. Claire vomited, unable to avoid thinking of the moments she had hated them. Even Lucy and Mary, had she told them she loved them? She couldn't remember and lurched over the sink again.

❈ ❈ ❈

Days later, the *Manasseh* was still pushing away or blasting Blackbird Yard debris in a grisly too-late defense of the Blackbird moon-base facilities. Families of the missing begged for the return of any encapsulated human remains. Every bit was scanned first for any life. The last survivors had been suited up and just starting a shift of EVA work when the attack struck and they were blown free. That pair had been found over four days ago. It was now five days after the total destruction of Blackbird Yard.

Claire alternated shuttle missions with burying herself in tactical simulations. Other ships arrived, taking over the remaining search missions, and setting up picket defenses around the system. Claire was rewarded with a day off that she spent sleeping.

She groggily awoke to a flashing light from a missed call and her stateroom terminal chiming politely to announce a call originating at Burdette Cathedral. She dragged on a clean uniform and answered.

A deacon in a cassock heavy with embroidery bowed his head and intoned a welcome at her. "Blessings, child of God. May the Tester grant you ease in your toils and strengthen your protector." Noah sat beside the older man with wide-eyed intensity.

The deacon was vaguely familiar to Claire as one of the lay ministers she'd spent her youth avoiding for their tendency to attempt to fix other people's lives without pausing to understand them. Her cousin's respectfully straight posture could only mean that this was his latest replacement father figure. He'd done worse before. She tried to process why they might be calling her.

"Good night. Good morning?" Claire blinked at them.

The deacon nudged Noah.

"Hi Claire-Claire, it's afternoon."

The deacon elbowed him again.

"And you've got to come home now."

Her mind was mush. "Huh?"

"Your repentance," the deacon prompted.

"Claire," Noah flushed. "Look, I'm really sorry. I should not made you go do stuff with the Navy. I know you hate it, and it was wrong, and I should never have made you do any of it, especially all that time at the Manticore Academy. So I did, you know, a confession, and it's okay for you to come home now."

"I what?"

The deacon nodded approvingly at Noah. To Claire, he added, "Young miss, your protector has informed you of his will to retract permission for work outside the home. You will be returning to your family on the next available shuttle."

Dazed, Claire shook her head.

The deacon sighed and closed his eyes. "Merciful Tester. Defend our hearts in these dark times from the scourges of greed and iniquity. Teach us to root and sustain ourselves in the tranquility of the home. Bless this daughter before you. Gentle her hardened heart and open it to Your true glory." He took a breath and Claire hoped he was done.

He wasn't. "Let the scales fall from her eyes that she might see the sins of Your people. That she might know her own sin and seek restoration into Your holy presence. That she might recognize the iniquity of our leaders, which has led to this holy vengeance."

Noah peeked one eye open. The spit dried in her mouth as Claire tried to find the words.

"Tester, grant her the wholeness of heart to turn away from the footsteps of harlotry traveled by her departed cousins." Noah exchanged a horrified look with her at the mention of Mary and Lucy as whores. They just danced. Really. They just danced naked for money from lonely men not used to being without their wives.

The deacon continued his prayer. "Forgive her sins of pride and envy. Forgive her as her family has forgiven her. Return this, Your daughter, to her home and to the bosom of her family."

Speechless, she flicked the power switch off on the console, disconnecting the call.

Cecelie sat on the other side of the room wide-eyed.

※ ※ ※

Claire went to CIC to think and found Lieutenant Loyd running Blackbird attack recordings from the shuttle logs and what little the surviving sensors had captured. There was nothing in them but missiles and death. Treacherous tears welled up. Emotions would be the excuse for kicking her out of the Service, Claire was sure. Now that there was no Blackbird, the Grayson space industry might well be in a recession for a generation. She'd have to go back to Burdette Steading. Claire choked back vomit. How had she grown so cold that all these people were dead and she was still mourning her own silly dreams?

Lieutenant Loyd looked up and froze the recording, beckoning her to sit down.

Claire used the tissues that now claimed a permanent pocket in her skinsuit but left the space sickness bag in its pocket. "I've got a problem, Sir."

That got a dark laugh from Lieutenant Loyd.

Claire found herself smiling back at the ridiculousness of having just one problem when the entire Grayson Space Navy equipment and weapons supply system had been torn to shreds, her star nation had been brutally attacked by who knew who, and at least half the civilian populace was screaming for blood without recognizing that no one knew who to go kill.

"It's a family problem," she said.

That sobered up Lieutenant Loyd quick enough. "Lockhart didn't—" He choked on the words and it took Claire a few moments to fill in the assumptions.

"Oh no. Not a pregnancy kind of family problem. A teenage head-of-household met the wrong new father figure kind of family problem." Claire clenched her fists.

Lieutenant Loyd cocked his head to the side, clearly baffled.

Claire repressed a sigh. People didn't understand how much the rule of law could suck when they'd never lived on the bottom of it. She explained about how Noah had signed the initial authorization for her to work for the Academy stint and about the pay transfers.

His eyebrows rose.

With a blush, Claire admitted to hiding the pay bump that came with a promotion to ensign. And she summarized the Burdette Steading altar call for a return to pious family values that had led to Noah's intent to revoke Claire's authorization to work.

Lieutenant Loyd's eyebrows stayed up. After a lengthy pause the sum total of his response was, "Wow." He shook his head and repeated himself, "Wow."

Claire felt compelled to point out, "You did say I was supposed to tell you about problems as they came up. That that was what department heads were for."

Lieutenant Loyd snorted. "Remind me never to say stuff like that again." He shook his head. "I've got no idea . . ." Then he stilled. "Oh, yeah, that'll work. You've heard what our latest orders are, right?"

Claire rubbed her forehead, vaguely remembering a navigation brief for the transit to Grayson, but she'd been given a day without watch to catch up on sleep and lost track of what the ship was doing.

Her department head shrugged. "I'm sure the wardroom gossip has it by now. The VIP we are picking up on Grayson is Michael Mayhew. We're taking his staff to Manticore. With the attack and all, I guess the Protector prefers to have him travel in a warship rather than their usual yacht."

Loyd broke off the conversation for a few moments to monitor *Manasseh*'s final approach into orbit around Grayson,

Once they were in a stable orbit, Commander Greentree's voice rang over the ship's announcing system. "*Manasseh*, We're about to bring aboard a very important member of the Mayhew family. Please welcome him and support his staff as you would the Protector himself. I'm sure you'll do me proud.

"We've been attacked, and you all know how much we've been hurt. The Protector is sending his brother to Queen Elizabeth to plan this new war, and he chose the *Manasseh* to get him there. Grayson and Manticore have some enemies out there due a full measure of retribution. This is the first step in delivering it."

The crew in CIC burst into spontaneous applause.

The usual ceremony of shuttles and personnel transfer went off flawlessly. Only Mayhew and a few staff members came onboard. The rest of his staff were still on Grayson engaged in last-minute preparations for the trip and would embark on later shuttles after the *Manasseh's* crew had rearranged workstations and berthing assignments to make room on the warship for the elite passengers.

From the craning necks at the nearby consoles, Claire realized that the official party was actually touring the ship with Commander Greentree leading them around and introducing the crew rather than going directly to their cabins. The CO performed the introductions naming every spacer in CIC, and the tour stopped. Michael Mayhew chatted with several petty officers eager shake his hand, so that one day they could tell grandchildren that they had actually met a Mayhew.

Mayhew worked his way around with polished elegance, staying just long enough with each spacer to exchange a few words but not so long that any appeared uncomfortable in his company.

Claire was ready with a fake smile when he reached out to shake her hand.

"Ensign Lecroix," he said. "A pleasure to meet you. Commander Greentree speaks highly of your work in the recovery efforts."

"Thank you, Sir."

Then he dropped the conversational grenade. "So tell me about your cousin Noah."

She looked from him to the CO to her department head. Word traveled fast.

"Sir, my cousin is my head-of-household in Burdette. He signed an Authorization to Work Outside the Home when I entered Saganami, but he's been talked into revoking it."

"So I heard. And does Steadholder Burdette generally feel he can undermine obligated service to Grayson in a time of war?"

"Sir, it was just my cousin and, well, a churchman who seems to be telling him what to do. The steadholder wasn't involved at all."

"They're his laws," Mayhew said, with the set of his jaw implying he held the steadholder personally responsible for their legal application. He looked at her for another moment, then inhaled sharply. "Would you be good enough to accompany me to the wardroom, Ensign?"

Claire was so dumbfounded—not to mention flustered—as she was ushered up to the wardroom that she almost missed the introduction that the silver-haired woman trailing Mayhew was Elsabeta Greentree, the commander's wife and a member of Michael Mayhew's legal counsel. It seemed ridiculous that the Protector's own brother could worry himself with *her* problems, especially at a time like this, but Mayhew and Elsabeta proceeded to pepper her with questions about Noah, the Bedlam family, and the Burdette Steading legal system.

Claire had answers about the first two and didn't want to share them. For the third, she didn't know, but it hardly mattered. Michael Mayhew and Elsabeta between them drew statutes and rulings from their legal libraries quite without needing any input or encouragement from Claire.

Cecelie Rustin's curly blond head popped around the corner of the wardroom just long enough to see the group, smile beatifically, and vanish. Claire nailed her roommate as the tattler. The Navy was quite as bad as a family at planning your life without consulting you.

Claire rubbed her eyes to block out images of Lucy's and Mary's faces, superimposed on the corpses found by her shuttle team and ghosting around the wardroom, as Elsabeta plotted stratagems to not only cut off Noah but to charge the family to repay Claire's past wages under some loose historical claim that an officer was legally a gentleman. Gentlemen were not dependents of one another under Burdette law, and thus the withdrawals from Claire's bank account were invalid.

Mayhew looked skeptical.

The other members of the diplomatic party had arrayed themselves around the wardroom, likely doing the work actually needed for the visit to Manticore.

Claire coughed and drew the whole room's attention. "Excuse me, I'm sure that my own little problems aren't worth, I mean, the alliance with Manticore and all is so much more important." Claire swallowed, and, uncertain of quite the right address, stuck with military courtesies. "Sir, Ma'am, I would like to try to reach Lord Burdette, if I might." Commander Greentree had taken care of Lockhart well enough once he was actually told. What if her Lord Steadholder just didn't really know what his laws were doing? Claire crushed the small part of her mind that insisted that if Lord Burdette didn't know then he was too much of an idiot to respond to reason.

Mayhew rubbed his lips, concealing a small smile as his eyes lit. Claire rather wondered if she had totally botched the honorific for the Protector's brother. "Sir" was such a useful catchall for military people whose titles you didn't quite know.

"Master Mayhew," she tried again, "My Lord Steadholder did nominate me to Saganami Island and all. It seems only fair to, well, give him a chance to fix things. I mean, it's his job."

The small smile broke loose, flickering around the corners of Mayhew's mouth.

This time the conversation actually expanded to include Claire. Elsabeta wanted to see Noah served with papers first, but Mayhew recommended the legal suit be held in reserve. Claire held out for a call to Burdette Steading to request to be put on Lord Burdette's schedule once the *Manasseh* returned from Manticore. Claire ruthlessly planned to borrow the cost of the call from Rustin. It was the least her roommate could do after airing Bedlam dirty laundry so publicly.

Commander Greentree offered his office for an immediate call. Elsabeta offered to write a script of legal talking points for it.

Thankfully the space was too small for the whole staff to follow along. Only Claire and Mayhew sat in front of the screen, with Commander Greentree and Elsabeta to the side off-screen watching as Michael Mayhew typed in a private code and reached the Burdette Steading without a single one of the usual screeners or automated recordings asking the nature of their business with Lord Burdette.

Steadholder Burdette's third wife answered immediately. She looked surprised to see Michael Mayhew but smiled broadly at Claire, chattering about how nice proper skirts looked on a woman in uniform.

Claire thanked her and thanked her again for the gift of the uniforms. The heavy material soaked the sweat from her hands without darkening the fabric.

An older woman with a decidedly pinched set to her lips, who Claire recognized as one of Steadholder Burdette's mothers, joined the screen. She made a short acknowledgement of Michael Mayhew and then skewered Claire with a frigid glare.

"Miss Lecroix," said the dowager. In Burdette, there had never been any acceptance that a military rank could replace the primacy of *miss* or *madam* in a woman's titling, Claire recalled. "Explain to me, if you please, why it is that months have passed since you received the gift of proper uniforms from my daughters-in-law and not a one of them has yet to receive a thank-you." The dowager lady steadholder's pink-glossed lips disappeared in a creased line with whitened edges as she glared.

Claire thought of hiding behind the disaster of Blackbird, but in exasperation just told the truth. "I didn't have the funds to have them hemmed, let alone send back a letter."

The dowager lady steadholder's lips made a reappearance, and the other two daughter-in-laws' faces showed at the edges of the screen as well. Apparently the Burdette Lady Steadholders had arrived in mass to hear what Claire had to say.

Tester only knew if anyone had even been sent to tell Steadholder Burdette himself about the call at all. The dowager shut down the babble of questions with one sharp look and patted her divan to have all three of her son's wives join her.

With significantly more concern, the dowager asked, "Has your father passed recently then, dear?"

Claire laughed. "Oh no, Dad passed on when I was nine and Mother didn't recover so well without him. I was raised by my aunts on my mother's side. Anyway, on the Bedlam side we've never had much success with pregnancies, especially for boys. Our head-of-household is my cousin, Noah." Claire automatically edited to leave out the family predilection for unmarried pregnancies.

The dowager seemed to recognize Claire's meaning without her needing to spell it out.

The dowager asked, "That wouldn't be the Noah Bedlam who created the civil disturbance a few years back by trying to run a watercraft on the aquaculture ponds, would it?"

Claire watched the eye contact between the steadholder ladies as they acknowledged to each other exactly which family the Bedlams were and quite pointedly did not ask who Noah's father was. It would have been on the paperwork for the arrest warrant. "Father: unknown."

She just closed her eyes.

"There was a wrecked boat involved. I wasn't privy to the details since I was at Saganami Island at the time. I just know that it took ten months for the account with my midshipwoman pay to show a positive balance. After that I learned to ask the bank not to permit overdrafts. There was some sort of fine, I assume?"

"A large one," the dowager acknowledged. "The pond was contaminated. Apparently he'd tried the boat on an open stream first and the hijinks with the pond-farm was in response to family concerns for his health if he kept trying to boat on our planet's toxic natural waters." The dowager shrugged. "I just know that my boy said he blamed his mother's nagging when the judge asked him why he did it."

Claire couldn't help but snort a laugh. "I suppose that was true." Gripping her skirts to keep her hands from shaking, she tried to refocus the discussion. "Do you think you could arrange for me to speak to Lord Burdette sometime, Ma'am? I'd like to request to be made legally independent. Noah would like me to resign from the Service, you see, and this isn't really the time. I have a service obligation for my schooling." And there was Blackbird. "And we're likely at war with someone."

The dowager was shaking her head. "We can't allow that. I'm sorry, dear, but it would set a horrid precedent." She shifted her gaze. "Don't give me that look, Lord Mayhew. We have two applications for legal independence already from Miss Lucy Bedlam and Miss Mary Bedlam. Their applications say they are working as artisans, but not six weeks ago Miss Mary made a most apologetic confession that they are actually, er—"

"Strippers." Claire said. "They used to dance at a men's club called Birdies. I couldn't find their bodies."

The Burdette ladies gaped at her, even the dowager.

Mayhew recovered first, patting Claire's knotted fist lightly, "I'm sorry for your loss."

Claire released the skirts and rubbed one temple. "Yes, I'll especially miss Lucy. Noah did like the money they earned, but he liked to think the club was paying them to waitress and they were just doing the other because they wanted to instead of because it was the only reason the club hired women at all." She focused on the Burdette ladies. "They worked on Blackbird."

"Would you like to see your cousin charged with whore-mongering? I do believe that is outlawed in every steading of Grayson." Mayhew folded his hands lightly and glanced from Claire to the dowager and back.

Claire blanched. She wasn't sure what the sentence for that offense was, but it would tear the family apart to see Noah in a prison somewhere. Or executed. Defaming the dignity of a woman through forced prostitution could be a capital offense.

"Nonsense." The dowager lady steadholder held up a hand. "Those two young women have passed on. It isn't right to sully the names of the dead." She pinched her lips and gave lie to the fine words. "Anyway, the last formal documents we have in their names call them artisans. It would be near impossible now to find evidence that they did or did not engage in the work willingly or of their own accord without their head-of-household's approval. The authorization to work outside the home, which I had checked, quite clearly states that they have positions as waitstaff at an entirely different venue, The Gym, I believe."

The second wife's crimson blush revealed that she somehow knew different. Claire wondered who had told her.

Claire shook her head, "It's the same venue, Madam Steadholder. It's much like bars called The Library situated outside colleges. The Blackbird Gymnasium. The customers call it Birdies among themselves and 'The Gym' to their wives, I understand.

"Could you see clear to letting my Aunt Jezzy Bedlam know about Lucy and Mary passing? I haven't been able to afford a call to let her and the rest of the family know. They'll know they're missing already, but I took part in the rescue. They might be thinking that there's still a chance. I saw. There's no way. It was really awful. There aren't going to be any more names added to the survivor list—especially not from Birdies' part of the yards."

Mayhew remained entirely blank-faced as Claire glanced at him. The existence of gentlemen's clubs was likely not something one normally discussed in mixed company. Mayhew seemed to be dealing with it by ignoring that part of the discussion, and the Burdette ladies were in turn ignoring his presence for that awkward piece.

Claire gripped her skirts again. "I had hoped to avoid all this awkwardness Madam Burdette. Please convey my continued gratitude to your son for the appointment to the Service. I remain honored to have been a daughter of Burdette Steading, but I shall have to apply for a transfer of citizenship to another steading now."

Claire froze her neck muscles with an iron will to keep from checking Mayhew for a reaction. If he was acting appalled at the suggestion, they would never believe that another steadholder might take her in. But if he just kept that blank face a few moments longer . . .

The dowager raised her eyebrows and glared past Claire's shoulder at Mayhew. With an abrupt command she sent the youngest daughter-in-law off to fetch the steadholder. Was it a call for reinforcements to crush an uppity steader or a decision to save a weakening city's dome by releasing just a little pressure?

Claire repeated her bid for freedom. "Madam, I have an obligation of service. I just ask that—"

The Burdette ladies vanished. Lord Nathan Fitzclarence, with the Seal of Burdette Steading carved in his study wall behind him, leaned forward and stared intently. "Yes, yes. You've had your questions. Now I have mine."

Had he been watching the conversation the whole time, waiting to see what a Mayhew with one of his steaders was doing calling a private line? Claire checked Mayhew's response. It seemed yes.

Entirely unflappable, Master Mayhew said, "A pleasant morning to you, Nathan. Glad you could join us."

Claire ducked her head in a seated bow. "Tester's blessings, Steadholder."

Lord Burdette made a flicking motion with his right hand as though to brush away all the usual courtesies. "This is quite a mess you've brought me, Michael."

The arch to Mayhew's eyebrows implied he didn't think that he'd brought the mess at all.

Claire felt the blood rise up in her ears in a familiar feeling of shame mixed with frustration that usually went with public notice of her family. "It's not Noah's fault he never had a dad." Claire glared at both men daring them to contradict her. "So what if he doesn't know how to grow up? He never had anyone to show him! That's your fault. If you'd just let some of the women around him be adults, we could have taught him.

"Instead, he went straight from a baby to a dictator without ever the chance to make mistakes that didn't leave half the family in hock and make my two cousins have to go off and strip on Blackbird just to cover the debts and then end up dead with nothing but folk looking down their noses at them as if they didn't do all that they had to do because there wasn't no better way." Claire flushed as she realized her Saganami Island grammar had abandoned her in her fury. She wasn't done, though.

She darted a look at Mayhew and then back at her Steadholder. "There's no way I'll be leaving the steading legally. And the GSN doesn't allow law breaking in the officer corps, so don't you worry, Sir. My life is well and fully ruined, because some idiot leeched onto Noah's guilt to get him to rescind my authorization to work outside the home."

Her two listening steadholders were dead silent. Claire wanted to vomit. "But, Lord Steadholder, you could have had a whole troublesome family that might have finally amounted to something. Tester knows that Aunt Jezzy, Lucy, Mary and the rest thought that with the Saganami Island appointment you'd decided to save us all. It was going to be a leg up for the whole family."

Steadholder Burdette shifted uncomfortably.

Claire held her peace, focusing on the fine weave skimming over her knees. Maybe she could keep the skirted uniforms after her discharge and wear them for Founding Day parades or something, just to remember that for a while she'd served.

Lord Burdette said, "I suppose I could grant just you legal independence, but I don't see how that could do much for any of the rest. If they just had one strong man to keep them from falling quite so much..."

Oxygen flooded in through Claire's gasping open mouth, and then the words came pouring out.

"Give them to *me*," she pleaded leaning towards the screen and nearly kneeling. "I've been managing a whole division of techs for a year and a half now, and I've done well enough they made me an ensign. There aren't but six or eight left in my extended family now, depending on who was actually on Blackbird in the end. I know them. If you give me charge of myself, I can take charge of them too."

Mayhew muttered something near inaudible about every man's responsibility for meeting his own Test. Claire gritted her teeth, and Lord Burdette slowly nodded, "I suppose I could make you Noah's guardian in lieu of the appointed paroleman, and his dependents would come with that. But what would you have them do? You'll be away most of the time. That's no way to run a family."

Elsabeta and Commander Greentree both bristled in Claire's peripheral vision.

"I'll do what the GSN has done for ages and leave Aunt Jezzy to run things. But like the officers do, I'll leave her the actual power to do so. And," Claire added almost in spite of herself, "I mean to leave the service after this tour. I had wanted to work on the shipyard. I suppose I'll have to help rebuild it first.

"We're going to need it to go after whoever did this to us. Whoever our enemies are, they know how important Blackbird Yard's industries were, or they would have hit our population instead. But we can rebuild the station, and we will. They *should* have hit Grayson; they just don't know it yet.

"Some of my cousins aren't too bad at schooling. If Noah weren't raiding my funds anymore, I could get them into some decent trade schools. Maybe enroll Noah in one, too. He could stand to learn a thing or two and do something useful, so he'd have something of his own to be proud of. Maybe we'll have a company in a few years for the rebuilding. The GSN is going to need it, and shouldn't Burdette have more space industry anyway?"

"Why not?" The edges of a smile tipped Steadholder Burdette's lips. "Your legal manumission will be in the next care package from my wives. And congratulations on the promotion, Ensign."

❀ ❀ ❀

The gleaming clean corridors from the captain's cabin back to Claire's stateroom held the usual bustle of crew members, but either Cecelie's stories had extended only as far as those she'd believed could help or the crew genuinely didn't object to Claire trying to break from whatever it was that could stamp a teenager as protector to his mother and female cousins. There were boys who could do it. Probably. Noah just wasn't one of them.

Claire recorded a message to Aunt Jezzy and saved it. Rustin would lend her something to get it passed. Tester knew she couldn't count on Aunt Jezzy getting a payable-on-receipt message without pawning the restaurant cookware. Doubt curled in her stomach. Lord Burdette would reconsider, or somehow she would flub up worse than Noah ever did.

Claire walked back into the wardroom to find Cecelie, Commander Greentree, and Elsabeta talking avidly about the implications for Burdette law of stretching head-of-household to include a female officer and what it would mean if Lord Burdette's judges decided to apply the precedent.

Lieutenant Loyd smiled a greeting at Claire and offered a seat next to her roommate.

Claire sank into the soft, stiff-backed chair and nodded tightly at Elsabeta's congratulations.

Cecelie's fair-to-bouncing-out-of-the-seat excitement stilled. "Claire, what's wrong? Your Steadholder didn't take it back, did he? It was witnessed, he couldn't!"

With a quick shake of her head, Claire hugged herself. "What if I blow it? My family, they aren't easy. They aren't like crew with skills and training and believing that directions can be trusted and generally followed as long as the officer isn't being too much of an idiot about it."

Commander Greentree shared a knowing smile with Lieutenant Loyd at the description of junior-officer leadership. "You'll do okay," he assured her.

"Of course you will." Cecelie smiled and got a little bit of the bounce back. "You should hear the crazy stories my chief tells about officer families. He says he's been bored with me, because I haven't got any wives to spend every cent or kids to flunk out of school."

Elsabeta added, "And of course, the wives' club does extend membership to extended family for whatever crises come up. We're around when the rest of you are off chasing down pirates, Havenites, or whatever." She flicked a wrist towards a group of the embassy staff as almost an afterthought acknowledgement of the Blackbird Yard destruction.

"Strengthening family support is one of the things a command team does." Commander Greentree said. "I don't see why your family should be left out."

"You'll help me?" Claire nearly stuttered, staring around the wardroom. She read their faces and believed them.

Lieutenant Loyd just grinned at her. "The slogan does say, 'Join the GSN. We'll make a man out of you.'"